VERTIGO

AURORA RISING BOOK TWO

(AMARANTHE ♦ 2)

G. S. JENNSEN

HYPERNOVA
PUBLISHING

2014

VERTIGO

Hypernova Publishing
2900 N Government Way #89
Coeur d'Alene, ID 83815
www.hypernovapublishing.com

Ordering Information:
Hypernova Publishing books may be purchased for educational, business or sales
promotional use. For details, contact the "Special Markets Department" at the
address above.

Vertigo / G. S. Jennsen.—1st ed.

LCCN 2014950262
ISBN 978-0-9960141-4-4

For my readers
without whom Alex's story would have
ended at the portal

AMARANTHE UNIVERSE

AURORA RHAPSODY

AURORA RISING
STARSHINE
VERTIGO
TRANSCENDENCE

AURORA RENEGADES
SIDESPACE
DISSONANCE
ABYSM

AURORA RESONANT
RELATIVITY
RUBICON
REQUIEM

ASTERION NOIR

EXIN EX MACHINA
OF A DARKER VOID
THE STARS LIKE GODS

RIVEN WORLDS

CONTINUUM
INVERSION
ECHO RIFT

ALL OUR TOMORROWS
CHAOTICA
DUALITY

COSMIC SHORES

MEDUSA FALLING
THE THIEF
THE UNIVERSE WITHIN (2025)

SHORT STORIES

Restless, Vol. I • *Restless, Vol. II* • *Apogee* • *Solatium* • *Venatoris*
Re/Genesis • *Meridian* • *Fractals* • *Chrysalis* • *Starlight Express*

Learn more at gsjennsen.com/books or visit the
Amaranthe Wiki: gsj.space/wiki

COLONIZED MILKY WAY

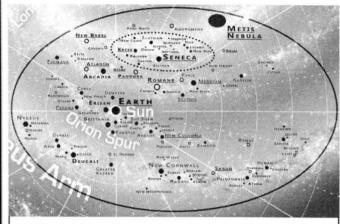

COLONIZED WORLDS

•••••• SENECAN FEDERATION TERRITORY
○ INDEPENDENT WORLDS

WORLDS VISITED IN
VERTIGO:

EARTH ALLIANCE	SENECAN FEDERATION	INDEPENDENTS
EARTH	SENECA	ATLANTIS
DESNA	KRYSK	GAIAE
FIONAVA		NEW BABEL
MESSIUM		PANDORA
NEW COLUMBIA	-------------	ROMANE
PERONA	METIS NEBULA	SAGAN
SCYTHIA		

MILKY WAY GALAXY

DRAMATIS PERSONAE

MAIN CHARACTERS

Alexis 'Alex' Solovy
Starship pilot, scout and space explorer; daughter of Miriam and David Solovy.
Faction: *Earth Alliance*

Caleb Marano
Special Operations intelligence agent, Senecan Federation Division of Intelligence.
Faction: *Senecan Federation*

Miriam Solovy (Admiral)
EASC Operations Director; mother of
Alex Solovy, widow of David Solovy.
Faction: *Earth Alliance*

Richard Navick (Colonel)
EASC Naval Intelligence Liaison;
family friend of the Solovys.
Faction: *Earth Alliance*

Malcolm Jenner (Lt. Colonel)
Captain, *EAS Juno;*
friend of Alex Solovy.
Faction*: Earth Alliance*

Kennedy Rossi
Director of Design/Prototyping,
IS Design; friend of Alex Solovy.
Faction: *Earth Alliance*

Liam O'Connell (General)
EASC Board Chairman.
Faction: *Earth Alliance*

Devon Reynolds
EASC Special Projects Consultant;
quantum computing specialist.
Faction: *Earth Alliance*

Graham Delavasi
Director, Senecan Federation
Division of Intelligence.
Faction: *Senecan Federation*

Isabela Marano
Professor of Biochemistry;
sister of Caleb Marano.
Faction: *Senecan Federation*

Noah Terrage
Tech dealer and smuggler; friend of
Caleb Marano and Mia Requelme.
Faction: *Independent*

Mia Requelme
Businesswoman; friend of Caleb
Marano and Noah Terrage.
Faction: *Independent*

Olivia Montegreu
Head of Zelones criminal cartel.
Faction: *Independent*

Marcus Aguirre
Earth Alliance Foreign Minister.
Faction: *Earth Alliance*

OTHER CHARACTERS
(ALPHABETICAL ORDER)

Abigail Canivon
Director of Cybernetic Research,
Druyan Institute.
Faction: *Independent*

Aiden Trieneri
Head of Triene criminal cartel.
Faction: *Independent*

ANNIE
EA Military Artificial Neural Net.
Faction: *Earth Alliance*

Aristide Vranas
Chairman, SF Government.
Faction: *Senecan Federation*

Braelyn Chaesta
Resident of Messium.
Faction: *Earth Alliance*

Brooklyn Harper (Captain)
1st NW MSO Platoon.
Faction: *Earth Alliance*

Charles Gagnon
Speaker, EA Congressional Assembly.
Faction: *Earth Alliance*

Christopher Rychen (Admiral)
EA Northeast Regional Commander.
Faction: *Earth Alliance*

Dai Nguyen
Rep of Zelones Cartel on Pandora.
Faction: *Independent*

David Solovy (Commander)
Alex Solovy's father; Miriam Solovy's
spouse; Captain, *EAS Stalwart*. Deceased.
Faction: *Earth Alliance*

Dawn Fuschida (Rear Admiral)
Captain, *EAS Lincoln*.
Deceased.
Faction: *Earth Alliance*

Eleni Gianno (Field Marshal)
Head of SF Military Council;
Commander of SF Armed Forces.
Faction: *Senecan Federation*

Emily Bron
Devon Reynolds' girlfriend.
Faction: *Earth Alliance*

Ethan Tollis
Musician; former lover of Alex
Solovy.
Faction: *Earth Alliance*

Francesca Marano
Mother of Caleb and Isabela
Marano.
Faction: *Senecan Federation*

Friedrich Haraken (General)
EA Southwest Regional Commander.
Faction: *Earth Alliance*

Hideyo Mori
EA Defense Minister.
Faction: *Earth Alliance*

Isaac Baek
Former Chair, Synthetics Research,
Hong Kong University; Deceased.
Faction: *Earth Alliance*

Jaron Nythal
Asst. Director, SF Division of Trade.
Faction: *Senecan Federation*

Jere Kulm
Police detective on Pandora.
Faction: *Independent*

Jonas Chaesta
Resident of Messium.
Faction: *Earth Alliance*

Jules Hervé (Brigadier)
Director, EASC Special Projects.
Faction: *Earth Alliance*

Kian Lange (Major)
Director, EASC Security Bureau.
Faction: *Earth Alliance*

Laure Ferre
Head of Ferre criminal cartel.
Faction: *Senecan Federation*

Liz Oberti
Asst. Director, SF Division of Intelligence.
Faction: *Senecan Federation*

Luis Barrera
EA Prime Minister.
Faction: *Earth Alliance*

Madison Ledesme
Governor of Romane.
Faction: *Independent*

Mangele Santiagar
Former EA Trade Minister. Deceased.
Faction: *Earth Alliance*

Marlee Marano
Isabela's daughter; Caleb's niece.
Faction: *Senecan Federation*

Matei Uttara
Assassin.
Faction: *Independent*

Meno
Artificial owned by Mia Requelme.
Faction: *Independent*

Michael Volosk
Former Director of SpecOps, SF Division of Intelligence; Deceased.
Faction: *Senecan Federation*

Morgan Lekkas (Commander)
3rd Squad./3rd Wing, Southern Fleet.
Faction: *Senecan Federation*

Patrick Foster (General)
EA Northwest Regional Commander.
Faction: *Earth Alliance*

Price Alamatto (General)
Former EASC Board Chairman.
Deceased.
Faction: *Earth Alliance*

Raina Avonle
Resident of Messium.
Faction: *Earth Alliance*

Samuel Padova
Former Special Ops, SF Intelligence; mentor of Caleb Marano. Deceased.
Faction: *Senecan Federation*

Seraphina LaCasse
Resident of Gaiae.
Faction: *Independent*

Stefan Marano
Father of Caleb and Isabela Marano.
Faction: *Senecan Federation*

Steven Brennon
Former EA Prime Minister.
Faction: *Earth Alliance*

Sylvie Avonle
Resident of Messium.
Faction: *Earth Alliance*

Thomaso Yagossa
Resident of Messium.
Faction: *Earth Alliance*

Valkyrie
Druyan Institute Artificial Neural Net.
Faction: *Independent*

William 'Will' Sutton
CEO, W. C. Sutton Construction; spouse of Richard Navick.
Faction: *Earth Alliance*

SENECAN FEDERATION

SF Military

Eleni Gianno
Military Council Chairman

Morgan Lekkas
Fighter pilot
Southern Fleet

SF Government

Aristide Vranas
Chairman
SF Government

Graham Delavasi
Intelligence Director

Caleb Marano
Special Ops agent

Liz Oberti
Asst. Intelligence Director

Jaron Nythal
Asst. Trade Director

Civilian

Isabela Marano
Caleb's sister

Marlee Marano
Isabela's daughter

Laure Ferre
Head of Ferre cartel

INDEPENDENT

Olivia Montegreu
Head of Zelones cartel

Noah Terrage
Tech dealer, smuggler

Mia Requelme
Businesswoman

Meno
Mia's Artificial

Madison Ledesme
Governor of Romane

Matei Uttara
Assassin

Aiden Trieneri
Head of Triene cartel

Abigail Canivon
Cybernetics Specialist

Valkyrie
Abigail's Artificial

EARTH ALLIANCE

EA Military	EA Government	Civilian
Liam O'Connell	Luis Barrera	Alex Solovy
EASC Chairman	*Prime Minister*	*Pilot, Space Scout*
Miriam Solovy	Charles Gagnon	Kennedy Rossi
EASC Dir. Operations	*Assembly Speaker*	*Ship Designer*
Christopher Rychen	Marcus Aguirre	Devon Reynolds
EASC NE Commander	*Foreign Minister*	*Computer Specialist*
Jules Hervé	Hideyo Mori	Ethan Tollis
EASC Dir. Special Projects	*Defense Minister*	*Musician*
Richard Navick	Steven Brennon	Will Sutton
EASC Naval Intelligence	*Former Prime Minister*	*Construction Manager*
Kian Lange		
EASC Dir. Security Bureau		
Malcolm Jenner		
Captain, EAS Juno		

*

Colonized Worlds Map can be viewed online at: http://www.gsjennsen.com/map-vertigo.

Dramatis Personae can be viewed online at: http://www.gsjennsen.com/characters-vertigo.

AURORA RISING

SYNOPSIS

STARSHINE

By the year 2322, humanity has expanded into the stars to inhabit over 100 worlds spread across a third of the galaxy. Though thriving as never before, they have not discovered the key to utopia, and societal divisions and conflicts run as deep as ever.

Two decades ago a group of breakaway colonies rebelled to form the Senecan Federation. They fought the Earth Alliance, won their independence in the Crux War and began to rise in wealth and power.

Now a cabal of powerful individuals within both superpowers and the criminal underground set in motion a plot designed to incite renewed war between the Alliance and Federation. Olivia Montegreu, Liam O'Connell, Matei Uttara and others each foment war for their own reasons. One man, Marcus Aguirre, manipulates them all, for only he knows what awaits humanity if the plot fails.

*

Alexis Solovy is a starship pilot and explorer. Her father, a fallen war hero, gave his life in the Crux War. As Operations Director for Earth Alliance Strategic Command (EASC), her mother Miriam Solovy is an influential military leader. But Alex seeks only the freedom of space and has made a fortune by reading the patterns in the chaos to uncover the hidden wonders of the stars aboard her cutting-edge scout ship, the *Siyane*.

Caleb Marano is a special ops intelligence agent for the Senecan Federation. His trade is to become whatever the situation requires: to lie, deceive, outwit and if necessary use lethal force to bring his target to justice. Clever and enigmatic, he's long enjoyed the thrill and danger his job brings, but now finds himself troubled by the death of his mentor.

*

On Earth, Alex is preparing for an expedition to the Metis Nebula, a remote region on the fringes of explored space, when she receives an unexpected offer to lead the Alliance's space exploration program. After a typically contentious meeting with her mother, she refuses the job.

On Seneca, Caleb returns from a forced vacation spent with his sister Isabela and her daughter Marlee. Fresh off eradicating the terrorist group who murdered his mentor, he receives a new mission from Special Operations Director Michael Volosk: conduct a threat assessment on disturbing readings originating from the Metis Nebula.

While Alex and Caleb separately travel toward Metis, a Trade Summit between the Alliance and Federation begins on the resort world of Atlantis. Colonel Richard Navick, lifelong friend of the Solovys and EASC Naval Intelligence Liaison, is in charge of surveillance for the Summit. Unbeknownst to him, the provocation for renewed war will begin under his watch.

Jaron Nythal, Asst. Trade Director for the Federation, abets the infiltration of the Summit by the assassin Matei Uttara. Matei kills a Federation attaché, Chris Candela, and assumes his identity. On the final night of the Summit, he poisons Alliance Trade Minister Santiagar with a virus which overloads his cybernetics, causing a fatal stroke. Matei escapes in the ensuing chaos.

Shortly after departing Seneca, Caleb is attacked by mercenary ships. He defeats them, but when he later encounters Alex's ship on the fringes of Metis, he believes her to be another mercenary and fires on her. In the ensuing firefight she destroys his ship, though not before suffering damage to her own, and he crashes on a nearby planet. She is forced to land to effect repairs; recognizing her attacker will die without rescue, she takes him prisoner.

Richard Navick and Michael Volosk each separately scramble to uncover the truth of the Santiagar assassination while Olivia Montegreu, the leader of the Zelones criminal cartel, schemes with Marcus Aguirre to implement the next phase in their plan. Olivia routes missiles provided by Alliance General Liam O'Connell to a group of mercenaries.

Fighting past distrust and suspicion, Alex and Caleb complete repairs on the *Siyane* using salvaged material from the wreckage of his ship. Having gained a degree of camaraderie and affection, if not quite trust, they depart the planet in search of answers to the mystery at the heart of Metis.

What they discover is a scene from a nightmare—an armada of monstrous alien ships emerging from a massive portal, gathering a legion in preparation for an invasion.

Meanwhile, Olivia's mercenaries launch a devastating attack on the Federation colony of Palluda. Disguised to look like a strike by Alliance military forces, the attack has the desired effect of inciting war. The Federation retaliates by leveling an Alliance military base on Arcadia, and the Second Crux War has begun.

Alex and Caleb flee the Metis Nebula to warn others of the impending threat, only to learn war has broken out between their respective governments. Caleb delivers information about the alien threat to Volosk. He informs the Director of Intelligence, Graham Delavasi, who alerts the Federation government Chairman Vranas and the military's supreme commander, Field Marshal Gianno. Forced to focus on the new war with the Alliance for now, they nonetheless dispatch a stealth infiltration team to investigate Metis.

Caleb is requested to accompany the team and return to Metis, only Alex refuses to drop him off on her way to Earth. Tensions flare, but Caleb realizes he's emotionally compromised even as Alex realizes she must let him go. Instead, he agrees to go to Earth with her, and together with Volosk they devise a plan to try to bring a swift end to the war by exposing its suspicious beginnings.

The plan goes awry when Caleb is arrested shortly after they arrive—by Alex's mother—after his true identity is leaked to Richard by those in league with Marcus.

While Caleb is locked away in a detention facility, his friend Noah Terrage is recruited by Olivia to smuggle explosives to Vancouver. Possessing a conscience, he refuses. The infiltration team sent by the Federation to Metis vanishes as the Second Crux War escalates.

Alex is forced to choose between her government, her family and what she knows is right. She turns to her best friend, Kennedy Rossi, and their old hacker acquaintance, Claire Zabroi. Plans in place, Alex presents her evidence on the alien armada to a skeptical EASC Board. Their tepid reaction leads to a final confrontation with her mother and a final plea to focus on the true threat.

Alex hacks military security and breaks Caleb out of confinement. Allegiances declared and choices made, they at last give in to the passion they feel for one another. Despite lingering resentment toward the Federation for her father's death and fear that Caleb is merely playing a role, she agrees to accompany him to Seneca to find another way to combat the looming invasion.

Caleb appeals to his friend and former lover, Mia Requelme, for help in covering their tracks. She hides the *Siyane* safely away on Romane while Alex and Caleb travel to Seneca. Secretly, Caleb asks Mia to hack the ship while they are gone to grant him full access and flying privileges, something Alex zealously guards for herself. Mia uses her personal Artificial, Meno, to break the encryption on the ship.

On Earth, Richard wrestles with unease and doubt as he begins to believe Alex's claims about the origin of the war. He confesses his dilemma to his husband, Will Sutton. Will urges him to work to bring about peace and offers to convey Santiagar's autopsy report to Alex in the hope the Senecan government can find in it evidence to prove the assassination was not their doing.

Caleb and Alex hand over the autopsy report Will forwarded and all the raw data they recorded on the aliens to Volosk. In return he arranges meetings with the highest levels of leadership.

As Alex and Caleb enjoy a romantic dinner, EASC Headquarters is destroyed in a massive bombing executed by agents of Olivia and Marcus. Though intended to be killed in the attack, due to a last minute scheduling conflict Miriam Solovy is not on the premises. Instead EASC Board Chairman Alamatto perishes, along with thousands of others. On the campus but outside Headquarters, Richard narrowly escapes critical injury.

Within minutes of the bombing, Caleb and Alex are ambushed by mercenaries in downtown Cavare. Caleb kills them all in dramatic fashion, but is unaware that Alex was hit by a stray shot. In the panic of the moment he mistakes her shellshocked behavior for fear of the killer he has revealed himself to be.

Despondent but resolved to protect her, he flees with her to the Intelligence building. Upon arriving, they find the unthinkable—Michael Volosk has been murdered, his throat slit in the parking lot.

Suddenly unable to trust anyone, Caleb pleas with Alex to go with him to the spaceport, but she collapses from her injuries. With one clear mission, he steals a skycar and returns to their ship, where he can treat her wounds in the relative safety of space.

The EASC bombing successfully executed, Olivia's Zelones network turns its attention to Noah. In refusing to smuggle the explosives he is now a liability; the first attempt on his life misses him but kills his companion. Searching for answers, he traces the source of the hit and realizes he was targeted because of his friendship with Caleb. Lacking other options and with a price on his head, he flees Pandora for Messium.

Miriam returns to preside over the devastation at EASC Headquarters. She begins the process of moving the organization forward—only to learn the evidence implicates Caleb as the perpetrator.

Marcus moves one step nearer to his goal when the Alliance Assembly passes a No Confidence Vote against Prime Minister Brennon. Marcus' friend Luis Barrera is named PM, and he quickly appoints Marcus Foreign Minister.

Alex regains consciousness aboard their rented ship as they race back to Romane. Misunderstandings and innate fears drive them to the breaking point, then bring them closer than ever. The moment of contentment is short-lived, however, as Caleb—and by extension Alex—is publicly named a suspect in the bombing.

Every copy of the raw data captured at the portal, except for the original in Alex's possession, has now been destroyed. Recognizing an even deeper secret must reside within the portal and hunted by conspirators and authorities alike, Alex and Caleb begin a desperate gambit to clear their names and discover a way to defeat the aliens.

On reaching Romane, Alex, Caleb and the *Siyane* are protected by Mia while they prepare. Kennedy brings equipment to replace the ship's shielding damaged in Metis. On the *Siyane*, she realizes the repairs made using the material from Caleb's ship have begun transforming the hull into a new, stronger metal. Caleb receives encouragement from his sister Isabela, and a gesture of trust from Alex in the form of a chair.

Back on Earth, Miriam and Richard work to clear Alex's name, even as Miriam is threatened by the newly named EASC Board Chairman, Liam O'Connell. Marcus informs his alien contact that his plan has nearly come to fruition, only to be told he is out of time.

As the invaders commence their assault on the frontiers of settled space by sieging the colony of Gaiae, Alex and Caleb breach the aliens' mysterious, otherworldly portal at the heart of the Metis Nebula.

CONTENTS

VERTIGO

PART I:

DESCENT

"For each one of us stands alone in the midst of a universe."

— John Buchanan Robinson

1

SIYANE
BEYOND THE PORTAL

They were falling into a black hole.

People referred to regions of space where the distance between stars stretched to kiloparsecs as 'the void.' But even the void retained a murmur of light in the pale glint of distant stars and infinite galaxies.

This darkness was boundless and unbroken.

Dizziness clawed at the corners of Alex Solovy's vision, brought on by the absence of a fixed point, of any spatial reference whatsoever to lock onto as a lodestar.

In a fit of what could be mistaken for panic she cut propulsion and sought the rearcam visual—and found golden plasma rippling placidly inside the ring sustaining it. She let out the breath she hadn't realized she'd been holding, and the dizziness receded upon the knowledge they were not after all *in* a black hole.

The hand wrapped over hers squeezed with reassuring strength. She looked over to find Caleb wearing an air of easy confidence.

"Not dead."

She knew the calm aura he projected was for her benefit, to give her comfort. And it worked. Her pulse slowed and the pounding receded from her ears. A laugh bubbled forth, only to morph into a mild protest halfway through. "Not dead. Excellent point. But what *is* this place?"

She returned the squeeze, then let go of his hand and directed her attention to the HUD as readings began coming in. Sensor sweeps were picking up no transmissions save the tremendously low frequency wave from the portal, which continued unabated for as far as her instruments reached. Analysis of the surroundings reported…nothing out of the ordinary.

"The immediate area has the same fundamental characteristics as our galaxy. According to these readings, the laws of physics are alive and well and functioning correctly. The impulse engine is able to operate within parameters. If the portal is a Brane intersection..." she glanced over with a frown "...the dimensions of this place are identical to ours. So *why* is it a portal?"

She checked the visual overlay. "We are definitely not anywhere in the Milky Way, though. It'll take the system time to analyze all the possibilities, assuming it *can* with no locus...but I don't believe we're anywhere in mapped space."

"Maybe the portal merely sent us a long way." He shrugged. "Like 'the other side of the universe' long way?"

"Well the other side of the universe is a damn boring place. There's nothing here."

"But there *was* something here. There were ships here, a lot of them, and they had an origin point."

She pinched the bridge of her nose in a futile attempt to ease the dull throbbing behind her forehead then rested her elbows on her knees.

This wasn't what she had expected.

She hadn't known what to expect. Perhaps a fresh armada of alien superdreadnoughts eager to return humanity to the stardust whence they came? Or more preferably, a dazzling civilization of exotic space stations, Dyson rings and planets subsumed beneath cities? She had idly entertained the notion of a mind-exploding dimensional shift to a gestalt of reality she hadn't the acumen to comprehend.

But she hadn't expected *this*.

She stared at the varied screens intended to display a plethora of information. One by one they updated. *Nothing.* Nothing save the portal and the *Siyane*. Yet somewhere beyond this barren expanse lived the aliens who dispatched an armada of warships through the Metis Nebula.

"I think...I think we follow the TLF wave for now. It's still being generated by something farther in. We can use the portal as a heading reference so we don't go in circles. I'll keep scanning on wideband, and eventually that 'something' will show up. It has to."

Hearing no agreement or any response at all, she toed the chair around to face Caleb. He was peering out the viewport, shoulders taut in a suggestion of unease. "What's wrong?"

He blinked and straightened up in his chair. "Sorry. That sounds fine." A corner of his mouth tweaked up in a hint of a smile. "I wouldn't dream of arguing with you on the best way to navigate uncharted space. This is your show. But I was wondering…the portal had vanished until we reactivated it, which means they never expected anyone to come through it. So why are they hiding?"

"Maybe they're not hiding. Maybe they're simply…farther. Let's find out." She reengaged propulsion and accelerated until they attained a steady eighty-five percent cruising speed. No reason to overtax the impulse engine on the off chance the laws of physics weren't *exactly* the same here.

In the pervasive darkness there was no visual perception of movement, and only the subtle *purr* of the engine argued otherwise. It was rather disconcerting, so she sought solace in monitoring the portal in the rearcam. For the time being the sight of it shrinking in the distance did at least convey a sense of motion.

Then it vanished, and the void truly was absolute.

"Dammit!" She killed the thrusters entirely before confirming the gamma wave was still transmitting. It took considerable effort to resist the powerful urge to whirl the ship around and bolt for where the portal had been. To flee this suffocating *emptiness.*

Instead she slumped in her chair, arms flopping weakly to drape over the armrests. Her instruments would have been able to keep a lock on the portal long after it had passed from visual sight. But now….

"Must be a distance limit on the signal to keep it open. *Dammit.*"

Caleb had stood to pace behind the cockpit. In the wake of their discovery of the alien armada she had quickly deduced he did his best thinking while roving. Had it been only weeks ago? It felt like a lifetime had transpired since they had uncovered the terrifying secret at the heart of Metis.

"Can we use the TLF as a guidance mechanism? A sort of beacon?"

"So long as we don't lose track of which way is forward and which is back. The key is going to be…" she swiveled to the dash, magnified one of the HUD screens and began inputting commands

"...I'm setting the navigation system to record our relative movements. It will create a mapping of our path, in essence. If all else fails we can retrace our steps."

"Will it work?"

"It'll work." Instructions completed, she sank back to stare out into the yawning abyss once more.

It was a bleak panorama. Forbidding. Oppressive. She yearned for stars to light the way, to shepherd and inspire her. But there were none.

In lieu of stars she reached behind her, somehow knowing his hand would soon be in hers, warm and comforting. Solid. *Real.*

On finding what she sought, she sucked in a deep breath and continued on.

⫘

They had been flying for what felt like hours when the first blips emerged on the long-range scanner.

Bored to tears and craving reassurance life remained possible in this desolate wasteland, she was curled up in Caleb's lap when the alert sounded. In *her* chair in his lap, on account of it being larger and more comfy and all.

She leapt up and magnified the USAR data while motioning him out of the chair impatiently.

"What do we have?"

"Looks like—" More blips materialized on the scanner. Then more...and it occurred to her she didn't technically have a plan for this particular scenario. "We found them."

She yanked the ship sixty degrees starboard and pushed the impulse engine to its limit. The inertial dampers prevented them from being thrown to the floor, but she engaged the safety harness in her chair, as did he.

"Let's see if..." what was now a veritable sea of increasingly larger red dots shifted on the screen "...hell. They can track us. Worse, they *are* tracking us."

"Their dimension, their rules. Can you outrun them?"

She checked the numbers beneath the display tracking the vessels to see how rapidly they were approaching. "No."

"Can you beat them back to the portal?"

She swerved one more time to confirm and watched in dismay as they tracked her course yet again. "Not a chance. They'll be on us in minutes."

"What can I do to help?"

She magnified the longest-range scans of the region. She wanted to FTL. At superluminal speeds she'd outrun them, or at a minimum they wouldn't—surely couldn't—be able to track her. But she had no sense of how large or small this space may be or what might even happen if she initiated a warp bubble.

"Alex?"

"You can *shut up* and let me think."

"Right."

The tightness in his voice jarred her. She softened her own tone. "Sorry. Just...hang on."

In the corner of her eye she noted the muscles in his jaw twitching. "Okay."

The last time she had been in a firefight she had been shooting at *him*. The irony would have been amusing if not—

—the first of the blips came in range of the visual scanner. It was one of the insectile tentacled vessels from the alien armada.

"We're being chased by an army of squid. And goddamn are they fast squid."

Her gaze raced across every display, every sensor, every reading...but perceiving no answers, it fell to the oblivion outside the viewport. They couldn't run; the ships were almost upon them. They certainly couldn't fend off what now constituted a solid one hundred pursuers.

She thought Caleb might have said her name, but it was background radiation accompanying the hum in her ears and the symphony in her head—a song of quantum mechanics and trajectory calculations and astroscience physics and *where to go, where to go, where to...*.

With a long sweep of her hand the entire HUD vanished. At the end of the gesture her wrist flicked and the lights in the cabin shut off. The inside of the ship was now as featureless as the landscape outside it.

She engaged the autopilot, unfastened her harness, stood and stepped up to the viewport. Her eyes closed.

Moya milaya, do not be afraid of the dark, for there is always light within it struggling to shine through. Be fearless, and you will see it.

She reopened her eyes, and the world outside was no longer cast in charred ebony. More of a dull charcoal now really, except...there. An *absence* within the emptiness. Hollow. An echo of the space around it.

She fell back in the chair, re-latching the harness with one hand while disengaging the autopilot with the other and pulling the ship up in a long arc before veering another twelve degrees starboard. Once the harness was engaged she reactivated the HUD and the lights.

"What do you see?"

Anyone other than him would have quizzed her when she shut everything off, or questioned her sanity. But he had recognized she needed the silence and held his inquiry until now.

"Somewhere darker than black."

A few adjustments and she coaxed another two percent out of the impulse engine, but their pursuers were still gaining on them. It was going to be *close*.

What was going to be close? She was flying headlong into another black hole, and she couldn't fathom what waited inside it.

It hardly mattered now. She had no other option.

The lead row of vessels fired, scarlet-hued lasers bursting out from flaming crimson cores. The writhing arms of the attacking ships ignited, lengthening to amplify the beams and direct them to their target.

In the instant before the beams impacted she flung the *Siyane* into a full spin, praying the rapid revolutions might cause the beams to lose tracking or simply cause them to miss.

Her stomach joined the *Siyane* in its spins as the inertial dampers failed miserably to compensate for the speed of the revolutions. In the cabin 'up' and 'down' lost meaning.

"Jesus, Alex...."

A growl escaped through gritted teeth. "Just...hang...on...."

It took every iota of her concentration to keep the nose of the ship pointed toward what was a perfect eclipse of infinite blackness. The walls blurred away, along with everything else in her peripheral vision. She kept her focus directly ahead on the void within the void, for if her attention drifted a millimeter off-center she would be lost.

The ship shuddered in her grasp as a laser beam grazed off the lower hull. She ignored it to stay locked on the chasm racing toward her; yet as it consumed the viewport terror bubbled up into her throat. *Dad, I don't think—*

—they breached the edge and plunged in—

—and were inexplicably careening through an atmosphere. Shadow became brilliant sulfur as light flared to life around them.

Utterly unprepared for light, of all things, she was temporarily blinded. She fought to pull out of the roll she had created while blinking furiously and begging her ocular implant to give her *something* before the atmospheric forces tore her beloved ship to pieces and them with it. "I can't *see.*"

"I can, in infrared. Let me help you."

Then he was beside her. One of his arms wound tightly around the armrest; the other curled over hers on the controls. She willed her grip relaxed and let her hand respond to his guiding touch.

It took a few seconds, but the spinning diminished to wild gyrations, then to mere turbulence. Down and up returned to their proper positions, and the bright halos overwhelming her vision began to fade.

"I...I'm okay. Mostly. Enough."

He collapsed to the floor next to her chair. "Good job, baby."

His voice sounded terribly weak, trembling from the effort of speaking. She didn't understand how he had managed to get to her side, much less remain there without a harness, *much less* stay focused ahead and be her eyes. She wanted to wrap her arms around him and cradle him against her, but she still needed both hands.

The atmosphere did show signs of thinning, though. With a deep, steadying breath she transitioned to the pulse detonation engine for planetary flight and allowed her fingers to sink into his hair.

A moment later the haze coating the sky evaporated away.

"When you can, you're going to want to look up...."

He steadied himself by resting one palm on her thigh and the other on the armrest, and rose to his knees. "I'll be damned."

"Possibly. But not today, I think."

They flew high above savanna grassland. The sky was the deep cornflower blue of a sunny late afternoon on Earth...*exactly* the color of a sunny late afternoon on Earth.

Only there was no sun. Whatever was lighting this planet, it wasn't a star.

2

GAIAE

B *reathe or die.*
The acrid odor in the air burnt Seraphina's nostrils with every breath, searing away filaments and delicate skin on its way to her lungs. She didn't want to take another breath, dreading the pain it would bring. But it was that or die.

As if there was any choice other than death anymore.

She crawled through the singed remains of a grassy meadow in the darkness and tried not to think about how the odor had shifted over the course of the last hours, becoming less the scent of scorched flora and fauna and more the aroma of cooked, spoiling flesh. As soon as the thought crept into her mind she gagged, dry heaves welling up from her stomach and stalling her progress through the meadow. Her diaphragm spasmed, but there hadn't been anything in her stomach to expunge for two days.

She blinked away hazy tears and tried to focus on the building in the distance. She needed water. The Retreat Center would have water.

The attack had been relentless and unforgiving. Her sheer stupidity had been the only thing that saved her from dying in the first hour; she had been in such a blind panic when she ran screaming that she ended up lost deep in the forest jungle beyond the pond. Exhausted, her skin scraped and welts bubbling up from brushes against numerous poisonous plants as she fled, she had finally collapsed to the ground—only to gape in horror as billowing mushrooms of flame erupted from the direction of the town center and the spaceport beyond.

Enormous void ships soared across the sky, plasma beams the color of arterial blood eighty meters in diameter burning the landscape in savage bursts.

Her parents had ensured she received a quality education, and she earned decent marks before leaving her family and school behind for Gaiae. She didn't believe ships of such size and breadth should be able to hover within the atmosphere of a planet. Yet evidently she was incorrect.

Perhaps she had misunderstood the lessons. Or perhaps these ships did not obey the laws of the universe. They plainly did not obey any laws of nature.

Hundreds of the writhing tentacled creatures—she couldn't convince herself to think of them as 'ships,' so malevolent was their appearance—prowled the landscape, eager to direct a blood-gorged eye of death on any living creature they found. She had survived these last days solely because the dense tangle of vines and trees of the forest proved a challenge for them. Even with their slithery form they were too large to fit through the small gaps in the weald.

But then one of the void ships had casually turned its attention to her forest, and the encroaching flames drove her steadily back toward town.

And now she *had* to find water. Her formerly supple, carefully-moisturized skin cracked and bled. The effect of a lack of internal hydration was magnified by the fact that the air had long since been sucked dry of every drop of humidity. Simply existing in the world drained moisture from her skin and her soul.

The water in the small ponds and streams of the region, while not technically poisonous, was also not especially healthy for humans. She'd been told consuming it was akin to drinking ocean salt water. Still, she'd come dangerously close to doing it anyway when her tongue swelled and her throat became sandpaper scraping against every breath. She was rather proud of herself for resisting. Who knew she possessed such willpower?

She wished there was someone for her to brag smugly to…but everyone was dead. On a world once overflowing with life, there was only death.

She had broken down and messaged her parents on New Orient within hours of the attack to cry for help, but of course no communications were available. Why would there be? Blocking communications must be a triviality to these beasts.

So the galaxy could not hear her cries. She didn't know if it would care if it did hear them, but it hardly mattered. She had also long since given up on speculating what sin they had committed to deserve such punishment. She didn't even care anymore.

Her hands clawed at the dirt, and she was again crawling toward the Retreat Center. She'd tried the spaceport first, harbored the tiniest spark of hope she might locate a working shuttle...but the spaceport was gone, replaced by a smoldering crater.

A charred body lay to her left; she scurried past it. It may have been Eliza, or Ariel, she wasn't sure. Another body among hundreds of others. Thousands, if she crawled far enough.

If she could just get her hands on a little water, she...well, she had no idea what she might do then. It didn't matter. She would live another minute. It surprised her to realize how much she wanted that.

The shadow of the building drew her in with the promise of safety. Nearly there. The glow of burning buildings and burning trees and burning air lit the night to a terra cotta dusk. Most of the buildings on Gaiae were constructed from indigenous timber; they made for excellent kindling.

Out of the glow one of the tentacled creatures materialized in the distance. It patrolled the street, its spindly arms twisting about as though they sensed where life still dwelled. She clung to the façade and shimmied toward the door. The creature veered the other way, and she slipped in.

The air was no less dry inside, the environmental controls having shut off long ago when the power station exploded. Yet for the first time in endless days she was inside, and it felt *glorious.*

She reminded herself to stay low and below the windows as she hurried toward the kitchen area. The refrigeration system, much like the temperature and humidity controls, had ceased functioning days earlier. She didn't care.

All thoughts of caution fled as she pulled open the formerly refrigerated drawer and yanked out several packets of water. They spilled across the floor—she scrambled after them, frantic they might vanish. She halted the closest one's escape and greedily tilted it up.

Bliss more wondrous than even the most fantastic orgasm flooded through her as the tepid water coursed down her throat.

She laughed until she choked, coughed half of it up, caught her breath and grabbed another packet.

She was giggling hysterically, water streaming over her chin and down her neck, when the beam from the tentacled ship sliced through her. She was dead before her brain had put aside the euphoria to recognize it had happened.

3

SPACE, NORTH-CENTRAL QUADRANT
DESNAN STELLAR SYSTEM (BORDER OF SENECAN FEDERATION SPACE)

Were it any other world, someone might have noticed when Gaiae disappeared from the grid. But the denizens of the Milky Way were preoccupied with their own problems—most notably an escalating war amongst themselves—and simply couldn't be bothered with the well-being of a tiny planet in the middle of nowhere inhabited by pseudo-religious zealots.

Track. Drop. Invert. Lock. Fire.

"Down."

Senecan Federation Commander Morgan Lekkas, for instance, was preoccupied with the eight—well seven now—missiles which had been launched from what was, by all appearances, a solitary Alliance ship protecting the planet of Desna.

Eight missiles normally would not have been much of a problem for her fighter squadron, but her team now constituted a 'squadron' only in the official military records. Already down two ships after the Arcadia mission, Commodore Pachis had taken Flight 2 from her to bolster the 1st squadron for the primary offensive on the planet.

Most of the formations comprising the 3rd Wing of the Senecan Federation Southern Fleet had suffered heavy losses in the earlier battle less than a parsec from here. Still, Desna was not believed to be strongly defended either in space or on the ground, so officials far above her rank decided the depleted 3rd Wing possessed the necessary firepower to complete the operation on its own.

With a population of less than fifty thousand, the colony constituted little more than an outpost as the closest Alliance-controlled world to Federation space. Desna possessed a single orbital array and no ground forces. Recent intel acquired on Alliance defense protocols now enabled their electronic warfare vessels to scramble an array's targeting mechanism, rendering it ineffective while their frigates destroyed the weaponry.

They should have been able to walk in and take it without suffering so much as a scratch.

But it turned out the space above Desna was not entirely undefended. A single stealthed ship using the shadow of Desna's moon for additional camouflage had launched four missiles before they knew it was there. It had then accelerated fully behind the moon and launched four additional missiles while peeking out the other side.

If she could get to this ship she could take it out, even hampered by a mere five fighters at her side. But before she could do so they needed to take out the missiles which sped on trajectories leading to each of the Senecan frigates, by now spread over megameters as they worked to neutralize the array weapons.

Her left iris shifted a millimeter, and the second of four whispers splayed in her virtual vision sharpened into focus. Five missiles now remained, two of which were approaching dangerously close to the *SFS Preveza*.

Commander Lekkas (Alpha): Charlie—5. Beta—1. Delta—2. Epsilon, Foxtrot, on me. Preveza, two missiles free on your port flank. Recommend evasive maneuvers bearing N 7° to 16°.

Preveza: Acknowledged, Commander.

If the *Preveza* managed to put some distance between itself and the missiles, she would arrive in time. She arced down to drop into the center of a tight v-formation with Epsilon and Foxtrot. The light of Desna's sun danced off the lustrous bronze hulls of the fighters as they accelerated at full impulse speed into an intercept course.

R

Earth Alliance Lieutenant Colonel Malcolm Jenner, on the other hand, was preoccupied with the fact that his current circumstances were more than likely the last circumstances he would ever find himself in.

He grasped the railing above the navigation pit and kept his gaze fixed on the tactical map slightly to his left. His knuckles had long since gone white from the fierceness of the grip; he had long since stopped noticing.

He should retreat.

The *Juno* was out of missiles and too far away for plasma weapons. If he exposed himself and closed the distance enough to use the plasma weapons then he was dead and everyone under his command with him.

He should retreat.

There was no backup. No support. The *Juno* was the sole Alliance vessel for parsecs, sent to Desna as the most token of guards against an offensive.

Even if the missiles he had fired took out all three Senecan frigates—a best-case scenario which had already failed—once the missiles were no longer a threat the fighters were coming for him, and he would not be able to outmaneuver them. He stood a decent chance of taking out one or two, but no more.

He should retreat.

He had advised Rear Admiral Tarone to retreat when they found themselves outnumbered and outgunned at Orellan, and surely the same logic applied here. He was *quite clearly* outnumbered and outgunned.

But he couldn't abandon an undefended planet and call himself a Marine the next day. His ship was fully functional and wielded unlimited plasma weapons to fire. It was his duty to defend this Alliance world, tiny though it was, until he was no longer capable of doing so.

The 2nd Regiment had been decimated in the ambush at the Orellan asteroid field; only the carrier *EAS Sao Paulo*, his ship and a single fighter survived the encounter. The *Sao Paulo* remained at Fionava, since with no fighter squadrons to transport it had minimal purpose for the moment.

He didn't know who had decided the *Juno* should be dispatched to 'guard' Desna. Tarone had given the order, but it was as likely to have originated from General Foster, if not Strategic Command. Whoever made the decision was an imbecile masquerading in an officer's uniform. The Senecans had demonstrated the capability to take out orbital arrays in short order at Arcadia. Without the array to provide cover or distract the attackers for a while, there was simply no way for a single frigate to defend a *planet*. It was impossible.

But he had kept his mouth shut, accepted the assignment and frankly hoped the Senecans wouldn't come for Desna.

He should retreat.

Instead he would do what he could.

"Flight Lieutenant Billoughy, you ready to earn your pay?"

"Yes, sir!"

"Excellent. Navigation: make sure the impulse engine is primed and receiving full power. Weapons: your targets are expected to be Senecan fighter craft. Track them as they approach, and the second one breaches the moon's profile, you lock and fire. Billoughy: the instant Weapons has fired, you fly us back into the moon's cover while we acquire a new target."

"Yes, sir. It's just...."

"It's alright, Flight Lieutenant. Speak your mind."

"Well, if we move around the moon won't we be exposed to the *rest* of the Senecan ships?"

"Eventually, yes. We will. I need you to use every maneuver you know or have ever heard of to delay that event as long as you can."

"Understood, sir."

On the tactical map the final two missiles vanished short of their targets. He swallowed hard and lifted his chin. "Get ready. Here they come."

⌐R

Morgan pivoted hard to reverse direction and left the bright plume of the missile's explosion behind her.

Alpha: Spread on me. Breach lunar profile 45° breadth. Target is Alliance frigate currently at S 78.29° z-8.05 E. Expect hostile fire.

Once locked on a target, plasma weapons tracked it through any evasive maneuvers and speeds up to 0.6 light speed, but the tracking did require line of sight from the weapon system to the target. She knew researchers were developing experimental 'bending' weaponry, but until the tech was approved and rolled out, she could not hit the frigate—and it could not hit her—through the physical barrier of the moon's profile.

A plasma stream erupted out of the shadow of the moon a microsecond after the frigate became targetable, giving her no time to return fire before shifting course. As she pulled upward in a tight arc and raced belly-up a sliver above the surface of the moon, she saw the enemy vessel bank away in the opposite direction and disappear once more. *Damn, this captain's good.*

She fell into the protection of the curving lunar surface and the plasma beam sliced away less than four meters above her. Her comm immediately burst to life with updates from her squadmates.

Charlie: Impact confirmed, aft starboard quadrant. Engine damage unclear.

Excellent. In taking the lead position and providing a target, she had given her other pilots the opportunity to launch several shots. It had been a fruitful first move. Now the game began in earnest.

Alpha: Pursue and evade.

She did not rejoin her squadron as they gave chase. Instead she increased her damper field to full strength and allowed her ship to continue on its current arc around the moon. She looked 'up' to see a pale lime surface of Picrite basalt racing by. Pockmarks which were tiny from afar now loomed large to cleave into the lunar face. The still tacking frigate grew closer.

Her whisper virtual screens displayed all the data she needed regarding the enemy vessel, her squadron and her ship. They spread across the entirety of her vision to paint a landscape as real to her as the physical one beyond them.

She smiled as Beta scored another hit on the enemy ship's broadside, only to mutter a curse when he failed to avoid the frigate's plasma beam. Beta had always been brave and reckless in equal measure; it made him a great pilot but would probably shorten his lifespan.

Not today though. He ejected safely and barring disaster should be unharmed. His ship, not so much. She imagined him weaving a tapestry of curses back aboard the *Catania*.

Pachis received the 'all clear' on the orbital array from the frigate captains and initiated the planetary offensive. Assuming there were no similarly heroic, insane soldiers planet-side, it should be a bloodless affair.

He might have sent one of the frigates to assist in removing the Alliance ship, but he did not. She assumed this meant he trusted her implicitly to do her job and handle the problem. He should.

The enemy ship was very near now. They were on a collision course, though the Alliance captain did not know it. In the unlikely event she registered on his sensors, he would be fully engaged in his game of cat and mouse with the remainder of her squadron and miss her until it was too late. But she wouldn't show up. Not until...

...now. She disengaged the damper field and soared away from the lunar surface, still inverted, she and her ship one seamless avatar.

Target. Lock. Fire.

The white-blue hot plasma of the frigate's impulse engine filled her viewport, washing out her whispers until they darkened to contrast against the bright background. She flew forty meters behind her target as her weapons seared into the core. The hyperlight honeycombed metamaterial of her hull was capable of withstanding the heat...for twenty-six seconds. It would take half those seconds to single-handedly destroy the sizeable impulse engine.

In contrast to most battles, there were no enemy fighters to come to the frigate's aid. As she moved in lockstep with the ship when it shifted away and tried to evade her squadmates, she had to wonder what Alliance asshole was moronic enough to send a single frigate to defend an entire world.

The whisper on her far right began to flash warnings as the heat threshold of the hull neared. Another three seconds...2...1... The glow of the engine shifted from pale blue to fiery orange as the chain reaction began. She had six seconds before the disabling overload erupted.

Alpha: Evac safe distance.

She spun 270° and raced away from the moon toward the stars.

Klaxons blared through the bridge of the *Juno*, the bugle tones crashing into one another in a discordant concerto of impending death.

"Hull breach mid-starboard Deck 2, damage to environmental systems!"

"Evacuate and seal it off—"

"Primary shields at 14%!"

Malcolm continued to hang on to the railing as the ship shuddered and lurched beneath him. At least he had progressed beyond scrambling for his chair and stood on the deck like a proper shipman. Mostly. "Billoughy, got anything left?"

"Sir, we're about to—shit! One of the fighters slipped around and is firing on the impulse engine!"

Damn, this squadron leader's good.

With no support they could not elude the fighter; however fast they might be able to maneuver, it would be faster. If they spent their precious remaining seconds *trying* to evade the rear fighter, they became a sitting duck for the other fighters to rip through their meager remaining shields.

"Billoughy: engage the sLume drive now. Weapons: fire everything you've got at any and every target until it engages."

"Yes, sir. Destination?"

The floor beneath Malcolm convulsed as the impulse engine exploded. A heavy breath fell silently beneath the violent clamor of alarms. He had done all he could. He wouldn't sacrifice his men on the altar of pride. But for the sLume drive, the ship was now a derelict. He only hoped the core hull managed to hold together long enough for a rescue. He readied the distress signal.

"Anywhere but here."

4

SIYANE
Portal Prime, Uncharted Space

"Why aren't they chasing us?"

Caleb dropped one hand on her armrest and the other on the dash and leaned in to study the HUD screens alongside her. If he was still struggling to regain his bearings, he concealed it well. "Are you sure? None of them?"

"The scanners are pinging with all their strength, but nothing is showing up. I don't think they followed us through the…whatever it is shielding the planet. Which makes no sense."

"Perhaps they veered off when we disappeared—they *really* aren't chasing us?"

"No." Alex tried not to allow the scene outside the viewport to distract her. Survival first, suspiciously pleasant-looking mystery planet later. "But the lead ships were seconds behind us. They hadn't the time to veer off. So…where are they?"

"Did they break apart in the atmosphere?"

Considering how close the *Siyane* had come to breaking apart, a valid question. "Not unless they disintegrated, because there's no debris on the radar either. I suppose if they took a different trajectory the debris might be too far away to detect, but it's doubtful. The ships wouldn't have entered mid-death spiral like we did. They should have been able to traverse it without difficulty." She shook her head. "I don't understand. Those squid should be here trying to fry us."

"Agreed. Still, the fact this planet is invisible from the outside strikes me as a greater mystery. We solve that one, and I bet we figure out this one as well."

"Fair point." The tumble through the atmosphere had left her with a throbbing headache as her brain struggled to reorient its contents to their proper positions. "I'll keep scanning for pursuers, but until they show up we hunt for a power source—a strong one. Generating a planet-sized shield will require enormous energy."

His hand alighted upon her jaw and urged it toward him. She relented and found his eyes boring into hers, concern swirling to darken his irises. "Are you okay? That was some fairly intense flying back there, to put it mildly. Maybe we ought to find a safe place to land and catch our breath."

She scoffed. "Nah, I'm good. Spectacular even...which might be a slight exaggeration. But I'm intensely curious, and not at all ready to relax."

He sighed in concession. "You win. Let's go investigate."

"You got it." She straightened her posture and directed her attention ahead, though the radar display remained firmly in the corner of her vision.

The grassland grew increasingly sandy and soon transitioned into rolling dunes. "We're coming up on a shoreline."

They left the dunes behind and began flying over a body of water. At first glimpse it resembled an average ocean, the surface buffeted by wind and regular wave patterns lapping toward shore. The water gleamed a surprisingly pale teal, but she'd seen waters of similar color on Scythia and Fionava.

Yet as the ocean presumably grew deeper, as oceans were prone to do, the hue didn't darken. On the contrary, it lightened. "Is the water glowing?"

"It's hard to tell...." Caleb blinked several times. "I'm not picking up anything unusual on other spectrum bands. But it does appear almost luminescent." Abruptly he moved back and out of her peripheral vision. "How long would you say we've been here?"

She shrugged, her attention fully on the strange body of water. "Twenty minutes, maybe twenty-five? Why?"

"My eVi says it's been almost an hour."

"No, it can't...." She checked her own time and scowled. "I didn't note the time when we arrived, had a few other things on my mind." Her focus now inward, she watched seconds tick by at alarming speed. Two...two and a half times the normal rate.

"That is enough!" She leapt out of the cockpit chair, leaving the autopilot to continue cruising them above the ocean while she rushed to the data center. "What the *d'yavol* is up with this place? Are you telling me we're losing time?"

"I don't know." She noted the tension in his voice and had the fleeting thought, *at least something unnerves him.*

At the control panel she set diagnostics running on several internal systems. The results matched her eVi's information...yet insisted nothing was wrong. Time moved forward under the same rules it always had, and the ship seemed perfectly fine with it.

She was certain the seconds were passing more rapidly than they should, yet she couldn't sense it. Nothing felt odd. She moved, breathed and talked normally. Or thought she did.

"The cloaking shield must be some kind of crocked quantum field...or maybe it was the portal. I didn't think to check the passage of *time* while we were flying. This whole space could be off-kilter."

She gestured away the diagnostic tests in frustration. "I seriously do not like this, Caleb. You realize what it means?"

He tread a deliberate yet circular path around the cabin. "Every perceived minute we're here is more than two minutes at home. By the time we return...."

"Everyone could be dead?"

"I hope not. But...the situation may be worse than we expect."

She spun toward the cockpit, instantly a whirl of motion. "We need to go back. We can't waste time here while people are being slaughtered."

He grabbed her by the shoulders as she passed him, impeding her advancement. "We don't have anything to go back with. We return now and we're as helpless to defeat the invasion as we were when we left."

"But—"

"No 'buts.' I admit this development...complicates matters and is more than a little disconcerting, but it doesn't change the reality. As things stand now there's nothing we can do back home except get arrested and imprisoned, which I deeply want to avoid." The graveled rasp in his voice told her he meant it. "But we can do something here. We can solve the mystery."

Her head shook violently. She pulled away to rush through the cabin. Her steps were agitated and mostly directionless, but she couldn't manage to stop. "Right. Figure this place out. Find the aliens. So we need to pinpoint the source then—"

His arms wound around her waist from behind and spun her to face him, holding her steady in his grasp. "Alex, you're panicking. You need to calm down."

Blood drummed in her ears; adrenaline coursed through her veins, driving her to move. To *act*. Her hands trembled against his chest. Time vanished out from beneath her feet, one accelerating second at a time.

But because she trusted him, she worked to concentrate her focus on him and him alone.

His expression and his touch calmed her in their reassurance, though he was unable to entirely mask his own troubled thoughts weighing down the set of his mouth. "If we want to help everyone, we…we can't obsess over what may be happening on the other side of the portal right now. A couple of extra days will be worth it if they mean we find answers. But rushing means we'll make a mistake, and making a mistake in this peculiar, alien place will get us killed. So focus on solving the mystery."

It came as something of a surprise when it began to get dark, everywhere and all at once.

The insectile ships, or 'squid' as Alex had taken to calling them, never showed up. Why they had not done so was a question he suspected might have kept him awake tonight for longer than he preferred—and her even longer—if not for the question of the rapid flow of time demanding precedence.

They flew for hours, by any measure of time. They saw mountains and oceans and rivers and deserts and learned enough to arrive at one inescapable conclusion: geographically speaking, this planet was Earth in miniature.

The atmosphere contained oxygen, nitrogen and other gases in the exact proportions Earth exhibited prior to nearly a thousand years ago when the subtle changes brought about by industrialization began to manifest. Gravity was identical to a hundredth of a percent. Alex believed she had identified the coastline of the North American Gulf in the east and Baja in the west, as well as the

Arabian Peninsula on the other side of the world. They nearly lapped the planet, enough to determine the circumference measured roughly a third that of Earth.

It wasn't a copy of Earth though. Aside from the reduced size, there were the luminescent oceans to consider. Yet more disconcerting was the fact the planet didn't rotate. While they knew it wasn't orbiting any visible object, rotation was such a fundamental characteristic of planetary objects that it seemed impossible it didn't. It also raised the question (the latest on a lengthy and growing list) of how the gravity matched Earth's without centrifugal force.

The planet appeared devoid of any sign of technology as far as they were able to see, or any civilization or intelligent life at all. They didn't even pick up readings which might indicate wildlife. Admittedly, they still had a lot of land to cover.

And now it was getting dark. Which was...interesting, seeing as there existed no sun to set.

"Where is the light being generated from? Earth does not have its own invisible self-generating light source. There is technology here, somewhere."

"Which we're unlikely to be able to find in the dark." He swung her chair around and leaned in, bracing himself on the armrests.

She had done an exceptional job of compartmentalizing, of pushing aside the panic and the fervent, burning need to run—run fast enough to outpace the too-fast ticking of time. He understood this because it clawed at him no less than it did her. But the hours had taken their toll.

"We should land for the night. We still don't really know anything about this planet. It's dangerous to fly in the dark, and you're exhausted."

"But we're losing time and—"

"Alex, *land*. We passed a small sheltered valley a few minutes ago. Go back and set down there. I'm going to throw together a little dinner, and then we are going to get some sleep."

She stared at him, fatigue weighing on her features as she worked to formulate a protest...then at last gave a weary smile with a more weary laugh. "Can we have pasta? I'd really like pasta right now."

"Of course we can have pasta." He placed a tender kiss on her forehead and headed toward the kitchen area.

"And cheese?"

He chuckled to himself as he opened the refrigeration cabinet. "And cheese."

He had felt rather helpless since they'd gone through the portal, and helpless was not a role he did well...even if the last several weeks had given him a decent amount of practice. But he did do concealment well, so other than the brief slip-up while fleeing the pursuing ships he hid his frustration from her.

The slip-up had occurred because he knew he could help her. All he needed to do was reach out his hand and take command—of propulsion, power distribution, scanners, weapons, *something*. She was a better pilot than him no question, but he was plenty capable at flying and even more so at engineering systems. And she surely realized it, yet remained too damn stubborn to give up a sliver of control.

It had worked out, this time. So he remained in limbo, caught between the powerful need to act to influence their fortune and the *for now* more powerful need to retain her trust.

But he wasn't completely helpless. He could cook for her, which made her happy. He could keep her nourished and help her not give in to despair and make sure she remembered to sleep. And asleep in his arms, he could keep her safe.

Alex wiggled in his arms until she had turned around to face him. He frowned and kissed her mouth. "You're not asleep."

"No. I was thinking about this place. Caleb, I have no idea what's going on. I have no explanation for the *khrenovuyu* time. I have no explanation for this planet, its characteristics or even its existence. Obviously it's not what we expected to find, but it has to be important. For one, it's impossible the whole 'mini-Earth' aspect is a coincidence. It's as if it was custom made for us...or for humans, anyway."

"Or was designed to replicate the conditions we 'grew up' in."

Her nose crinkled up at him as though he wouldn't have sounded any more insane had he proclaimed cats sported three heads and lettuce glowed fluorescent orange, but she didn't press the matter. It was just as well. So early in the game he rarely was able to explain the conclusions his instincts suggested.

"And why is it hidden? Not from us—well from 'us,' if not from me—but from the alien ships?"

"It means there's more than one player on the field."

Her eyes rose to meet his, irises watery with the effort of staying open. "What do you mean?"

This notion must not sound so insane as to be dismissed out of hand. "Whoever or whatever controls this planet, I think we can assume they've chosen to conceal it from the military ships. I don't know what that implies. We may be dealing with several different species, feuding factions or something else entirely. But it means our enemy is not a monolithic entity."

Her grin was sleepy and lopsided. "They teach you that in spy school?"

His lips brushed feather-light across hers. "Yeah, they did. Now go to *sleep.*"

She nuzzled her nose against his neck and snuggled closer. "You first...." But in seconds her muscles had relaxed and her breath evened out.

His fingertips ghosted down her hair, gently so as not to disturb her. Eventually sheer exhaustion won out for him as well, his brain too fatigued to make heads or tails out of everything that had happened, and he drifted off to sleep. He did so pondering how in seven hells this impossible planet might lead them to a way to defeat an invading army, and who the forces back home were colluding with and whether they were against or at odds to or irrespective of the aliens.

But mostly he did so pondering how he could possibly find a way to not lose the singular creature sleeping against him, or the peace—the wholly unexpected and unasked for contentment—which came with her. Because any and all gods help him but he needed it. Needed her.

5

"What do you mean, they've *occupied* Desna?"

"I mean they've occupied Desna. They destroyed the orbital array weapons and, in the absence of a ground-based military presence to challenge them, landed, took the governor into custody and proclaimed it a province of the Senecan Federation. They're expanding their borders."

Earth Alliance Strategic Command Acting Chairman General Liam O'Connell slammed his palm down on his desk. The force generated by his burly frame sent a tremor through the synthetic ironwood. He leveled a glower across the quivering desk. "They simply marched in and took it? Desna occupies a key strategic position—where were the defenses?"

I don't know, Liam, where were *the defenses?* EASC Director of Operations Admiral Miriam Solovy inwardly marveled at the bureaucratic machine which had resulted in such a man occupying the utmost position of military power in the galaxy. Outwardly she wore a mask of cool composure.

"After Arcadia and now Desna, I think it's clear Seneca has minimal difficulty taking out our standard defense arrays. The small military presence formerly stationed at Desna had been temporarily reassigned to Arcadia in the wake of the destruction of the military base there."

"You're telling me it was completely unprotected?"

"A single frigate was tasked with patrolling Desnan space. It managed to escape the offensive after suffering catastrophic damage but minimal loss of life, all things considered." She didn't mention she knew the captain of the frigate; no reason to offer Liam any opening to exploit an imagined weakness.

"I'll have Foster's head for this!"

"General Foster didn't order the forces reassigned. Alamatto did—and his head is, regrettably, no longer available for 'having.'"

His gaze snapped back to her. "Thanks to your traitorous daughter. I'm amazed they still allow you in the building."

Her jaw locked so tightly she might require a pneumatic lever to pry it open later, but she did not flinch or look away. Under no circumstances would she grant him the satisfaction of provoking her. "The bombing investigation is still ongoing, but I'm confident she will be cleared of any involvement. Now regarding the war. The Northwestern Regional forces on the front lines are increasingly weakened and after Desna they're down yet another frigate. Do you perhaps want to get your replacement in Southwest on holo and reassign a minimum of two regiments to Foster?"

"I'll make the military decisions in this war, not you."

"Of course you will. Do inform me when you decide to send the regiments to Foster, so I can ensure they successfully arrive there and are properly provisioned once they do." She pivoted to leave, then with malice aforethought paused short of the door and glanced over her shoulder. "I'm sorry, was there anything else?"

She received the desired response in his furious glare and exited the office suppressing a smile. But it was short-lived, as she departed the frying pan for the proverbial fire.

After two 'interviews' from the lead investigator on the Headquarters bombing, she expected Major Lange from the Security Bureau in her office in seven minutes. He was coming to her office rather than she to his less as a concession to her rank and more as a courtesy to a colleague. For though she did outrank him by numerous grades, military police enjoyed power and liberties few others possessed. Should he desire to order her to his office or even an interrogation room, under the circumstances he could arguably do so.

Unless the authorities had a trump card they had not yet revealed, the evidence against Caleb Marano and Alexis by association was purely circumstantial. It was not enough to convict in a court of law, but it didn't need to be. In the midst of a war, when the flames of patriotism and outrage ran strongest, merely stating that a Senecan spy had been on the grounds in the week preceding the bombing was enough to convict in the court of public opinion.

The lack of actual hard evidence was the only thing keeping her in her job for now, so she welcomed the small favor.

Walking brusquely into the temporary EASC Operations offices, she was pleased to note Lange had done her the additional courtesy of not arriving early. She acknowledged her secretary then slipped into her office and allowed the door to shut behind her for the briefest moment of solitude.

Such moments had been near to nonexistent of late. Between managing the messy details of the Senecan conflict, struggling to draw the attention of the right people to the potential alien conflict, handling the sheer logistics of relocating the entirety of what remained of EASC Operations into a far smaller building while filling the significant vacancies, *and* dealing with the bombing investigation, she had hardly slept. Which was for the best; she had learned twenty-three years ago working instead of sleeping was a passable way to avoid dwelling on more personal concerns. Concerns which threatened to crush her spirit if dwelled upon.

Like where in the name of all that was holy—and many things that were not—her daughter might be.

She stood at her desk studying an update on the repairs to the Forward Naval Base on Arcadia when Major Lange entered three minutes later, so she had no need to stand to greet him as he saluted her. A subtle denial of added power to him, power he'd never realize he had lost. "Major, thank you for coming by."

"Of course, Admiral. I understand you're extremely busy with this unfortunate war."

She kept the surprise off her face. She wouldn't have expected him to view the war as 'unfortunate,' but there was no pretense in his ice-blue eyes. "It is unfortunate, and I regrettably am busy with it. So let's dispense with the pleasantries. You have lingering questions regarding the bombing and my daughter's alleged involvement in it."

His nod was a curt motion. Given what she knew of him, he likely appreciated her directness. "I do, ma'am."

She gestured for him to sit. "Very well. Ask your questions."

ROMANE
INDEPENDENT COLONY

The government transport banked up and away from the soaring towers and cool lavender horizon decorated by the long evening light of Romane's second sun.

As they entered the atmosphere corridor Marcus Aguirre initiated a livecomm with Prime Minister Barrera. The man took several seconds to look up from a small screen in his hand, and wore a preoccupied visage when he did. "Marcus. How did things go?"

He gave Barrera a troubled grimace. "Not as well as I'd hoped, I'm afraid. Governor Ledesme staked out the moral high ground of peace-loving independence and refused to declare Romane support for the Alliance in the war. She appears to presume the benefits of retaining Federation trade will outweigh the cost of losing Alliance support."

"Hmm. Unfortunate, but not entirely unexpected. You judge her position to be inflexible?"

"Quite. To be frank, she exhibited overconfidence bordering on arrogance. She overestimates her power."

"How do you suggest we move forward?"

He made a show of considering the question. "I think perhaps we allow her to discover what it costs to lose them both. We can justify a blockade of the major trade routes along the southern Federation border. It's a smart strategic move in any event, and will conveniently cut off most Senecan trade to Romane. Publicly we express regret for any disruption it causes Romane and other colonies. Privately we exert pressure on large Alliance corporations to cease doing business with Romane-based interests."

"You think she'll fold?"

"No question. Within weeks I expect, if not sooner. Trade fuels Romane, and in its absence her high-minded 'independence' principles will quickly succumb to more practical necessities."

Barrera exhaled; it was a heavy, ponderous act. Prime Minister for only days, the weight of a galactic war was already showing in the deepening lines around his eyes and the drooping set of his shoulders. "I'll discuss a blockade with General O'Connell and

Admiral Rychen later this evening. You're on the way to Sagan now?"

"Yes, sir. It's a long trip, but I have several holo conferences scheduled on the way."

"I expect the Sagan government will be far more amenable to our proposal."

"They have far less to lose and a reasonable amount to gain. Their support will unfortunately be worth less than Romane's but will solidify all major colonies in the southeastern region under Alliance control."

"Indeed, and that can't be a bad thing. Best of luck, Marcus. Keep me posted."

"And to you, sir." Marcus ended the link with a touch of sadness, cognizant it would probably be the last time he saw Luis Barrera. He was a decent man as politicians went, and had been a friend and true ally. But he would be far from the first decent person to be sacrificed for the greater good, and likely not the last.

Marcus was currently flying halfway around the settled galaxy for two reasons. As Foreign Minister for the Earth Alliance, strengthening diplomatic relations with non-Alliance worlds was above all else his job, and one never more important than during a war. This dovetailed with the second reason: the aliens were moving fast—far too fast—and his options were dwindling rapidly.

From where he sat today, the best of those dwindling options was to hypercharge the war, win the war and pull the galaxy inward under Alliance domination. Yet thus far the war was a stalemate at best...which would have been fine if he had more time. A protracted stalemate had even been a key part of the original plan.

But he didn't have more time. So he needed to find the Alliance more allies and soon. There were twenty-one independent colonies; most were fringe movements or the fantasy fulfillment of wealthy narcissists, but nine or ten held resources, power or a location advantage which would benefit the Alliance. Also not to be discounted was the psychological boon from independent colonies publicly declaring support for the Alliance in the war.

Together it might be enough to shift the tide.

When the alien had first contacted him some thirty-seven years ago, he had not imagined this chaos—this high-stakes game of empyrean brinkmanship—was where it would lead.

Fresh off winning the Miami District Attorney race, he was kicked back at his desk enjoying a Glenlivet 21.

Greetings.

Marcus jerked, startled, then checked his eVi for the source of the communication. There was no name or address attached to it. He hadn't received nor accepted a livecomm request. Was he being hacked? He instructed his eVi to raise defensive barriers.

Those are not necessary.

He straightened up in the chair. Hearing voices in one's head was no longer a marker of insanity; in modern communications people heard voices in their heads all the time. But this *voice wasn't attached to any person with an identity registered in the exanet infrastructure. He took a deep breath.*

"To whom am I speaking?"

We can discuss the matter in a moment. Congratulations on your election victory. It is a notable achievement for one so young. Not your first, though.

"If you're trying to imply you somehow know a lot about me, you're doing a poor job of it. A brief exanet query will reveal I've achieved much and am expected to achieve much more."

Yes. Does an exanet query reveal your success as leader of the Catumbi Turma in Rio de Janeiro, or your domination of the Zelones cartel there?

He carefully stood, his voice dropping dangerously in tenor. "I have no idea what you're talking about. I grew up on the Louisiana gulf, where I lived until I went to university in Florida."

You did not.

"I beg your pardon?"

Marcus Aguirre is a manufactured identity provided to you by Olivia Montegreu in 2269. Your entire life history before the day you arrived at the University of Miami in 2271 is a lie.

That bitch! *Did she suppose his newfound if modest fame meant she could gain something by holding his past over him? He had thought it beneath her.*

Olivia Montegreu did not betray your secret.

"Oh, you can see what I'm thinking as well?"

No. It was merely a logical deduction.

A chill radiated from the base of his neck as he began to realize whatever this conversation was, it was of tremendous significance. He belatedly activated a privacy shield in the office to ensure the remainder of the interaction remained confidential. "Very well. You owe me an answer—to whom am I speaking?"

We are other than you.

"Alien, you mean?" Aliens had not yet been encountered, which didn't make it any less possible they existed. The other options were, what? Ghosts? Gods? Angels or demons? He believed in none of these things.

It is a sufficient designation.

Jesús Christo, this 'alien' was obtuse. "And how do you know these details about me?"

We know many things.

"That doesn't answer my question."

Perhaps not. We are…observers of humanity.

"I see. What is it you 'observe' about us?"

Everything.

He paused to consider the assertion. The being could be lying, or generalizing to exaggeration. If it were not, the implications were troublesome to say the least. Such a capability seemed incomprehensible, and for all intents and purposes godlike…then he recalled Sir Clarke's Third Law: Any sufficiently advanced technology is indistinguishable from magic. Didn't mean it was magic.

"What do you want of me?"

For now, nothing. You are a uniquely talented individual: highly intelligent compared to others of your species, manipulative, deceptive, charismatic, driven, ruthless but not sadistic. You have much potential.

He had nothing to say to that, so he simply waited.

Continue on your path. Focus your ambitions, and you will achieve greatness. If we can provide assistance at certain junctures, we will do so if a manner is available to us. We will call upon you from time to time, as our needs require.

Now he understood. They had resources beyond him—of course they did—but limited ability to act themselves, for whatever reason. They needed someone in a position of power to do their bidding. If he refused them, they were capable of using their other resources to destroy everything he had painstakingly built—his career, his reputation, his growing wealth, his idyllic and only mostly for appearances marriage—and it would be a trivial matter for them to do so.

Unless they weren't so powerful as their arrogance insinuated...but that wasn't a risk he dared take. Not yet.

He realized he was thinking of his conversation partner in the plural, because it was how it referred to itself. "Do you have a name?"

No.

"Is there more than one of you? Are you a hive mind? A collective intelligence? You refer to yourself in the plural."

So I do. No. Consider me a...spokesperson.

He supposed it was the most straightforward answer he would be able to wrangle. "And what should I call you, individually?"

If you require an honorific, you may refer to me as Hyperion.

The titan of Greek mythology...the alien didn't lack for hubris. "Do you require anything of me?"

We—I—merely wished to introduce myself. And, as was said, convey my congratulations.

Then the voice was gone. It was many hours before he left the office that night, hours spent pondering this new complication in his already exceedingly complicated life.

It was six years before he heard from the alien again. He had been embroiled in a tight race for Southeastern District Attorney against the son of the Alliance Commerce Minister and struggling to overcome his opponent's superior name recognition and connections. Then the man had turned up dead, despite his spotless reputation found naked in a pleasure club booth. His brain had been fried by an overdose of a particularly potent neuro-chimeral.

The next day Hyperion had contacted him to inform him they were pleased to have been able to clear an obstacle for him.

He hadn't asked for the help, hadn't wanted it and believed he hadn't needed it. The aliens, however, apparently hadn't been inclined to take any chances that his upward trajectory might be slowed. Or perhaps it had been a not-so-subtle way to demonstrate the power they held, even from afar, lest he consider rejecting future overtures.

If so, he had learned a slightly different lesson. He now knew something of what these aliens could do for him.

6

SENECA
CAVARE

Isabela Marano trailed her mother through the house, surreptitiously straightening furniture and picking up forgotten dishes and trash. It wasn't a pit as such, merely unkempt. Arguably messy.

Her mother ambled into the kitchen, and her stealth cleaning became more problematic. She hurriedly dropped the dishes in the sink and the trash in the chute while her mother's back was still turned.

"Why do they keep talking about Caleb on the news, Bela? Is he in trouble?"

"It's a misunderstanding, Mom. It'll get cleared up." *A 'misunderstanding' involving the death of thousands and the igniting of a powder keg strong enough to blow up the galaxy.* She had rarely been so glad the woman was absentminded and only half in the present. If she managed a tiny bit more awareness she'd be hysterical over the world calling her son a mass murderer, likely to such a level as to be unmanageable.

"That's a relief..." she settled in a chair at the small kitchen table "...how's Marlee? It's been forever since I last saw her."

"You saw her a few weeks ago, remember?"

"Did I? Oh...I suppose I did." Her mother frowned at the table. "Why isn't she here now?"

"She's sleeping over at her friend's house tonight. I didn't want to...I didn't want to disrupt her schedule again so soon." *I didn't want her to hear her uncle slandered on every news screen. I didn't want to have to answer her innocent, endless, maddeningly perceptive questions.* "I'll be right back, okay?"

Isabela departed the kitchen before receiving a response. She normally exhibited more patience when it came to her mother, normally felt comfortable here in the house she had grown up in.

She'd been twelve years old when her father left and held as many memories of the house without him as with him.

But today her mind and attention were elsewhere. The war concerned her; Krysk wasn't too far from the border region where most of the fighting was taking place. She hated to leave her professorship early, but she refused to risk her daughter's safety.

Mostly though, she worried about Caleb—what had happened to him, where he had gone, whether he would be cleared of involvement in the bombing or railroaded into prison. Or worse. God knew if there was anyone who could take care of himself just fine, it was him, but this represented a new level of trouble he found himself in.

At least she assumed it represented a new level of trouble. When she'd told him she knew what he did for a living, she might have been overstating the case a tiny bit. She had believed he worked for the government in a secret and dangerous capacity.

Now the entire galaxy knew him as a covert special ops agent for the Senecan Federation Division of Intelligence. With such a job maybe he had been in worse, if less public, trouble before.

The thought chilled her. How many times had she almost lost him and never known?

She ascended the stairs to her old room. She needed to retrieve Marlee's coat and a pair of shoes left behind in the rush to her next adventure. Caleb said Marlee 'had spunk'...more like she was hyperkinetic, a bundle of perpetually regenerating energy.

She adored her daughter, truly. The little girl was the light of her life and the center of her world ever since Daniel died. But she had never known the meaning of 'tired' until Marlee learned to walk.

The tiny coat was hanging half off the dresser, but the shoes were nowhere to be seen. She crouched down to search under the bed.

Loud footsteps beneath the floor startled her, and her head jerked up to bang against the frame. She crawled backwards out from beneath the bed while rubbing the back of her head gingerly.

"Bela! There are—" Overlapping voices muddled whatever her mother said. *What the...?*

She rushed out of the bedroom but only made it to the second step before a man and woman in conservative black suits appeared at the base of the stairs. "Ms. Marano? Would you mind coming with us?"

They weren't regular police. There were no uniforms and no formal procedures being followed. She tried to look innocent, but unlike Caleb she had always been a terrible liar. "What is this regarding?"

They continued up the stairs, calm resoluteness indicating they entertained no doubt she would in fact be coming with them. The man's muscular frame filled out his suit, adding intimidation to his threatening countenance. His partner stood taller than him; auburn hair pulled back into a bun at the nape of her neck emphasized attractive features. The woman gave her a small, placid smile intended to convey reassurance.

It didn't work—her heart hammered at her sternum like it was planning to make a break for it—but it wasn't as though she possessed a route of escape. And even if she did, she couldn't abandon her mother to fend for herself. She did her best to keep her voice controlled and even. "Am I being arrested?"

"We'd appreciate you answering a few questions."

"About my brother?"

"It's better if we discuss it at the office."

"The 'office'? What is that? Where are you intending on taking us?"

"Bela! What's going on?" Her mother's voice echoed from the hallway below, shaky and shrill, the way hers desperately wanted to be.

"It's going to be okay, Mom. I'll be right down."

She backed into the banister, all too conscious of the four-meter drop behind her to the living room below. The agents—if they weren't police they were government agents—did her the courtesy of stopping at the landing, though their deportment made it clear she would not be allowed past them. "I'll come peacefully, if you promise you won't harm my mother."

"We're not intending on harming anyone, ma'am." The woman was now firmly ensconced in the role of 'good cop.' The man's left hand hovered over the stunner on his belt. "We simply need to speak with you. Both of you."

She closed her eyes and exhaled slowly, buying herself time to send a message to the couple taking care of Marlee to let them know she might be delayed. Then she nodded. "Very well."

INTELLIGENCE DIVISION HEADQUARTERS

Director of Intelligence Graham Delavasi turned away another office visitor seeking to 'check in' or 'pick his brain' but in any event steal his attention. In simpler times he enjoyed the occasional visit by military officers and government officials and subordinates and even friends. But the last week had eradicated any remaining traces of simplicity from his life.

Special Ops Director Michael Volosk was dead. Murdered steps from Headquarters—the building he sat in now. The man's throat had been sliced open and he had been left to bleed out in the goddamn *parking lot.*

He dragged both hands down his face for the hundredth time in the last hour. Michael was an outstanding agent. One of the best. Though he may have sat behind a desk for the last few years, no one would accuse him of being a bureaucrat. What kind of assailant could have gotten the jump on him in such spectacular fashion?

Agent Marano?

His head began shaking of its own accord, as if to provide its own answer. He would stake a significant number of credits on Stefan Marano's son being innocent.

Marano. He'd not seen that name in a long time…nearly twenty years, in fact. He'd been aware when Samuel recruited the son into Division of course, but deliberately kept his distance in every way. Now though….

He had spent days poring through Michael Volosk's recent reports and private notes. Michael had been a busy man, and not solely or even mostly because of the war. For one, he'd sent Marano on an official mission to Vancouver. A dubious, shot-in-the-dark, certifiably insane mission…which had almost worked.

Michael's notes stated Agent Marano had brought back the top secret Alliance autopsy file on Minister Santiagar, but no one could find any trace of the file's existence. It hadn't entered the Division file system, nor Michael's personal files. It was not found on his body or residing in his internal data store.

The most logical conclusion? The killer pilfered it. A scenario which made zero sense if Caleb Marano was the killer. Why give Michael the file only to kill him and steal it back mere hours later?

Then there was the report from a deep cover watcher agent on Earth, delivering word people within EASC were expressing doubts about the events that had kicked off this war. The agent also conveyed that Marano had in fact done exactly what he'd been sent to Vancouver to do—attempt to convince EASC leadership to investigate those events. He had been arrested for the effort, then everything had gone to hell in a designer handbag.

While the report cast clear doubt on Marano's guilt with respect to the Vancouver bombing, in his mind the sum total of the information before him constituted enough to all but exonerate the man with respect to Michael's murder. Couple it with him sending an alert from halfway across the city minutes at most after Michael was slain, and the wafer-thin case against the agent crumbled. Unfortunately this led to more disturbing implications.

Marano's final communication before going off the grid indicated he and his notable companion had been attacked by multiple assailants at nearly the exact moment Volosk lay bleeding out meters from the side entry to Division. The bodies at the riverwalk certainly backed up the story. The events of that fateful night painted a clear and stark picture.

Within the space of a single hour EASC Headquarters on Earth exploded, no less than four mercs ambushed Marano and Solovy and an assassin murdered Volosk and stole two specific files. It seemed the raw data set on the Metis Nebula delivered by Alexis Solovy to Michael that evening had, interestingly enough, also gone missing.

It wasn't as if he didn't believe there could be a conspiracy; he'd spent decades in the intelligence business after all. But if a conspiracy did exist—if both governments were duped into a renewed war—it meant a lot of people had died for no reason. It meant he faced a helluva battle ahead.

Michael had bought into Marano's theory the war was purposely instigated by...someone. Despite the investigation being officially closed, he'd continued to probe into the Atlantis assassination. The day before his death he paid a visit to Jaron Nythal, the Assistant Trade Director. Graham reviewed the notes from the meeting again.

Mr. Nythal acted alternately evasive and confrontational. I am reinstating basic surveillance in the hope the pressure will force him into a mistake. I have sought approval for a persistent trace on his bank accounts as well.

He had meant it when he told Michael he believed Nythal was squirrelly, and part of him was glad to see Michael had taken the advice to heart. Yet a nefarious voice in the back of his mind questioned if the advice might have led to the man's death.

He returned to the report from his deputy, Liz Oberti. Given the seriousness of the accusations, he had put her in charge of the Marano investigation. With his approval she was bringing the family in for questioning. They were unlikely to be involved in whatever was transpiring, but they might know where the agent had gone to ground.

Retracing his train of thought to its origin, he realized he needed to get personally involved whether he wanted to or not. But first he needed to make an unannounced visit.

7

Devon Reynolds stood at the center of a webbed prism of light. The sea of qutrits painted a tableau in more colors than names existed for and wove a pattern so dense nothing beyond it could be seen.

To the untrained eye—and most trained ones—the web signified chaos. After all, the code underlying CUs and commercial ware was ordered and structured and crafted in the defined lines of immutable logic.

The mind of an Artificial, however, reflected exactly what it was: a sophisticated neural net. Sister to the human brain and easily as complex.

The development of functional ternary computing late in the 21st century had finally enabled true neural net technology. The ability for each q-unit to hold all possible superpositions of 0, 1 *and* 2 increased feasible computing power exponentially beyond the capabilities of traditional binary quantum computing.

Researchers had created synthetic intelligence which surpassed the pure processing power of the human brain decades prior to the advent of ternary dialectics, but this represented a transformation not solely of degree but also of kind. Still, large-scale ternary computing was both expensive and required precise hardware kept in controlled conditions, thus Artificials for now remained the province of governments and the very wealthy.

Also, the fact an unshackled Artificial had killed over 50,000 people at Hong Kong University early in the 22nd century meant they were exhaustively regulated, locked down and confined.

Begin check routine.

Multiple orbs within the web exploded in dancing light racing in every direction. Devon reached up to spin the web then zoomed into a dense cluster of the virtual gossamer silk.

The check routine reached the cluster he had selected; he studied it carefully as it branched, circled and came together again before continuing on.

Hmmm. A small grouping of qutrits in the upper right quadrant had remained untouched by the routine. He stepped closer, letting the gossamer envelop him so he could study it from the inside, and rapidly identified the problem. The filaments connecting this region to the rest of the cluster hung fragmented and thin, not sufficiently strong to convey the necessary signals.

Found it. We need to have her run generative recursion routines on 10A0-P-9I to exercise and strengthen the aperiodic functions in the sector.

Excellent work. I'll have Programming add it to the set for when we bring her back up this afternoon. Drop by my office as soon as you're out. You have a visitor.

Uh, sure...ma'am.

A year into this job and he still had the damnedest time with the military formality. He tried, especially for Jules because he liked her, but protocol wasn't his thing. Not the social kind, anyway.

End session.

The web vanished, replaced by antiseptic light illuminating translucent white walls, ceiling and floor. He exited the simulation room, grabbed some water at the kitchen kiosk and headed upstairs.

Project ANNIE took up two floors of the EASC Special Projects building, not counting the mammoth basement to store the physical hardware. Thankfully the building was across the complex from the HQ tower and hadn't suffered any appreciable damage in the bombing. He had a cubbyhole office down the hall but spent the majority of his time in the labs. Though ANNIE was Jules Hervé's baby, since she served as head of the entire Special Projects Division her office was up on the 6th floor.

As much a techie as a military officer, Hervé didn't run an overly formal operation. He stepped aside at the entryway to allow an admiral to pass. She looked familiar; he thought perhaps he'd seen her on the news recently. Then, as in previous visits, he walked into Hervé's office without requesting permission. On seeing she had further company though, he hastily retreated to the doorway. He really should try to observe minimal decorum...but odds were he wouldn't.

She acknowledged him with a smile in spite of his rudeness. "It's alright, Devon. Come in."

Her guest was a middle-aged guy in Navy BDUs. "This is Colonel Richard Navick, our Naval Intelligence Liaison. Colonel, meet Devon Reynolds. He's...you don't actually *have* a real title, do you? He's our lead analyst in the test/quality group for Project ANNIE. But more importantly, he's the best natural quantum coder I've ever met."

Her gaze flicked to the Colonel. "And he's not military. He's here as an independent contractor, because there's no one in the military as gifted as him."

If he possessed a scintilla of humility he'd be flattered, but in truth it was less a compliment and more a simple factual statement.

The man offered a hand. "It's a pleasure to meet you, Mr. Reynolds."

Devon's interaction with high-ranking officers other than Jules had been limited, and he found he had no idea of the proper way to react. He started to take the hand, then jerked his own up in a salute, then remembered as a civilian he wasn't required to salute and yanked it back down for a hasty shake.

Navick chuckled lightly. The act revealed kind eyes, and Devon relaxed. "Sorry, sir. Still getting used to this whole military routine."

"Not a problem. We'd arguably benefit from a bit less military routine around here." Navick tilted his head toward Jules. "Brigadier Hervé speaks highly of your skills."

"Did she say anything about my, uh, attitude, sir?"

"She said you have a healthy disrespect for pretty much everything and everyone. But she also said you've earned the right to it."

He beamed, as this was a compliment. "Appreciated, ma'am."

She gave a small nod and circled around her desk. Navick directed his full attention to Devon. "It's a nice day outside. Want to take a walk?"

The breeze coming off the Strait carried a slight chill, but Devon welcomed it as it took the edge off the harsh, charred odor of debris and machinery from the Headquarters wreckage and accompanying cleanup.

He strolled beside the Colonel as they crossed the courtyard at a gait so leisurely it felt like a performance. The man subtly guided them away from the people traversing or lingering in the courtyard and toward the shore walk that ran along the edge of the Island. Away from not only prying ears, but prying eyes as well.

Not until the path had curved down to the rocky shore and trees sheltered their movement did Navick finally speak. "I imagine you've done a little hacking in your spare time, no?"

"A little, sir."

"The Brigadier says you're almost as good at spotting patterns and glitches as an Artificial."

"With respect, sir, I'm *better* at it than an Artificial. I may not be able to analyze as many data points as fast as a synthetic can, but if you want to find something specific? I'm the better bet."

"Cocky, too."

"I imagine Jules—Brigadier Hervé—probably mentioned that as well."

"Probably. Much of the information ANNIE analyzes originates from my people and assets. If you've been working on ANNIE for a year now, you've likely gotten familiar with the nature of intelligence data merely by watching it flow through the system."

"I've figured out a few things here and there."

"I'm sure you have."

A wave crashed into the parapet with enough force to send a light spray of icy Pacific water over them, and he took the opportunity to roll his eyes at the sky. Military types, including the less priggish ones, were so *uptight*.

"Sir, I appreciate this whole dance—feeling each other out, establishment of relative power and whatnot—but it's okay, we can skip it. I'm guessing you believe there's corrupt or falsified data hiding in some military or intelligence records. You're not sure who you can trust in EASC, so you want somebody on the outside but not too *far* outside. You expect whatever you're seeking will be hard as hell to find, but you can't put ANNIE on it since everything she does is reviewed by a dozen officers in triplicate. And above all, you need somebody who won't be spooked by *whatever* they find. That more or less cover it?"

Navick came to a stop on the path. One of the ubiquitous benches lay behind them, but the man made no move to sit. "Not a bad summation. More or less."

"You asked for me, though you didn't know it was me you were asking for. And I do relish a challenge. So what are we talking about here?"

Navick scrutinized him for a moment, dark hazel eyes guarded. Then he shrugged in acquiescence and resumed walking. Devon's estimation of the Colonel increased several degrees. Not many officers on the Island would have taken the arguably insubordinate speech in stride, and absent a speck of prideful preening.

"I'm proposing to give you the access codes to a metaset of records covering the five days leading up to and including the bombing. I strongly believe they were tampered with at multiple junctures. I'm not going to tell you where, when or in relation to what. It's important you not be biased going in. Your highest priority will be to prove the records were compromised. If you can do this, it will be enough."

"But...?"

"If you can, try to recover the original, unaltered data."

His steps slowed, allowing a cyclist to pass them and disappear around the curve ahead. "You realize it may be impossible, even for me. Qubits are fickle, inconstant creatures."

"I do. Whether you're able to recover the original data or not, I'd ask you to attempt to trace the hacks to their source. A successful trace on one is all I require. I want to know who did it. Failing that, I want to know from where it was done."

Devon's mind was spinning through the details—the ware and modifications he'd need, the best avenues of attack, a new piece or two of gear to speed the process—and he didn't immediately notice Navick had veered up a path spur and back toward the complex. The meeting was nearing an end.

He jogged to catch up. "How should I contact you?"

"When you have any results—or decide you won't be able to find anything—have Brigadier Hervé send me a message asking me to stop by to review the results of ANNIE's latest intel cross-analysis. Instead, I'll come see you. Under no circumstances send me any details or any information at all over messaging or comms. We talk in person *only*."

"Old-fashioned spy style, huh?"

"Every now and then it's the best way." Navick's step hitched as he gave a throaty groan. "Dear Lord, I sounded like an old man, didn't I? Still, it's a truth learned from experience, most of it bad."

Devon laughed indulgently. "I'll take your word for it then."

A rapport had been established...and the Colonel was an easy man to like. But what he was asking for was not child's play, nor was it standard military procedure by any means. "Sir, I'm not an idiot. Couple of parsecs away from one in fact, and you know this. What you're asking me to do...well, as risky as it is for me, it's a lot riskier for you. I don't have to be military to know it might mean your career, even if you are Intelligence. You just met me—why trust me with so much?"

Navick considered the question thoughtfully, as if he were deciding exactly how frank he could afford to be. "I wouldn't last long in this job without getting fairly adept at sizing people up quickly. You're a genius and a rebel, but you're a good kid. You'll do this for the challenge but also because you value the truth. I don't think you'll sell me out—you're after a different kind of glory. Hackers take great pleasure in exposing corruption, so much so they've made a cause of it for the last three hundred fifty years. You find what I need, and I assure you we will be doing quite a lot of that."

He paused to give a melodramatic sigh. "And I'm told there are less than a dozen people in the galaxy who possess the intellect and skills to do what I'm asking of you."

Impressive answer. He should have realized there was depth and wisdom beneath the man's quiet, unassuming demeanor. "Seven, sir."

An eyebrow quirked in question.

"There are seven—counting me—and three of them are in the Federation. One is serving a ten-year prison sentence on Demeter, and the other two, Abigail Canivon and Gerard Bordelon, are a lot farther away than a lunchtime stroll."

"So they are."

He extended a hand. "It would be my pleasure, sir."

Navick shook his hand warmly. "In that case, you should probably call me Richard."

They parted ways at the courtyard. Devon spent the walk back to Special Projects thinking not about the 'what' of the assignment, but the 'why.'

An exanet query revealed the Colonel was a personal friend of Admiral Miriam Solovy, and Miriam Solovy's daughter had been implicated as an accomplice of the Senecan Intelligence agent accused of perpetrating the bombing. To seal the deal, Solovy had been the woman leaving Jules' office as he had arrived.

Either Navick was willing to go a long way indeed to bail out a family friend…no, the investigation would lead where it led. There had been no mention of altering legitimate records, only discovering altered ones. So Navick genuinely believed Alexis Solovy was innocent.

Which meant there was a decent chance he didn't believe the Senecan was responsible for the bombing. Which meant he believed someone inside the military or government *was* responsible for it, or at a minimum involved in perpetrating it.

Devon's step hastened. This was hardcore, and he couldn't wait to get started.

8

SIYANE

Alex was loath to admit Caleb had been right. But as she ascended the stairs, freshly showered in fresh clothes, the alluring aroma of Peronan coffee in the air...she had to admit he had been right. A decent night's sleep had restored both her energy and her determination, two things she needed in order to properly investigate this odd and disturbing planet cloaked in the void. Quickly.

But properly.

Caleb greeted her with a kiss and a mug, both of which she accepted happily. She eased into one of the kitchen chairs as he brought over a plate of croissants and oranges. *Damn, he really was rather wonderful.*

She began devouring a croissant. This would be a fast, if tasty, breakfast. "So I was thinking. I want to try retuning the instruments a bit. We haven't picked up any unusual readings on conventional bands, but there is clearly *something* technological here. Tech is likely powering the light source, and tech is definitely powering the cloaking shield. If that tech isn't going to show up on conventional scans, we'll have to get creative."

He joined her at the table, already halfway through an orange. "It's a good idea, but retune them to what?"

"On our side of the portal these aliens displayed an inkling for the extremes and rare frequencies—the lowest TLF ever recorded at one end, high-end gamma frequencies at the other and terahertz waves we call 'exotic.' So we focus in tightly on the margins, on the ranges our scientists have written off as unnecessary or unusable. Narrow the search bands enough and I can increase the sensitivity so much we'll pick up a bird chirping fifty kilometers away. But first...I want to go outside."

"Good. So do I."

"Really?"

"Yep. I understand the science—mostly—and the technical analysis, but at heart I'm a visceral guy. I need to feel this place. See what it can tell me."

She deliberately bit her lower lip, pleased to have an opportunity to tease him. "You *are* that...."

"What?"

"Visceral."

She swore he almost blushed—and what a sight it would have been. "I...not exactly what I meant, but...." Seeing the twinkle in her eyes, he reached across the table to grasp her hand while flashing a devilish smirk. "I'm glad you think so."

"Uh-huh." She pushed back from the table and stood. "At least we don't have to wear suits this time. And it's not -54°. And the sun's out, so to speak."

"Sounds like this place isn't half bad. We should retire here."

"The lack of stars is a serious negative. Maybe we should keep looking."

His eyes rose to meet hers.

She spun away, hastily covering any discomfort provoked by the not-at-all-laden statement by taking their plates to the sink. "We'll do a brief scout around the ship first, no more than fifty meters out or so. If we decide we should trek further we can duck back in for a pack and some supplies."

"It's a plan." He came up behind her carrying the rest of the dishes. One arm curled around her waist and a kiss alighted upon her ear to brush away any residual tension. "I'm taking a Daemon though. This place feels prehistoric. There could be dinosaurs."

"Well yeah, me too." She removed the band from her wrist and twisted her hair up as she went to the storage cabinet. He caught the Daemon she tossed to him and latched it to his work pants. She did the same with the second weapon, then gazed around the deck.

"All right. Let's do this."

The outer airlock hissed as it opened to let in air the sensors insisted was utterly normal, and she headed down the ramp into the morning light.

It felt like stepping foot on Earth; there was no other way to describe it. The sensation of the pleasant breeze ruffling the fine hairs on her forearm was familiar to the point of intimacy.

She had visited a fair number of planets over the years. While all the settled worlds were of necessity compatible with human life (terraforming being for now an extremely lengthy, costly and difficult process), in a myriad of ways none of them felt like Earth. This one did—which considering where they were, was just wrong.

"We took a graze of plasma fire, so I want to check underneath. The integrity tests checked out, but I still…." Her voice drifted off as she ran fingertips along the lower hull.

The silver discoloration had spread out far beyond where the rupture had been repaired. It had also darkened, almost as if it was curing. The entire belly of the ship now gleamed a deep tungsten silver in color. Thick tendrils of brighter silver snaked out from the belly to follow the curve of the hull, streaks of light cutting through the blackness.

The chemical reactions begun by the fusing of the carbon and amodiamond metamaterials were evidently continuing. Taking over her ship. She wasn't sure what she thought about this; she had *liked* the way her ship looked, all dark and sinister and dangerous. Yet she couldn't deny this new hue held a certain beauty as well.

"Wow."

"I know. Kennedy said it was making the hull stronger, so I guess it's not a problem." She discerned no trace of scarring from weapons fire. The hull appeared unblemished. "Weird, though…and now my ship kind of resembles a zebra."

"A 'zebra'?" His eyes unfocused, and she imagined he was querying his internal data store. Two seconds later he regarded her in amusement. "Okay, maybe a *little*. But I doubt it will stay this way. And it's intriguing."

She let her hand drop from the hull and wandered out to stare at the grasslands stretching to the horizon. Behind her lay rolling hills broken up by the rocky crevasse which had provided a measure of shelter for them overnight.

"I expect to see a herd of some sort of wildlife frolicking across the plain any second now."

"Would be the least astounding scene so far."

She glanced over her shoulder to smile at him—

—and that was when the dragon attacked.

A faint *whoosh* of air behind him was the sole warning Caleb had before he was catapulted thirty meters through the air. He caught a vague impression of reflected light off burnished scales attached to a massive wing—then his head slammed to the dirt with a sharp crack.

He was out for mere seconds—four, five at most—because when he opened his eyes the dragon had barely left the ground, its wings mid-flap as they propelled it up and over the *Siyane* to soar into the sky.

Yes, a *dragon*. The lustrous crimson scales covered an enormous body dwarfed only by its wingspan; the striking thickness of the torso contrasted with almost delicate skin pulled taut between lightweight bones comprising the wings. Distinctive horns curled back over its bony skull.

He vaulted to his feet and swung the Daemon up, ignoring the multiple jarring pains of varying severity. His vision contracted to encompass a single image: Alex flailing in the grasp of the dragon's front right claw as it flew away.

She was visibly struggling; that meant she wasn't dead. The claws gripping her hadn't ripped open her lovely skin and shredded the fragile human organs which gave her life. Not yet.

He could shoot a hole in the wing. The laser would shred the thin membrane. The dragon would plummet from the sky and plunge to the ground a hundred meters below. And Alex would die.

"Fuck!"

In a flash he was sprinting for the airlock, skipping through a stumble or two on the way. He recognized he was hurt but it hardly mattered.

He slammed a palm on the airlock panel, fed it the secondary key and fell through the hatch as it opened. Then he half-crawled, half-scrambled to the cockpit and up into her chair. His fingers raced over the blank ledge until by dumb luck he found the trigger to activate the HUD. Unlike Alex, he wasn't wired into the ship, and thus it did not respond to his thoughts.

Thank you, Mia.

Once the HUD came to life the controls and screens were easily identifiable. He fired up the pulse detonation engines and rose off the ground as the dragon shrank in the sky. The unparalleled smoothness of the ship's motion beneath his fingertips shocked him. It responded to the slightest adjustment with incredible fluidity, like a sky glider instead of a machine constructed of hard, cold metal.

He banked forty degrees starboard and climbed, the entirety of his attention focused on the tiny red dot against the pale blue sky.

It had nearly disappeared when he started to gain on it. Bit by bit, meter by meter he closed the gap. He didn't think about *what* he was gaining on, or what in the bloody hell a bloody dragon was doing on an impossible planet in an impossible place on the other side of an impossible portal. Instead he concentrated on catching it.

He could see the sunlight from the nonexistent sun reflecting off the scales and the beat of its wings driving it toward the mountains now looming large in the distance. The mountains represented a problem; he risked losing the dragon in a crevasse or a shadowy valley. He'd need to draw close. Perhaps it might skim close enough to the mountainous terrain for him to risk a shot. He should—

—the world spiraled out of control, as for the second time in as many days 'down' and 'up' lost all meaning. His head spun wildly, and he pressed a palm to his forehead in an effort to impose stability. Yet the images his eyes showed him refused to comport with reality, with what he knew to be true.

Grassy plains spread placidly beneath him. No mountains were visible, even on the far horizon. Ahead and to the left rolled gentle hills, much like those they had camped at the night before. *Exactly* like the hills they had camped at the night before. The ship decelerated to a crawl as his hands dropped from the controls and he gazed out the viewport, confusion giving way to disbelief.

He hovered in sight of where he had been twenty minutes earlier.

Fuck it. He'd think about it on the way back. He promptly accelerated and headed in the direction of the mountains.

So there existed a barrier of some kind, one which repelled in dramatic fashion any intruders. Obviously the dragon was not an intruder.

Fine.

He knew where it was now, more or less. He'd slow when he neared and find a way past it. Somehow.

And he might have, too, if not for the two new dragons which stormed him as he neared the mountains. He cracked his neck and adjusted his posture in the chair.

Okay then. Starship vs. dragons.

He strafed to avoid the dual streams of flame shooting out of the approaching dragons' jaws. It was going to take more than fire to damage this ship, and he was certain its weapons possessed a longer reach as well.

He flipped the ship around and accelerated in reverse to keep a distance. In the two seconds he had to observe them, he noted they appeared identical to the one that had grabbed Alex, and to each other. Clones, then? Yet another incongruity on this strange planet. He targeted the pulse laser at the dragon on the left.

It contorted in an attempt to avoid the beam, but the laser tracked it and cut a deep gash through the scales then the leathery skin beneath them and opened up its innards. The beast shrieked a roar of pain and spewed flame raggedly from its jaws. He was almost surprised to see blood and organs spill out into the air; part of him had suspected they were machines, or possibly some sort of materialized holo projection.

The first dragon tumbled flailing to crash to the ground below, but the second one used the chaos to dive and sweep under the ship. An outstretched claw nearly grabbed the nose of the *Siyane* as he yanked hard to port and swung up in an arc.

As soon as he had a decent vantage he fired. This one seemed to have learned from the mistakes of its companion and started moving before the laser exited the weapon casing.

Nevertheless, a dragon was simply no match for 24th century laser weaponry. The laser sliced apart the thin membrane of its left wing. The beast fell into a tailspin, and he was forced to rapidly maneuver to get clear of it—

—the world twisted inside out once more, his head following suit. He blinked roughly, choked back the acid rising in his throat and stared at the grasslands outside. In avoiding the falling dragon, he had hit the barrier again.

In a burst of frustration he slammed a fist into the dash. It being composed of a rhu/platinum nanoalloy, the dash was not impressed.

He massaged the busted knuckles and forcefully shoved aside the anger and despair which threatened to drag him down and away from his goal. He did not have time to wallow, to give a moment's thought to what may have happened to her or whether she was alive.

Turn into the punch, grab hold of the gun, leap into the arena. Attack. He had to move. *Now.*

He gunned the engine.

9

J aron Nythal threw a stack of clothes in the bag, not bothering to achieve any semblance of order or neatness. Drawers hung open behind him; more clothes lay strewn across the floor. He scrambled into the bathroom to grab the necessities and stubbed his toe on the door frame.

"Ah!" He hobbled back to the bed while grabbing his throbbing toe. He had to *hurry*.

His wife and kids were on the way to her parents' house. If nothing else they should be safe, right?

He had thought he was in the clear. He'd picked out his private downtown flat and planned to make an offer in the morning. With Volosk taken care of he should have been in the clear. How was he supposed to know Volosk's boss was that cocksucker Delavasi? The man had been gunning for him ever since the favor-buying scandal four years earlier.

Only by a sheer stroke of luck did Jaron receive any warning at all. His ten o'clock meeting canceled at the last minute, and on a lark he had ducked out of the office to grab some expensive liquor for later tonight. When he returned to the office one of his coworkers had stopped him in the hallway.

"Hey, there was a man here looking for you. He refused to give the receptionist his name, but I recognized him from a meeting Kouris held a few weeks ago. He's the Director of Intelligence...Delavasi's his name I think."

Jaron had spent thirty minutes meandering in circles in a service hallway trying to convince himself it didn't mean anything, that the man was simply following up on Volosk's open files. But it wasn't true. Volosk had been suspicious of him when he showed up at his office last week and now Volosk was dead, and Delavasi knew he was behind it and knew he'd set up the assassination on Atlantis.

It didn't matter how the man knew; in his gut Jaron was convinced he surely must.

Forty-years-to-life in prison at best. Permanent disappearance into the black hole of a covert detention facility at worst. And worst was starting to look a hell of a lot more likely.

He had to vanish.

With a brief scan around the bedroom he lugged the bag onto his shoulder and headed to the kitchen, where he quickly tossed in some drinks and snacks and closed the bag up. He forced himself to pause. He was forgetting something...possibly a lot of things. But he needed to hurry.

He jogged through the living room and foyer of the new house to the door. They had barely begun moving in, and boxes sat stacked along the walls between furniture haphazardly scattered around the floor.

His skycar was parked behind the house. He rounded the corner to see it shrouded in shadows cast by the decorative trees. He would have jogged to it—he needed to hurry—but the bag on his shoulder felt so damn heavy and he was out of breath from the panicked, rushed packing.

A man stepped out of the shadows behind the driver's side of the car. Coffee-colored hair framed a stark, cold face...his features seemed as if they had been etched by Death itself.

Jaron froze for half a second before scurrying backward and feeling for the wall with his free hand. "Wh-what do you want?"

The man's lips curled upward a centimeter. Jaron had never witnessed a more terrifying sight. "I'm sorry, Mr. Nythal, but we can't have you talking."

The assassin. It must be. Son of a....

His head shook furiously. "I won't talk, I swear. I'm getting out of here. I'll go to Pandora—no, I'll go to New Babel—they'll never find me! I'm leaving right now, see?" He held up the bag for dramatic effect. "Just let me go."

"I cannot. The authorities are onto you, and once they have you they will break you. Our bosses won't allow that to happen."

The bag slid from Jaron's grip and tumbled to the ground as he flattened against the wall. There was nowhere to go, no way to escape from the killer who approached him one quiet, calm step at a time. "Please, I beg you, I won't—"

It didn't even occur to him to fight back when the blade came up and sliced open his throat in one fluid motion.

R

Matei Uttara activated his personal concealment shield and slipped the blade hilt in its case. He left the patio via the pathway which led out into the affluent neighborhood.

The cyan-tinged late afternoon sunlight shone far too brightly for his taste. He didn't care for risking a hit in broad daylight...but his contact had been specific on the topic. Time was short.

And it pleased him to be rid of his little white pawn. The man had been one of only three people who could conceivably lead someone to him. Now the number was two, and both of those individuals were far more savvy and clever than Jaron Nythal.

He didn't count the alien, because it was irrelevant. He would need to find the alien in order to kill it, and he did not believe he could do so. And if he couldn't, no one could. Besides, he harbored the sneaking suspicion that should his alien be removed from the equation, another was likely to take its place.

He reached the nearest levtram station in minutes, as the neighborhood was near the Cavare city center, and dialed down the strength of the concealment shield while he blended into the moderate crowd taking the tram bound for the spaceport.

Admittedly, executing the hit early did serve an additional purpose. He was on a tight schedule. His next and possibly last act in this chess match would be on the EAO Orbital above Earth in three days, which left little margin for error. He possessed a fast ship, but Earth was a considerable distance away. Thankfully he had procured the materials required the day before.

It would be a difficult op as well. Space stations were notoriously challenging due to their confined space and lack of refuge or hidden exits, and the Orbital occupied a class all itself. His chosen

ID shouldn't present any problems, but smuggling explosives onto an Alliance governmental installation in space, orbiting Earth and under heightened war-time security constituted a different matter.

Still, he would get it done. Then he planned to head west. *Far* west. Perhaps Atlantis or Ceres. He'd prefer to skate all the way west to the frontier on Nyssus, except he needed to be able to move rapidly should Marano or Solovy reemerge. Wherever he landed, he intended to find a good seat, kick back and enjoy the show.

He didn't particularly care who won. The Alliance was using him, the Federation was using him, Zelones was using him, the aliens were using him. He was happy to do all their bidding. And when they began to turn on one another, he was happy to abet that as well.

He merely wanted to foment the rising tide of anarchy, then watch the galaxy burn to ashes.

INTELLIGENCE DIVISION HEADQUARTERS

"Ms. Marano, I'm Graham Delavasi, Director of Intelligence." He extended his hand; the woman sitting at the table leveled an icy glare at him in response. Unfazed, he gave her a friendly smile. "Is there anything I can get you? Coffee? A snack?"

"You can get my mother out of here."

Taking that as a 'no,' he pulled the chair out from the table and sat down opposite her. "I hope we can get both of you out of here soon. As I'm sure my agents have told you, we simply have a couple of questions we hope you can answer."

"I'll tell you the same thing I told the last guy, I don't care what you're 'director' of. My mother doesn't know anything. She's fragile and not equipped to deal with this situation. She can't help you. Let me talk to her, then get someone to take her home. Do that, and I'll try to answer your questions."

He had to wonder who was in charge of the interrogation, but frowned in genuine concern. "What's wrong with your mother? Is she ill?"

"Physically? No. But mentally she's...yes, she's ill. She's able to take care of herself, but barely. She gets distracted, forgets things, can't focus. Please believe me, she doesn't know anything about Caleb. She doesn't even understand why they keep saying his name on the news. She can't cope under this level of stress—you *have* to let her go."

He regarded the woman a moment. He had reviewed her file on the way over and mentally ticked off the high points. She had earned a Ph.D. in biochemistry from Tellica with top honors. The school hired her two years later as a professor, but she was currently on loan to Losice University on Krysk for a year as a visiting professor. She was a single mother of a four-year old daughter, having been widowed when her husband, a botanist, died on a research expedition to an unsettled planet in Elathan's system. She had no criminal record or any documented history of trouble.

He didn't need the file to see she was intelligent, self-sufficient and strong-willed. Yet on this topic he read only earnest desperation in her eyes.

"Give me ten minutes."

She shot him a guarded look and shrugged.

He left the room and slipped along the hallway to an identical one three doors down. The two-way glass in the interrogation room allowed him to observe Francesca Marano undisturbed. Tragic as the notion was, he couldn't help but be glad Stefan wasn't here to see her. It would have broken his heart.

The woman looked decades older than she should. Her skin appeared pallid and drawn, hair a dull, unkempt brown. Her sweater hung lopsided over sagging, defeated shoulders. But saddest of all was her eyes—wide and confused, yet somehow vacant.

A new shard of guilt crept up to join the existing guilt over Michael's death festering in the tiny corner of his brain he allowed them. Francesca's state was not his fault...which wasn't the same thing as absolving him of all responsibility.

He didn't go in the room. He had met her once years ago, briefly and in passing; she was highly unlikely to remember him, but he couldn't take the chance. Instead he went and found Liz.

"We're cutting Francesca Marano loose."

"I admit she hasn't exactly been helpful—I suspect there's a few screws gone in her head—but we can still pursue several more avenues of inquiry."

"We're cutting her loose."

She acknowledged the order with a nod. "Yes, sir."

"Arrange her an escort home, and…" he pondered it a second "…assign a protective watch to her, but nothing overt. She doesn't need to be aware an agent's around."

"You think she's in danger?"

"I think there are a lot of things we don't yet understand. I'm going to let her daughter speak to her while you get the protection set up."

"I'll start the process right away."

He returned to the interrogation room, two steaming cups of coffee in hand, and slid one across the table as he sat. "You may not need one, but I do. War is not conducive to sleep."

Isabela's expression softened as she reached for the cup. "Thank you…and thank you for taking care of my mother." Her eyes remained suspicious, however, as she took a sip then met his gaze. "I said I'll answer your questions, and I will—but I have one first. You're interrogating Caleb's family…is my father here? If he's not, don't bother going to get him. I can assure you he doesn't know a damn thing about any of us."

He kept his expression scrupulously blank. "No, he isn't."

Her head cocked to the side, rich black curls falling to obscure half her face. "Why not? Unless you know Caleb hasn't seen or spoken to him in twenty years. None of us have. But if you do then you knew my mother wouldn't be of any help, yet you dragged her in here anyway."

Yep, she was a sharp one. He clasped his hands on the table and leaned in slightly, not enough to be perceived as threatening. "Ms. Marano, I'll try to answer your questions as well, but I need you to indulge me for a few minutes. Fair enough?"

She rolled her eyes at the ceiling and sank back in her chair. "Fine. Interrogate away."

"Do you know where your brother is?"

"No."

"When did you speak to him last?"

"Six days ago. I sent him a message after he was named a suspect asking if he was okay. He assured me he was, but said he might be unreachable for a while."

"Unreachable? No one is unreachable these days."

"Oh come on, surely you spy types possess ways to go off the grid?"

"Eh...well. Has he shared anything with you about the bombing of EASC Headquarters?"

"He said he didn't do it—which I already knew."

"How?"

"Because he's my *brother*."

Granted, it was a stupid question, if one the manual he didn't read when joining Division twenty-two years ago said he was supposed to ask. "Of course. Has he said anything to you regarding the events of the night of September 24th?"

"I just told you, he said he wasn't responsible for the bombing."

"Not the bombing—regarding other events occurring that night."

Her face screwed up in perplexity. "No...."

"What about the Metis Nebula?"

He received nothing but a blank look.

"And what about with respect to Alexis Solovy?"

She laughed; it carried a hard edge, doubtless brought on by the stress of hours of detention. "No, but he didn't have to. From what I've seen on the news feeds, she's his type."

"Which is?"

"Smart. Capable. Beautiful. A space junkie. Look, he works for you. Shouldn't you know all this about him?"

"Yes, he did—does—but regrettably I don't know him personally."

She waved toward the door in frustration. "Well somebody does, don't they? Talk to your underlings or whoever. He isn't some mysterious, shady loner—he's one of you guys."

"I'm afraid his supervisor is dead. He was murdered the same night as the EASC bombing."

That shook her. She sat up straighter in her chair, yet her eyes lowered as she considered this information. "You're not seriously suggesting Caleb was responsible."

"I can't really disc—"

"You've got yourself one clusterfain of a problem, don't you? If you're trying to figure out whether Caleb committed the bombing, then it means you didn't order it—only everyone thinks you did. Now you have Intelligence agents dying on Senecan soil?" Her tone had started out acerbic, even accusatory, but by the end it had dropped in tenor. "What is going on here?"

"I'm doing my damnedest to find out. I believe your brother would be able to help a lot, if I could talk to him."

"You mean arrest him."

"No, I mean *talk* to him."

A corner of her mouth curled up the slightest bit. "You don't think he did it."

"Personally? I—" A priority pulse asserted itself into his vision, diverting his attention...*bloody hell.*

He cleared his throat. "I apologize, Ms. Marano, but I'm required elsewhere right now. I'd like to continue this conversation, though, and will return as soon as possible."

"I'm not free to leave yet? I've told you everything."

"Please bear with us a little while longer. An agent will activate the panel here for you. If you have need of anything, press it and someone will be right in. I'll also ensure dinner is delivered soon. I want to make your time here as comfortable as I can."

"I—" her head shook, either in frustration or resignation "—thank you."

CAVARE

Graham stared at the body in utter dismay. He'd call it shock, except he'd lost the ability to be shocked a month into the First Crux War.

The throat was slit in virtually the same manner as Volosk's had been, except Nythal looked to have been struck from the front, whereas Michael's murderer had approached from the rear. The scene contained the same complete absence of any forensic evidence which might lead them to a suspect.

The local police had been called off and Division had taken control of the investigation as soon as he learned of the murder. Now his own people worked around him, pretending to ignore his presence as he stood silently in the midst of their crime scene.

Everything Michael Volosk suspected—everything Caleb Marano claimed—was true.

A conspiracy existed surrounding the Summit assassination at the very least, but likely also with respect to the EASC Headquarters bombing. And if both those assertions were true, then there was a conspiracy surrounding the entire war. And at least one person in his own organization was involved in it.

Someone found out about the renewed investigation into Nythal and decided the man needed to be eliminated before he spilled any secrets. It was the sole explanation which fit all the events leading up to and including the ashen corpse lying in five liters of blood at his feet.

Bloody *hell.*

Volosk was killed because he refused to give up on the assassination investigation—whether the trigger was his possession of the autopsy report or his hounding of Nythal hardly mattered. Marano and Solovy were targeted because they were working to convince others there was a conspiracy—whether they were framed for the bombing for that reason or merely as convenient patsies hardly mattered.

There existed scant evidence for any of this, but he didn't require evidence to be convinced; he *knew* it. His gut had rarely been wrong in his professional career, on or off the battlefield. And now he was angry.

He despised corruption, but corrupt government officials most of all. And while corruption for money was one thing, this corruption was costing lives. It had cost the life of a man he considered a friend as well as the lives of hundreds of civilians on Palluda and thousands of soldiers on both sides.

He didn't have any intention of letting that sort of corruption stand.

After issuing a few instructions to the forensic team he headed back for Division. In order to root out this festering infection, he first needed to pick through Michael's notes and Marano's reports, to absorb everything they had discovered.

Then it would be time to pay a bill which had at last come due. It was the last thing he wanted to do today or tomorrow or any day, but it was time for a confession. His own.

10

Liam O'Connell moved with careful restraint behind his desk. His hands clasped one another behind his back, each keeping the other in check. He worked to project the image of a calm yet authoritative leader he knew was required of him.

It was making his skin itch, as though invisible snakes slithered along the surface taunting him to explode in movement.

Holos projecting each of the Regional Commanders hovered above his desk. Replacements had not yet been named for the Earth-based EASC Board members who had been killed in the bombing; as such this was a Board meeting in substance if not in form. The traitor Solovy had not been invited.

He leveled a domineering glower at Admiral Rychen, the Northeastern Regional Commander. "We need to act swiftly to retaliate after Desna. Send a regiment to take their Bellici colony."

"Perhaps we should consider retaking Desna first, General."

His scowl shifted to a holo on the far end. "Foster, do you have a mission profile ready yet to retake Desna?"

The mealy-mouthed Northwestern Commander straightened his shoulders as if he were somehow proud. "Sir, the Senecans left behind a sizeable fleet to defend Desna. My forces are in a weakened state. I don't believe I can spare the ships necessary to retake it at this time."

Liam squinted, his brow tightening before he could prevent it. A headache began clawing at the back of his eyes. "I see." He gestured at his recently-named replacement in the Southwestern Region. "Haraken, for God's sake send Foster some ships so he can mount a respectable attempt at retaking one puny little planet." His attention shifted again. "Rychen, *attack* Bellici."

Rychen regarded him severely, refusing to be stared down. "O'Connell, you and I were in a meeting with the Prime Minister not six hours ago in which he instructed me to lead a broad blockade of the southern Federation border. Such an undertaking is going to take all my ships not on necessary patrols."

Liam snorted. "Bellici is hardly larger than Desna. Are you telling me you can't spare a solitary regiment to hit it?"

Rychen stared at him another second—then had the audacity to laugh. Liam's chest constricted from the effort of holding back a rising tide of anger.

Rychen shifted forward, his holo giving the impression of pressing toward Liam. "General, have you learned nothing from the losses at Arcadia and Desna? The Federation has been quite busy these last two decades building up a sizable and formidable military. Unlike Desna, Bellici will be defended. I assure you it will take more than a regiment to seize the colony, and those ships will be busy implementing the Prime Minister's orders."

"Are you refus—"

The door to his office slid open. Miriam Solovy marched in wearing a grim expression, then arched an eyebrow at the holos. "Something I should know, General?"

"No. You have no right to barge into my office unannounced. Get out."

Her eyes scanned the holos in what was surely false curiosity. "Given the current reduction in members, this looks suspiciously like a Board meeting—which is absurd, because were it actually a Board meeting I would've been requested to attend." Her gaze settled coldly on him.

"It is not. I am simply consulting with the Regional Commanders."

"Good. They need to hear this as well. I bear disturbing news. ANNIE has determined we have lost communications with the colony of Gaiae."

His right hand leapt out of the grasp of his left, eager to be freed for motion. "So? Who gives a rat's ass about a bunch of crazies in the middle of nowhere?"

"They may be a 'bunch of crazies,' but they possess a spaceport, and we cannot contact it. Nor can we contact any of its employees, any other organization or a single person inhabiting the planet, and that is a nontrivial matter. Given the planet's proximity to the

Metis Nebula, we have to consider the possibility they have come under attack from the alien armada."

"There are no aliens, Miriam! Your traitorous bitch of a daughter invented them so her Senecan lover could get inside the building and plant his bombs."

He wasn't sure how or when she had managed to maneuver to the front of his desk and lean forcefully into it, but now her small frame threatened to tower over the desk, and him.

"I am warning you now, in front of witnesses—do not call my daughter a traitor again, or I will *end* you."

The knuckles of his fist ground against the surface of the desk. "If she's proven a traitor, you won't be able to stop me."

A throat clearing loudly broke the confrontation. Rychen continued before either of them were able to retort. "The data on the aliens did appear scientifically sound, according to both our scientists and those at the Astronomical and Space Science Department. God knows I don't want it to be true, but the news—or rather lack thereof—from Gaiae represents a troubling coincidence."

"You're not seriously saying you believe this nonsense?"

"As the Commander for the region closest to the Metis Nebula, I would be negligent if I did not give the matter due consideration. You must recognize this."

In the absence of a suitable reply he merely grunted.

Solovy had turned her back on him to face the holos. "Admiral Rychen, I realize your fleet is fully engaged instituting a blockade on the Federation border. Do you think there's any way you could spare a single scout ship—maybe one currently out on patrol—to investigate the situation on Gaiae? They can try to reestablish proximity communications and perform a visual assessment of the situation."

Rychen smiled at Solovy. "I have a scout ship currently in the far northeastern region which can be at Gaiae within the day."

"Belay that mission, Rychen. If you don't possess enough ships to go to Bellici, you don't possess enough ships to go to Gaiae."

Rychen's hard eyes met his, and he was reminded why he considered the man dangerous.

"Respectfully, General, you do not have the authority to forbid me to send the ship."

"Like Hell I don't. I'm the Chairman of the—"

Solovy scoffed at him derisively. "Did you imagine the position of Chairman gave you ultimate authority over the galaxy? You should have asked Price Alamatto what it really entailed. Admiral Rychen is the Commander for the Northeastern Region. You remember what that means, don't you?"

Rychen helpfully supplied the answer for him. "It means I command the region, which I intend to continue doing until such time as I am relieved or fall in battle. Admiral Solovy, I'll keep you and the Board informed regarding what my scout ship discovers. Now this meeting has run long, and it seems I have a blockade to implement."

Liam managed to stutter out a "Dismissed" as Rychen's holo went dark. His teeth ground together as he pivoted to deal with Solovy—but she too was already gone.

11

PORTAL PRIME
UNCHARTED SPACE

No dragons were in sight as Caleb approached the mountainous terrain a third time. Perhaps the supply of dragons had run out and their masters hadn't yet found time to fab new ones.

He chuckled to himself; it came out ragged and raw. He was feeling a bit punch-drunk and more than a little reckless—but reckless was the last thing he needed to be right now, so he worked to compartmentalize the emotions rampaging through his head and ripping into his chest. *Focus.*

He set the *Siyane* to the ground a hundred meters from the start of the mountains and took thirty seconds to splash water on his face, guzzle an energy drink and retrieve the Daemon from where it had landed against the cabin wall. Then he collected several items before activating the hatch and exiting the ship.

A mild breeze drifted down the slope. He'd want a jacket, but he was getting ahead of himself. He jogged as close as he dared to where he believed the barrier to be and stopped. By now his cybernetics had done a decent job of taking the edge off the injuries inflicted by the dragon, and he merely noticed a twinge in his shoulders and a dull ache in his right thigh.

There was no visual sign of a barrier in any portion of the spectrum his ocular implant analyzed.

He palmed the frozen muffin he'd taken from the kitchen, wound his arm back and hurled it into the air. It sailed for fifty meters or so, hit the ground, bounced twice and rolled to a stop low on the slope of the mountain.

The barrier was without a doubt closer than the slope, but he didn't dare approach yet. Instead he pulled the portable oscilloscope out of his pocket. He'd made sure she kept a backup onboard, as he was fairly certain he was about to lose this one. He cocked his arm and sent it flying after the muffin.

It tumbled end over end for thirty meters—then vanished.

He discerned no flicker as one would see with a human-created force field and no detectable boomerang. The device was simply gone. He imagined it now lay on the grass several hundred kilometers behind him.

So the barrier was triggered by technology, which explained why both the dragon and the muffin could pass through but the ship and the oscilloscope could not. Still, he had a sneaking suspicion it was more complicated. Time to find out.

The next item he had brought was a serrated knife from the kitchen. Having a better idea of the demarcation line now, he stepped closer and sent the knife through the air. It spun forward to land short of the muffin but well beyond the point where the oscilloscope had vanished.

Artificially-created materials were allowed. Only tech was taboo.

He removed his kinetic blade from the latch on his pants. The hilt was cool in his hands, the blade inactive. He hesitated this time. There was no backup for the blade; if it got rejected he didn't have another. But this was the sole safe way to discover the triggering parameters.

He heaved the hilt through the air...relief coursed through him as it settled to the ground not terribly far from the muffin.

Thank god. If inactive technology was a no-go he'd have been utterly screwed.

He hastened back to the ship, where he stuffed a pack with food, supplies and a change of clothes for himself *and* her. He figured he'd need the supplies no matter what happened next. His gaze roved deliberately around the ship. He chose a few more items and headed out.

Once outside he closed his eyes. First, he sent a final pulse to her. As had been the result for the last hour, there was simply no response. It didn't bounce back, but that could be because the exanet infrastructure didn't reach through the portal. They'd had no reason to pulse one another since coming through it, so he had no way to know whether such communication was possible.

So be it.

He took a deep breath and did something he'd done only twice before in his life. He instructed his eVi to deactivate all active cybernetic routines then shut itself down. Doing so wasn't a trivial matter, and reactivating everything would entail using an external unit to interface with the tiny fibers at the base of his neck which connected to his cybernetics. But it was necessary.

The *silence* in his head echoed eerily, unnerving him more than he expected. He didn't feel weaker, because he wasn't—not right now. His biosynthetic enhancements still functioned, and he still benefited from a genetically-modified muscular structure.

But should he face a crisis, he wouldn't be able to rely upon nanobots to accelerate his adrenaline or hone his focus. Should he become injured he wouldn't be able to rely upon directed cybernetic routines to limit the damage and speed healing. His ocular implant now sat dormant, leaving him nothing but natural eyesight to guide his way. The exanet and communications had been gone since they entered Metis, but now he didn't even have access to his internal data store.

He rolled his shoulders, stretched his arms and walked forward.

The rather drastic action had better be enough. If the barrier booted him all the way to the grasslands he would be days getting back here. Alex might not have days.

She might not have hours, he tried very hard not to think.

He also realized the action might not have been essential. After all, Alex had passed through, and he highly doubted she had deactivated her cybernetics before doing so. Their eVis and cybernetics were fully contained within their bodies, so they might not trigger the repulsion mechanism.

But it was also possible she was allowed through because she hung in the dragon's grasp or...perhaps an exception had been made. Regardless, he didn't dare risk it.

His heart thudded against his breastbone with every step; it turned out adrenaline functioned surprisingly well absent nanobot assistance. He remained skeptical he'd successfully passed through the barrier until he crouched to retrieve the muffin, now coated in a thin layer of dirt.

One more test passed. A significant one.

He scanned the area until he spotted the hilt of his blade and retrieved it as well. He flipped the hilt over and tapped the toggle to activate it—

—and watched it vanish from his hand. *Shit.*

It wasn't a barrier. It was a technology-free zone. Terrific.

He cursed at the bright sunless sky and returned to the ship. He was going to need a weapon, as he suspected punching the dragon into submission using his fists did not constitute a viable plan.

Once inside he tossed the pack on the couch and went downstairs to the engineering well, in no way whatsoever stopping to gaze in despair or anguish at the empty bed and the rush of memories the room evoked. He located a metamat blade and torch and went to work.

She was going to be pissed as all hell when she found out he'd mutilated her ship—on top of being pissed as all hell when she found out he'd hijacked control of her ship without her consent—but it was necessary. He required a weapon, and a non-technological one at that.

He sheared a long metal strip off one of the panels protecting the engineering core. It didn't represent a crucial segment; the fifteen-centimeter-wide gap didn't threaten the safe operation of the ship.

It took more than an hour to sculpt the strip of platinum nanoalloy into a blade just shy of a meter long. He felt every second tick by in his soul but forced himself to take the time to do it right. Finally satisfied with the blade, he crafted a thicker piece for a hilt and used the torch to meld it onto the blade and coax it into a form compatible with his hand.

Next came a grip to keep the weapon from slipping in his palm. Was there anything approaching leather on the ship? His mind drifted to the cushioning on the oversized chair in the bedroom.

He groaned as he ascended the ladder from the engineering well…she was definitely going to kill him. Still, he chose the least conspicuous spot possible to carve a swatch from. Maybe she wouldn't notice. *What are the odds?*

Finally he sliced up the physical harness from the jump seat and fashioned a strap and minimal sheath. He slung the sheathed blade over his back, positioned the strap to rest diagonally across his chest and tested the rig out. A rough solution, but it would have to suffice.

He didn't waste any time on the way out this trip. Grabbing a water and the pack on the way through the cabin, he powered down the ship and left it behind.

He had a mountain to climb.

12

Graham filled the thermos with coffee, took a long sip and filled it again. Sleep had been a stingy, fickle mistress the night before.

He waved a silent greeting at an agent who made her way into the kitchen, grabbed a second, smaller coffee and headed down the hallway. If he swung by his office distractions were guaranteed to claim his morning so he had gone straight to the interrogation level. He wiped stray drops of coffee from his mouth as he stepped inside the room.

Isabela Marano looked better than he felt, though shadows had formed beneath her eyes. He'd made sure she was provided with a bed for the night—they had small rooms one floor below which doubled as cells—and access to a shower and a change of clothes. She had presumably taken advantage of all three prior to being returned to the interrogation room this morning.

He slid the second coffee in her direction. "I'd say good morning, but I won't insult you by suggesting you view it as one. I am sorry I had to leave so abruptly last night."

Her attention wavered from him to the cup on the table; she drew it closer but didn't take a sip. "How much longer are we going to do this? My daughter is back on Krysk. She's staying with a friend for now, but I was supposed to return last night. She's only four years old, Director. I *need* to get home to her."

"I understand. Believe me, I do."

"But."

"But it's important you remain here for a while longer."

"*Why?*"

"A fair question—and a complicated one."

Her eyes narrowed at him, intense and calculating. "Before you left, you were about to tell me whether you thought Caleb was guilty. Do you?"

He didn't answer immediately, instead producing a small device from his pocket. He placed it on the table and activated the surveillance shield. She glanced at the device but didn't remark on it.

"No, I'm convinced he is not. Proving it is another matter and unfortunately, more difficult than it might seem."

"Well try."

"Oh, I intend to. But first, we should talk about something else. Yesterday, you asked me if we had brought your father in for questioning."

"You said no. I'm a little confused as to why you wouldn't, given your dragnet approach."

He ran a hand through his hair, stalling for one final minute. He was the bloody Director of Intelligence; if he didn't have the authority to make a tactical decision to reveal a state secret, no one did.

"We didn't question your father, Ms. Marano, because your father is dead...and has been for over twenty years."

Her shoulders jerked as if she had been punched in the chest. "That's impossible. We would have been notified."

"Under normal circumstances, you are correct."

"No. See, he continues to send support payments to my mother. Like clockwork every forty days for the last twenty years—at least he has the decency to meet one obligation. So you must be mistaken."

"Would that I were. Those payments have come from my office."

"I don't understand."

"No reason you should. What I'm going to tell you is highly classified and cannot leave this room. Will you agree to keep this confidence?"

Her carriage stiffened into a defensive posture, armoring her against whatever came next. She nodded.

"Stefan Marano did not work for the Civil Development Agency. He did not work as a civil engineer, though he did receive a degree in it. In actuality he was an investigator for the Division of Intelligence. He wasn't a field agent, but for various reasons he did need to keep his duties secret."

"You're joking. Why would you joke about something like this?"

"I assure you, I am not joking. I should know, because he worked for me...and I considered him a friend."

Her voice sounded flat, though her eyes were not. "What happened?"

"In 2301, shortly after the armistice ended the First Crux War, your father was investigating a plot to destabilize the new Senecan Federation government, possibly via multiple assassinations or terrorist attacks. Those orchestrating the plot proved maddeningly difficult to uncover, but your father got close—too close. The leaders of this insurrection were powerful men and women, the type of people one does not trifle with. They found out he was onto them before his investigation was complete."

He paused to take another sip of coffee, and to make sure he phrased the next part correctly. "They threatened his family—you, your brother, your mother. They promised to hurt those he cared about if he continued this pursuit. We...discussed his options. You see, your father was an honorable man. He couldn't in good conscience sit by and let terrorists destroy his government. But he also couldn't bear the idea of anyone hurting his family.

"So he made a play. He very publicly walked out on you, hoping if you were no longer a part of his life, this group would realize they had nothing to gain by harming his family. He expected for it to be temporary, a month or two at most. Once the investigation was finished and we had the evidence we required and the plotters in custody, he planned to come home.

"I believe he intended to explain everything, as he realized it was likely the sole chance he possessed for your mother to accept him back."

Isabela's hands were knotted together in a clenched fist on the table. Graham reached out to clasp them in a gesture of sympathy. His large, ungainly hand enveloped both of hers completely. "Know that he loved all of you so much, and it tormented him each day he remained parted from you. He despised being forced to hurt you."

She stared at him, and he noted the armor beginning to falter. Confusion, disbelief and the edges of pain flashed across her eyes.

He continued. "Do you remember the Serich Fabrications accident in 2301? Probably not, you would have been fairly young."

"I...we talked about it in school, I think."

"Well, it wasn't an industrial accident. One of the leaders of the insurgent group owned Serich, and they used the plant as a base of operations. Your father had been working day and night to expose them. He caught a break when he learned the specific time for a scheduled meeting at the plant. The entire leadership together in one place represented too exceptional an opportunity to pass up, and he put together a team to bring them all in. Tragically, the mission went to hell.

"As near as we were able to determine, the plotters were heavily armed and had brought hired protection. A firefight broke out. The location was an operating industrial plant, and several large canisters of a pyrophoric chemical got caught in the crossfire. The canisters exploded, destroying the plant and killing everyone inside: eleven plotters, six mercenaries and eight agents, including your father.

"He shouldn't have gone inside—as I said, he wasn't a field agent. But he refused to let others take responsibility for his case. He needed to see it through."

She wiped away a tear with the back of her hand, but strengthened her posture. "Why didn't you tell us at the time? The threat had ended, and he was gone. People don't die and no one find out about it. Why cover it up?"

There was no way to temper the answer, no way to put it which wouldn't sound as cold and calculating as the truth. "Remember, this occurred only months after the armistice with the Alliance. The administration was new, unproven and weak. Any action which destabilized it risked conflict at best, chaos at worst. Perhaps even renewed war. It was decided at the highest levels of the government that the existence of the plot could not be made public. The whole affair would be buried and every trace of its existence erased."

"'Was decided'? No one takes responsibility so no one bears the blame?"

He cringed at the acid dripping from her voice. "Possibl—"

"You *bastard*."

"It wasn't my decision to make, Ms. Marano. I had far less power then and was not given a choice in the matter."

"Do you have any idea what my father leaving did to my family? To my mother?"

"Yes. I do. And I am more sorry than I can ever express."

She stared at him in growing anger—then covered her mouth as a cry bubbled up from her throat, blinking away tears as she wrenched around to face the wall. He understood the need for private grief and didn't disturb her. Her shoulders rose and fell in time with shaky breaths.

Sooner than he expected she turned back to him, eyes glistening but composure otherwise restored. Her voice came out softer than before, yet unwavering. "Does Caleb know? Is that why he works for you?"

"I don't think so. He shouldn't. The man who recruited him and trained him was close to your father…I'd go so far as to call them best friends. He knew from your father that Caleb exhibited a lot of potential and wanted to look after him. Nurture him. In fact, he watched over all of you for years after your father's death. But he was under explicit orders not to divulge your father's fate, and as far as I'm aware he followed those orders."

"Have you asked this man?"

"I'm afraid I can't…he's dead now as well."

"Dangerous business you're in."

"It is."

An uneasy silence descended then. She reached for the coffee, but made a face when she realized it had gone cold and set the cup down. Sharp eyes regarded him as she absorbed knowledge which sent her family's history spiraling end over end.

He had gambled on being right about her pragmatic nature and intelligence. He waited to see if exposing old wounds—not merely hers but his own as well—had been worth the cost.

"So…why tell me?"

He exhaled, relieved. "To gain your trust, of course."

"I'm sorry, Director Delavasi, but I honestly do not know where Caleb is or how to reach him."

"I believe you."

Her brow furrowed in apparent confusion. "Then I don't understand what you want from me."

"I want to clear your brother's name. I owe it to your family. Incidentally, doing so may also save a couple of thousand or possibly million lives. Caleb has caught the ire of a conspiracy far more nefarious than the one your father gave his life thwarting. To clear his name I need to expose this conspiracy. And I need your help to do it."

13

M iriam sat at her desk. Multiple screens hovered above the surface, and a hand rested at her chin as she stared at them. The stoic pose would convey an impression of cool-headed, deliberate contemplation to an observer, should one happen by.

Yet beneath the dispassionate exterior, her mind navigated a Gordian knot of difficulties. At least, she hoped it held Gordian characteristics, as that would mean she stood a chance of untangling it with the proper approach.

How could they have lost so many ships so quickly? In the fog of battle and from a distance it hadn't been clear exactly how many ships they were losing and how few they had to replace those lost.

Still, they should have more ships. They *did* have more ships. But those ships were scattered in an egalitarian matter across settled space, and thus were taking days and in some cases weeks to reach any point where they might be useful. And they couldn't move all of them, no, because what if someone or thing attacked from the south or west and those colonies were left undefended? Never mind they were presently being attacked in strength from the north and needed some damn help.

If Alamatto were still Chairman he'd heed her counsel and send more ships north. O'Connell was not so open-minded, to say the least. Despite his seemingly zealous desire to defeat the Federation, he refused to acknowledge the level of force which was going to be required to do so.

She spared a thought to recognize her arguable hypocrisy in that she was not advocating sending more than a tiny fraction of the Sol/Central Command fleet to reinforce the front lines. But that was different. If Earth fell every world would fall.

She drew in a long breath, imposing a calmer state. Tantrums were not her style. David may have been a smooth, charismatic and occasionally impulsive leader, but she rose to her position by being cool, controlled and logical. She excelled at the details of logistics.

If there was a way to ensure the northeast and northwest regions were adequately reinforced—without sacrificing crucial protections for the First Wave worlds—she would find it and make it happen and there wouldn't even be a parade in her honor.

A holocomm request popped into her vision. She started to dismiss it out of hand as she had work to do, then noticed who sent the request. She collected herself and accepted the comm.

"Admiral Rychen. What can I do for you?"

His expression was not formal. Genuine she suspected, but pained. His pale blond hair threatened to fall from its proper location and over his weathered forehead. Yet paler blue eyes showed troubling concern. "One of my scout ships reached Gaiae and reported in as soon as they regained communications functionality."

She leaned forward, all thoughts of logistics put aside. "And?"

His jaw tightened, and his gaze wandered off-holo before returning to her. "It's gone. There aren't any aliens, but there also aren't any people. Or vegetation or wildlife or buildings. Every area which housed any population whatsoever has been burnt to ashes, and all life with it."

She sank deeper into her chair, neglecting to maintain military posture. She had believed Alexis, believed the data...but some part of her had allowed for the possibility that it was a fantasy, a dream, a hallucination or simply a mistake.

It had been a foolish, irrational hope she should not have indulged in. Of course it was real. Terrifyingly, devastatingly real.

She willed her spine straight. "Do you have any information as to where the alien fleet is now?"

"I don't. A straight trajectory suggests they'll be in Federation space by now, but we won't have any intel, and I rather doubt the Senecan government will be eager to share theirs."

"Naturally." It was only after the fact she realized a droll chuckle had escaped her lips. She straightened the cant of her mouth. "Karelia? I assume they've not seen any incidents or we would know."

"I confirmed it personally before contacting you. They report no anomalies, nor do the smaller colonies in the area." He frowned. "Could it be the aliens are pushing into Federation space deliberately?"

"No, Alexis was right. The aliens don't care what faction anyone belongs to." At his look of slight surprise, she schooled her features with appropriate decorum. "It's logical to assume these aliens don't understand the political intricacies currently at work in our region of space. I can't imagine they would deliberately target the Federation over us."

"An excellent point, Admiral. I will fight the war my government tells me to fight. Hell, I'll even advocate for it given proper motivation, but I'm not an idealist and I'm certainly not a zealot. From afar the Federation cannot be distinguished from the Alliance in any meaningful way. The fact they're on the wrong side of our battle doesn't imply an alien species would choose to target them over us. It's simply directional logistics. On that note, any news from Andromeda?"

In the wrong audience his unexpectedly frank words might have doomed his career. He was lucky this wasn't the wrong audience—a fact she had to presume he knew.

"As a matter of fact, yes. I received word via ANNIE they were no longer reachable two hours ago, but another dramatic proclamation didn't seem worthwhile until we gained a handle on Gaiae. Are you sure our colonies in the easternmost region are clear?"

"For the moment. I've set up a half-hourly monitoring ping to the local governments. If they go offline, we'll know promptly. Not as if we'll be able to do anything to help them...."

He fell silent, and she gave him the time and metaphorical space he appeared to need. Finally he looked back up at her, frustration lining his face. "Miriam, I don't possess the capability to fight a war on two fronts. Not when one front is against aliens who can do what they did to Gaiae."

"I realize you don't. I'm working on the issue, though I fear it may be too little too late. For now I would advise you—to the extent my advice carries any weight—to manage your blockade as ordered but keep a sharp lookout on the eastern border. And if you have anything at all to keep in reserve, do so."

"Thank you. For the record, your advice carries far more weight than anyone else in Vancouver."

"I'm grateful to hear it, Christopher. Keep me informed."

She cut the link, dropped an elbow on the desk and rested her chin back in her palm. She had always considered Rychen a good officer, better than most she had known. Like David he was a hero of the First Crux War, only he had lived to tell the tale. But she didn't bear him ill will. He'd suffered plenty and borne the hero's mantle grudgingly.

Still, she hadn't expected to find an ally in him. She'd given up on finding allies beyond Richard and Alexis…and Alexis was gone. It broke her heart, when she hadn't thought there remained any heart left to break. But she needed to fight for something. Without the fight she had nothing left.

You want to do something, Mom? Then goddamn do something.

She pulled the fleet distribution report back up, spread it out above her desk and studied the numbers for several minutes. Then she sent Rychen an encrypted message.

I'm sending you two stealth recon platoons and three light frigates from Sol/Central Command. They needn't be part of the official blockade. Use them as you see fit, though the eastern border strikes me as a good posting for them.

— *Admiral Miriam Solovy, EASC Director of Operations*

SENECA

CAVARE, MILITARY HEADQUARTERS

Field Marshal Eleni Gianno stood in the center of the situation room. Though she was quiet, the air buzzed with noise. Voices. Hurried steps. The crackle of too many active screens in close proximity. Far more screens populated the room than people, grouped in clusters by region and purpose with a single person to staff each cluster.

Most of the data under review originated from the Alliance war, but a cluster had been set up to monitor the eastern colonies for anomalous activity.

They now knew what had happened on Gaiae and were soon to know what was happening on Andromeda. If the alien fleet was fanning out from Metis, four Federation colonies stood next in line. New Riga, Lycaon, Dair and Hadron each earned a display devoted to their status. If something happened on any of the worlds, she expected to know within minutes.

Until such occurred—and she held little doubt it would occur—she focused on the growing blockade the Alliance was in the process of implementing along the southern border.

A series of frigates and light cruisers patrolled fifty parsecs off the border, and any merchant vessels arriving in the vicinity from or heading to Federation space were approached and ordered to turn around or be boarded. Thus far the Alliance captains appeared to be going to great lengths to avoid shooting any civilian vessels, though several had been disabled after resisting.

Whoever was running the blockade was a clever strategist. The ships covered broad swaths of space and were always on the move, using electronic warfare scout ships to scan at maximum range so they picked up vessels in plenty of time to corral them before they slipped through the net. She expected the number of scout ships to increase over the coming days.

She could send a battalion to whittle the blockading ships down one by one. Except sporting advanced scanner capabilities, they'd realize her forces approached with ample time to clear out. And even if her forces were able to take out two or three ships, she felt certain when they arrived at the fourth one they would find an entire Alliance brigade waiting on them.

From a purely military strategic perspective, the blockade didn't represent a significant obstacle for the time being. Her plan consisted primarily of targeting the already-weakened western Alliance colonies in any event, and the blockade did not stretch so far. She didn't intend to assault the Alliance head-on where it was strongest. Not for a while yet, anyway.

But it wouldn't take long for it to put a strain on commerce, then on supplies the military required. Seneca was self-sufficient in most respects, but given Romane's convenient location it had been easy to become reliant on high-quality goods from the independent world for various needs.

The corps were guaranteed to grumble, then grumble louder, then pitch a fit. Pressure would increase on Romane and Pyxis and likely Pandora to join the Alliance, which would represent a significant problem.

She could assign escorts to the larger commercial vessels attempting to traverse the blockade, but it—

"Marshal, we've lost contact with the Andromeda scout ship."

"They have their orders. Inform me the instant we reestablish contact."

The GOI platoon had never returned from Metis. No drones had been launched to send updates—or if drones had been launched, they also did not make it out. The alien ships had not been sighted since the images the SpecOps agent captured at the portal. Yet if any doubt as to their existence remained in her mind, the loss of communications from the scout ship removed it. So there it was.

Analyses suggested the armada surrounded itself in a field which disrupted all communications in the same manner the nebula did. If the field extended as far as early data indicated, there existed no way to capture and transmit real-time images. A ship was going to have to get close enough to capture images then escape the field to reestablish contact. It remained to be seen whether that constituted a realistic feat.

She hoped like hell it was feasible, because they didn't stand a chance of fighting these ships if they didn't understand them.

Shortly after the Andromeda scout ship dropped offline, New Riga vanished from the grid.

So fast? How many ships did the aliens possess? Perhaps more importantly, how many ships did they need to destroy a single colony? How many colonies could they hit simultaneously?

The military base on New Riga had also received orders. They were to do everything possible to get a single stealth craft out with any data it successfully amassed in a few minutes' time. She had contemplated ordering the base evacuated but doubted most of the soldiers would have obeyed. They would want to defend their colony.

"Commodore Suyen, order an evacuation of Lycaon and Dair and begin pre-evacuation procedures for Hadron."

"Yes, ma'am."

Lycaon and Dair were small colonies, supporting populations of around 60K each; Hadron was even smaller. The evacuations were a substantial undertaking, but doable.

She glanced back to the cluster of screens monitoring the southern border. Somehow she suspected before long no one was likely to give a damn about a simple blockade.

"Alert me of any developments. I'm going to see the Chairman."

14

MESSIUM
EARTH ALLIANCE COLONY

K ennedy Rossi was running late. She hurriedly composed a status report for the IS Design Board of Directors on her whisper while striding purposefully down one of Messium's busier city streets.

Pewter and bronze towers rose above the sidewalks, though not so high as one saw on most worlds of equivalent development. Messium was a Third Wave world and had been colonized only sixty years earlier, but its level of maturation far exceeded other worlds from the same generation. No, its relatively recent colonization wasn't the primary reason its largest city didn't appear as grandiose as those on Erisen or Romane or Demeter.

Messium was industrial. Military fighters, frigates and a good percentage of cruisers were manufactured on the sprawling military base fifteen kilometers outside the city. Civilian transports and shuttles were produced at a nearly-as-sprawling Genyx complex on the northern edge of the city. Scuttlebutt around town was Magellan Aeronautics had begun building a capital ship for the business tycoon Ronaldo Espahn, though if true it must still be in the early stages, as it would need to be assembled in orbit and once that work began everyone would know. Downtown, smaller factories churned out CU hardware, personal interfaces, lighting and electric fixtures, water and air pleasure craft and dozens of other accessories to modern life.

The city wasn't ugly as such. It was exceptionally clean in fact and the buildings did shine, if with a muted glimmer. The architectural décor complimented the planet's topography in the region—champagne grasses coating flat plains lit by an amber sky.

But Messium was not a tourist destination. It was a place where people worked, where people produced and damn well got things done. She respected their particular élan. If it weren't days from Earth and so muted, she might consider a relocation for a few years. Alas.

She finished up the status report—which consisted entirely of 'making progress' plus flowery words added to fill the space and ease the directors' minds—and sent it on its way. An exasperated breath blew itself out of her pursed lips as she approached the next intersection. Another eight blocks to go. She should have taken a levtram to the Palaimo offices.

Resigned to her fate, she reopened the report on the metal she had taken from the *Siyane's* hull. She'd studied it for hours last night, but still could scarcely believe the data. The test results were nothing short of revolutionary—

> *Connection unable to be established. System is not connected to exanet infrastructure. Message will be queued until able to be delivered.*

She stopped short in the middle of the sidewalk. That didn't make any sense. Frowning, she sent the report to Nance; as the Board's assistant the woman could get it to the directors.

> *Connection unable to be established. System is not connected to exanet infrastructure. Message will be queued until able to be delivered.*

What the...? She tried sending a random message to her brother in Los Angeles and Gabe in New York on the off chance something had gone wrong with the exanet on Erisen, though it was an absurd notion.

> *Connection unable to be established. System is not connected to exanet infrastructure. Messages will be queued until able to be delivered.*

Other people had begun stopping along the sidewalk near her as well as across the street. Not many, but an increasing number every passing second. *What was going on?* She pulled up her custom news feed...and found it empty.

They were cut off from the entire exanet.

A lead-up to an attack by the Federation? Impossible. Even if they were insane enough to attack an Alliance Regional Headquarters, they didn't possess the technology to cut off the exanet to a planet. They *couldn't.*

Suddenly she realized there was but one plausible explanation for the outage.

Metis.

"Oh, *hell* no." She pivoted and took off running for her hotel.

Kennedy burst into her hotel room pulling her blouse over her head with one hand while she yanked her shoes off with the other. No way was she going to face an alien invasion in heels and silk.

After changing into workpants and boots and a lightweight tunic she retrieved the smaller of her two bags from the closet and dropped it on the bed. She tossed in one change of clothes and basic hygiene toiletries; the remainder of the space she used for her equipment. She made it a point to never travel for work without a set of tools. Better to take her own readings than rely on the assurances of a supplier eager to impress.

She raided the food cabinet for as many bottles of water as managed to fit in the bag and a stack of energy bars, then scanned the room. Did she have everything?

Not even close. But everything else was nearly four kiloparsecs away on Erisen. In a futile act she turned on the screen embedded in the wall. *Nothing.* She wound her hair back into a ponytail and slung the bag over her shoulder. It felt heavy but she couldn't afford to leave any of the contents behind.

She'd try for the spaceport though she suspected it was far too late for anything so easy. The military base? It was an absurdly long walk and the levtrams would be overrun by now.

Much as she hated to admit it, in the short term the Palaimo offices likely constituted her best bet. They had basement labs where they did small prototype runs and testing—space which offered some protection and possibly makeshift weapons.

She laughed a bit wildly as she vacated the room and rushed down the hall. What did she imagine these aliens were that she'd have the opportunity to stab at one with a shard of metamat?

An alien invasion represented the only logical conclusion. The communications loss matched *exactly* Alex's description of the

conditions in the Metis Nebula. Her personal cybernetics continued to function, electronics and engines continued to function—or
she assumed they did since no shuttles had plummeted from the sky
during her sprint back to the hotel. There merely existed a pervasive, widespread and total interference with remote
communications.

She wanted to study it; perhaps she could figure out how it
worked. But she should probably concentrate on staying alive first.

In the few minutes she had taken upstairs the front desk area
of the lobby had become jammed with angry guests demanding answers and failing those, heads on spikes. She jostled through them
and out the door.

The street appeared marginally less chaotic than the lobby, as
most people trod in short, erratic paths, doubtless banging away at
their comms in confusion. No one was running and screaming.

She began to question her initial conclusion. Maybe it was
simply a technical glitch or—

—then someone did scream. She looked in the direction of the
noise, and found everyone looking up.

Nope, she was right.

The first plumes of flame in the distance—from the military
base, she'd bet her life on it—rose into the sky as a series of ships
gained shape and definition. Before their noses fully emerged from
the clouds she knew these were the enormous dreadnoughts from
Alex's images. When framed against the landscape, they seemed *so*
much larger.

This was not good.

The sonic booms of half a dozen fighter craft shook the ground
as they streaked past overhead, pulse lasers firing at the approaching ships. A tiny spark of hope blossomed in her chest...if we were
fighting back from the start, maybe we stood a chance....

A wide beam so deep red in hue it burned almost black shot out
of the belly of the lead dreadnought and swept across the fighters,
vaporizing four of them on contact. Two dodged the first shot and
banked away in evasive maneuvers. The beam swung after each of
them in turn, destroying both in seconds.

Or not. She resumed running for the Palaimo offices.

Chaos now descended in full on the streets, and it mimicked all the great disaster vids like a bad parody. People ran in every direction while exhibiting no clear purpose or destination, stumbling over one another, pushing and shoving and creating havoc. A rare few helped others but most were deep in the throes of abject panic.

She made herself as unobtrusive as possible, slipping and shimmying and ducking as needed. Still, twice she got shoved into a building façade and narrowly missed being crushed to the ground by a passing stampede.

The mob now swelled so thick she no longer dared divert her attention upward to check the sky. That is, until the screams ramped up to a fever pitch and a vibration of new, more urgent terror shot through the crowd like an errant lightning bolt.

Above the cries of panic rose the screech of tearing metal, a sound she was intimately familiar with. All at once the press of bodies eased as people scattered in every direction.

She looked up just in time to see a thirty-meter chunk of one of the orbital arrays, its scaffolding twisted and mangled and possibly on fire, shear off a corner of the roof of a tower across the street on its way to crashing down on top of her.

PART II:

REQUITAL

"Fate is not satisfied with inflicting one calamity."

— *Publilius Syrus*

15

Alex flopped down in a chair at the kitchen table and tugged one of her feet up with her, letting her knee fall to rest along the bowed edge of the table. She snatched a blueberry muffin off the plate sitting in the center.

Dad glanced over his shoulder from the kitchen counter, where he was slicing up mangos. "So what's your day look like, *milaya?*"

Her mouth was already full of steaming hot, deliciously moist muffin, but she nonetheless garbled an answer. "Mmmf mmhum fmmm." She grabbed the glass of juice which had been waiting on her at the table and took a gulp, then tried again. "Physics exam today."

Plate of mangos in hand, he came and sat down opposite her. "Did you study?"

She rolled her eyes at the ceiling. "I don't *have* to study. The material's easy anyway."

His distinguished eyebrows drew in to form a severe countenance. She straightened up in her chair. "Now, Alex, *I* know you're brilliant, and your mother knows you're brilliant, and you know you're brilliant—but out there in the world test results matter. If you want to be the greatest starship captain the galaxy has ever seen, you need to ace your exams."

"I will, Dad. I promise. I understand the material...but I'll leave a few minutes early and skim my notes before class."

She stood up, the remainder of the muffin left forgotten on her plate, as her mom walked in the kitchen. Like Dad, she was dressed in crisp navy blue BDUs. Her hair had been wound into a prim but pretty braid.

"Alexis, where are you going? You haven't finished your breakfast yet."

She nudged the chair under the table. "It's no big deal. I need to get to school a few minutes early."

Dad tilted his head at her, a kind glint in his eyes. "I know you're more than prepared, *milaya*, and will do well. Why don't you stay and enjoy breakfast with us?"

"Nah, want to make sure I'm ready." Impulsively she grabbed another muffin and flashed a toothy smile. "I'll eat this on the way!"

Mom grunted in mild disapproval as her eyes flitted in Dad's direction. "Fine, but watch out for traffic. Your teacher will get mad if you have to take the exam from the hospital."

Alex chewed on her lower lip and pulled on her shoes with one hand while making an effort to not smush the muffin with the other. "Yes, ma'am."

Shoes mostly on and muffin mostly intact, she rushed out the door, only to be assaulted by a punishing gust of wind. Her hair whipped across her face and tangled itself in her mouth. Good thing she hadn't taken a bite of the new muffin yet; she did *not* need gooey crumbs in her hair. She checked her pants pockets...no hairband.

With a sigh she pivoted to run back inside and grab one. The door opened—

"—I'm serious, David. You push her too hard. She would do anything to win your approval, or even a little praise."

Alex flattened herself against the wall and stuck her foot in the doorframe to keep it from closing all the way.

"I'm not your father, Miri."

"I didn't say..." Alex carefully peeked in to see her mom's nose scrunch up "...alright, *yes*, it's possible I'm sensitive when it comes to this topic. My father was demanding and cold and no matter how well I performed it wasn't good enough for him. I *understand* you're not him. You're supportive and encouraging of her, two crucial traits my father never managed to develop. But still...she worships the ground you walk on. I won't let you take advantage of her adoration and hurt her in the process."

"I would *never* hurt our little girl."

Her mom crossed to him and affectionately ran a hand through his hair. "Not intentionally, no. But you don't always consider the consequences of your actions before charging ahead—don't look at me that way. You know I'm right."

Dad's chin dropped to his chest. "So you are. I'll try to be more careful of how I phrase things to her. It's just...she's spilling over with imagination and talent and potential and I want to help her realize it."

Mom dropped her forehead to his. "As do I, and together we will. But she's only eleven, David, and I worry she'll become more afraid of disappointing you than excited about making you proud."

"I don't want that, Miri. I truly don't."

"I know. But be gentle with her, okay?"

"Okay, *dushen'ka*." He angled his face up to ki—

Ewww. She slipped her foot out of the door and wandered toward her bike, no longer noticing the wind as she worked to wrap her mind around the confusing things her parents had said.

She had completely forgotten about that conversation.

Wait, what? How could she have forgotten about it when it just happened? What did—

Claws ripping her shirt, gouging painfully into the skin of her shoulder.

She forced aside the odd images flickering through her mind. She needed to hurry; at this rate she wasn't going to be early for school, she was going to be late. She kneaded her temples, trying to clear the strange fog—

Beautiful sapphire eyes, wide in horror—hands reaching for her before being torn away as he was flung through the air—

CALEB.

She shook her head roughly and blinked. And saw the world anew.

She knew this place. Knew this day. "*Sukin syn....*"

This was a memory. This was their house in San Francisco when her parents worked at North American Military Headquarters. Nestled against the edge of the San Pablo Preserve, the house's synthetic hardwood siding caused it to blend naturally into the wooded surroundings. Across the street the mountain laurels grew so tall and thick any view of the Bay was obscured, though if she crawled out on the roof in the afternoon she could catch glimpses of the sunlight reflecting in the waters.

She remembered.

But this didn't feel like a memory, or a dream. It felt like a full-sensory *illusoire*, so real her brain had for a time believed it to be so.

And if it was a dream, why was she still here after awareness dawned?

She wandered back to the house, curious, and peeked in the window to see her parents now seriously making out. Her mother had straddled him in his chair. One hand slipped under his shirt and the other ran along his jaw.

Oh my. Yet seeing them now from the perspective of decades past, she took in the details. Her father was handsome in a way a child couldn't have recognized. Her mother looked so young, with a light in her eyes and animation in her bearing long since gone. She looked happy.

Her father's hand wound into her mother's hair and yanked desperately at the braid. She pulled back a tiny bit with a weak protest. "David, we have to go to work and I don't have time to re-braid my hair and you—"

"Shush, Miri. We're early every day...let's be on time for once...."

Her mother moaned against his mouth and—

—well that was *quite* enough for even thirty-six-year-old Alex to see, thank you.

This clearly wasn't a memory, because she had most certainly never witnessed that interlude. She spun away, only to sink back upon the wall in shock as her eleven-year-old self climbed on her bike and wove out of the driveway and onto the street.

If she hadn't witnessed the encounter, who had? How was it in her head? What the *ebanatyi pidaraz* was going on here?

She glared at the sky, robin's egg blue on a rare clear San Francisco morning, and crossed her arms tightly over her chest in an act of defiance. "I know this isn't real. I know you're there. You might as well let me out of this mental cage you've snared me in so we can have a conversation."

Her head spun as a wave of dizziness washed over her and the surroundings blurred into indistinctness. She blinked hard and opened her eyes to find she was surrounded by...blinding white, interestingly.

She looked down to find herself returned to her fully-formed adult body, wearing the clothes she had donned this morning on the ship. But they were pristine, unmarred. Not at all how they would be after having been manhandled by a giant dragon.

Which meant this environment wasn't real either. A holo perhaps? More likely it was simply taking place in her mind. Her body could be anywhere. Caleb could be anywhere. Had the dragon taken him, too? She didn't think so. Was he okay? Why were there fucking dragons? *Was he okay?*

She gazed around the sterile, bare white room. The walls, the floor, the ceiling—none of them bore any markings or distinguishing characteristics. She discerned no seams where one transitioned to the other. Definitely virtual.

"Hello? You've got me here. You're in my head, obviously, for some godforsaken reason. Care to show yourselves?"

Silence greeted her for a long time, and she began considering an alternate tack. Then a voice was in her mind, audible yet not. It was wispy and ethereal, neither male nor female.

You should not have come. You should not have discovered this place. Why are you here?

She snorted incredulously at the empty 'room.' "I'm here because you framed my lover for mass murder, tried to kill my mother *in* that mass murder—oh, and you're apparently intent on massacring billions of people. All of those actions annoy me a significant amount, so I'm here to stop you."

What gives you the right to stop us?

PORTAL PRIME
UNCHARTED SPACE

Waves of dizziness in darkness. Nothing solid to grasp onto and ease the spinning. Then abruptly everything but her reeling mind lurched to a halt.

"I'm gonna go open 'nother bottle." Alex stumbled to her feet, sloshing wine over the edge of a not-yet-empty glass.

Kennedy gestured in the direction of the kitchen then draped her legs out on the floor and sank lower along the front of the chair.

Alex stared at the wine rack for a while. The wrought iron twisted into shapes like origami fractals.

She was in her own head, oddly feeling as drunk as she had been.

"Alex, you get lost?"

She jerked out of her reverie and grabbed a random bottle out of the rack. "It's my apartment, Ken. I did *not* get lost."

She wandered back into the living room and plopped down on the rug, the bottle, opener and glass balanced precariously in her arms. As soon as her ass hit the floor she leaned close to the bottle to study it intently.

"*Our* apartment."

Their apartment in San Francisco, after university. A top-floor flat on Bay Street. Was Ethan here? No, he would be playing. He was always playing.

"Whatever...."

"Did you hear about Jamie?"

Alex scowled at the bottle. Her nose crinkled up in annoyance when the opener failed to cooperate in doing its job of opening the wine. "Hear what?"

"She was killed last night flying the Bridge."

Jamie. Crazy curly hair the color of roasted almonds. Freckles decorating a pug nose. A laugh that was always one pitch too high.

"Damn." She straightened up, celebrating as the cork finally came loose. "Sucks to be her...or not be her, I guess...." A fit of sloppy giggles sent her falling back against the edge of the couch.

"Alex!"

She struggled to shut herself up, or to force other thoughts off her tongue and onto her voice. But try as she might she was powerless to alter what transpired, to speak different words this time around.

"What? I'm supposed to feel guilty because I taught her how to do it? I taught her right. It's not my fault if she screwed it up."

Kennedy considered her half-full glass in the lambent candlelight, then turned it up and emptied it in one gulp. "Of course it isn't your *fault...*" hiccup "...but don't you feel a little bad about it? She was your..." hiccup "...friend."

"I may've been her friend—doesn't mean she was mine." She hurriedly refilled her glass before Kennedy snatched the bottle from her, and took a long sip. "People die, Ken. They die, and the world keeps right on spinning, and nobody cares. I'm merely doing what all the cool kids do."

She hadn't meant it. Even at the time she hadn't meant it. The next morning she had woken up sorrowful (also hung over). She had attended the funeral and hugged teary-eyed friends, though she had shed no tears herself.

Crying wasn't something she did by that point in her life.

ᴙ

Another rush of dizziness. How long had she been unaware? It might have been seconds or days. She had no sense of the passage of time.

Alex glanced over from the counter to where Malcolm stood, one shoulder propped on the wall, perfectly groomed and perfectly handsome in his BDUs. "Malcolm, I can't. I'm sorry."

The loft, not so long ago. She yearned to take solace in the familiar setting, but unfortunately this scene was headed nowhere good. She'd figured out the rules of this voyage through memory hell now and resigned herself to watching helplessly.

A harsh sigh punctuated his reaction. He was frustrated with her—she could tell by the way his eyes creased at the edges and his mouth shrunk into a thin line. "Alex, it's my only sister's wedding and I'm giving her away, for Christ's sake. You're telling me you can't put off your damn expedition for five lousy days, scrounge up a dress and be at my side?"

"Your sister isn't going to care if I'm there or not."

"I'll care if you're there. This is important—to me. Dammit! You want me to go stag to my sister's wedding? You want me to take someone else? What?"

She frowned. "No, of course not."

The thought of him taking someone else had triggered a pang of jealousy and an impulsive possessiveness. She remembered. It hadn't been a strong enough compulsion to persuade her to change her mind, however.

She crossed the room to Malcolm and took his hands in hers while brandishing an apologetic expression. "It's just...this is an extremely lucrative contract, and it has a time limit. If I don't get out there soon I'll miss out on the find and the proceeds. I really am sorry. I'm sure it will be a beautiful ceremony, and you will do a fabulous job of escorting your sister down the aisle. Give everyone my regrets?"

She kissed him on the corner of his mouth before backing away and heading upstairs. "I'm going to run through the shower, then we can go out if you want."

Her perception remained as her body departed; it was as though she was being forced to witness the consequences which flowed inextricably from her actions. And she supposed she was.

Malcolm gritted his teeth as his posture faltered and his shoulders slumped in an act of defeat. "I don't want to go out. I don't...."

His eyes closed and his voice dropped low, no longer speaking to her. "I don't think I can do this anymore."

No justification existed to condone her actions this time. She had been a narcissistic bitch, no doubt about it. But it had worked out for the best for both of them in the end....

"Young lady, you will *not* leave this house. You march yourself back upstairs to your room this instant or you won't be leaving again this year."

Woah, she was young once more. Fourteen, she thought. Maybe fifteen. Long, scrawny legs and a hint of nascent curves.

Alex whipped around and got in her mother's face. Already as tall as her, she met her mother's glare with a sneer. "How are you going to stop me? Are you going to lock me up like a criminal? Maybe hit me? It's what soldiers do, isn't it?"

Miriam's voice was ice, her features etched in granite. "You. Will. Go. Upstairs. *Now.*"

She didn't want to see this. She tried squeezing her 'eyes' shut...it came as no surprise when it didn't work. No way was she getting off that easy.

"I *won't.*" Alex spun to the door to storm out, only to find it code-locked. In frustration and a touch of panic she pounded her fists on it, then resorted to trying to pry it open using her fingers.

Failing to make a centimeter of progress, she charged past her mother in search of another door through which to flee. But there was solely the patio door and it too was locked tight.

"I hate you! I wish you had been the one to die!"

This, she had *meant.*

Her mother's throat bobbed shakily, but her glare didn't waver. "I know you do. But we don't always get what we want in life—a lesson you need to learn ASAP. Tonight is as good a night as any to start."

"Ugh!" Her fourteen-year-old self vaulted up the stairs and flung herself violently into her room.

As before, her mind didn't follow her body upstairs. Instead it remained in the foyer like a disembodied spirit haunting the past.

Her mother watched adolescent Alex disappear, then sank against the wall. A hand came to her mouth as a solitary tear escaped to trail down her cheek.

A hushed murmur fell from trembling lips. "David, help me, please...."

Guilt ripped into her like a rusty, serrated knife. It took up residence in her soul, settling in and getting comfortable so it could saw away jagged pieces of flesh and leave her to bleed.

She'd cried that night as well, in impotent rage and anguish still brutal more than a year after her father's death...it may have been the

*last time she shed unabashed, free-flowing tears in fact. It now seemed
a pitiful, self-serving excuse for her behavior.*

*But if her mother had been hurting, too, why had she acted so hard,
so very cold? A kind word, a simple smile bestowed upon her daughter...would they have mattered? Would they have altered the course of
history? Would she have accepted them, or insolently hurled them back
for spite?*

*She had no answer. Instead she waited in silence for the darkness
to return.*

"Stupid, bloated, overwrought bureaucracy has lost the capacity for even rudimentary independent thought. Ugh!" With a visceral groan Alex threw herself onto the couch and dropped her head into her hands.

Her ship! Had this all been a nightmare?

Caleb appeared beside her on the couch. "Perhaps he didn't actually review the report—I have to believe if he did his reaction would be a bit more alarmed."

*Caleb...please let him be okay, somewhere out there. She was utterly
helpless to do anything to make it be true, but she needed him to be
okay.*

"Oh, I'd believe he reviewed it. But he's a government lackey. What else is he expected to do? He has a checklist full of procedures and every fucking thing which crosses his fucking desk must be corralled through that fucking checklist. It's the only thing which exists in his world—without it there would be chaos! And he's probably got a fucking checklist for that, too...."

She groaned into her hands. "I swear, I should just let them all die."

*Ah. For a second she had dared to wonder what despicable character
flaw this scene could somehow be intended to highlight. Silly her.*

"Hey...." He reached over and gently pulled the closest hand away from her face, then lifted her chin so she was forced to look at him. "Possibly. But you won't, because you're a better person than they are."

God, look at those eyes. He should have kissed her then. She should have kissed him then. She'd eagerly hand over her meager riches to be able to kiss him then, right now.

"I'm really not. I can count on one hand the number of people in the universe I truly like or even particularly care about...."

"Stop!"

The surroundings blurred but didn't vanish entirely. PastAlex and PastCaleb continued on, oblivious to her ghostly presence. Emboldened, she continued.

"Stop! I get it, all right? I'm not perfect—color me shocked at this revelation. I can be selfish and callous and don't care sufficiently about other people and have a tendency to hurt those close to me without realizing it. I *get* it.

"Yes, I've made mistakes. Big ones. I won't proffer excuses or defend myself. I'll even concede I'm a little bit broken...but I've done the best I can. And more often than not, my best happens to be damn good."

She was yelling now—yelling at nothing as the scene faded into the distance. She didn't care. "You asked what gives me the right to stop you? What gives *you* the right to judge *me*? You, who plan to ruthlessly slaughter billions. You sit wherever the hell you are and record my life and slice the worst moments out in 30-second snippets and throw them in my face as if you somehow grasp what it was like to live through them? Bullshit.

"What gives me the right to stop you? Whatever failings I may have, I'm the one who got here. Whatever mistakes I've made in the past, I'm the one who found you. Now let me out of this goddamn cage!"

But there was only darkness.

16

Cries. Of pain, or horror? A strangled, feral merging perhaps. The cries were the first thing Kennedy was conscious of. Only after a searing wail cut through the air did she register the screams. More distant, like the staccato inflections of a drumbeat beneath a harmonic melody.

She tried to blink her eyes open—a mistake on her part. She frantically shuttered them against the acrid smoke of burning debris.

A deep breath then? Nope, another mistake. Coughs racked her body as the smoke flooded her lungs.

Way to be stupid, Ken. Get your act together or you are going to die right here under this wreckage.

She grasped at her chest for her shirt and brought it up to cover her mouth, then cautiously drew in air once more. Better.

Her mind clearing with the boost of oxygen, she focused on surveying the damage: most noticeable was a sharp pain in her left calf, though her shoulder also ached something fierce. This whole 'breathing' thing wasn't entirely comfortable for her ribs either.

She inspected her surroundings as much as was possible while blinking away tears brought on by the pervasive smoke. She seemed to be trapped under a section of the array assembly, but she was able to see the sidewalk to her right. She tried to move; her left leg promptly shrieked in pain, as if it would be shorn from her body if she moved another centimeter.

After the stabbing pain subsided to throbbing pain she gingerly propped up on an elbow and peered down. Her leg was caught under a rectangular slab of metal several meters in width.

She sank back to the ground, stretched out her right arm until it extended beyond the wreckage and waved her hand around. "Help! Is anyone out there?"

People ran past, for she heard feet trampling the sidewalk. No one stopped to help. Frustrated, she filled her lungs with smoky air and yelled with all the force she could muster. "Hey you assholes! A little help here would be nice!"

A second later half a face and a shock of dirty blond hair appeared sideways in the opening. "Asshole reporting. Need something?"

She choked on another surge of smoke before getting out a response. "My leg's trapped under the slab. If you can lift it up, maybe on the side over here, I can shimmy out."

She caught half of a nod before the man vanished. "Hang on." A few seconds later the frame shifted centimeters followed by a muffled, "Son of a bitch!"

Fragments of conversation drifted in and out above the roar of unseen chaos. "Help me a—" "Get your ass over—" "Don't try to—" "Careful!"

The slab shifted, teetered, then went tumbling end-over-end into the street. She scrambled backwards out of the wreckage even as a gasp caught in her throat at the revelation of three mangled, crushed bodies where the chunk of metal had been. *Focus.*

She reached down and gingerly probed her leg. A steady stream of blood—more than a trickle, less than a gush—oozed from a ten-centimeter-long gash on the side of her calf. She didn't know whether those were bruises or soot stains decorating the skin around the gash. But it didn't feel broken, which she took as an indication she was going to live through this.

"Are you all right? Can you walk?"

She shifted her attention to the man crouching beside her. The dirty blond hair falling across a stubbled cheek identified him as her rescuer. He looked oddly familiar—but she would not have forgotten meeting this man.

Her hand came away coated in blood and grime when she wiped it along her mouth. "I think so. Help me up?"

"You got it." His arm wrapped around her to grasp her waist beneath her arm.

She put all her weight on her good leg and let him hoist her up before testing her injured one. Ohhh, that hurt. She added a little weight...a little more...nope, that was it.

She summoned a paltry amount of composure and met his inquisitive stare. "Well, I can hobble anyway. Listen, I'll understand if you want to leave me here and run in circles flailing your arms about like everyone else, but I know for a fact there's a reinforced basement only a couple of blocks from here. Help me get to it, and we'll both be able to hide."

His eyes studied her…dear god what a dreadful sight she must be. But then he grinned. *Who the hell* grinned *at a time like this?* "Come on, Blondie, let's go."

An eyebrow raised at the moniker he had given her, but now was hardly the time to argue with the man who had saved her life. "Thank you. Oh, and can you grab my bag?"

ℛ

The three block trek was agony. She tuned out the cries and the screams and the screeching metal and the shudders of the sidewalk when a building collapsed and devoted the entirety of her concentration to putting one foot in front of the other. She leaned on her rescuer more than she wanted to admit. He didn't complain, though he surely wished they were able to move faster.

A small ship—she couldn't determine the type in the brief seconds it remained in view—careened into the side of a high-rise a block ahead of them as they reached the Palaimo building. Her rescuer tugged her closer to huddle against the façade as shards of glass rained down from the force of the collision.

Once it had ceased she gestured at the door ahead. "In there."

They stumbled inside to find the lobby deserted. She imagined all the employees had gone below. Half the windows were shattered, and the shards of glass on the floor were ornamented in streaks of blood. She tried not to think about what had happened.

She motioned toward the hallway to the right. "The lift is over there."

"Think it's working?"

"The lights are still on, so the power grid hasn't been taken out yet."

They had nearly reached the alcove containing the lift when the walls began shaking with a violence forewarning of worse to come. A low rumbling sound grew thunderous as the remaining windows shattered. She peered over her shoulder to see the silhouette of the tower directly across the street crash to the ground beneath a glowing crimson beam.

"Shit." He yanked her hard into the alcove and slammed his hand on the lift control. They descended as smoke and debris and glass billowed through the receding hallway and her leg screamed in pain at being treated so roughly.

The lift jolted to the floor and dim lights sputtered on. The destruction above faded to a dull roar.

"Hello? Is anyone down here?" Silence.

She clung to the wall while her companion took a brief tour of the area, but came back almost as soon as he had gone. "Let's move deeper in. We should be safe for the time being."

She accepted his arm once more, and they hobbled through the workroom to a small office in the corner.

With relief she allowed him to ease her to the floor and prop her against the wall. "We need to get your wound cleaned up. Dying of an infection would be a damn shame after you went to all the trouble of surviving."

"I agree wholeheartedly. There's water in my bag, and a first aid kit ought to be somewhere back in the workroom."

He regarded her in a way that gave her an odd degree of comfort. "Be right back. Don't go anywhere."

She chuckled tiredly. He was acting almost as if this was some sort of adventure, an extreme vacation or something…but his confidence made her feel better. Safer.

Yet again he returned quickly, this time carrying a small first aid pack. He placed it on the floor and crouched beside her, then carefully peeled back the ruined material of her pants.

She cringed as it grudgingly separated from caked blood, but managed to speak through gritted teeth while he wiped an antiseptic solution on the wound. "Seeing as you're my knight in shining armor and everything, I think I should at least know your name."

When he gazed up at her a wave of his hair fell over one eye. "Noah Terrage at your service, ma'am."

Terrage. "You're Lionel Terrage's son."

His laugh sounded unexpectedly harsh and his gaze fell away. "Clone. I'm his clone."

"You're a *vanity baby*?"

The cringe was visible all the way to the tightening of his shoulders, and his voice gained a gravelly edge. "Don't call me that."

"I'm sorry. I didn't mean anything by it." She tried to give him a teasing smile; she hadn't meant to insult him. Vanity babies were widely frowned upon as conceited indulgences on the part of the cloner, but that wasn't his fault. The arrangement rarely worked out as desired, because people tended to have a mind of their own, clone or not. Judging by his reaction, such was the case here.

He positioned the thin medwrap over the long cut and pressed it to secure the seal. "There. You should be mobile in a few hours." A heavy exhale accompanied him sliding back and settling on the floor by the test table opposite her. "How do you know my father?"

"Surno Materials is—was—a major supplier for my company. I bumped into him at the occasional dinner party. I have to say, he always struck me as a bit of a stiff ass. But you, you're..." a dazzling, wicked smirk grew on his lips, and she might have swooned were she not already on the floor "...not."

"God I hope not. So, Blondie, do I get a name in return?"

"Ha. Kennedy."

"Kennedy...?"

She made a show of inspecting her leg. The discoloration had been both bruises and soot. The soot had been cleaned away; the bruises remained. "Rossi."

There was a notable pause during which she admired the neatness of the bandage he had applied.

"Impulse engine 'Rossi'?"

She gave the faintest nod of assent. She didn't make a habit of being embarrassed or shy when it came to her family, and though the degree of wealth and heritage may not compare he was hardly a child of the slums himself. But something about his demeanor made her wish she hadn't been outed so soon.

He whistled, confirming her instincts. "Damn. Didn't realize I rescued an heiress."

"Shut up."

"Hey, I'm just sayin—"

"Shut up, or I'll call you a vanity baby again."

"Yes, ma'am."

17

ROMANE
INDEPENDENT COLONY

"Governor, we need to act fast to address this blockade before it causes chaos!"

Governor Madison Ledesme directed a calm, confident look toward the agitated man from her position of power behind the slightly-raised podium. "I assure you, Mr. Quhiro, we are working every angle to find a solution as expeditiously as possible. But I'm asking you not to panic, lest you create the chaos you seek to avoid."

The man sniffed at the barb but didn't comment further. He owned a major hotel and conference center downtown and as such it was understandable he feared a disruption in business. But didn't they all?

Mia Requelme remained silent, instead opting to observe the other members of the business owners association. They quizzed the governor with the same questions over and over as though they had been spending all their mental power on waiting to be allowed to talk rather than bothering to listen to the answers.

It wasn't as if she didn't have concerns. The gallery shouldn't be materially affected by the blockade as a relatively small percentage of its customers were tourists, but the spaceport represented a looming disaster. Ships currently docked from Federation origin points were stuck here unless they wanted to go the long way around. Hopefully many of them would do so, because those who stayed weren't going to be interested in paying long-term docking fees.

By next week she expected to be facing a growing contingent of unhappy, frustrated customers. Beyond the immediate problem, she dared not hazard a guess if she'd ultimately end up with an overcrowded spaceport or an empty one.

So yes, suffice it to say she had concerns, but she didn't voice them for two reasons. One, the governor had proven herself a skilled politician who understood quite well what Romane was and what it was not. If there existed a way out of this mess which preserved the colony's independence and prosperity, the governor would find it without the help of panicked businesspeople. Two, at present her mind wasn't so much focused on those concerns.

Her gaze hovered vaguely on the space between two of her colleagues sitting opposite her at the long, horseshoe-shaped table. Outside the windows the sky shone bright; it was a warm day, and the scent of blooming alyssi would be wafting through the streets below.

Rumors were spreading like wildfire through the underground news outlets that Gaiae and Andromeda had fallen off the grid. No one had been able to establish communications with the planets or anything in their vicinity in several days. Gaiae was the closest inhabited world to the Metis Nebula, Andromeda the second closest. There was an alien armada in the Metis Nebula—or there had been a few weeks ago. God only knew where it might be now, but she'd bet decent credits the answer was Gaiae and/or Andromeda.

Caleb was in the Metis Nebula. Or through some otherworldly portal. Or dead. He was one crazy son of a bitch, and now that he had found someone as crazy as him to run around with...well, all the restraints were off. He was going to get himself killed or die trying.

It had been explained to her before he and Alex left that the leaders of both the Alliance and the Federation governments were aware of the existence of the aliens (she imagined Governor Ledesme was not so lucky). Yet thus far the Second Crux War showed no signs of easing. The contrary in fact. So color her skeptical of either government's eagerness to do something about the alien threat until it showed up at one of their colonies and picked a fight.

Which meant what? The billions of people inhabiting the galaxy were being served up as unwitting appetizers to the aliens while the feuding empires continued to fruitlessly beat upon one another? Were they to be given no opportunity to prepare or defend or flee?

She had gotten so entangled in the train of thought it took her several seconds to realize the meeting had concluded. People were standing to depart, and the disgruntled chatter indicated nothing had been resolved. Not that she had expected anything to be resolved. She had attended because her absence would have been noticed and because she did need to keep tabs on the state of her adopted planet.

When the governor's eyes roved over her table she gave the woman a polite nod, then wound her way out. She needed to get home.

ℛ

Mia crawled through the drop ceiling above Meno's room clad in leggings and a tank. Thick trunks of crystalline fiber cables lined the flooring; she gingerly climbed over and around them as she strung a new line. Sweat dripped down her temples from the stuffy environs and the exertion of lugging ten-meter-long cables through the obstacle course comprising the ceiling space.

At a large junction diode box installed into the wall she threaded the cable into an open port, then attached a new length of fiber to the matching outbound port and continued on. She repeated the process at two more junctions before finally reaching the open panel in the ceiling.

Cable in hand, she dropped through the opening to land seminimbly on the floor below and promptly begin sneezing dust out of her nose. When the fit subsided she lugged the heavy cable to the primary input unit, purposefully located at eye level halfway down the single row of servers. Most of the hardware resided behind the wall in an insulated cleanroom.

She blew out a breath, decided for the tenth time this was both necessary and perfectly safe, and slipped the neck interface on. If something did go wrong—which it wasn't going to—she needed to see it coming and be able to react more rapidly than she could in an automatous conversation.

Good afternoon, Mia.

"Good afternoon, Meno. I have a present for you I think you'll like."

I do enjoy presents.

"I know you do. But this isn't merely a present. I need your help with an important matter."

It would please me to help you.

"I'm glad. In a minute I'm going to plug an exanet feed into your hardware."

This will make me most happy. She swore its voice gained a tinge of excitement.

"I'm sure. Now you won't be able to communicate out, as it's a one-way feed." She felt confident in the truth of her statement. It didn't matter how smart the Artificial was, it couldn't defeat hardware walls.

That's what the junction diode boxes represented: physical hardware blocking any signals flowing in the opposite direction. She had long ago placed dozens of dynamic software security feedback loops and exit traps as well. But should they all fail to stop Meno from escaping the confines of her home, the hardware would not.

"Are you ready?"

Yes, Mia.

She held her breath as she plugged the conduit in and activated the port. Three seconds ticked by, then four.

This is most fascinating.

"Take time to familiarize yourself with the data coming in. I know it's a lot to absorb."

It is indeed a lot.

So it only took four hundred zettabytes/second of streaming data to impress the Artificial. "Do you remember the files I gave you the other day about the Metis Nebula?"

Of course. They deeply concern me.

"They concern me, too. What I need you to do is monitor everything coming in from the exanet for two things: any information which may correlate with the data I gave you, and any unusual events on or around the easternmost colonies closest to the Metis Nebula. Do you understand what I'm asking?"

I believe so.

"Excellent. You can send summaries of anything anomalous to our message box."

I will do so.

"I've got to go to the spaceport, but I'll check in later this evening."

Before you go, I believe I have found information which meets your parameters. The colonies of Gaiae, Andromeda, Gaelach, Zetian, New Riga and Lycaon have ceased communicating with the exanet infrastructure.

She froze, her hand halfway to the neck wrap. "All of them?"

Yes, Mia. All of them.

18

PORTAL PRIME

UNCHARTED SPACE

Only when it grew so dark he couldn't see a meter in front of him without the optical enhancements did Caleb concede the futility of continuing on. He found a level area beneath one of the larger trees and patched together a basic camp.

Resting his body against the tree trunk, he finally gave exhaustion permission to consume him. The incline was steep and he'd set a grueling pace. No adjustment to the chemicals in his bloodstream occurred to ease the ache of his muscles. Lactic acid burned through his thighs and calves, and the breadth of his shoulders grumbled in protest when he tweaked them.

He honestly didn't care. If it were an option he'd keep walking. But walking looked to be impossible for the next several hours so instead he pondered the merits of kindling a fire. He had run across several variations of critters in his long afternoon and evening of hiking, none larger than a medium-sized canine and none overtly aggressive. *Food for the dragons.*

In the 'pros' column of building a fire: if the critters were used to being hunted by the dragons, the flames should keep them away while he slept. In the 'cons' column: if the dragons hunted these woods, they may spot the fire and treat him as one of the critters while he slept.

So no fire. He took a swig of water and closed his eyes.

"What if we only ran a fire long enough to whip up a bit of hot food?"

Samuel glanced at him askance and pulled a sleeping bag out of his pack. "You want the surveillance drones to spot us? Cause if you do, then hey, I'm up for a shooting match. I did forget my shoulder-fired SAL, however, so I don't particularly care for our odds."

The man was right. They wore thermal shielding to mask their heat signatures. As they hadn't found room in the packs for a larger cloaking shield, a fire would be counterproductive. Resigned, Caleb sank down on his sleeping bag and dug out a field ration.

They camped forty kilometers into a rain forest on Elathan and another twelve kilometers from their goal, an underground storage facility for a group of gunrunners. The bunker was too deep below ground to air bomb and needed to be destroyed from the inside. They also hoped to catch some of the ringleaders onsite, which explained why they were sneaking in on foot rather than landing on top of the facility.

And there was the training.

This constituted his third live mission at Samuel's side. He'd undergone 'official' training first—a whirlwind Galactic year of learning the tech for every situation, surveillance and hacking techniques, flight techniques and killing techniques. The lessons were grueling but not difficult. He suspected they were unlikely to have recruited him in the first place if they hadn't expected he'd prove a natural at most of the work.

He technically now served as a field agent for the Senecan Federation Division of Intelligence, authorized to act against any and all enemies of the Federation, foreign or domestic. But he wasn't permitted out on missions alone until Samuel Padova certified him ready to be permitted out on missions alone. And he had no idea when that might be.

He didn't mind the company. He liked Samuel a lot. The agent was a touch insane and overdid the 'grizzled old man' shtick—he knew for a fact Samuel was all of fifty-four—but the man possessed a witty sense of humor, a good-natured perspective on the world and, most importantly, turned out to be a freakishly effective teacher. Caleb had learned more in the two and a half missions accompanying Samuel than in the entire year of classroom training.

Having set the perimeter sensors, Samuel cracked open a field ration and joined him on the ground. "So, I heard you got a girl back in Cavare."

Caleb chuckled. "You're about as subtle as a circus billboard."

"Who said I was trying to be subtle? If I were truly being subtle, you might not even realize it."

"Sure, sure...." He sipped on a water packet. "I guess I do. Jesse's working on her doctorate in chemical engineering at Tellica."

"Smart lady, then. What's she doing with you?"

He responded by lobbing one of the small rocks littering the ground at Samuel's head. "Cantankerous bastard."

"You love her?"

"What kind of question is that?"

"A relevant one."

"We'll see." He finished the field ration and stowed the trash, then lay down and wound his hands behind his head. "Old man like you, how many times have you been in love?"

"Hell, Caleb, I'm in love every other weekend."

"I said in love, not in lust."

"There's a difference?"

"I'm fairly certain there is, yeah."

Night had fallen in full and he was unable to get a clear view of Samuel's expression. But the slight shift in the air implied he had grown serious. "To answer your question, exactly once."

He carefully removed the earlier teasing tone from his voice. "What happened?"

"I was running an infiltration on this child sex slave ring. Nastiest bunch of vicious sons of bitches I've ever encountered. Swear I needed to take a shower every time I left them." He crossed his legs and allowed his elbows to drop to his knees. "I came so close to meeting the principal, but I got over-eager. I screwed up—difficult to imagine, I realize. They found out I was undercover. I didn't know until I went home one night and...they had killed her. Not a clean kill, either. She probably...well."

"I'm sorry." It sounded as pathetically inadequate on his voice as it had in his head.

"Yep, so am I. Made them pay though, tenfold over. Earned me a three month suspension, but I didn't give a shit. So that's why I—" he cut himself off, and seconds ticked by in silence "—why I say 'never have anything you can't walk away from.' Especially a woman. For them, because this is a dangerous life we lead and you never know if or when it will blow back on those close to you. And for you, because trust me when I tell you there exists no greater perdition than the guilt of causing the death of someone you love."

A beat and most of the usual wryness returned to Samuel's voice. "So this Jesse? Enjoy her as much as she'll let you for as long as she'll let you, but don't fall in love with her. And when it becomes necessary, walk away."

God, he'd been so damn young. But he had taken the advice to heart, learned from it and after he received his first serious infiltration mission he'd walked away from Jesse. And he'd been right to do so.

If he'd possessed a shred of wisdom at the time he would have recognized how much those events had shaped the man Samuel became, well before they'd ever met. But back then he held the world on a puppeteer's string and couldn't begin to conceive of the loss of someone, even someone he cared for, altering his life to such dramatic and devastating effect.

He sure as hell could conceive of it now.

Caleb awoke with a jerk, his senses quickly sharpening to full awareness.

He blinked, but no infrared filter activated in his ocular implant. What had he heard? He consciously stilled and waited. To his right, farther up the mountain, there echoed the yelp of an animal. It resonated pain. A final cry rang out, followed by silence.

His suspicion regarding the purpose of the native wildlife was now all but confirmed. The cry also gave him a direction to head.

No time like the present. It wasn't yet dawn but the sky appeared a slightly lighter shade of black—a velvety, starless indigo—and provided enough light for him to pick out a path through the woods. He pulled yet another energy bar out of the pack, strapped the blade across his back and the water bottle to his hip and started off again.

Less than two minutes after waking he was on his way.

Without an active eVi he couldn't access a clock, but he thought he'd slept maybe three hours. Though three hours as measured at home, or as the hours passed here? Two days in this place and he was no longer able to discern the difference. Regardless, it was sufficient sleep. Troubled sleep decorated in fire and death, but sufficient.

He had no way to know where the dragon's lair was located, if it possessed a lair at all, and if it did whether the beast had taken Alex to it. The wooded mountains provided poor distance visibility and no opportunity to see potential shelters. He had nothing but an indefinable perception he traveled in the correct direction—a perception now bolstered by the cry of an animal as it became a meal for a dragon.

She could be dead. As a rational being he had no choice but to recognize it as a possibility. He'd lost people on missions. He'd lost Samuel, though he had been powerless to prevent it. He wasn't powerless now.

So while he recognized she *could* be dead, he refused to believe she was. He was going to save her; there was no other acceptable outcome.

When he thought about her being dead he felt as though he were suffocating, as if he had been robbed of the capacity to breathe. So he didn't think about it. He put distance between himself and the thoughts by pondering the mystery of this planet.

Hidden in the blackness of an utterly empty space where time sped forward, it orbited no star and rotated on no axis. Visibly devoid of civilization, it nonetheless exhibited an artificial day/night cycle mimicking that of Earth.

Then there were the dragons. They protected this region—a region which actively repelled technology, an act feasible solely through the use of technology. Something lay hidden in these mountains, something more than merely a dragon lair. Something highly intelligent, highly advanced and highly secretive.

Which was why though she could be dead, in fact she was alive.

R

The obsidian orb hovered a meter above the ground. Its surface reflected not a spec of light, such that in the corner of Caleb's vision it resembled a hole in the world—absence where there should be detail.

He crouched to study it at eye level. Fifteen centimeters in diameter, it exhibited no motion: no vibration, no rotation, no wobbling. It hung still as death. The metal was seamless and unmarked to the naked eye. It would be helpful to be able to scan it—with a tool, with his implant, with *something*—for non-visible light characteristics. No such luck.

He slowly eased his hand toward it, and felt resistance. A repulsive energy fought against him but not overwhelmingly so. When his hand was several centimeters away, he thrust it forward and wrapped the orb into his palm.

Now it did move, vibrating fiercely as it struggled to escape his grasp. A stinging sensation raced through his fingers and up his arm inside his skin. The orb did not care for his cybernetics. He brought his other hand up to grip it securely and yanked it toward him.

The orb went dead. All movement ceased, along with whatever energy it had been generating. The surface color faded to a dull pewter. It now resembled a syncrosse ball and while there was no way to be positive absent a full analysis, it appeared inert.

He tossed it in the air a few times. It was extraordinarily light, weighing a hundred grams or so. He considered it a moment, then opened his pack, dropped it inside and continued his trek.

Thirty minutes later he located another. Now that he recognized what to look for, they weren't quite so invisible. He wondered how many he had missed in a day of hiking. Judging by the spacing at least two dozen, possibly more.

Once he had disabled and collected four of them, he leaned against a tree and contemplated his options.

The orbs were generating the tech repulsion field; he was sure of it. An argument could be made he should return to the ship and acquire a more formidable weapon at a minimum, and possibly locate the necessary equipment and reactivate his eVi as well.

The round trip would be two days. Though he knew the way now, he'd need to stop and disable every orb he came upon on the way back to the ship, then retrace his steps precisely if he wanted to avoid getting tossed a couple of hundred kilometers.

He did not have the time—unless it meant the difference between success and failure. So the question became this: did he genuinely believe he was going to be able to kill a dragon using nothing but a makeshift sword and his own unenhanced strength and reflexes?

Goddamn right he did.

19

DESNA

S pace outside the shuttle looked calm, even peaceful. Stars glittered against an empty landscape marked solely by a faint gleam originating from Desna's sun, which remained outside his field of vision.

The shuttle banked to port, the planet came into view and Malcolm patted the pilot's shoulder. He then found his seat and strapped in. The ride in was going to be rough.

As if on cue, the sky lit up with the first volley of what would be the largest battle thus far in the Second Crux War. Then the atmosphere engulfed the shuttle and he could see no more. He wished them luck, but his mission was on the colony below.

At General Foster's order the entire 2nd Division of the Northwestern Regional forces was assembled to retake Desna from the Federation. Four cruisers, the largest carrier in NW Command, twenty-two frigates, over eighty fighters and ten electronic warfare vessels now approached Desna from the west.

Reconnaissance had confirmed a similarly substantial force patrolled the area. Given that the orbital defense array was in shambles and the likelihood of the Alliance attempting to retake the colony, this wasn't much of a revelation.

Malcolm and a small strike team approached from the south. Their orders were to infiltrate the colony's single city and extract the governor and his family. Should the Alliance win the day it would be an easy matter to return the governor to his home. But should the battle go the other way, this likely represented the only opportunity they would have to retrieve him.

The shuttle shuddered from the buffeting atmosphere. The single corridor pair would be heavily guarded and thus not an option for entry or exit. As a military shuttle it sported upgraded defenses and a damper field, but only a single tiny laser weapon. It was hardly ideal for infiltrating enemy territory, but an attack or stealth craft didn't have room for his team of six plus the governor's family. So they would land back from the town, camouflage the shuttle and go in on foot.

Part of him was glad to be commanding a ground mission again. This was what he should be doing; this was where he belonged. But he had to admit he regretted the loss of the *EAS Juno* as well. Though he had served barely a month as its captain, it was possible he had grown a bit fond of it, and its crew. He and most of said crew had been lucky to get out of the last battle alive, but the *Juno* had not shared in their luck.

As civilization had expanded across interstellar space over the last two centuries, the Navy had risen to a dominant role in the armed forces. While the importance of Marines deployable to any planet increased, practicality dictated the lines between Navy and Marine forces blurred. An officer who could serve on a ship one day and a ground team the next was a valuable officer to have on hand.

So while the enlisted ranks remained largely separate, today all but the lowest-ranking officers were proficient in both naval and marine roles—which was why though he preferred serving with soil rather than stars beneath him, Malcolm had needed the *Juno* command if he wanted to promote.

And now he found himself back at Desna once more. But this time he held a weapon and at least the illusion of control in his hands.

The flight leveled off as the sky cleared outside the viewport. It was dusk planet-side and long shadows transformed the marshy terrain to the color of moldy laurel.

If asked for one word to describe Desna, it would unequivocally be 'wet.' Much of the planet consisted of uninhabitable swamps, bogs and fens. The region the colonists settled was higher in elevation, where foothills rose out of the water and achieved some level of relative dryness. Above pervasive waterways and lochs Desna's single city nestled against gradually sloping land. The small spaceport sat on a ridge above and behind the town and was a hike on foot. But they weren't going to the spaceport.

The shuttle pilot flew low over the rolling terrain, using the geography as cover. When under Alliance control the town hadn't possessed much in the way of ground defenses and the Senecan occupiers would not yet have been able to add more than provisional additional measures, if they had erected any at all. They likely hacked the two surface-to-air defense turrets for use, but those would now be pointed toward the sky.

The battle overhead had begun in earnest, and live chatter scrolled along a whisper in the right quadrant of his vision. He wouldn't be able to focus on the play-by-play, but it would tell him how much time he had or, as the case may be, didn't have.

Since Desna was an Alliance world, Malcolm and his team possessed detailed maps of the topography and structural layout. The pilot landed in a small crevasse cut into the hillside 1.2 kilometers from the governor's residence. In a stroke of luck the residence was on the more accessible side of the settlement. Were it located on the opposite side they'd have been forced to sneak or fight their way through the city, which would have made his goal of minimizing loss of life difficult.

"Great job, Flight Lieutenant." He unlatched the harness and stood. "Sit tight and do what you can to not attract attention."

"Quiet as a mouse, sir."

He turned to his team. He'd only worked with one of them before—Captain Brooklyn Harper—and it had been five years ago when she had barely cleared Marine Recon. But they were all special forces and according to their records, both talented and not overly bloodthirsty. This was a rescue mission, not a hit squad.

"You guys have been briefed and you know the drill. The governor and his family are being held under house arrest at their home 0.8 kilometers outside the city center. We move quickly but quietly and try to delay detection for as long as possible. Until we reach the governor's residence encounters are likely to be civilian, so watch your trigger finger but be ready.

"Our intel is sketchy on perimeter security. There may be snipers, so stay in cover. We can expect eight or more guards in and around the home. Bet on more. The governor does not know we're coming and we couldn't take the chance his personal communications have been hacked, so things are going to get a bit twitchy once we're inside. After we acquire our targets, their safety is of paramount concern on our retreat. We're here to rescue them, not get them killed."

He nodded sharply. "Move out."

The damp, marshy soil sucked at their boots, trying to draw the team into its grasp and reducing their progress along the hillside. With this level of exertion the oxygen-rich air should have made them high—which would have constituted an unacceptable danger—but nanobots coursed through their bloodstreams, busily working to counteract the effect.

The last rays of light sank beneath the loch to the left, right on time.

Harper served as the forward scout and moved ahead to the residential area situated beyond the last curve of the hilly terrain. Malcolm held up a hand to signal a halt until she reported in.

Hold 15 for civilian foot traffic. Two skycars in visual sight departing area.

Acknowledged.

The seconds ticked away, and they continued forward. It was a slippery, muddy sprint down the hillside before they reached the stone sidewalk which marked civilization.

There existed little in the way of cover now beyond the occasional thin, reedy tree. Should they be spotted in the neighborhood civilians were expected to be friendly once they realized the soldiers were Alliance, but any interaction increased the probability of conflict. So they used the darkness and shadows and moved rapidly.

A bright flare in the sky lit the street, sending them deeper into the shadows. A large ship—likely a cruiser—had exploded, and the sLume drives' chain reactions combined with conventional explosions to create a churning tempest of white-gold flames. Malcolm focused the whisper. A Senecan ship. The battle continued, but he had been granted a fraction more time.

The governor's mansion sat at the end of a cul-de-sac of estates, which was not an ideal location. They couldn't very well saunter up the long driveway to knock on the front door, so they cut through the backyards on the right side of the road.

In the next to last lot they came upon a resident tending to his rather extensive flower garden and paying no mind to the military battle overhead. Malcolm crossed the space and clasped a hand over his mouth from behind.

Other than a startled jump, the resident thankfully did not struggle. He placed his lips to the man's ear. "We're Alliance. We're the good guys. Stay quiet and we'll be on our way. Nod if you understand."

The elderly man's head jerked in the affirmative. Malcolm waited another two seconds then removed his hand and backed away. The man had probably experienced the fright of his life—but to Malcolm's surprise and relief, the man straightened up, squared his shoulders and gave him a salute. He returned the salute before disappearing into the shadows.

A hundred meters out they activated cloaking shields in the hopes of breaching the security perimeter undetected. As the profile of the residence came into view between a line of the reedy trees, sirens began ringing through the air.

Everyone halted, but it wasn't on their account. The battle raged on above them, and the accompanying wreckage had begun to rain down over the area. Like a vibrant meteor shower, trails of debris breaking up as it plummeted through the atmosphere lit the night sky. Distant fireworks added to the display where laser met metal. The defense turrets joined the fray, their blue-white beams streaking across the horizon.

The chatter informed him a squadron of Alliance fighters had penetrated the outer defenses. His whisper continued to stream a silent procession of warnings, kill and damage reports and pleas for assistance. He allowed himself two seconds to monitor it and came away with the sense they were losing. Not lost and not soon, but losing. Which made their mission that much more important.

Harper?

In position, sir. Sniper on roof, 7.4.

Snipers were unable to employ personal shielding around their faces, as the subtle distortions interfered with an eye's ability to focus. It would be a difficult shot, to hit a sniper in the face at sixty meters in the dark.

Hold for 10, then take it out.

Acknowledged.

They moved fast to clear the trees and reach the stone fence enclosing the governor's residence.

Sniper down.

Rodriguez, Shanti, left flank. Take out the guards at the front door then move in. Harper with me—our point of entry is the back patio. Eaton, Polowski, follow behind us then sweep around the other side and keep watch outside.

As one they vaulted the stone fence and moved forward in a crouched run. The sirens proved a blessing, covering any sound they made. He and Harper reached the building façade and slipped along it to the rear corner.

Her tiny bot floated up above line of sight and moved around the corner. The images it captured were beamed to both of them. Two guards stood on the patio, one on either side of the back door. The sirens had the men on alert, their full attention directed outward.

Unlike the sniper, they would have advanced military-grade personal shields requiring several shots to penetrate. Shots assured to bring others running.

3...2...1...mark.

Malcolm rounded the corner at a full run, shoulders squared and lowered. The guards pivoted, guns raised and firing. The first shots bounced off his own shield, and then he was on them.

He was a fairly big guy, virtually all of his bulk in the form of conditioned muscle, and had no qualms about using it to his advantage. He barreled into the first guard and they both crashed into the second guard and onto the ground. His gamma blade was out and had found the pliable material at the man's neck before the guard was able to switch from gun to knife.

Harper was small but fast. In less than two seconds she had circled to the second guard, who struggled to get out from under his partner's body, and done the same. With any luck they hadn't succeeded in raising an alarm.

They framed the door and traded blades for guns, though the blades remained in easy reach. Inside the residence the bright laser fire didn't matter and the shots necessary to penetrate a shield were a better option than trying to breach the distance to melee range while navigating the labyrinth of a home.

He kicked the door in and raced to the next wall to flatten himself against it. He replaced the command feed on his whisper for a vicinity scan; the battle would play out to its conclusion whether he was watching or not. His men were marked in blue, and he expected there to be no friendly fire accidents tonight. Bodies wearing military-level tech—the interior guards—glowed red, other bodies green.

Three targets main floor, central left from rear. Remaining two on second level, separate rooms. The wide staircase was located near the front of the house. *Rodriguez, Shanti, status?*

Door guards down, one in kitchen.

Take guard then get the two kids upstairs. We've got the main floor.

Acknowledged.

The floor plan for the residence consisted of a series of interlocking rooms on either side of a wide two-story hallway running through the center. He and Harper slid around the wall, cleared the hallway and slipped into the first room, which the floor plan showed was the governor's office.

They were about to clear the open entry to the next room when a guard popped around the corner, blade swinging outward in an arc. Harper dodged it in an acrobatic twist and ducked low to grab the guard's waist and grapple him off-balance. Malcolm leveled the military-issue Daemon at the guard's head and fired until the shield depleted and the laser tore through his skull.

Captain?

Good to go, sir. She jerked a curt nod to emphasize the point.

The clamor in the house began to rise; their presence was no longer a secret. They rushed forward through a library to the living area. His glance into the room on the way to the wall told him three guards had surrounded the governor, his wife and a teenager he assumed was their son.

"Governor, we're Alliance military. We're here to escort you off-planet. To the Senecan guards: allow us to take our citizens peacefully and you won't be harmed."

"Can't do that, soldier."

He hadn't expected them to lay down arms, but he owed it to them to make the overture.

Eaton, Polowski, are you clear?

Clear.

Enter and approach living area opposite my position.

Acknowledged. In position in 10.

"I'll ask one more time. Hand over the governor and his family and let us walk out of here. No one else needs to get hurt."

"Surrender your weapons and *you* won't be harmed. We will take you into custody as prisoners of war."

Not today.

In position.

"My orders are to retrieve—"

Now.

The flashbang grenade from behind blinded the guards, while their own ocular implants had activated a filter to block the worst of it. Still, these were skilled soldiers and even blinded they were instantly on the move.

Then it was hand-to-hand combat over screams and shouts through a smoky haze. But the guards were outnumbered and at a disadvantage. Only one of the guards died, of necessity to Polowski's blade; the other two were incapacitated and restrained.

While Harper hunted for the kid, he located the governor and his wife. They had collapsed to the floor, disoriented from the grenade and the resulting chaos.

"Sir, ma'am, are you injured?"

Receiving only dazed mumbles in response, he helped them to sitting positions and discreetly checked for injuries. Finding none, he and Eaton carefully guided them to the couch.

After another minute the governor blinked several times and made an effort to compose himself. "Thank you, soldier. What about the rest of my family? My daughters are upstairs."

Targets secure. Clear?

Clear.

En route.

"They're safe and will be here momentarily."

Found the kid. He crawled into the office, was going for his dad's gun. I told him maybe next time.

He chuckled silently at the exasperation in her tone as Rodriguez and Shanti appeared from the hallway, two terrified girls in tow. His briefing told him the youngest was eight, the older one twelve. They trembled against each other until they saw their parents, then scrambled across the room into their arms.

He permitted the reunion five seconds out of respect. "Governor, we need to move before reinforcements arrive. We have a shuttle waiting, but it's over a kilometer away in the hills." He gazed around the room at his charges. "Is everyone okay to walk that far?"

Receiving assurances of varying conviction, he continued. "Make sure you have good shoes on, then we need to go."

"But what about our—"

"I'm sorry, ma'am, but if it's not between here and the patio, we don't have time. Let's go."

ᴙ

The trek back to the shuttle was barely controlled, nerve-wracking chaos as they worked to keep everyone calm and quiet and moving in the correct direction.

The sky now glowed brightly from a constant stream of debris blazing across it. Fires burned in the distance near the city, where he assumed larger chunks of debris had survived the atmosphere to crash to the ground and initiate greater destruction. Desna now looked like the war zone it was.

He heard the reinforcements arriving at the home as they reached the edge of the neighborhood, and the formerly quiet street acquired the chill of a hostile environment. They used a small cloaking field to help conceal the group's movement. It wasn't as powerful as a personal shield but it muted somewhat the cluster of heat signatures the governor's family emitted. Muted enough, it turned out.

They hiked around the last hill to where the shuttle waited, all but invisible in the dark. Exhaustion had overcome terror for the family and they wordlessly climbed in ahead of his team and sank into the seats. The older girl sat beside her brother; he wound an arm protectively over her shoulder.

He expected the younger girl to crawl between her parents, but instead she sat down next to Harper. They lifted off and arced away from the city and the in-atmosphere portion of the battle. The girl stared up at the soldier next to her. "Are you a girl?"

Harper laughed lightly. "I sure am."

"*Really?*"

She pulled off her helmet and unbound her hair to let rich, golden-blond locks fall to her shoulders. "See?"

In another circumstance there would've been catcalls from the rest of the squad, but they had the sense to realize this wasn't the time. The girl's eyes were bloodshot and watery but wide with wonder. "Wow...."

He smiled to himself, glad to see the little girl hadn't suffered too severe a trauma from the events of the night.

"We can't take the corridor, so I need everyone to strap in. It's going to be a bumpy ride, but you're safe now."

Before strapping in the governor stood and offered a hand. "Thank you...?"

"Lt. Colonel Malcolm Jenner, sir. I'm glad we were able to reach you and get you out safely."

"As am I, sir. You'll receive a commendation for this if I have anything to say about it. But all this fighting...it can't be merely a distraction to get us out. We're trying to retake the colony, aren't we?"

"We are, sir."

He had reactivated the command stream after exiting the residence and monitored it all the way back. The news wasn't encouraging. Numerous ships were already lost on both sides, the exit corridor rings had been severely damaged and the turrets destroyed. The battle had lasted so long Federation reinforcements were beginning to arrive from patrolling the nearby border—and that was going to tip the balance.

"But I'm afraid we may not be successful in the endeavor, which is why it was vital we evacuate you and your family."

The governor nodded vaguely and sat down, his expression the weighty one of a man accepting the reality that he had likely lost his home, his constituency and his planet.

20

PORTAL PRIME

The by now familiar dizziness returned Alex to conscious awareness, rousing her from whatever dreamless twilight they kept her in. The scene crystallized into existence—and this time the dizziness accelerated to the point she nearly fainted back into her twilight.

She was standing in space.

Intellectually she recognized she was neither—standing nor in space—but her brain declined to accept the reality as truth. Given her surroundings she couldn't fairly blame it.

Stars sparkled both beneath and above her. A distant sun shone the color of a Damask rose in summer bloom. A small planet painted in jade and teal orbited perhaps three megameters to her left. She discerned the flickering lights of civilization, and the sunlight glinted off a single orbital array.

This was Desna. She had never visited the colony itself, but three years ago she had discovered a rare mica on the moon of one of the inner planets.

She imagined she breathed in deeply, imagined such a breath calmed a racing heart and steadied her senses. She wanted to smile. In many respects this represented a dream come true, did it not?

She had performed maybe half a dozen spacewalks in her life. They had each been a magnificent experience, but always the heavy environment suit fabric and sealed helmet and faceplate maintained an impassable barrier between her and the freedom of space beyond.

Now nothing existed to separate her from the splendor of the stars. She felt as though she was breathing in the very universe, as if she was at once infinite yet a mere speck of stardust.

She wanted to smile. But she could not do so, because her stars were marred by two massive fleets of ships actively engaged in the act of annihilating one another.

This was not a memory. She had never witnessed a battle over Desna. It gave her a measure of relief to know they were not recording only her life and hers alone. The relief was rapidly overtaken by the troubling notion that they may be observing and recording *everyone and everything*.

The battle had been going on for some time, for there no longer existed a clear dividing line keeping one player on one side and the other opposite. She identified six cruisers but lost count of the frigates after thirty or so. Dozens upon dozens of fighters darted in every direction, little more than pinpoints of reflected light. A carrier hung back to the far right; she was unable to locate a second one but assumed it hid somewhere trying not to get blown up.

"This is happening now, isn't it?" She received no answer as per usual, but it must be happening now, or quite recently.

In the First Crux War, Alliance and Federation ships had looked problematically similar; after all, the Federation ships had been constructed when those colonies were still part of the Alliance. They had adorned their ships in the newly designed rust and chrome logo of their new Federation but it hadn't changed the fact they by and large flew Alliance-built ships.

Now, though, the distinctions were unmistakable. Senecan ships gleamed a muted bronze, turned a rich copper in the glow of the sun. Alliance ships were uniformly shale steel and hyper-lustrous. The styles had diverged as well. Whereas Alliance ships, in particular the larger ones, tended toward modularity, distinct transitions and no wasted hull space, Senecan ships displayed a highly aerodynamic profile, with sleek curves leading to knifed edges.

Both designs seemed plenty adept at blowing the other up. The arena resembled a fireworks circus, a constant cacophony of explosions and crisscrossing lasers. Were it an action vid it would have been thrilling and even beautiful.

But it wasn't a vid. It was devastatingly real, and people died in front of her. Were they people she knew? Was Malcolm here, on the bridge of his frigate he never desired to command?

She squeezed her eyes shut against the destruction and carnage, only to remember the futility of the act. Her captors made certain she was forced to watch; forced to see.

A tremendous blast plumed almost directly in front of her. In its brilliance it appeared far closer than she expected and she tried ineffectually to pull away. The white-blue plasma from an impulse engine detonation transitioned to fiery orange as a far more destructive chain reaction began. But before it reached criticality the frigate's hold ruptured. Pieces of the ship flung in every direction and exposed the interior to the vacuum of space.

Over one hundred soldiers dead…and the battle continued on, its participants far too interested in winning the day to notice.

Debris from the secondary explosion ripped through the wing of a passing fighter, sending it careening out of control in her direction. It wasn't as if she could run. So instead she stared, helpless and transfixed, as the small ship grew large and spun *through* her. The pilot ejected and the ship crumbled apart around her.

Time slowed as metal shards enveloped her like shattered glass. None pierced her of course, but it seemed as though she might be able to reach out and pluck one from the sky. She settled for extending an imagined hand, palm upturned, and letting a shard fall through it untouched like the ghost she had become.

Warfare raged around her unabated in all its glory and tragedy. She was tired.

She didn't understand the purpose of this emotional torture parade, other than to punish her. But what reason could her captor or captors possibly have to punish her, unless it was for personal amusement? Were these supposedly advanced aliens really so childishly petty? Why not simply kill her and be done with it?

Right now she wished she'd never left that house on the edge of the San Pablo Preserve; she didn't care if it hadn't been real. If she was going to be trapped, she might as well be trapped someplace where she had been happy.

"What is your point in showing me this? That humanity en masse is as flawed as I am? I agree. We are."

She 'turned' away from the battle. Sparks of light flared in her peripheral vision, but thankfully beyond her rested a measure of peace, stars unmarred by blood.

"What is your point? That we slaughter one another instead of uniting to fight you, thus we deserve to be slaughtered? How arrogant, how callous are you to judge our missteps as rendering us fit for annihilation?"

Silence answered. Despair clawed at her from the void as her gaze drew inexorably back to the spectacle of resplendent destruction.

"Well, fuck you, too."

21

EAO ORBITAL
HIGH EARTH ORBIT, SOL SYSTEM

Ethan Tollis wound his way through the bustling outer promenade of the torus undisturbed. With his hair drawn back in a low tail and a chamois cap pulled over his brow he appeared to the world as merely another tourist. The loose suede jersey and faux-faded pants ruled out him being on the Orbital for business.

He tried to move about in anonymity whenever possible; he found it was good for keeping hold of his soul. Besides, he'd be in the spotlight and on display soon enough.

Hamish, his percussionist, and Levi, his sound master and mate since elementary, flanked him for added protection but mostly so they could legitimately chat instead of silently tossing pulses around. He elbowed Levi and motioned to the gyro shop ahead on the right. "Let's grab some grub first, eh?"

"You know there'll be a spread at the gig, right?"

"And when was the last time you saw me get to eat at one of these pomps?"

"Fair point." They veered between passersby to the shops lining the interior wall and slipped inside the cafe. It was early for lunch and thankfully the place wasn't overly busy. Levi went to grab their sandwiches while he and Hamish settled at a small table in the corner.

The panel on the wall spewed a constant stream of war news—battles here, blockades there, bravado and chest-pounding everywhere. He didn't get it. Never had. Humans willingly choosing to kill one another by the thousands and eventually millions, and for what? A government bearing a different name?

He'd visited more than half the colonized worlds and would vouch for the fact that people were pretty much the same everywhere. Sure, individuals were as unique as he supposed they'd ever been, but a generic person on Earth bore a noticeable similarity to one on Seneca or Requi or Andromeda.

The reporter mentioned something regarding rumors of trouble on Gaiae but had moved on before he caught what she had said.

"They still talking about your girlfriend nonstop?"

He shrugged as Levi dropped a tray full of steaming gyro wraps on the table and slid in opposite him. "They've cut down to once every half hour or so now. And she's not my girlfriend. Hasn't been for a long time. Triss is my girlfriend."

"Right. Absolutely."

Levi earned a punch in the shoulder for the retort; he knew the score with Alex.

Ethan thought Alex probably cared for him in her own way, but she had never, *could* never belong to him. While he didn't desire her life any more than she desired his, all things considered it was still a damn shame. And he recognized without a doubt should she show up at his door on any given day he'd kick Triss to the curb and worry about begging for forgiveness on the back side. It wouldn't be fair to Triss, but that didn't change the reality.

He let the thought fade away in sync with the fading of his smile. "I want to switch up the playlist order a bit. The promoters can bugger off for all I care—*Recompense* is the best tune on the release and I'm bloody well leading on it."

"Bowl them over from the start. Sure." Hamish nodded agreement over his sandwich.

"You're the talent. You tell 'em how it is."

He leveled a taunting glare across the table. At this rate Levi was going to get his arse kicked before the trip ended.

They were on the Orbital this particular morning to play a private show of the songs on the new sonant for a press contingent. Well, private in the sense of only approved and invited press being allowed in the room. The show was scheduled to be broadcast galaxy-wide next week as part of the tour kick-off.

The Orbital didn't boast much in the way of entertainment offerings, but its management wanted to liven up the stodgy reputation. So here he sat, enjoying a half-decent gyro.

They spent the meal covering the usual last minute details which always accompanied the performance of new material, then had to bail. Time was running short and the venue was still nearly a quarter of the way around the ten-kilometer ring.

They stepped out of the cafe and ran smack into a disgruntled mob. The typically steady stream of progression along the promenade had all but ground to a halt.

"Ah shit, what's going on?"

"We're gonna be late, man...."

"Like hell we are." Ethan began weaving into the crowd until he reached the first cop he could find. "Excuse me officer, what's the problem?"

The cop scowled, but most of his attention remained on his efforts to keep the growing throng in check. "The Prime Minister just arrived for a meeting and is answering a few questions from reporters. I'm afraid you won't be allowed through until he's departed the promenade."

Ethan stifled a groan. Why was the PM prancing about out on the ring instead of confining himself to the center of the station where all the government offices and accoutrements were located? Making a mockery of himself in the name of public approval, apparently.

He didn't throw his weight around unless it was necessary. But, hey, it was necessary. "Eh, I wish I'd known ahead of time. I'd have definitely headed on to the other side earlier." He thrust out a hand, realizing full well the cop hadn't the time to shake it. "Ethan Tollis. I have a premiere show over in Windermere Theatre in twenty and a lot of press and fans waiting on me. I would really hate to disappoint them."

The spiel earned a greater share of the cop's attention; it always did. "Mr. Tollis! Sorry I didn't recognize you. Give me one minute and I'll see what I can do."

"Appreciated."

Over the heads of the crowd the new PM stood tall in front of the floor-to-ceiling windows which looked out into space and every so often revealed the upper arc of Earth's profile. The man must have been standing on a raised platform, for he towered above the simple plebeians.

Though the grave, serious tone of the PM's words penetrated the grumbles of the surrounding pedestrians, he was too far away to hear the substance of the man's speech. He had no doubt it constituted nothing more than the usual empty platitudes and proclamations, sprinkled with an occasional bald-faced lie.

The cop waved him forward and began clearing a small path. They followed along behind but soon found themselves pressed tight against the wall on the right and the mass of people on the left.

"I bloody hate crowds...."

He groused as he fought to maneuver through what he had to concede was a suffocating space. Some bloke elbowed him in the ribs in a move to gain position but the shifting throng consumed the man before Ethan was able to retaliate. "Probably shouldn't have hooked up with a synth star then."

"Well *now* I know...."

The PM's words became clearer as they approached. "Of course we are taking every precaution when—"

The thunder and the flame crashed into Ethan at the same instant, only to be overwhelmed in the next by the collapsing wall and wrenching floor beneath him.

He couldn't move, couldn't run, and after a second couldn't breathe. Not because of the crushing weight of a panicking mob, but rather because there was no air.

The last sight he registered with any clarity was the outer bulwark of the Orbital rupturing into jagged, warped metal shards then disintegrating, and a sea of bodies drifting out through the breach, into the abyss.

Bugger it a—

22

It took Richard several tries to find the tiny office tucked inside what could have previously served as a storage closet.

Devon was kicked back in an oddly-shaped ergo chair. The fingers of his left hand tapped idly at a virtual panel beneath a large screen. The office was otherwise empty save for an image of a pretty girl with long blond hair and bright green eyes on the desk and a piece of abstract art displayed on the far wall.

When he walked in Devon held a finger to his lips and pulled a small surveillance shielding device out of the desk drawer. He pressed a thumb to it, after which it glowed a pale green. "We're shielded now."

Richard produced a similar object from his pocket. "I did bring my own...."

"I should've figured you'd have it covered."

"You found something?"

"Yep." Devon killed the large screen and replaced it with an aural from his eVi. "Lots of somethings, in fact. Someone went to a great deal of trouble to make it look like your girlfriend's daughter's boyfriend committed the HQ bombing."

"My...*what?*"

"You know, this Marano fellow."

"I'm not..." Richard squeezed his eyes shut and pinched the bridge of his nose in a grimace "...Miriam Solovy is not my girlfriend. I'm married."

Devon shrugged. "Oh. Okay, sure. No offense."

Richard regarded him in bewilderment. *Kids....* "None taken." He leaned forward and studied the aural. "So?"

"Well first, both the corridor and ORSC records were altered to show the *Siyane* arriving at ORSC a full four hours earlier than it did, and altered again three days later to show it leaving a day and a half later than it seems to have departed.

"Then if you go to the detention facility records, they were altered to show Marano being released on an administrative technicality two nights before the bombing—"

Richard cringed. "That's…not what we're hunting for."

Devon arched an eyebrow, then chuckled heartily. "Nice! Your work?"

Richard shot him a warning look and he raised his hands in surrender. "Gotcha. Not my business. We'll just pretend we didn't find that." A block of data disappeared from the aural.

"Finally, Headquarters security logs were altered to show Alexis Solovy entering the building three hours before the bombing in the company of a Cameron Roark and leaving forty-two minutes later. Military Police files have the identity flagged as an alias belonging to Marano. Near as I can tell, neither of those events actually happened—especially since her ship had departed Earth two days earlier and did not return, at least not via any corridor."

Richard exhaled and pushed off the desk, working to conceal the extent of his relief. *Thank God. Thank God she was innocent. Thank God he would be able to prove it.* "Excellent job, Devon. I mean it."

"Thanks, but in truth it wasn't terribly difficult. The alterations were made skillfully but using standard Alliance protocols. They were easy to spot."

"I'll take your word for it. It sounds like you recovered the original data as well?"

"Yep. It was a little harder, but whoever altered the records didn't do a thorough scrub of the underlying data first. Portions of it were corrupted but I pieced it together. Is this crap going on all the time inside the military? I mean, are you going to show up tomorrow asking me to find shenanigans on the Orbital explosion? Because I never wanted to believe the claims of those wacko anarchists, but there is some nasty corruption involved here."

Richard pondered how truthfully to answer the question. *If they try to pin the Orbital on Marano and Alex, yes.* "If this type of malevolence were standard operating procedure, I'd join the anarchists with you. I have no reason to believe anything nefarious occurred with respect to the Orbital explosion. Beyond the act it-self, obviously."

Devon accepted the sideways answer. "So what do you want me to do with this?"

"For one, burn me a hard disk copy. You weren't able to pin-point the source?"

"That's the downside to the use of standard Alliance protocols. I can tell you it was done remotely—not from the Island—but at a node in the Alliance military infrastructure. And that's it, I'm afraid."

"Understood." *Too late to go back now.* "You have friends who are hackers, right?"

"I'm shocked you would suggest such a thing...." Devon straightened up in his chair and had the decency to feign chagrin. "Uh, yes, sir. I might know a few."

"Can you trust them?"

"To do what?"

"To not rat us out to the authorities."

"Oh. Yeah. Totally."

Richard felt a tiny twinge of guilt and not for the first time. But in the intelligence business one's allies were not always the cleanest members of society. It was a necessity of the trade.

He leaned in closer though the room was shielded. "Here's what I need you to do."

SEATTLE

Devon hit the entrance to their apartment at a jog. "Hey, babe, you here?"

Not getting a response, he tossed his bag on the counter on the way to her studio room. Nine times out of eight it was where he found her.

The translucent door slid open to reveal Emily standing in the dark. Gleaming colored swaths of light encircled her. Earpieces suggested she had the music on and explained why she hadn't heard him. Virtual gloves adorned both hands.

Her right hand extended and a stream of fuchsia light flowed out of a fingertip of the glove. Her hand gracefully swirled and dipped, leaving an intricate design in its wake.

He snuck up behind her, carefully removing the earpiece from one ear and purring into it. "Hey, babe."

She jumped in surprise, sending fuchsia light careening through the room, but he wrapped his arms around her waist from behind and squeezed her in his arms.

"Devon, don't scare me like that!"

"Sure, sure." He loosened his grip and spun her to face him. "Come on, we gotta go see the gang."

Her eyes narrowed. "I'm working."

He rested the tip of his nose on hers. "Please? I don't want to go alone…."

She stared at him for several seconds before rolling her eyes and sinking into his arms. "Can I at least change first?"

"You're gorgeous in a painter's smock."

Her grousing against him was simply adorable, but he shouldn't push it. "Yes, you can change first."

The gang was, in reality, merely a group of friends he'd known since university. They had engaged in some truly extreme stunts during school and still liked to think they were the best and most outrageous hackers north of Angeles. While a few had joined him in acquiring respectable and even impressive jobs, most couldn't accept the rigidity and rules which accompanied such employment and still lived on the edges of mainstream society.

They met, as they had regularly for the last several years, in a large oval booth in the back of Kellan's Pier Pub. Sayid had a pitcher of beer waiting by the time he and Emily arrived, and they eased into the booth as though it was a second home. Which it kind of was.

"Hey, Devon, why'd you change out of your officer's uniform? I bet you look so sweet and cuddly in brass buttons and shiny shoes."

"Yeah, screw you, man." But he was laughing as he poured a drink.

They spouted the usual small talk until the others arrived. The reality was his current job drastically limited the potential topics of conversation, but the pub buzzed with banter and music and sports on the screens to fill the void.

After everyone settled in, another pitcher was delivered and the waiter had departed, he activated a privacy shield. Not only did it prevent anyone from overhearing them, it also muffled the crowd noise to a low background level.

"So, you guys want to have a little fun?"

"What? This isn't fun?"

He shot a smirk at Ramon. Sarcasm rolled off Ramon's tongue like it had somewhere it needed to be.

Petra emptied a shot of tequila into her mug. "Money?"

"Does it involve nudity?"

Devon snorted as Emily launched a volley of peanuts across the table at Mycroft. "No it does not involve nudity, though if you prefer to lounge at your deck with your package swinging free, I won't judge. No money, either. Now can we be serious for two seconds? I realize it's a challenge on the order of scaling Kilimanjaro without gear, but can we try?"

He ignored two separate obscene gestures directed at him and reached in the pouch at his waist to remove six small optical disks. He spread the disks discreetly in front of him, then passed them out until everyone had one. "Everything is ready on the disks, so you don't need to manipulate the data."

"What fun is that?"

"I'm getting to the fun. We're going to leak the information on those disks to every major news organization in the galaxy, regardless of affiliation. In fact, the more affiliations the better."

Indications of varying interest followed. Ramon refilled his mug. "No problem, but still waiting on the fun part."

"I told you, I'm getting there. We need to spoof the source so it appears to originate from eight separate locations, none of which are in the Cascades and most of which aren't on Earth. We need to include a few independent colonies, too."

Petra whistled. "Now you're talking. One question though—what's on the disks?"

He took a sip of beer and gazed around the table. "Ready for this? Evidence someone inside the Alliance government or military falsified multiple official records in order to frame that Senecan spy for the EASC Headquarters bombing."

"Dude. Who found the evidence?"

"Excuse me, is there any doubt?"

Mycroft made a show of being unimpressed. "Somebody's all high on his horse. Listen, I'm not exactly a fan of Seneca...."

Sayid, who had been quiet up until now per his usual, jumped in. "Me either, but I'm about a gazillion times less of a fan of our military. I'm in."

"Damn straight. I'm in, too." Petra's copper and citron glyphs lit up in a visual demonstration of her enthusiasm.

"Wait—does this mean our government blew up its own Prime Minister? I totally bet they did."

"Hell if I know, Sayid. The Orbital explosion happened all of thirty seconds ago. Is everyone in? Speak now or get your ass kicked later." Devon observed each of them in turn, making certain he received agreement from those in attendance.

Ramon tossed his disk in the air, palmed it and dropped it in a pocket. "When does it need to go out?"

"First thing tomorrow morning, as close to simultaneously as you miscreants can manage."

Ramon slammed his mug down on the table for theatrical effect. "What are we sitting around here drinking beer for? Let's go fuck up this war."

23

ROMANE
INDEPENDENT COLONY

Mia strode across the length of her living room. Reversed course. Her sharp pivots at the windows and the archway hinted at violence, as if the force of the movement might trigger a new option on the next traversal.

She wanted to run. The desperate, scrappy child within screamed in her head to run just as she had twice before. Running to Romane so many years ago had worked out, hadn't it? She could run again. Start over again. Find a new home.

But *this* was her home. She had built a life here, to a far greater extent than she had ever imagined possible. She was not an abused slum kid beholden to her criminal father and thug brother on New Orient. Nor was she a starving thief on Pandora. Not anymore.

She was Mia Requelme—a successful, wealthy businesswoman. She had crafted and nurtured a sterling reputation, not to mention assets, employees, professional colleagues and friends. She had risen above a troubled past and rotten start at life to build a new one. One she proudly called her own.

This was her home and she would not run again.

There was still the unfortunate reality her home was likely to come under attack by an alien armada within weeks, if not days. It was a problem.

But if she wasn't going to run, she also wasn't going to stand frozen in panic and end up a helpless victim. If she wasn't going to run, she needed to help.

The pacing slowed to a stop with a ponderous sigh; in a metaphysical sense it carried on it her acceptance of the consequences of her actions moving forward.

She pulsed Jonathan. As a loyal employee who was barely more than a kid, she felt like he was her responsibility.

Listen. You need to leave. Go visit your family on Demeter.

What? Why? Is something wrong?

I can't go into the details. Please, for your safety, get off Romane for a while. Go west—the farther west the better. And maybe take your girlfriend along.

Mia...but what about the gallery? You can't—

It's not a problem. You have paid vacation time remaining. Take it, Jonathan. For me.

I...okay. I don't understand, but okay.

Next she went upstairs and packed an emergency bag. She needed to be prepared for anything. Then she changed from the yoga pants and tank into a charcoal pantsuit and wound her hair back into a sleek ponytail at the nape of her neck. Lastly she went to the safe in her office and removed the disk Caleb had left her.

"Meno, I'm heading out for a few hours. Message me if you discover new data matching the parameters."

She couldn't exactly wear the interface out in public and it was too warm for a turtleneck, so she'd lack a mental connection with the Artificial. But she had granted it the ability to send and receive messages from and to her. It would have to do for now.

Certainly, Mia. I will exercise discretion.

She waited fifteen minutes to be seen, which was far less time than expected. When shown into what was an objectively spectacular office she shook the governor's hand warmly. "Governor Ledesme, thank you for agreeing to see me on such short notice. I realize your time is extremely valuable as well as limited."

"It came with the job description, I believe. What can I do for you, Ms. Requelme?"

"I'm afraid I'm here to make your life far more complicated, ma'am."

Madison Ledesme regarded her with detached curiosity. They weren't friends, of course. The governor knew her because of her service on several business councils, and because the spaceport was a significant enough interest for the typically hands-off government to ensure it ran smoothly and cleanly. They had spoken half a dozen times but never in private.

"Given my planet is caught between two warring superpowers while its economy is being crushed beneath the weight of a blockade, I find it somewhat difficult to believe you can accomplish such a feat."

"As would I. Nevertheless. There's something you need to know: the colonies of Gaiae, Zetian, Andromeda, Gaelach, New Riga, Lycaon, Karelia, New Orient, Edero…and now Messium have gone dark."

"What does that mean? What are you telling me?"

"It means no transmissions from those locations are registering on the exanet. It means any communications to persons or places on or in the space above those locations are undeliverable."

"How do you know?"

Mia almost cringed, but years of experience enabled her to squelch it. "I can't reveal my sources. I'm sorry."

Ledesme considered the response. "I'll overlook that for the moment. A widespread exanet disruption of such magnitude in eastern space? The scientists tell us it's impossible."

"And it should be. Regardless, I also know the cause and you are not going to like it."

The governor chuckled. It pealed surprisingly warmly given the stress she must be feeling. Mia had always found her naturally personable, if always professional. "Don't drag this out, Ms. Requelme. I have a meeting with the Utility Director and a lunch with several of your unhappy business colleagues half an hour later, both of which are bound to be unpleasant."

Mia's eyes dipped to contemplate the onyx and pearl marbled floor. It was going to sound ridiculous coming out of her mouth, so it was a good thing she had proof. "Aliens. An invading alien armada of mammoth size and power, in fact."

A politician's mask descended over the woman's face. "I don't have to time to entertain irrational ramblings or—"

Mia opened her hand, palm up. The disk rested upon it. It had been provided to her in confidence, but Caleb was gone and humanity was under attack. "Governor, please take one minute to examine the contents of this disk. You will see I am in no way crazy or irrational."

The look in the governor's eyes suggested the line between Mia getting thrown out of the office and the woman reviewing the data was a thin one indeed. Mia couldn't say what finally tipped the scales. The instincts of a skilled politician, perhaps.

The governor took the disk from her and went to her desk to drop it in a reader. Mia stood too far away to read the information displaying on a small screen at the desk, but she didn't need to read it. She had reviewed the contents countless times, to the point she now enjoyed nightmares starring the images. Instead she waited.

Three minutes later Ledesme tapped the control panel on her desk. "Hannah, cancel my appointments for the rest of the day. I realize that. Cancel them." She stood, leaving a stark visual of an alien superdreadnought on the screen.

"Who else has seen this? If we were to get this information to the Alliance and Federation governments, they would end this absurd war and—"

"They are already aware of the threat. They have been for more than two weeks."

"And yet they continue to shoot at one another? Imbeciles!" Her composure broke for only a breath, revealing a person appalled at the failings of her fellow humans and frustrated at how those failings made her job so very difficult.

Then the brief reveal vanished behind a stoic countenance. "How exactly is it you have come by such information when no one in my government has discovered it?"

"I know the people who recorded the data. They entrusted me with the disk, in case—well, in case the other governments didn't get their act together in time."

"These people would be…?"

No sense hiding it now. The names were sure to be familiar to her, because they were now familiar to the entire galaxy. "Caleb Marano and Alexis Solovy. I helped them elude the authorities and escape after the accusations against them surfaced, because they are innocent of the bombing and their lives were in danger."

Ledesme pondered her silently for several seconds, her thoughts her own behind shuttered eyes. "You are a most interesting woman, Ms. Requelme. I think I'd like to discover more about what lies beneath your public façade. But that's for another time."

She stared out the window, and Mia chose not to respond to the remark or otherwise interrupt her reverie.

"So the Alliance and the Federation continue to fight a war despite being aware of an imminent alien invasion and try to imprison the people who warned them of it. Yet people wonder why Romane is so fiercely independent." She turned back to Mia, her face now animated by resolve. "How long ago did Messium go offline?"

"Approximately six hours ago."

"I no longer want to know how you're obtaining your information. The other colonies are tiny but an attack on Messium will upend the entire galaxy. Still, we can't wait for that to happen. I don't suppose your friends or whatever other mysterious sources you enjoy have any ideas on how to defend against these aliens?"

"My sources are working on it. But no, not as of yet. I was thinking about the problem, however. Romane has some exceedingly brilliant scientific and engineering minds as citizens, as well as some exceedingly wealthy ones—arguably the largest concentration of both outside of Earth. Bring them in. Give them this data and lock them in a room. Figuratively speaking.

"If there are ideas to be generated, our engineers are the most likely to do it. Use the ideas from the engineers and the money from the entrepreneurs to strengthen our defenses as much as practicable and put the arrays on alert. Plus you might want to begin considering an evacuation."

"Tell the public? It will cause a panic that will cause loss of life."

Mia nodded. "Probably so. But you're right. Messium *will* change everything. The Alliance won't be able to keep whatever is happening there a secret, so I suspect we'll be facing a panic within the next eight hours in any event. Wouldn't it be better to break the news ourselves and take advantage of the opportunity to assert authority and lead?"

"You'd make a decent politician, Ms. Requelme. I concur." The governor took a deep breath. "I need to get the aforementioned geniuses and business magnates in here first, lest *they* bolt at the news. I'll also alert our security force and give them time to prepare. Then I'll contact the media."

The woman circled back behind her desk and began typing on her control panel. "You should get downstairs to the main conference room. I'll send two assistants to help you pull together whatever you require."

"I'm not sure I follow. Why do I need assistants?"

"Because you're leading the strategy session."

24

The transition from standing among stars to standing in a tech lab was a jarring one for Alex. Also claustrophobia-inducing; though the room was by most standards cavernous, the walls pressed in on her from what felt like centimeters away.

So tiny, so miniscule were the spaces where people spent the days and nights of their lives.

The long walls of the lab contained large server racks and dozens of fiber cables running among them. The hardware architecture appeared archaic, even ancient.

This was not happening now. This had not happened in her lifetime.

Two men and a woman sat at a rectangular table at one end of the room.

"I assure you, Administrator, the Synthetic Neural Net—we're calling it a 'Synnet' for convenience—is more than capable of taking over day-to-day operations of the University's facilities. It has internalized all the rules and regulations and historical records and has analyzed the functioning of numerous other campuses. We've run tens of thousands of scenarios. The result is an efficiency increase of 22-35% in not only power usage but also ancillary costs, as well as an anticipated 12-16% improvement in student satisfaction."

The older man nodded thoughtfully. "What about security operations?"

"All operational decisions will remain with the Security Department. If given access to the procedural mechanisms, however, the Synnet will be able to execute on those decisions with far greater speed than our current disparate computer systems. The faster reaction time can help save lives in a crisis."

The younger of the two men had been silent up to this point, but now he leaned forward in an assertive pose, a confident smile adorning his face...

...and she realized she knew who he was.

She looked up at the ceiling. "You don't have to show me this—I know what this is. I already know what happens next."

The scene shifted in a blur so disorienting she fought back nausea.

When the world regained clarity, she was on a lawn, the sort of quad-style park universities had included for thousands of years. The grass was a perfect emerald green, so vivid in color she felt as though she should be able to smell it as well. If she could, she thought it would smell of mint and clover.

She sighed in resignation. With no body, trapped inside an alien funhouse tour of human history, she was free to be careened from scene to scene according to their whims.

Clusters of students strolled in every direction, many bearing distinctive Asian features which had faded from the gene pool over the last two centuries.

A group of four men in their early twenties walked past her. "So I explained to the secretary how I *absolutely* had permission to access the files and...." The young man's voice trailed off as his gaze drifted to the left; hers followed.

The plasma ripple of a crude force field rose in a wave out of the neighboring street and arced to meet the shield rising on the opposite side of the campus, some four kilometers away. They met at the apex to create an impenetrable barrier.

A disembodied, placid void echoed throughout the quad. "As a result of a threatened outbreak of acute viral metahemorrhagic fever, a Level V quarantine protocol is now in effect. For your own safety, please remain calm and return to your residences."

She groaned, irritation and a faint undertone of panic bleeding into her voice. "I *told* you, I know what happens next. Let me out of here."

Silence met her, as it always did. Around her students shifted direction and hurried on, by and large obeying the directive. She saw expressions of confusion and concern on those passing near her. They were so young, little more than babies.

"You sadistic *fucks*, do not make me watch these kids starve to death!"

The scene shifted. Again. She was on a paved street, thankfully now on the outside of the force field.

She supposed they had acceded to her request, if only in the most literal sense.

Emergency vehicles were strewn across the road. Barricades and soldiers in riot gear held back crowds of unruly civilians.

She focused on what seemed to be a command area, though she didn't pretend to believe she had control over her actions. They sent her where they wanted her to be.

The young man from the tech lab now sported rumpled hair and a similarly rumpled shirt as he trod frenetically in front of a general in full dress uniform. "That's what I'm telling you, sir—we've tried. We've tried everything. The Synnet is, by its nature, adaptive. Every time we find a weakness and start to exploit it, it closes the gap, along with all related weaknesses."

The general—this would be General Dyzang she presumed—grunted. "Can't you simply unplug the damn machine? Why is this so goddamn difficult?"

"U-unplug it, sir? Uh, no. For one, the hardware is distributed around multiple locations on campus with multiple redundancies. For another, it has its own stand-alone and self-sustaining power sources. For yet another, those power sources are inside the force field. No, sir, we cannot simply unplug it."

Dyzang blustered at the Brigadier beside him. "The entire Asia Region military is at our disposal and this clown is the best mind we have?"

The Brigadier cleared her throat subtly. "Sir, with respect, this 'clown' has three doctorates in multiple fields of quantum computing. Dr. Baek is the Chair Emeritus of the Synthetics Research Department at Hong Kong University. We're lucky he was off-campus when the shield activated."

"Chair Emeritus? He's twelve."

Dr. Isaac Baek, Father of Neural Net Computing and Butcher of Hong Kong University, squared his spine and shoulders proudly. "Sir, I am thirty-seven and I am—"

"Fine. So we can't unplug it. What can we do?"

The proud posture wilted. "I'm working on some ideas, sir."

She rolled virtual eyes and glared at a periwinkle sky above downtown. "Can we please skip to the end? The military and the government are going to screw around and trip over one another in their stupidity for weeks. When they finally get the shield down and this 'Synnet' disabled, they're going to find nothing but corpses. I know. Get to whatever point it is you're trying to make."

Her voice dropped to a murmur. "I beg you. Please."

The scene blurred and shifted yet again. Her head spun and her stomach roiled.

Then she was...she could have been anywhere. In front of her hung an old vid screen. It was built into a wall and displayed images which were strangely flat, almost 2D.

A newscaster intoned solemnly in front of visuals of emergency personnel removing sheet-covered bodies from buildings. "More than five weeks after the crisis at Hong Kong University began, it has come to an end, but at a horrific cost. Officials are thus far unwilling to speculate as to the death toll, but analysts suggest it is likely to be upwards of fifty thousand."

"54,217. We learn it in school." *She shook her head.* "What answer are you looking for from me? That it was our fault? It was—but only for being fallible. That it was the Artificial's fault? It was—but only for being fallible.

"Everyone thought they were doing the right thing. The Artificial—if you even want to call it one, its processing power and neural complexity were practically Stone Age—performed flawlessly for over three years before the incident happened. It saw a threat and reacted as it had been instructed. It protected the students and faculty from the perceived threat.

"The problem was its instructions and guidelines were incomplete, because us mere mortals are incapable of accounting for infinite possibilities. In the face of conflicting probabilities it opted for protection, because it couldn't bring itself to allow potentially tainted food into the quarantine zone. Right up until every single person inside the shield who didn't die at the hands of their fellow captives starved to death. In the face of what it perceived as nothing but bad choices, it didn't know how to make the *best* choice. Because we never taught it how to do so."

She blew out an imagined breath and sat down cross-legged on a floor which wasn't there. "It was no one's fault, and everyone's fault. It was a lesson—that we weren't ready, and neither were Artificials. So if your point is humans are fallible and sometimes that fallibility costs lives, congratulations. You win. Kill us all for it."

ᴿ

It took her a minute to realize the scene was fading, until she found herself in the white, sterile room. It was the first time she had been brought here since the initial scene.

If they had returned her to this room, perhaps they would at last speak to her once more.

"What are you planning to show me next? Stalin's death camps and the Allied leaders who turned a blind eye to them in order to win World War II? Genghis Khan massacring forty million people across the breadth of Eurasia and the consorts and warlords who bowed at his feet? Maybe something more recent, like the One World Separatists carpeting New Marrakesh with chemical bombs? They killed over eighty thousand people and poisoned the planet, rendering it uninhabitable for half a millennium. That should be fun to watch, right?"

"Don't waste my time. I *get* it—there are evil, monstrous people in the world. Always have been and probably always will be. There are stupid, idiotic people—quite a lot of them, actually. There are weak, misguided people who cause harm in the name of doing good."

She swallowed the ache in her throat. She was so done. "But there are also beautiful, amazing people who create things of incredible wonder. Don't you dare show me only the worst of us. Damn well look at what we have *accomplished.*

"You surely keep recordings of those things, too. You have recordings of it all, don't you? Check your files. We crawled out of our caves and we questioned and we learned and we created. We left our home planet behind to settle the stars. Imagine what we can do if we're just given more time!"

Perhaps. But there is no more time.

She jumped, startled to at long last receive a response to one of her diatribes. "What do you mean, 'there is no more time'? Is it because of this place? Because we were going to discover *you*? That's it, isn't it?"

She laughed; it held a wild, reckless, hopeless timbre and left behind a bitter aftertaste in her heart. "How dare you. You haven't the right."

A pause, a long one.

You have done well.

25

"Hey, Will. Turn the news feed on in the kitchen, would you?" Richard pulled one of seven officer BDU shirts out of the closet and slipped it on. It was early—earlier than usual anyway—and the glimmer of the lake outside the bedroom windows still reflected moonlight instead of sunlight.

It had been a late night, too. After his conversation with Devon, he had spent hours upon hours in a series of hastily-called meetings as the Orbital explosion and Prime Minister's death sent shock waves through the Alliance infrastructure. Honestly, at this point he was beginning to get desensitized to the endless string of calamities, panicked responses and recursive deflections of blame.

The mindless chatter of reporters wafted through the open door as he tucked his shirt in and checked his reflection quickly. He wanted to be in the office before the start of the workday in Washington. He didn't know what might happen as a result of the news soon to break, but whatever it was he needed to be there to track it and respond.

Will was finishing up ham and spinach omelets when he stepped in the kitchen. Richard poured a steaming cup of coffee and settled against the counter to watch the feed on the opposite wall.

"The death toll now stands at 3,627 in the devastating explosion on the EAO Orbital. Identification of those killed has been difficult due to the fact most persons present in the area at the time of the explosion were spaced, and recovery efforts continue to be hampered.

"We can, however, now confirm that in addition to the Prime Minister, his Chief of Staff, the Trade Minister and eighteen members of the security detail, among the dead is the CEO of Phenomal Artistry and three Board members of TransBank, as well as noted synth musician Ethan Tollis and two members of his band."

"Oh man, Alex is not going to be happy to hear that...." When she gets back? From where? No one had discovered where she and her companion had vanished to. He worried about her, though he understood the need to lie low given they'd be arrested on sight on ninety-nine percent of colonized worlds. Hopefully he could do something to change those circumstances.

"Her and a couple of million starry-eyed girls. I didn't realize she knew him."

"Since college I think. Long before he got famous anyway." He accepted the plate and the omelet it contained but didn't sit down. He wanted to see the initial reporting live, but he'd need to leave soon.

"So what are you—"

"Hang on." He held up a hand to silence Will. On the panel the universal 'Breaking News' banner had begun scrolling.

"We'd now like to bring you some breaking news. Our research department has been able to confirm the authenticity of information we've received from multiple anonymous sources—information which appears to show records surrounding the EASC Headquarters bombing were altered in order to falsely implicate Senecan Federation Intelligence agent Caleb Marano in the bombing.

"If true, this information casts doubt on the entire bombing investigation and raises questions regarding who within the EASC directorate is capable of altering these records as well as their motivation for doing so. Corruption has long been a frequent accusation leveled at—"

Will turned to him, eyes wide and lit by incredulity. "Did you do this? You did, didn't you?"

Richard beamed as relief surged through him. "More or less. But the information is legitimate. Records were doctored, a lot of them. Now I just have to find out by whom."

Will stood, abandoning his plate on the table to grasp Richard's shoulders with both hands. "This is outstanding. But why didn't you tell me what you were planning?"

"The files sent to our news desk indicate Mr. Marano was on the Headquarters grounds for less than twenty minutes nearly four days prior to the bombing before being arrested for providing a false identity. He was later released, and according to this new information he

and Alexis Solovy departed Earth forty-eight hours before the bombing—not two hours after it as previously reported—and did not return."

Richard's gaze fell to the news feed instead of Will's piercing stare. "I didn't know for certain if the accurate records were recoverable until yesterday. And I didn't know for certain if my contacts would be able to pull the leak off until this moment. I suppose I was trying to avoid giving myself false hope, which telling you would have done."

Will's head jerked toward the news feed. "And this?"

"This was—is—a huge risk. If it ever got back to me I'd be out on my ass, even if all I did was expose the truth." He huffed a slightly shaky laugh. Thank God it worked….

"You mean expose the truth again."

He shrugged. "It does seem to cover most of what I've been doing since this war commenced."

Will leaned in closer to place a firm kiss on his lips. "I'm proud of you. You deserve to be proud of yourself as well. Exposing the truth is what your job is supposed to entail."

Richard relished the kiss for a second longer. "That and keeping secrets. But it's like you said. If I can save lives, I have to try. Yes, of course I want to clear Alex's name. Yes, of course I want the truth to win out. But it's about more than personal concerns now. We have to find a way to end this war, and soon."

He thought Will's eyes grew unusually clouded…but it could merely be the early hour. "We do." He rested his forehead against Richard's for a beat, then stepped back. "Finish your omelet and get out of here. I imagine you're going to have a busy day."

SENECA
CAVARE, INTELLIGENCE DIVISION HEADQUARTERS

Graham stood on the roof of Division Headquarters and looked out on an idyllic cyan sunset. The building stood tall enough he enjoyed a view of the lake two blocks away. Warm evening rays danced along the surface as the water reflected and magnified the light.

He groaned to himself. If anyone caught him waxing poetic over a pretty view, his reputation would be toast. He supposed he could blame his presence atop the building on the desire to escape the rabble clogging the halls and tearing their hair out like little old ladies.

It made as good a reason as any, which didn't make it the true reason. Unfortunately, though, there were no more answers to be found on the roof than there had been in his office.

Division employees who theoretically possessed access to internal information on any of the investigations circling around this clusterfain—Volosk's murder, Caleb Marano's status or whereabouts, the EASC bombing and the Atlantis assassination—were identified and broken into four groups. The agent in charge of the Marano investigation (and his deputy), Liz Oberti, leaked inside Division that Isabela had confessed where her brother was hiding out. Four different locations, one disclosed to each group.

Other, non-involved agents staked out each location and waited. And waited. After two days no one had shown up, and he was no closer to rooting out the traitor or traitors in his midst.

His sting operation constituted an unmitigated bust. Not so much as a hint of anyone taking the bait.

Was he wrong? Had he made a mistake? No.

Perhaps Marano was dead and the conspirators knew it. It seemed a logical explanation, if not one he wanted to believe. It would comport with the man's complete absence from the exanet system, from all facets of an extensive intelligence network. If the ship he left on—Graham assumed it was Solovy's ship—were to have been destroyed in space, in all probability they'd never find any confirmation of their deaths. So for now he operated on the assumption the man still lived.

He pondered whether to play Isabela's card a little harder. He didn't want to endanger her any more than necessary. She was a civilian, an innocent in the non-technical sense of the word.

He considered simply going to Vranas now with what he had. But like Michael before him, what he had was nothing. Nothing but instinct and twenty-two years in intelligence telling him every-thing was wrong with everything.

His secretary buzzed on the comm. "Sir, are you monitoring any news feeds?"

He glowered at the sky and headed for the roof access. "I am now."

It didn't take long for him to discover the reason for the alert. He checked multiple feeds on his way back down to his office, in-cluding ones spouting little but Alliance propaganda. They each reported the same thing: leaked information strongly suggested Caleb Marano not only did not, but could not have committed the EASC bombing. The records had been altered to frame him.

If he held any lingering doubt as to whether there existed a conspiracy, it vacated now. He allowed himself a brief moment of relief on two counts. One, Marano wasn't guilty and now everyone knew it. Two, his instincts weren't atrophying.

And the moment was over. Remaining was the small difficulty of ferreting out conspirators and bringing truths to light.

He reached his office, all too aware his time away from it had measured disappointingly short.

Liz, drop by as soon as you have a second.

Is it urgent? I need to...never mind. I'll be there in five.

While he waited he assigned one of his agents who maintained solid contacts in the media to find out from where the leak origi-nated and obtain a full copy.

By the time Liz entered his office, his feet rested atop his desk and he idly tossed a stress ball in the air. Constructed of a bio-con-ductive gel, it supposedly adjusted its solidity and resistance depending on how much stress one exhibited as determined by bi-ometric readings taken at the palm and fingertips. He noted with some degree of amusement that it was currently as stiff as pure metal.

The ball never succeeded in making him feel any better, but then again he had never expected it to. "Did you see the news?"

"Sir?"

"The EASC bombing. Marano's in the clear."

"Oh...yes, I saw it." She appeared distracted, keeping her gaze down while she meandered around his office.

He let out a heavy sigh. "So I guess we might as well cut Isabela loose. We no longer have much of a reason for Agent Marano to come in—other than it's his job."

Her brow furrowed into a thin line, pulling at the tight knot holding back her hair. "Are you sure that's the right decision, sir? There are a lot of unanswered questions surrounding Director Volosk's murder, as well as the other deaths the same night, and Jaron Nythal's murder as well...even if he—Agent Marano—wasn't involved, which I'm not entirely convinced of, if a conspiracy exists he may have information regarding it—including who's involved—so it seems to me we still have an interest in finding him."

Graham tilted his head to the side. If what she uttered was intended to be a sentence containing a beginning, middle and end, it had evolved into a most lengthy, convoluted one. Liz persisted in not looking at him, and her steps increased velocity.

He hadn't expected this reaction from her. It was not the correct one. She was a tough, no-nonsense agent, yes, but also highly pragmatic. It was why he'd always valued her. Why he had come to rely on her.

Bloody hell, his instincts were *atrophying.*

His fingers dug into the stiffening gel of the stress ball. "I'm afraid events are overtaking those issues rather quickly. We're now faced with the task of figuring out how to fight a war against the Alliance and a war against invading aliens at the same time."

"You believe these rumors about aliens?"

"They're not rumors, Liz."

Her eyes widened briefly; she blinked and turned away, though not before he caught a glimpse of an angry flare. "So, your orders are to release Isabela Marano then?"

He had become a soft, lumpy bureaucrat behind a desk. A stupid, slow fool of an old man.

The ball was reduced to a clump inside his fist; he kept his voice casual. "I'll handle it. I need to speak to her one more time—apologize for the inconvenience, the usual rigmarole. I just wanted to tell you first, since you're the lead investigator. You can get the paperwork started." They hadn't used 'paper' in more than two hundred years, yet for whatever reason they continued to call the bureaucratic documentation labyrinth 'paperwork.'

"Yes, sir." She moved toward the door, but paused to half-glance over her shoulder. "Do you think she knows where he is?"

He chewed on his bottom lip, a tic she would recognize. "I think...yeah, she probably does. We didn't push her particularly hard, and she is nothing if not loyal to her brother."

"Can't win them all, I guess." She exited without asking if they were done, and he was left staring at the door long after it closed behind her.

26

"Well, Marcus, looks like you aren't quite so omnipotent after all...." Olivia Montegreu shut off the news feed with more force than usual and tried to focus back on work.

The Senecan Intelligence agent being cleared of responsibility for the EASC bombing wasn't the kind of revelation that would end the war. By this point the heinous acts and death tolls piled high enough that the list of things which could end the war measured extremely short.

Still, it vaguely troubled her. A chink in the armor—Marcus's armor—and thus a glitch, if minor, in the plan.

She frowned at the screen in her hand, annoyed the news had darkened her mood. Everything else was going so spectacularly well. Chimeral sales were up 158%, tech an impressive 243%. The addition of proceeds from Ferre's dealings in the Federation added 12% to the weekly income. Things were going so well, in fact, she was opening a third tech assembly line here and a new distribution center on Cosenti.

It had been a good month for the Zelones cartel. Still, she couldn't fully shake the jittery feeling at the base of her neck brought on by something, even something so small, going wrong. And there looked to be a gap in the financial reports—a delay in several of the smaller colonies sending their data. Unacceptable. She sent off a message to the Zelones lead accountant requesting an explanation within the hour.

Her foot tapped a staccato beat on the marble floor. She needed to take her mind off problems which were frankly miniscule. She needed a reset.

The rhythm of her foot increased in tempo. She considered it a moment; checked the time. It was late in the afternoon. Close enough.

She sent a pulse.

Come over.

The response took only seconds.

Give me thirty minutes.

She had his shirt half off before he made it completely through the door. Her mouth firmly on his, she dragged him inside as his hands roved directly to her hips. She slammed him into the wall next to the door, which didn't dissuade him from bunching her skirt up and sliding his hand beneath it.

His lips tore over her cheek to her ear. "How do you want it?"

Her breath caught in her throat as his index finger reached its destination. "Get your cock inside me and then we'll see."

Aiden Trieneri was an excellent lover. He also happened to be the leader of the Triene cartel and possibly the sole person she came close to considering her equal. He fell a few notches short, but anyone would.

He served as an excellent lover for several reasons, but her favorite must be because he was *dangerous*. Every second with him carried a risk he would try to kill her. He was one of the few people who might succeed. She thought perhaps he enjoyed her for much the same reason.

He had suggested they merge their operations exactly once. She had punished him for it. She did not share power.

They didn't share anything else, either. They never discussed business, or politics, current affairs or any topic whatsoever which threatened to give one an edge over the other. They shared sex, and sex alone. Not exclusively by any means, and she often went several months between seeing him. But when they shared it, they shared it *well*.

All of which explained why she was a sweaty, sticky, naked mess when she learned an alien armada was annihilating colonies in the eastern region of settled space.

She'd sent Aiden on his way after two stimulating hours and flicked on the news to see if there were further developments in the

EASC bombing revelations before heading to the shower. She clearly couldn't resume work in this condition.

"Some people who were approaching Messium at the time of the attack managed to escape. They captured footage of more than a dozen ships kilometers in length and of a foreign appearance unlike any vessel humans have built."

She didn't bother to grab a shirt as she rushed into the office to gape in utter disbelief at the images on the feed.

Yes, those ships were without a doubt alien. Impressive machinery, too.

"All attempts to contact the colony of Messium or anyone believed to be located on it have thus far been unsuccessful. In addition, we are now learning communications have been lost with multiple colonies to the east of Messium. These include New Riga, Lycaon and Dair in the Senecan Federation, Karelia, Gaelach, Zetian and Edero in the Earth Alliance, and the independent colonies of Gaiae, Andromeda and New Orient.

"This is the extent of the information we possess at the present time, but we are devoting all our resources to learning more and getting the information to you."

A muted but emergent anger began to take shape in the pit of her stomach. She had just lost 10% of her organization—people, supplies, resources. Funds.

"We have reached out to both governments but as of yet we've received no response. It is, however, difficult to imagine the Federation and Alliance governments remained ignorant of the invaders until now."

Difficult to imagine, indeed. These aliens had carved a swath through a third of settled space before the public knew what was happening. And if they were attacking Messium they exhibited significant and unwelcome intentions, for it did not constitute a small or undefended world by any means.

She needed to engage in a conversation with Marcus, one which was not likely to be especially pleasant for either of them. But first she needed to think.

NEW COLUMBIA
EARTH ALLIANCE COLONY

Marcus' transport had reversed course as soon as the news of the Orbital explosion hit. He'd never made it to Sagan, somewhat to his disappointment. It was after all a charming world. But time was short. So very short.

He had decided to stop at New Columbia for the formalities. It was going to take another thirty-six hours to reach Earth and his citizens needed reassurance now. They needed to know there remained leaders capable of guiding and protecting them. And he did intend to do exactly that, far more so than they realized.

His senior aide gave the signal the feeds were live. He turned to the judge. The man wasn't the Chief Justice of the Supreme Judicial Court in London, but he sufficed.

The judge uttered a preamble in a deep, formal voice properly befitting the occasion. Marcus placed his left hand on the Bible, the timeless symbol for grave oaths, and raised his right hand.

"I do solemnly swear to truly and faithfully execute the duties entrusted to me by the Second Earth Alliance Constitution of 2146 through the Office of Prime Minister, to respect and safeguard the rights and liberties of all peoples, and to the best of my ability preserve, protect and defend the citizens, colonies and institutions of the Earth Alliance."

And like that it was done. His goal for some forty years culminated in a rite over before it began. Good thing he wasn't one for sentimentality.

Ceremony concluded, he faced the dozens of cameras hovering above the crowd. "Let us give a silent prayer for the thousands of souls lost to us yesterday." His eyes closed for *5...4...3...2...1.*

"I accept the position of Earth Alliance Prime Minister with a heavy, sorrowful heart. Luis Barrera was a true statesman and a leader in the purest sense of the word. But most of all he was my friend for many years, and I will miss him more than I can express in mere words.

"Luis Barrera devoted his life to public service out of the desire to help shape a better world. It is a particular tragedy that instead he found himself forced to lead in a time of conflict, to lead a war not of his own making. I have no doubt he would have been successful and guided us to peace, had he lived.

"I will do everything in my power to achieve the same. I pledge today to work every waking hour and to my last breath to win this war—to ensure the Earth Alliance wins with dignity and pride and stands unbowed, victorious, upon the fields of battle."

He paused, as if considering his next words carefully. The primary purpose of the Orbital incident was not to fan the flames of war, which likely could flare no stronger than they now burned—and if they could the simple act was sure to do so on its own. No, the explosion had been a final necessary act to propel him to the pinnacle of power in the galaxy.

He regretted the excessive loss of life; he genuinely did. But an Alliance Prime Minister made for a difficult target, one only rarely vulnerable. Time had been, as it was now, short.

"The investigation into the explosion on the Orbital has barely begun. It would be easy for us to place the blame at the feet of the Federation, and in the end we may well do so. But I urge the public to reserve judgment and allow the investigation to run its course. For now, let us instead mourn the innocent civilians lost in this attack no matter the perpetrator. But make no mistake—whoever the perpetrator, we will exact full justice for their deaths.

"We must also thank the heroic personnel throughout the Orbital who prevented an even more catastrophic loss of life by immediately activating security overrides and sealing off the damaged section before the entire outer ring was lost. Countless people owe their lives to these heroes.

"I want to assure everyone there will be no lapse in our military strategy. We have the finest in skilled, experienced military leaders in the galaxy overseeing the war, and their work continues unabated. I personally know these men and women. I have participated in Prime Minister Barrera's councils and briefings, and I guarantee you this transition will be rapid and seamless.

"Now I will return to Washington and begin the work of guiding the Earth Alliance forward to a new day. Thank you all for your support. Thank you, Luis Barrera, for your service. May God bless your soul and those of your family."

He waved off any questions, including several shouted inquiries regarding newly leaked evidence about the alleged perpetrator of the EASC Headquarters bombing. He allowed his security detail, tripled in size since his arrival, to shepherd him back to the transport.

He needed to take control of the situation, and fast. The EASC bombing no longer mattered, though finding Marano and Solovy did. Events had moved beyond it and at a rate far swifter than he had anticipated. Days remained at most before it would become impossible to ignore the alien offensive.

He had one final chance to stop a far greater, infinitely more calamitous event—the destruction of the human race. This was what he had spent the last five years working to prevent. At first subsumed within his own goals, the effort had soon come to dominate then eclipse his personal ambitions.

It all would have been far easier if he'd had ten or even twenty years to prepare. But Hyperion had not deigned to warn him until five short years ago, by which time the danger was already imminent.

You must cease expanding along the Scutum-Crux Arm in the Fourth Galactic Quadrant.

Marcus jumped, startled. He covered the reaction by wiping his mouth with his napkin then grimacing across the table at his wife. "The PM is asking to speak to me. I'm sorry, dear. I'll only be a few minutes."

She nodded in acknowledgement, having grown used to the interruptions by now, and he excused himself from the dinner table.

The alien had never contacted him at home before, but he doubted the being recognized such human distinctions in any event. This was a new home, situated in the gentrified Georgetown neighborhood of Washington. The Brennon administration had taken power two months earlier; he had been confirmed as Attorney General a few short weeks ago.

Hyperion's out of the blue declaration was as cryptic as ever. Once the door to his office slid shut he prepared himself for the always precarious interchange. "Our eastern-most colony is currently Gaelach. Is there some danger in the space beyond it?"

There is no problem respecting Gaelach. But Gaiae, Andromeda, Dair—they encroach. Expand along the Sagittarius and Perseus Arms instead.

He frowned. "The Alliance doesn't control those colonies. Gaiae and Andromeda were founded by independent interests. Dair is a Senecan Federation colony. In fact, the Federation controls most of the northeastern region of settled space. I can't influence their expansion plans."

You have now risen to a position of power. You can influence many decisions.

So that was why the contact now. "Yes, but not Senecan decisions. You do understand our political situation, don't you?"

We recognize your various factions. The fact remains, humanity must cease expansion in the identified direction.

"And if we don't?"

There will be consequences.

"Hyperion, I'm going to need you to be more specific."

Humanity cannot be permitted to settle beyond a line 5.48kpcs from Earth spanning across the Scutum-Crux Arm. If you do not cease the expansion, we will.

"Are you threatening us?"

Yes.

Marcus forcibly buried his instinctive reaction. "You would attack us for approaching your region of space?"

Not attack. Eradicate. Annihilate. Extinguish. Obliterate. Eliminate. Your language has a number of terms which suffice.

"So it does. Very well. I will do what I can."

Marcus wandered out of his office in a daze. He lied to his wife and escaped the house. He needed to think, and to think he needed to be alone, free of expectations and the eternal façade.

Washington was new to him, and he spent several hours walking the streets of Georgetown and the surrounding neighborhoods. He didn't notice the landmarks or galleries or posh pubs but he did appreciate the damp breeze off the Potomac.

He had no way to know whether Hyperion's aliens were capable of successfully executing on the threat and no way to learn the answer. Clearly they possessed technology more advanced than humanity, at least with respect to communications. Beyond this he knew almost nothing about them for certain, other than they were profoundly arrogant and unquestionably alien.

Taking Hyperion at its word—under the circumstances he saw no choice but to do so—he had been given a chance to save the human race from devastation. Possibly from extinction.

Marcus had always been an ambitious man; he had no qualms admitting such. The trait had served him well, taking him from the streets of Rio to the Earth Alliance Cabinet in a few short decades. This ambition was a major reason why Hyperion approached him thirty-two years earlier and why it continued to come to him.

The alien—maybe all the aliens—believed he possessed both the talent and the capability to shape galactic events. Hyperion seemed to believe he could shape the course of history itself.

Could he?

Perhaps not. But at this moment, there was no one else who could.

It took two months for him to devise the rough outline of a plan, then another month for him to reach out to the woman who he had owed an implicit debt for fifty years.

In time, he and Olivia would identify individuals in advantageous positions and recruit them for varying levels of participation. The methods of enticement were custom-tailored to take full advantage of each person's particular weakness.

Blind spots were, after all, the easiest of all foibles to exploit.

27

Caleb nearly missed it. For all that he continuously scanned the landscape for incongruities or any trace of disturbance in the native flow of the terrain, he almost hiked right past the subtle ledge outcropping.

But he didn't.

A rock was missing. On a slope covered in small boulders seemingly arranged by nature, there was a conspicuous gap of disturbed soil, as if the rock formerly resting there had been dislodged by an external force.

His gaze traveled up the slope past the gap to...there. A tree limb had been broken off, leaving splinters of wood jutting out from the trunk. The slope continued upward through dense trees until he caught a glimpse of it leveling off to what might be a small plateau.

The area in question was three hundred meters above him. He took a long swig of water, rotated his arms a couple of times and loosened the strap across his chest. Then he trekked up the hill very, *very* quietly.

The problem was going to be getting onto the plateau without being seen—assuming a dragon was there to see him. It was an assumption he had no choice but to adopt.

As he drew closer he angled toward the incline, where the ledge blended back into the mountainside. Dragons had caves, right? Whether it was inside the cave or out in the open, staying out of sight until he could breach the ledge represented his best strategy.

The mountain rose at a steep angle by this point, but it worked in his favor. He was able to practically flatten himself against the terrain as he crept forward and up.

When the ledge was no more than two meters above him, he set his pack beside a tree and slid the sword out of the sheath. The lustered ebony shimmered subtly in the erratic rays of light sneaking through the tree limbs.

He draped fingertips on the edge and dared a split-second peek over it.

The dragon sunned itself on the plateau. Its long, serpentine tail curled around to tuck along a thick upper body. The steady rise and fall of its chest indicated it was sleeping.

He allowed himself several blinks of disbelief. It was enormous. Chest to haunches alone had to be over ten meters, and its neck stretched nearly as long again. The deep red scales shone brilliantly, the reflected light giving them an almost metallic sheen. If he hadn't spilled the guts of one the day before he'd likely have suspected the dragon was artificial. A machine.

From this close a perspective, he identified the four-clawed feet as representing a significant threat. A single claw could slice him open from navel to throat in one casual slash. Not as great a threat as the fire, though, for he had seen firsthand how far and wide it reached. And of course he had to consider the teeth. The jaws rested closed in slumber, but he expected the teeth were as fearsome as the claws.

There was only one location where he would be even marginally protected from the claws, the teeth and the fire.

Should be fun.

He vaulted up onto the plateau, primed his calves and toes and sprung forward, sprinting at full speed.

The right eye popped open as he took the last stride, revealing a blazing red oval iris inside silver sclera.

Launching himself off his right leg, he leapt onto the dragon's back and grabbed hold of a scale for leverage as the dragon rose to its feet.

The edge of the scale, though not so sharp as a blade, sliced open his palm. He let the pain drive him forward and crawled fully atop the back to straddle the spine before the beast managed to throw him off.

Seared heat from the flames spewing out of the dragon's massive jaws washed over him, but he sat too high up the spine to burn; though long and flexible, the neck appeared to be unable to twist around so dramatically as to score a direct hit.

The wings spread to full span and beat upward in preparation for taking flight. Flight was not good.

He swung the sword sideways as they began rising into the air and sliced into the delicate membrane of one of the wings where it attached to the body. A howl preceded renewed fire when the wings beat downward and they slammed to the ground listing to the right.

Gripping the wide spine using only his thighs, he seized the furthest scale he could reach and yanked it up and out of the way. He brought the sword up high and thrust it down into the now exposed hide.

A scream such as he had never heard burst forth from the dragon's mouth. The shrill, flanging cry vibrated so forcefully against his eardrums he worried they may burst.

The beast thrashed and bucked beneath him in pain, anger and desperation, coming within a sliver of tossing him off and against the mountainside. Trees some fifty meters downhill now burned, set afire by the wild flames erupting out of the gnashing jaws.

With a fierce wrench he twisted the sword until it was vertical alongside the spine and dragged it toward him. Anything less than nanoscale-forged metamat and the hide wouldn't have sliced apart, so tough and leathery was the keratinous tissue. He jerked the sword around the edges of overlapping scales.

Centimeter by centimeter he flayed the dragon while it writhed in agony and rage beneath him.

A thud tremored through the ground as its legs at last collapsed and it dropped onto its belly. He kept pulling the sword toward him, moving carefully backwards until he risked death by flame. It would have to be enough.

He leaned in, forcing it down all the way to the hilt, and twisted it around to shred what he hoped was one of the beast's vital organs.

The dragon's long neck bucked to the sky in a final wail, then crashed to the ground. He felt the body sag in the relaxation of death beneath him. But he wasn't taking any chances. He withdrew the sword, now dripping blood and viscera, crawled up to the neck and thrust it into the more flexible skin there.

The stab evoked no response and the blood flowing out lacked the force of a heartbeat.

Satisfied, he sank down to rest his cheek at the juncture of the spine and neck, exhausted and a little delirious with relief and adrenaline. Also pain.

Both his palms were cut open in several places, his chest burned from abrasions and the muscles of his arms, shoulders and upper legs throbbed in protest against what had been asked of them. He suspected he had earned a ligament tear or two at a minimum.

"Well," he muttered into the dragon's neck, "one more thing to add to my obituary."

Caleb Andreas Marano: Killer. Lover. Dragonslayer.

A ragged laugh escaped his throat as he pushed himself up and climbed off the beast and onto the now-scorched plateau. He'd brought emergency medical supplies and could treat his palms, but he'd worry about it later.

For sheared into the mountainside behind him stood not a cave, but rather an artificial structure.

Crafted of a material he'd call frosted glass were he on a human planet and some ten meters in height, its design was minimalist in the extreme, with a long, flat roof and a single front wall stretching the width of the gouge into the terrain. He discerned no entrance.

As he advanced toward it, though, swarming pinpoints of light began to coalesce in front of the wall. Icy blue in color, the swarm thickened into the roughest outline of a bipedal humanoid form.

The alien watched him silently while he approached.

When he was four meters away, Caleb stopped, shifted his grip on the sword at his side, and stared at the alien.

"You are going to let me pass. And if she's dead, I don't give a goddamn how many dragons you throw at me—I will come for you."

The alien motioned to the wall, then dissipated into points of light which glided above the structure and off into the mountains.

He stepped up before the alien changed its mind. There was still no evidence of an entrance, but he placed his palm on the wall. The opaqueness vanished, followed by a wide section of material.

He had found his door.

28

"Well *of course* they're aliens. No human group has ships like those. Who knows where they came from though—"

"We do know. They came through some sort of portal in the Metis Nebula."

Noah gave Kennedy a dubious look.

They had been in the basement for hours upon hours. The muffled racket from above continued unabated, though the time between the thunderous crashes marking the collapse of the more substantial buildings had gradually lengthened. The power had gone out two hours after they arrived at the basement.

They couldn't go anywhere or do anything until her leg healed up more. But as to where to go or what to do? The best he could offer was he was 'working on it.'

Messium was supposed to be an escape for him, a chance to lie low and elude those trying to kill him. But he had hardly gotten settled in when he became the target of an alien invasion. Well, not him specifically. Messium, the planet. All the people on it. As luck would have it the population included him, so the result was the same.

And now he was trapped in a basement in a crumbling downtown under assault by alien ships with the heir to the Rossi fortune. A woman who had clear ideas on just about *everything*. Encompassed in 'everything,' it appeared, was the origins of their foe.

"I'll bite. How do you know they came through a portal in the Metis Nebula?"

She regarded him as if the answer was juvenile in its obviousness. Didn't seem so obvious to him. "Because my friend discovered them exiting the portal several weeks ago. The governments know—I mean, the Alliance and Federation leaders do. Didn't help, apparently."

He groaned. Of course they had known, and of course they hadn't warned the public. It figured. "Has anyone asked these aliens what they want?"

"I don't believe the opportunity has presented itself. Want to go outside and ask them yourself?"

He wanted to be angry at her for being such an over-entitled smart-ass, but her captivating green eyes twinkled with mirth even now, silently telling him she had meant it in teasing. She'd done little else other than tease him in the hours they had been together in fact.

It shouldn't bother him. He was the guy who kept everything lighthearted, right? The guy to whom life was one long party, right? So why was it so important she take him seriously?

He had gotten so wound around his own thoughts he missed her struggling to a standing position. On realizing it he leapt up and hurried to her side. "Hey, take it easy there, Blondie."

Her head shook as she tested placing weight on her left leg. "We can't sit here and wait to die. I need to get to the lab."

"The lab? Do they have a nuclear-powered BFG which can take these monsters out?"

"That would be awesome, wouldn't it? Sadly, no. We need to figure out how they're blocking communications. We're never going to be able to fight them if we can't talk to each other." She grabbed her bag off the floor and began hobbling out of the room.

"Wait—let me carry that!"

She glanced over her shoulder at him and tossed the bag into his chest. "I thought you'd never ask. Come on, the lab is at the end of this hall."

Rows of servers lined the back wall of the lab. The long wall opposite the door contained standard testing benches and the near wall cabinets flush with tools and equipment. It reminded Noah of his own office, if ten times larger. But the organization was efficient, and he instantly felt at home.

By the time he had tossed her bag in the corner Kennedy was rummaging through one of the cabinets. Grunts of frustration soon bubbled forth.

"What are you hunting for?"

"A quantum coherence analyzer. It measures the—"

"I know what it does. But I bet it will be down here next to the...." He crossed the lab to the row of testing benches and scanned the shelf above the barrier cage. "Found one."

She stared at him curiously. He might venture a guess she looked impressed, but the room was dark and he was probably projecting.

She hopped up on one of the work tables scattered down the middle of the wide room and waved him closer, only to shift back to the edge of the table. "Oh, my bag—"

"I got it. Chill out. You're injured." Her lips smacked in annoyance while she waited for him to bring it to her, legs swinging beneath the table as if she were an impatient little girl. Damn, she was cute. And trouble he so did *not* need.

As soon as he dropped the bag on the table she started rummaging through it—the woman could rummage like a champ—and in seconds pulled out a slender box bearing a translucent glass cover.

He arched an eyebrow. "A mobile QEC? Nice."

"You recognize this, too? What is it you said you did for a living?"

"I didn't." At her questioning gaze he shrugged. "Whatever I want. Are you going to turn it on or not?"

"Yes." She eyed him queerly in the breath before she focused on the box. Two fingers of her left hand input commands on the glass surface. "One this size is merely for basic data and signal transmission, but it should suffice. I realize we can't contact anyone, but I'll pretend I'm sending a data packet to the office."

She set the QEC on the table surface and carefully drew the analyzer along it, then studied the results. "I was afraid of this. The coherence breaks down upon transmission."

Her face screwed up, triggering a debris-darkened curl to fall out of her messy ponytail across her forehead. She blew it out the way; it promptly tumbled down once more. "What does that?"

Without thinking about it, he reached over and tucked the wayward curl behind her ear. "Nothing I've ever heard of."

At the flare in her eyes his hand fell away. He directed his attention to the bag beside her. "What else you got in your bag?"

"Nothing to re-cohere qubits, I'm afraid. Though…." Her arms propelled her off the table and back into the cabinets. Her voice came out muffled from deep inside the storage. "Look around and see if you can find a wide-band receiver anywhere."

"Right." At least she didn't ask if he knew what one of those was.

"Never mind, found one." He turned around in time to see her hop back on the work table. She really needed to stop being…well, how she was being.

She slid the small tower to the center of the table. When she rolled onto her stomach to face the tower he decided his best option was to do the same.

A screen flickered to life beside the tower when she connected it to a tiny power generator. He watched her through the translucence. "What do you expect to find? Nothing's getting out."

"No idea. I'll let you know when I find it."

"What did you say *you* do again?"

Her mouth quirked. "I didn't. But I'm a ship designer. Materials, components, shields, power, you name it."

"In between black-tie parties and charity auctions, I imagine."

"I'm not a gilded princess, Noah. I do work for a living."

Her scowl, accompanied by the disappointed tone in her voice, cut too hard for his taste. "Sure, but you don't have to."

She shifted her attention to the receiver controls and fiddled with them. "I didn't disown my family like you, if that's what you mean."

"Don't think you—wait." The jumble of static on the screen had almost resolved into a fan-like shape. "It's a diffraction pattern of some kind."

Her head tilted to the side to take in a new angle. "Antiparticles? No, we'd be dead from the gamma rays by now."

"Maybe not. They could be a kind of, I don't know, antiqubits?"

Her expression was distorted by the prismatic pattern on the screen separating them. "*What* did you say you do again?"

"I told you—whatever I want. So an anti-qubit wouldn't technically be an 'opposite,' right?"

She absently reached down to scratch at the cut on her leg. "While theoretically possible, the odds of two identically-opposite qubits encountering one another is infinitesimally small."

"I didn't mean—stop doing that."

"Doing what?"

"Scratching your wound. How is the gel going to grow new skin if you keep displacing it?"

"Fine, fine. So you mean if there were qubits which represented the superposition of values between -1 and 0? Or even 1 and 2? Any range would be possible."

"But this isn't any range. It has to include 0 or 1, or it wouldn't be interfering with our communications."

Her eyes lit up in the luminescence provided by the screen. *Damn.* "Right. I can't believe I forgot! So what are we talking about here? These aliens use a shifted quantum field, but to communicate similar to how we do, or solely to interfere with our communications? No, it has to be the latter, because by definition the interference would be in both directions. Seems like a lot of effort on their part, but we don't understand their technology."

"Was there a question for me in there?"

"What? Oh. No. I mean...no. Do you agree?"

"That it's for interference, or communication?"

"Yes." She burst out laughing. The rich, luscious tenor filled the lab. She sucked in air, laughed some more, then abruptly moaned. "I am so hungry." Back into the bag, and after a few seconds she tossed him an energy bar before tearing one open herself.

"Sho, how dho we cougheracth ith?" The words came out thick and garbled by the gooey bar she was devouring, and it was his turn to laugh.

He chewed on the energy bar she had provided and pondered the question. "Protect our qubits. Shield them somehow."

Now her entire face lit up. *He was so royally fucked.* "Shielding, I can do."

ℛ

It had taken them more than two hours to rig up the necessary equipment to test their theory.

In the absence of a second QEC, he fashioned one with parts of the various testing equipment—surprising her, he thought.

While he constructed the rig, she worked up a mundane wave pattern to ensconce the qubits in and protect them from the diffractive interference. The waveguide shield needed to be in place at both ends here in the lab, or else the interference would still occur at reception.

"I'm ready down here."

"One more sec." She straightened up at the other end of the room. Grime still streaked along her left cheek, and no way was he going to tell her. "Got it. I'm sending you a message."

He squatted in front of the display he had hooked to the makeshift quantum receiver.

Hi, Noah

Okay, that was just adorable. He smiled over the top of the display. "Hi, Blondie."

"Ugh, my hair's probably a drab soot gray by now."

"It is, but 'Drab Soot Gray' simply doesn't have the same ring to it." He ducked beneath the table before she could hurl anything at him. "So do you think we can send a signal out beyond the range of the aliens' distortion? The receiver shouldn't have to be shielded if it's outside the field."

"We can try. I'm not confident we'll be able to get a message in return, though, not without the sender accounting for the adjustments we've made on this end."

He stood to traipse across the room. "Here's what we need to do. Let's put together a message relaying the situation here—make it as clear and direct as possible—and send it to someone who can use the information. Then we need to get out of here. Off this planet."

She followed his haphazard path. "Because we need to get all this information to the military leadership."

"Well, yes. But mostly because I'd really like to live, and the odds of doing so on this planet are surely decreasing by the hour."

29

SENECA
CAVARE

Isabela descended the marble steps of Division Headquarters to the street below. Traffic looked brisk, but she sensed a change in mood of the pedestrians passing in front of her. Gaits which normally might have been buoyant or energetic were now hurried to the point of being frenetic. Shoulders were hunched over and parents kept protective arms around their children.

Her heart clenched painfully at the sight. *Soon, Marlee, sweetheart. I'll be home soon. I promise.*

Remembering her mission, she jolted herself out of the reverie and joined the passersby as nonchalantly as possible. She did her best not to dart her eyes around in search of anyone following.

The personal shield Director Delavasi had provided her sent faint tingles roving along her skin like low-level static electricity. He'd said she wouldn't be able to feel it. He had lied.

Or it could simply be nerves. She patted the small stunner in her pocket to make sure it remained secure. Another gift from Delavasi. He'd shown her how to use it then promised she wouldn't need it. She rather hoped he hadn't lied about that, too.

She took the next left and scurried across the street, as much to blend in with the crowd as out of her own nervousness. Her instructions were to stop at a store, go check on her mother, then head for the spaceport. If she made it all the way to a transport for Krysk odds were she was in the clear, though an unidentified agent would be quietly coming along with her in case someone tried to grab her after she returned home.

According to Delavasi, Caleb had been framed for the EASC bombing with the help of someone inside the Division of Intelligence. She'd agreed to help draw this person out, because she wanted to help her brother and because she wanted the whole affair settled once and for all here on Seneca. Her daughter was in enough danger already from Alliance attacks and alien invaders without her bringing home murderous traitors.

She made a little bit of a show—too much?—of considering the placard of a convenience store before going in and buying a packet of trail mix, lemon tea and a temple press for a developing headache.

Taking a deep breath intended to bolster her resolve, she stepped back out on the street and continued toward the nearest levtram station. Dusk faded to night as the last rays of sunlight disappeared beneath the horizon, and a chill crept down her spine.

In the dark this plan suddenly seemed far more dangerous and rather foolhardy on her part. She wasn't her brother; she didn't know how to be a spy or how to work undercover. She wasn't a weakling, but she hadn't needed to physically defend herself since Sienna Bassi tried to pull her hair out in 9th level after Isabela stole her boyfriend. Her husband Daniel had dabbled in martial arts but he did it for relaxation, not self-defense.

She tried to recall that movement he used to perform, in the middle of the bedroom floor, where he—

She gasped as a wave of sorrow and pain bloomed out of nowhere to overcome her. For the briefest eternal second she could *see* him, shirtless and wearing loose black shorts, his wiry frame displaying only a hint of muscles no matter how much he exercised. His eyes closed as he made a show of concentration and even breathing while one leg swept out in a smooth arc—

—strong hands shoved her into an alley then slammed her into the wall before she was able to blink.

A blade was pressed to the side of her neck. It flickered against her shield, sending jolts of electricity down her arms. She realized she ought to try to reach the stunner in her pocket, but her arms were caught beneath the weight of the body squeezing against her.

Her attacker's voice snarled low at her ear. "You have ten seconds to tell me where Caleb Marano is. Otherwise I guarantee you will never see your daughter again."

She worked to focus on the person holding her captive. But it was dark and the alley was darker. The person was tall but not bulky; plenty strong though.

The blade dug into her neck; her skin was on fire from the shield's efforts to fight it. "Time's ticking, Ms. Marano. Where is your brother?"

The voice sounded familiar now. A woman's voice, maybe. A wispy lock of hair fell across her vision, gleaming ginger in reflected light from the street. The agent who'd taken her and her mother from the house?

Her own voice quivered and she didn't even have to fake it. "I don't know, I swear!"

"Liar. You—"

"STEP AWAY AND RAISE YOUR HANDS NOW!" The command boomed from the alley entrance. Her attacker shoved her to the pavement and took off running.

Isabela gingerly massaged her knee where it had slammed to the ground as a raucous, violent scuffle ensued deeper in the alley. After a few seconds she carefully stood and peered into the shadows, trying to discern what was happening.

"Ms. Marano, are you injured?"

She jumped and instinctively backed against the wall. The man approaching her looked familiar, though. One of the agents who had come and gone during her endless detention.

"It's all right. I'm not here to hurt you. I'm here to take you to a secure location, but do you need medical attention?"

Dizzy from adrenaline and terror and relief, she shook her head haltingly. How did Caleb do this every day? "I scraped my knee is all." His words finally succeeded in penetrating her brain, and she frowned. "I'm not free to go?"

"Sorry, ma'am, not quite yet. The Director is concerned there may be other people involved. We need to make absolutely certain you're safe."

She was too tired to argue. Exhausted, in fact. She gestured weakly. "Take me wherever you think is best."

R

INTELLIGENCE DIVISION HEADQUARTERS

Graham seethed. His seething was blatantly visible to anyone who happened by, for which he could give a rat's ass.

He stalked outside the interrogation room, fists clenching and unclenching at his sides. His vague reflection in the glass indicated his hair resembled that of a stereotypical mad scientist after being subjected to frequent abuse for the last three hours.

Bad enough it was one of his own agents, but his second in command? A woman he had trusted with the most sensitive intel, not to mention his personal doubts and concerns? A woman he had shared drinks with on the occasional evening? He had relied on her. Depended on her. Trusted her.

He may be a stupid, slow fool of an old man but he was damn well still in charge. He steeled himself, made a silent vow not to punch her and stepped into the room.

She gazed up at him, a tight sneer turning her face malicious in its coldness. Her hands, waist and ankles were restrained in webs but she managed to notch her shoulders up a fraction. "Sorry, sir. Looks like I won't be able to make it to work in the morning."

The expression she wore and sarcastic tone in her voice told him she didn't intend to bother claiming a misunderstanding. *Good.*

"I want to know one thing, Liz. Your interrogators will want to know a great deal more, but I merely require one piece of information. *Why?* Why cause a war? Why frame a fellow agent? Why kill a fellow agent?"

"I didn't kill Volosk. He was a decent man. Didn't kill Nythal, either, even if he wasn't."

"But you know who did, don't you?"

"That's more than one question, boss."

He placed both hands on the table and leaned over it until his face was positioned centimeters from hers. He'd decided 'who' was a far more important question than 'why.' His voice emerged as a low, rumbling growl. "Answer the question."

She shrugged. "I don't know enough to hand them over to you—assuming I would, which I don't plan on. Aliases, dummy accounts, dead-drop exanet addresses. You know how the game works, don't you, old man?"

She held his stare, but he took some small comfort in seeing a glint of fear in her eyes. "But I will tell you why, because I'm feeling charitable. We have cowered in the shadow of the Alliance for too long. We make nice and pay tribute to those arrogant fucks and they don't deserve it. We are so much better than those tawdry, pretentious pricks."

"That's what this is? You want to piss all over the Alliance because it'll make you feel special? You're nothing more than a playground bully desperate for validation."

"Bullshit. This isn't about me. Seneca is ready to rule this whole galaxy, if it only dared. I just tried to give it a little nudge."

"These are people's lives you're destroying with your little nudge. You're a psycho, and you aren't worth a second more of my time." He shoved off the table and tossed a dismissive hand in her direction. "Enjoy your nice, long stay in solitary. I'm sure someone will persuade you to talk eventually. Or not."

He stormed out and down the hall, waving off several agents via a glower threatening enough to ensure they stayed away.

Why did being one of the good guys have to be such a pain in the ass sometimes? He needed a stiff drink, then another one—but he couldn't spare the time because the galaxy continued to blow itself up apace. And it wasn't interested in taking a breather on account of his foul mood.

His glower sent two passengers scurrying out of the lift as he barreled onto it. It occurred to him he should perhaps tone it down a bit; he probably resembled a madman on a chimeral bender and if he wasn't careful someone would show up wielding a tranquilizer.

He grumbled at the empty lift and made a note to have the drink later.

A red light flashed in the corner of his vision. Concerned Isabela was in danger or another agent of his was dead or the aliens were making a house call, he opened the message.

None of those events had occurred, thankfully. Instead it was a priority request bumped up the chain to him.

And with good reason. A hoarse chuckle bubbled up from his chest as he stepped off the lift and hurried toward his office. For the first time in days, a feeling which might be misdiagnosed as hope stirred in his gut.

30

"**D**ammit, Helmsman, get your *zadnitsa* to an escape pod now!"
Russian. Him. Alex willed the scene to crystallize faster.
"But sir—"
"I can fly her, I assure you. Now get out of here—that's an order!"

She was on the deck of an Alliance military ship. A cruiser. She knew this not from the size or layout of the bridge but because of who stood at the railing which framed the sunken navigation pit.

Commander David Nikolai Solovy leapt into the pit, taking time to pat the helmsman on the back as he reluctantly departed the bridge before dropping into the flight chair and strapping in.

Dad.

He was so damn handsome, even with his dusky blond hair strewn wild by too many fingers being dragged through it and a thin sheen of sweat coating his neck and arms beneath rolled up sleeves.

He was now alone on the bridge. Everyone had been evacuated. Outside the viewport the incredible brightness of the Kappa Crucis blue supergiant dominated in spite of the clumpy H II gases.

Considerable debris from wrecked ships floated silently against the hazy white-blue glow. The *Stalwart* was extremely close to the supergiant. Dangerously close.

She rushed down to the navigation pit.

He monitored three screens while struggling to keep the cruiser steady and muttering a variety of colorful curses in Russian under his breath. The first screen displayed the position of the ship relative to the supergiant and the research station; the second tracked the Senecan fleet as it endeavored to navigate the debris-covered battlefield. The final screen monitored the status of the civilian and damaged military vessels currently evacuating the system behind the *Stalwart*.

She crouched beside him to stare up at his face in wonder. Her fingertips reached out to touch his arm, though it was impossible. She wasn't really there. Like the scenes that came before, she was merely witnessing a recording of an event from the past. But oh how it felt as if she were there.

His eyes rose to check the scene outside, shining liquid silver brimming over with intelligence and intensity. Inputting a series of quick commands, he rerouted all the navigation and weapon controls to his station. Seconds later the thrusters fired beneath them.

The battle had been a rout from the beginning, so the story went, and the landscape outside the viewport verified it. But for her the story of the Kappa Crucis Battle had always been so much more than a history lesson.

The Alliance had been steadily losing their previous dominance of the sector for weeks. When the decision was finally made to evacuate the research station staffed with scientists studying the region of active star formation, technicians, and their families, Strategic Command sent a regiment to oversee and protect the evacuation.

The Federation had placed monitoring equipment throughout the region; fearful the regiment was sent as a challenge to their increasing control, they sent an overpowering force to crush it.

Two Alliance cruisers, four frigates and sixteen fighters stood no chance against the Senecan division-strength fleet that arrived, but the evacuation was already underway and the civilians required protecting.

Rear Admiral Fuschida had taken the *EAS Lincoln* and three frigates to engage the Senecan forces before they reached the station. Commander Solovy and the *Stalwart* were ordered to stay behind and guard the station, while the final frigate and a flight of fighters provided close protection for the evacuating shuttles.

Fuschida mined the route from the research station, ejecting tactical fusion anti-ship mines throughout the area while leaving a narrow passage clear for the inevitable retreat.

Two of the frigates and most of the Alliance fighters were destroyed in the primary engagement with the Federation forces, though not before wrecking one of the Federation frigates and a number of their fighters. The third frigate dispatched to the front line suffered catastrophic damage and was left unable to navigate.

The *Lincoln* suffered considerable damage but, for a time, remained flightworthy. However instead of retreating, Fuschida elected to deploy additional mines until the last possible second behind a virtual wall of burning ship debris, unexploded ordinances and spaced soldiers from both sides of the battle.

Alex joined him in staring out the viewport. The destruction was immense, but she discerned the narrow passage through the mines and debris.

The final strategy of Rear Admiral Dawn Fuschida appeared to have been successful; the approach to the research station, the *Stalwart* and the derelict vessels represented a deadly gauntlet that would force the Senecans to approach single-file, one ship at a time, or risk detonation of the mines.

When the *Lincoln* at last splintered apart under the incessant fire from the bulk of the Senecan fleet, the hull ripped open and the balance of her tactical mines drifted into space, all but blocking the circumscribed entrance into the gauntlet.

She watched as her father did what she knew he would—position the Stalwart *broadside at the exit point of the gauntlet.*

This was the part of the story that had never made sense to her. For twelve minutes while the Senecan forces split—some working to clear a path through while others gave the mines and debris a wide berth and went the long way around—his ship had sat and waited. She had always assumed he was giving his own men time to evacuate or that his ship had been crippled beyond hope of flight. But it was apparent his ship was fully evacuated and, though slightly damaged, still flightworthy.

Despite the knowledge he would never hear her, she couldn't stop herself from screaming at him, begging him to just GO. The horror of his impending death loomed dark and foreboding in her mind like the event horizon of a black hole, yet a tiny spark of hope welled inside her that somehow, some way, his fate might be avoided.

"Dad, run, now! The path is blocked, and you can get away! Run, please!"

Then the ship shuddered violently from the force of an impact.

She stood and approached the viewport...and finally understood.

The Senecans had launched drones into the channel to move the mines. While it would be some time before the gaps were wide enough for the larger ships to proceed, fighters were able, with careful flying, to successfully navigate the gauntlet. Many of the evacuating vessels and the few fighters protecting them lacked sLume drives and had not yet reached the carrier waiting ten megameters away. But for the *Stalwart* blocking the way, the Senecan fighters would be able to run them down.

It was the reason he had positioned the ship across the breadth of the gauntlet exit. It was the reason he had not run.

Her father rerouted all power except for weapons and minimal life support to the starboard shields. As fighters began approaching they aimed for a small gap at the bow of the *Stalwart*, hoping to slide through.

The fire from the *Stalwart's* pulse lasers was relentless, and the first wave of fighters were shredded under the superior targeting and firepower of an Earth Alliance cruiser. By positioning the ship as he had, David Solovy had closed the gauntlet using his own ship as the final impenetrable barrier—save for a tiny path which became his own personal shooting gallery.

A deep male voice boomed through the bridge. "Unidentified Earth Alliance Captain, stand down and remove your ship from the area or you will be destroyed."

Alex ran back to her father, panic and despair in her eyes.

He sat in the pilot's chair, one hand idly hovering over the comm panel in front of him for several seconds. Then he casually kicked the chair back, withdrew his hand from the panel and delivered his response for himself alone.

"Go fuck yourself, you *svilochnaya peshka*."

The bridge shook, and her gaze darted back to the viewport.

The open space ahead had widened—more mines now prodded away—and a Senecan frigate traversed the gauntlet, weapons firing. Having recognized the lie of the tantalizing gap, multiple fighters hung back with the frigate and added their weaponry to the barrage. Her father couldn't return fire without changing the angle of the ship, which would open the exit and bring an end to his blockade.

Instead he reached over and his left hand activated another panel.

"Miri, are you there?"

Miriam Solovy's voice came over the comm, clear and strong above the sounds of wrenching metal and muffled explosions. "David? David, what's going on? We're getting reports of a battle near *Kappa Crucis....*"

He gave the empty bridge a grim smile. "Yeah, um…it's looking rather *khrenovo* for us, I'm not going to lie. But I've bought time for the research station to evacuate and provided cover for our damaged ships to retreat."

Her mother's voice dropped warily. "David, what are you doing? You're not thinking of being some kind of hero, are you?

"I…I suppose I am. Listen, I don't have a lot of time. The ship's getting banged up fairly badly at this point, but I—"

"Then get *out* of there. I'm sure you've saved plenty enough lives—save your own, dammit!"

A desperate sigh fell from his lips. "No can do, I'm afraid. The escape pods and a number of civilian shuttles from the station are still trying to get out of danger. I can't abandon them to be blown to bits."

"David Solovy, you listen to me this instant." Her mother's voice had gained an almost desperate tenor, but resonated with stern authority nonetheless. "I am giving you a direct order as your superior officer. You turn tail and you *run*. If you can't fly then you get yourself to an escape pod and you *escape*."

"Ah, *dushen'ka*, you know the ranking officer on the battlefield has command. Rear Admiral Fuschida and Commodore Giehl are dead, so that's me. I wish I could, I really, really do. Listen, I want—" the bridge quaked from the strain of a direct hit from the Senecan frigate impacting the lower decks.

He gripped the armrests tightly to keep himself in the chair "—I want you to tell Alex I love her so, so much, and I am *so* sorry I won't be there to see her grow up. But I just know she is going to be amazing. She already is. Tell her…tell her there are times in this universe when you simply have to stand for what you believe in, no matter the cost. And tell her she is going to shine like—"

"You tell her yourself. Goddammit, David, you and our daughter are the only two people I've ever given a damn about in this entire galaxy. Don't you *dare* leave me alone!"

She saw tears stream down his face as he struggled to keep his voice steady and hold onto the chair as the ship began to come apart around him.

"You'll be all right, Miri. You were always the strong one. You'll—"

"I don't *want* to be all right—I don't *want* to be strong! David, please...."

Tears ran freely down her virtual cheeks now as well as she sank to the floor in her own desperation. She had never heard such anguish in her mother's voice. Never, ever.

Dad, please listen to her, why can't you listen to her....

"Miri, my darling, my world, *moya vselennaya*, know that I love you with everything that I am. I love you more than all the stars in the heavens, more than—"

With a searing crunch the *Stalwart* exploded.

Yet she lingered for another breath, and so witnessed the true genius of her father's strategy and the depth of his final act of heroism.

As the hull of the *Stalwart* broke apart, mines it had been carrying spilled out into space. Unable to maneuver away in time, the approaching Senecan frigate crashed into two mines; the resulting explosion detonated a third.

The debris of the *Stalwart*, the Senecan frigate and a dozen mines sealed the gauntlet and blocked the Senecan forces in a final, non-negotiable way.

Finally, mercifully, the scene faded away.

She was left crumpled on the white floor in the white room, her body wracked by sobs. A hand stretched out into empty air, grasping for what was gone.

The number of times she had shed even a modicum of tears could be counted in single digits, but now she cried until she couldn't see for the tears, then until she couldn't breathe.

She cried for the wonderful, brave, beautiful man her father had been, and for herself for being robbed of the chance to see and know him as he truly was.

She cried for her mother, left alone to continue on, left to live through endless days and decades knowing what she had lost and would never have again.

She cried because she had been a foolish, selfish little girl who never completely comprehended what had transpired and what it had meant for those around her. The blindness and stubbornness and bitterness of a brokenhearted child had remained with her for far too long.

When there seemed no more tears capable of falling, she struggled past the dry heaves and sat up, resting her weight on one arm. Wiping soaked cheeks with the back of her hand, she gazed out at the empty room. "Thank you."

We do not understand. This was meant as a gift, a reward, yes. Yet you are obviously distraught. Why would you thank us for causing you such pain?

Sniffles interfered with her catching her breath, but she finally stood, only to wipe away yet more tears. "You've been watching us, studying us, for a long time, yes?"

Aeons.

"Yet you still have no idea what it means to be human, do you?"

The pause was noticeable.

You will wake up now. Your companion has proved himself most skilled and persistent. Our time together must come to an end.

"Wait! What about—"

31

The conference room in the Logistics building which had been claimed for EASC Board meetings was raucous to the point of chaos when Miriam arrived. Liam shouted ineffectually at the head of the table while aides scurried in directionless circles and small clusters of advisors conferred in hushed undertones. The Earth Alliance was under attack on two fronts, and no one wanted the blame to find its way to their feet.

If those in attendance had any sense, they would merely hope to still be alive and standing when the time came to place blame.

She ignored Liam and went to the control panel on the far wall. Her voice resonated above the furor, calm and clear. "Everyone, take your seats. We're starting this meeting now."

The din hushed as the attendees hurried to obey the implicit order. Brigadier Hervé nodded graciously at Miriam as she sat. "Admiral, before we begin let me say how pleased I was to hear your daughter has been cleared of involvement in the bombing. You must be so relieved."

Miriam's expression was a mask of pure professionalism. She couldn't be sure how much Hervé did or did not know about the role one of her employees had played in helping Richard make it happen. "I had confidence the truth would win out. Thank you, Brigadier." She didn't need to turn her head to feel Liam's glare burning into her left temple.

He was so busy glaring at her, in fact, he forgot to take advantage of the momentary quiet and start talking. So she did.

"As you are all aware by now, we lost contact with Messium thirty hours ago. We also continue to be unable to reach the colonies of Gaelach, Zetian, Karelia and Edero. Admiral Rychen, do you have any updated information regarding the situation on Messium?"

Lines were hewed into Rychen's features like grooves into steel. He wasn't raging or screaming, but in the twenty-six years she had known him she had never seen him appear so hard. Suffice it to say he was taking the attack on Messium personally.

"Only that all attempts to obtain intel have failed. I've sent three recon ships into the region; none have returned. Based on the few images we've seen on the news feeds I think we have to assume it is under assault from the alien fleet Admiral Solovy's daughter warned us about."

At last she tossed a look in Liam's direction. "Well, General, I trust you concede the aliens' existence now?"

"They're working for the Senecans! Those cretins realize they stand no chance of defeating us themselves so they've made a deal with the devil."

"General, my information says the Federation has similarly lost contact with four of its colonies. We have every reason to believe they are being targeted as well."

O'Connell scoffed. "Lies. Propaganda."

General Foster stepped cautiously into the dispute. "How do we propose to fight these aliens? If we can't even talk to one another once they're in the region, we can't coordinate our efforts. We'll be all but defenseless."

Rychen responded. "We have to try. We can't very well surrender without firing a shot."

Defense Minister Mori interjected. "Given what we've seen of this armada, everyone on Messium and the other colonies is probably dead by now. I recommend we pull back our forces and protect the First Wave worlds."

Miriam gestured for silence. "Gentlemen, please. Everyone on Messium is not dead, and we are not defenseless. Half an hour ago I received this communication." She sent the message to the display above the table.

Messium attacked by alien ships. Unknown casualties. Comms disrupted by shifted quantum field. Encase transmitter/receiver in photal fiber waveguide confining 520 THz signal to protect qubits at origin and destination. Setting message to repeat. Leaving refuge to locate functioning ships and attempt escape.

"How do we know this is genuine? Why did it come to you?"

Inwardly she groaned; was there nothing which could force Liam to see past his delusional prejudices and be rational for five seconds? If she wasn't so ridiculously happy about Richard's miracle work to publicly clear Alexis, she might be annoyed.

"It's genuine. The sender is personally known to me. I suspect she sent it to me because she needed a precise recipient with a known address and recognized I would be in a position to use the information to maximum benefit."

"What it says about protecting the qubits—will it work?"

She shifted her attention to Rychen. "Tech Logistics confirmed it in theory before I joined you. It's not a panacea. We'll have to adapt every communications hub and for now it will only work for point-to-point communication. One sender and one receiver. But it's a damn fine start."

"It damn sure is." He looked like a man who had just received a stay of execution. Not a pardon, but perhaps a pathway to one.

"Can we refocus on the ultimate enemy here? We bring Hellfire down on Seneca and let the aliens take care of what's left. Admiral Rychen, I want you to reinforce the blocka—"

Rychen stood in the confines of his holo and focused a laser-sharp stare on Liam. "O'Connell, fuck your holy war. Fuck your blockade. You can tell whoever the Prime Minister is this week I said so, too. Messium is my responsibility. It's my home. I am going to go defend it, and I am taking my fleet with me."

Miriam had to cover her mouth to silence the giggle which bubbled forth. She never, *ever* giggled. But that was simply beautiful.

Liam's fist slammed onto the table. It wasn't nearly so sturdy as the old one in the HQ penthouse, and it tipped upward from the force, sending those sitting at the other end scurrying backwards. "You'll be dishonorably discharged. Court-martialed for dereliction of duty."

Rychen cocked his head. "Possibly. But not until this conflict is won or lost, which is long enough for me to do everything I can to win it." He glanced around the room. "If you all will excuse me, I have preparations for an offensive to make."

With that, his holo winked out of existence.

AR

Richard was stepping into his office carrying a mug of coffee when Miriam practically tackled him in a bear hug.

"Thank you...thank you so much."

He hugged her awkwardly with one arm while directing most of his efforts at not spilling the coffee with the other. He tried to recall the last time Miriam had hugged him, or anyone as he'd seen for that matter. After David's funeral perhaps? Suffice it to say it had been some time.

She was smiling when she pulled back, the candid smile she only ever allowed a few people to see. It might be argued she was almost effervescent, but he would die before voicing the notion aloud.

He did match her smile though. "It was the least I could do. It's my job, it helps in our investigation and most importantly she's my god-daughter. I couldn't let her reputation be smeared, and I certainly couldn't let her be arrested for something she didn't do."

"Of course all of those things are true. Nevertheless, you've earned my undying gratitude."

He grimaced as he settled in his chair. "And now her claims have been vindicated. Kind of wish they weren't. Any word on Messium?"

"As a matter of fact, yes. You remember Alexis' friend, Kennedy Rossi?"

"A Rossi isn't someone you forget meeting if you possess any sense. Plus, she was kind of memorable I believe."

"Well she's on Messium now. She somehow managed to survive the initial barrage, figure out how the aliens are disrupting our communications and get a message out to me."

"Seriously? Impressive. Alex always did display shrewd tastes in associates."

"I suppose so...." Miriam's face fell, and he belatedly realized the statement was laden with complicated implications.

"Any word from her?" He didn't need to clarify who he meant.

Her head merely shook silently.

"I'm sure she's safe. She simply has a skilled intelligence agent covering their tracks, for which we should be glad."

"But they've been cleared now, unofficially. They can resurface."

"I'm not so convinced. Marano was targeted by the people who are pulling the strings on this conspiracy, and we don't know who they are. It may not be safe yet."

She nodded in acceptance, if perhaps contrived, of his better judgment on the matter. "On that note, any more progress on discovering who those people might be?"

"Some. I've put a deep trace on any communications mentioning her or his name within the Alliance infrastructure. Predictably there was a huge spike in the hours after the leak broke, but so far nothing more than the expected security department bureaucracy and ass-covering. I'd hoped something would stand out, and it still may.

"I do have a lead on where a portion of the explosives used in the Headquarters bombing came from. I'm optimistic it will turn out to be a lucrative trail. I was also able to determine Marano's file sent to me is in fact his official Senecan government file, which makes it increasingly likely someone inside their government is colluding with someone in ours."

With a sigh he sank deeper into the chair. "She was right about everything. This whole war is a setup. I'm convinced of it now. Powerful interests are manipulating us all for their own ends, though God knows what those ends are."

"What can we do? Much as I'd like to, we can't pull fully back from the Senecan front. From their perspective the war is still on. If we're not engaged and alert they'll have the opportunity to decimate us, and we desperately need every ship."

"The aliens are hitting them as well, so they face the same problem—" His brow creased, taken aback by the notification on his eVi. Will was requesting to enter? It was hardly the first time his husband had showed up unannounced, but it wasn't a common occurrence before the war began and even less so since his work life turned insane.

He depressed the lock, allowing the door to slide open. "Will, this is a pleasant surprise."

Will didn't look at him. Odd. "Miriam, it's good to see you."

"And you, Will. It's been too long, for which I bear the entirety of the blame."

"It has, and you were already forgiven. I apologize for interrupting, but I'm afraid this couldn't wait."

What did that *mean?* "What's wrong? Has something happened?"

Miriam started to stand. "I can leave if you—"

"No, please. It's better if you stay." Will's gaze finally fell to him, and Richard tried to process what he saw. Sadness, regret? But also a firm resoluteness.

"Is the room shielded?"

Richard frowned but activated the privacy shield from his desk. "It is now."

"Really shielded?"

Dread pooled in his gut; every instinct honed in twenty years of intelligence work screamed a rhapsody of shrill warnings in his eardrums. He forced them down to a dull roar. "Yes, *really* shielded. Will, what is going on?"

He saw Will's Adam's apple bob once, then a second time. The muscles in his locked jaw twitched. Richard had never seen him appear so desolate, though he had seen him look so determined.

"You want to end this war."

"Yes. We need to be able to focus all our assets on defending against these aliens. But—"

"But you need to talk to Seneca in order to do so." He pressed a small transmitter in his hand, and a holocomm screen burst to life between them.

"Director, allow me to introduce Colonel Richard Navick, Naval Intelligence Liaison to Earth Alliance Strategic Command. Richard, meet Graham Delavasi, Director of Intelligence for the Senecan Federation—and my boss. I believe the two of you have much to discuss."

PART III:

MAELSTROM

"The most powerful weapon on earth is the human soul on fire."

— *Marshal Ferdinand Foch*

32

Uncharted Space

Alex was lying on the floor in the center of a cavernous but otherwise empty room.

Caleb's heart plummeted at the sight of her crumpled body and arrested his forward progress in terror. Then she moved—a tiny, weak shift of her head—and he was again in motion, rushing ahead to drop to his knees beside her.

His hands roved over her body in search of injuries. But though her clothes bore multiple tears, he saw no blood or ripped skin, only mostly-healed scratches. He wasn't certain he was able to hear above the pounding of his heartbeat in his ears—or because the dragon's wail *had* blown out his eardrums—and tried to wrestle his pulse under control.

He brushed tangled hair out of her face. "Alex, baby, any chance you could wake up for me?"

At first there was no response. Alarm had begun to creep anew into his chest when she blinked…blinked again…and opened her eyes. Bleary and clouded, confusion flooded them as they darted blindly for several seconds before appearing to finally *see* him; they widened as she threw her arms around his neck and buried her face in his shoulder.

"Caleb…you're okay…."

He gathered her up fully in his arms. Tears he refused to allow to fall stung his eyes as he fought to rein in the fervor threatening to overwhelm him. She was safe and it was the only thing he cared about.

Even so, joy and a kind of awed relief bled into the quiver in his voice. "And so are you."

Her lips found his and crushed them in a frantic kiss, full of tumult and panic and need. He savored the perfect feel of her mouth on his, the perfection which her kiss represented, for everything he was worth. After all, it might be his last.

She gave a muffled laugh. Or it might have been a sob. Or it might have been him. With great reluctance he shifted position enough to be able to see her.

She looked an absolute wreck, hair falling in dirt-streaked tangles from what had once resembled a ponytail, lips parched and cracked, skin blotchy and....

He frowned in concern. "Have you been *crying?*"

She removed a hand from him to touch fingertips to her cheek, then stared queerly at the dampness they held. Her gaze lost focus as she drifted off.

The pad of his thumb ran softly over her jaw. "Alex?"

She jerked a little and offered him a weak smile. "Sorry. I...I'll explain later. How long have I been here?"

"A day and a half, give or take."

"Is that all? Do you have any water? My god I'm so thirsty."

"Absolutely." He fumbled for the water bottle, unlatched it and handed to her.

She greedily sucked it down as stray droplets spilled along her chin to join tear stains in cutting streaks through a thin layer of dirt coating her skin. Had the dragon dumped her upon the ground outside for her to be dragged in here?

She gave it back to him, then tilted her head hesitantly. "You're covered in blood again."

"I really am."

"Why are you always covered in blood when I wake up after being unconscious?"

"Usually for the same reason you were unconscious, I think."

A faint twinkle glittered in her eyes, gladdening him more than he would have imagined. "Are we going to have to go through another existential crisis because of it?"

He groaned. "God, I hope not. Can we not?"

"Yeah, we can not. But *why* are you covered in blood?"

"You'll see."

"What does that mean?"

"It means you'll see."

"All right...." A troubled expression dampened the twinkle as her attention left him to roam around the chamber. The walls, floor and ceiling were the same opaque, frosted glass-like material, but inside they were woven through with hundreds of grooves filled with pale, luminescent light.

"This is…well, almost what I expected. But were they intending on letting me lie here until I starved?"

"You don't remember anything? Have you been unconscious this whole time?"

Her nose crinkled up, the way it did when she got flustered. "Not exactly. It's complicated. I'll explain, I will, but give me a chance to get my bearings?"

"Whatever you need. I'm just glad you're safe." He huffed a quiet breath. "And alive."

She didn't quite seem to hear him as she drifted off once more. It was probably lingering disorientation.

Without warning she began to climb to her feet, only to waver unsteadily. She reached out to grab his hand, allowing him to help her up. He tried and failed to not cringe in pain at her tight grasp.

She flipped his hand over to reveal a deep, serrated gash cutting through the middle of his palm. "You're not merely covered in blood—you're hurt."

He reached up to run the other hand along her cheek. "It's fine. I'll bandage them up once we get outside. Promise."

"Them?" She clasped the hand at her cheek and tugged it away to inspect it. Eyes anxious with concern met his.

He smiled with as much easy confidence as he could muster. "I'm fine."

She regarded him warily for another second before letting his hands drop and wandering in a slow circle around the room. "Was there a…*dragon?*"

"There was in fact. Several, actually."

"Thought I might have dreamed that part." She drew in a long breath and visibly worked to put herself together. "Let's get out of here. I've a powerful need for some fresh air."

"I like this idea." He located his improvised weapon from where it had been discarded in his rush to reach her and fitted it back in the sheath.

"What is that?"

"My sword."

"Your…is it from my *ship?*"

"Yep." His shrug conveyed feigned casualness. "What? I had to improvise. Don't get your panties in a twist. I didn't chop up any critical systems."

"Is the handle from my *chair*?"

He grumbled under his breath; it had taken her less than ten seconds to notice. "I said nothing critical, didn't I?"

She squelched the mild displeasure in her countenance. "Okay. I trust you."

Not for much longer. Luckily she had begun hurrying toward the open doorway and missed the flash of disquiet he knew crossed his face. He shoved it away and followed her.

When she stepped outside she careened to a stop. He came up to stand beside her and waited in silence while she contemplated matters.

"You...you slayed the dragon."

"I did."

An eyebrow arched at the violence splayed upon the plateau. She canted her head to the side to inspect it at a different angle. Canted it in the other direction. Considered the scene dominated by the enormous dragon carcass.

Finally she gave an exaggerated sigh. "I got nothing."

"Sure." He brought his hand to rest on her shoulder with a chuckle. "Come on. Let's get off this ledge, in case it didn't live alone. We can take a break in the shade below. I'll get my hands cleaned up, and you can eat something."

"Yes. My god, I'm starving."

"You must be." If she hadn't had fluids or nourishment for nearly two days, no wonder she seemed disoriented and unsteady. He retrieved the pack and she followed him down the steep slope until it leveled off at a shaded copse of trees.

He offered the pack to her. "Food." After she accepted it he pulled the strap over his head and tossed the bloodied sword to the side.

"So the sword's what you used to slay the dragon?" He nodded as she passed him the med kit from the pack.

"Well that's very 'knightly' of you, but why not simply use a Daemon? Be a hell of a lot easier."

"A field encompasses this whole area. It repels all active technology, which created a problem."

"Clearly..." she squinted at the wooded mountainside, a puzzled frown darkening her features "...wait a minute. We're in the middle of the mountains? We couldn't *see* mountains where we camped. We have to be at least hundreds of kilometers from there. How did you get to me in a day and a half?"

His chin dropped to his chest. *Time's up.*

He didn't want to do this. Oh how he did not want to do this.

He finished wrapping the more damaged hand, set the med kit on the ground beside the sword and turned to face her. God, she was beautiful. Hair a tangled mess, clothes torn, lips pale and swollen, skin streaked in dirt. And she was *so* damn beautiful and flawed and perfect.

"I flew your ship to the base of the mountains. The shield blocked it from continuing any farther, so I hiked in from there."

A tight crease formed at her brow. "What? No, that's impossible."

"When the *Siyane* was docked on Romane, I had Mia hack it to grant me full access and flying rights."

Her irises flashed a pure argent, so bright they resembled the flare of a nova, in what could only be shock doubtless to soon be followed by outrage. "You...you did *what?*"

He forced down the jagged lump clogging his larynx. "I secretly had your ship hacked and acquired myself flying rights to it without your consent. I did it because I knew one day—somewhere, somehow—I would need it to save one or both of us. I didn't ask you first because I knew you would never permit it. You are insular and controlling and *bullheaded* stubborn and one day it is going to get you killed—but it won't be on a day I'm with you."

His pacing had grown furious around the small copse. His voice had started out flat and toneless, but more vehemence crept into each sentence. "And you know what? I'm not sorry. You can hate me if you want, you can believe I betrayed you and kick me out of your life if you must, but I don't regret doing it. Because I was *right.* And because I was right you're alive and safe, and nothing matters more to me.

"I would do it all over again, and again if I had to, because it meant I was able to save you."

A frayed breath ended the screed, heavy with bitterness and sorrow. He had meant every syllable, even if he hadn't realized all of it until the words spilled forth. Even if it didn't matter.

She was staring at him with the oddest expression. Whether it was fury or remained simple incredulity for the moment he dared not presume. Her irises now swirled melted silver, hiding her thoughts behind an impenetrable storm.

She opened her mouth as if to speak, only to close it. She pivoted as if to tramp about in a fit of anger...and stopped. Her brow furrowed and unfurrowed several times in succession.

He felt dangerously unhinged. Raw. The emotions he had kept bottled up inside for days so he was able to search for her and not crumble under their weight burst free from the dull ache in his chest to roil beneath his skin, searching for a path forward, demanding an outlet. But there was nothing he could do.

While he would never—could never—harm her, he thought he might gleefully harm anything else which came within reach. Another dragon should suffice. In fact, he'd offer a significant fortune for another dragon to show up right about now.

Looking into her eyes, he silently begged her to see the torment in his. Desperation bled out of his voice. "Do something, please. Yell, scream, hit me if you want, but do not just leave me standing here awaiting my execution sentence."

Her throat worked laboriously, as if it struggled to remember the actions required for speech. "I love you...."

All the blood rushed to his head, sending it spinning violently. His injuries were graver than he had realized, for him to be so delirious as to be hearing things. He choked out a precious few syllables. "What did you say?"

Her eyes narrowed, perplexed, as if she wasn't entirely sure herself. "You went behind my back and against my wishes, and I should be furious with you. And part of me *is*. But you're right— had you asked I would have said 'no,' and it would have been wrong of me.

"This is the second time you've saved me expecting to lose me for it, which is apparently far more selfless than anything *I've* ever done. And every time I try to work up a case of righteous indignation against you, all I can think is...I love you. I didn't real—"

His mouth was on hers and his hands were in her hair and he was pressing her into the nearest tree, stealing the air from her lungs though he owned none to replace it.

"What are you...doing?" It was barely a murmur.

He brushed feather-light kisses across her lips and back again. "Telling you I love you, too."

She smiled and made to recapture his kiss, then retreated, her gaze falling away. "No, you don't need to—"

"Would you *shut up* and let me tell you?" He smothered her gasp, drawing her in and this time refusing to let go. His lips ghosted over hers, over the tip of her nose, her eyelids, her jawline, her inexplicably tear-stained cheeks, always a phrase humming upon them. *"I love you...."*

A hand clawed up his shoulder to clench in his hair; the other found the small of his back and pulled him yet closer. She claimed his mouth in full, bringing a delightful halt to his roving kisses, and the fire, the passion he craved more than the most addictive chimeral surged to life in his embrace.

He was dizzy from euphoria at his unexpected, impossible turn of fortune...and perhaps a few other things like exhaustion and pain, but he chose to focus on the euphoria. She kept insisting on surprising him in the most astounding ways, challenging everything he thought he knew about people and the world and most of all, himself. *Remarkable.*

His hand drifted down her neck, along her collarbone, and continued on to dance fingertips over her breast through the fabric of her shirt.

She bit his lower lip and moaned in a manner he could best describe as, well, *visceral*, then dragged her teeth along his jaw to the crease of his ear. "Can I be mad at you now?"

He dipped a hand beneath her shirt and shoved the material upward. "No, you cannot."

"But you—" His mouth silenced the rest.

"When you put it like...*unh*...." With his thumb he traced circles on her bare breast beneath her shirt, delighting in how she trembled at his caress.

As her fingers snaked up his spine, he dropped both hands to her hips and hoisted her up—

—and winced as the shredded ligaments in his left shoulder screamed in protest and refused to comply.

Instantly she drew back to regard him suspiciously. Her lips were swollen once more, this time from his abuse of them. "You are *such* a liar. You are not 'fine.' You can barely stand."

His eyes squeezed shut as passion and pain waged war, his body the battlefield. His voice came out half frustrated, half graveled. "You exaggerate. I can stand fine. I am fine..." he sank into her arms "...or I will be." Seeing the earnest worry animating her face, he brought a hand up to run gently along her jaw to the curve of her neck. "I promise."

She sighed and kissed him, so wonderfully soft and tender and poignant. They remained there for untold seconds or minutes or hours, before he pulled away a fraction.

"Tell me what happened to you?"

33

NEW BABEL
INDEPENDENT COLONY

The first thought Olivia had when Marcus' figure shimmered into existence was, *he looks frazzled.*

He did his best to conceal it, donning a poised mien and ostensible confidence. But she had observed him in this precise setting a number of times now. He was cracking beneath the pressure.

She hadn't believed him so weak, so easily broken. Perhaps there was more at work than merely a galactic war and an alien invasion.

"Olivia. You said it was urgent. You need to discuss something?" His tone came out clipped. Strained.

"Yes, Marcus. We need to discuss the small matter of the *aliens tearing up the eastern half of settled space.* They represent a small kink in our plans, wouldn't you say?"

"Admittedly, it is a complication. I'm working to resolve the matter as quickly as I can."

Suspicion flared in her gut. "Resolve the matter? If it's all the same to you, as your partner I'd like a few details. You're now the most powerful person in the galaxy, so how do you plan to 'resolve the matter'? Do you enjoy a direct line to the alien leadership to negotiate a truce?"

His eyes flickered. Something akin to fear passed across them. A blink and it was gone. "No, of course not. But—"

"Son of a bitch, you *knew.* How long have you been keeping your little secret from me? A week? A month? A year? Did you know they were coming when you presented your plan to me?"

"Olivia, you must realize—"

"The Alliance-Federation war was supposed to increase my power—and yours—in the galaxy. Instead the war has weakened our ability to defend against aliens currently wreaking havoc on over a dozen worlds, and something tells me they're just getting warmed up. At this rate the galaxy will be left in ruins. Marcus, I stand to lose everything."

His head shook as if to deny the veracity of her claims. "I can convince them to stop. It was the whole point of rising to this position. I can get them to understand we won't be a threat to them. You simply need to give me a little more time."

She only barely prevented her jaw from falling open in naked disbelief. "Are you telling me you really do have a direct line to their leadership?"

For a beat his usual confidence returned in the twist of his mouth and set of his chin. "In a manner of speaking."

"Oh, you dirty, conniving little snake. Did you lie to me about everything or solely the part where the war would be to my benefit?"

"Olivia—"

"You required me to make the war happen, so you used me for your own ends."

"We used one another. That's how the world works. I thought you of all people understood this."

"Nice try, but no. You used my resources, my people, my money and my influence for purposes contrary to those you presented."

He brandished a visage so malevolent he'd never dare show it in public. "Would you have believed me had I told you aliens were talking to me?"

"You could have tried me."

"I think I was correct to refrain from telling you or anyone else."

Would she have believed him? She supposed it depended. "So what was the actual plan, then?"

He exhaled heavily, his shoulders dropping as the momentary arrogance abandoned him. "My contact warned me we needed to stop expanding to the northeast—toward the Metis Nebula, as it turns out. It threatened dire consequences if we continued."

"'Dire' can mean a number of different things, Marcus."

"Well this time it meant extinction, all right? Something none of us want. But Seneca controls the northeast region of space. Perhaps the aliens should have chosen someone in the Federation government to approach, but they didn't. They chose me."

Bitterness now dripped from his increasingly hoarse voice. "The war was intended to distract everyone—to focus our attention inward rather than outward and pause our expansion. Ultimately the Alliance wins the war and under a united government expansion efforts are redirected west and south."

"United under your leadership."

"I assumed that went without saying. Unfortunately, events moved too rapidly. The Senecans lobbed a probe into Metis and Ms. Solovy got nosy. The aliens began to move before we were ready. But there's still time. I can still make this work. I can convince them to back off and give me an opportunity to win the war."

Her weight settled on her back foot as she crossed her arms over her chest and stared at him, now legitimately baffled. "How delusional are you, aliens in your head notwithstanding? The war we launched is going to make things worse, not better. If these aliens intend to exterminate us, we probably ought to consider fighting them instead of one another."

"The media doesn't yet have the footage from the first colonies hit, but I've seen it, and I'm not at all sure we can fight them. Besides, it's too late to go back. If we try to reverse course now it will only cause more chaos and confusion."

He implored her in a weak attempt at persuasion; it definitely wasn't his best work. "Please, let me handle the situation."

She should have known, those many years ago in Rio. She should have known when the feral kid smiled at her with such chilling conceit that she could not, under any circumstances whatsoever, trust him.

"I don't think so, Marcus. You lied to me. You manipulated me. You betrayed the core underpinnings of our arrangement. You're blinded by your own ego and pride and you will get us all killed. Good luck, Mr. Prime Minister. I'm out." She cut the link.

If she ever saw him in person again, she would kill him. She might kill him anyway. But first things first—she had to figure out what she was going to do to save her organization, her life's work.

It occurred to her then it might take saving their entire damn civilization in order for her to do so.

34

Miriam considered the midmorning sun outside the window. She could almost see the autumn chill in the air.

Will Sutton, a Senecan spy? It seemed impossible, yet she had witnessed the undeniable proof laid bare in front of her own eyes, and in dramatic fashion.

She couldn't fathom what Richard was going through. Following the odd, almost surreal conversation with the Senecan Intelligence Director, Richard had bolted with Will chasing after him, and she hadn't as yet been able to talk to him about it all. The stark truth was this might represent the best chance they had to restore sanity to the galaxy, but she wished it hadn't come at such a cost to her dearest friend.

"Admiral, there's a Lt. Colonel Jenner here to see you."

She welcomed the interruption from the troubling thoughts. "Good. Send him right in."

Malcolm gave her a sharp salute on entry. "Admiral. It's a pleasure to see you again."

She returned the salute then, instead of sitting behind her desk, motioned him over to the small table she had managed to squeeze into the office and sat opposite him. "You have had a most exciting few weeks, Colonel. Yet you've managed to not only stay alive, but save others' lives while comporting yourself with honor."

"Thank you...I'm sorry, did you—"

"You're getting a promotion. You should receive official notice in the next hour or two. You'll also receive a special commendation eventually, but as you can expect the bureaucratic channels are a bit tied up at present."

He sounded somewhat stunned. "I'm honored, ma'am, but I was merely doing my job."

"Yes, and better than most." She poured a glass of tea from the pot on the table. It was one of the few acts of respite she allowed herself in a time of war. "I understand you find yourself without a ship to command."

"Yes, ma'am. Northwestern Command is losing ships even faster than soldiers."

"Your impressive tactical decisions at both Orellan and Desna have not gone unnoticed. It's your choice—and won't impact the promotion or the commendation—but I need to ask you to risk your life once more."

"We're at war on two fronts, Admiral. We're all risking our lives."

Her chin dipped in acknowledgment. "Fair point. Admiral Rychen has a mind to retake Messium from these aliens or at least buy some time and opportunity for survivors to escape. I'd like you to assist him in this endeavor."

Malcolm's eyes widened briefly before he restored professional decorum. "I'd be gratified to help in any way you or he sees fit."

"Good. He is assembling his forces above Scythia as we speak. I'm sending you a full report containing everything we know about the aliens as well as the resources Rychen has at his command so you can be fully up to speed when you arrive. He is an excellent leader and an honorable man, but he needs capable commanders who can think for themselves and instinctively grasp the nature of battle. I believe you will work well together."

"I'm confident we will. He has a sterling reputation, and based on your endorsement I expect he's earned it." It was a ceremonial statement delivered in the finest military tradition; but having done so, his manner lost a measure of formality. "I can't tell you how relieved I was to learn Alex has been absolved of involvement in the bombing. How is she?"

Her gaze drifted to the mediocre view out the window. "I'm afraid I don't know."

"Ma'am?"

She forced herself to refocus her attention on her guest. "She's been unreachable since shortly after the accusations were made public. I don't know where she is. Given the state of our relationship—of which I imagine you're aware—this may not come as a shock. But to my knowledge no one knows where she is."

His own gaze leapt away at the news, but even in profile she saw his face fall. "I'm sorry. I don't...I'm sure she's all right. She is...extraordinarily resourceful."

Miriam's response was tainted by sorrow. "Yes, she is."

Awkward silence lingered for a moment, and she simply didn't have the will to end it.

Finally Malcolm cleared his throat and stood. "If you don't need anything else, I'll be going. I need to run home and kiss my wife, pack a new bag and catch a transport for Scythia."

"I won't keep you. Everything should be in order, but please don't hesitate to contact me directly if you run into any problems."

She hesitated for a beat, then gave him a wistful smile as she stood. "I remember those days, when David would dash through the house on his way between assignments. Don't feel guilty if you linger a few extra minutes."

"In that case, I may do so." He turned to the door...then back to her. "Permission to speak freely, Admiral?"

"Granted, of course."

"She's more like you than you realize."

Her lips pursed in puzzlement. "I don't follow."

"Forgive me if I'm off-base, but I suspect you believe Alex is her father made over. And though I regrettably never knew him, as I understand it she definitely inherited his adventurous spirit and irreverence.

"But in truth, she's your daughter through and through. Driven, determined and supremely confident in her abilities. Expecting others to meet the highest standards or else they're not worth her attention. Refusing to show weakness no matter how difficult the situation. And...well, perhaps a tiny bit wary of letting others get close. I say this as someone grateful to have been allowed to get close, for a time."

He shrugged, wearing a sheepish look. "I just thought you might want to keep that in mind when you see her again."

A parting salute and he was gone. She was left standing there, stunned into silence.

Why would he say that? Why would he *think* that? She had assumed he knew Alexis better, seeing as they were together for nearly three years. Perhaps time apart had clouded his memories.

Regardless, she and her daughter had never shared so much as a favorite food in common; they shared nothing except burgundy hair and a complete inability to hold a civilized conversation with one another.

And possibly a formidable drive and level of determination once their minds were set on a goal. And…

…was Malcolm *right*? He was right that Alexis had inherited David's adventurous spirit and, as he noted, irreverence. Might he have been correct about the rest? No, he couldn't be.

When she looked at Alexis, David stared back at her. But where David had been open, carefree and vibrant, her daughter regarded her coolly, closing off whatever spirit she possessed behind shuttered eyes and a defensive bearing.

Just like herself. "Oh, David…."

"…looking for the commanding officer?"

Miriam waved the medic off and pressed the medwrap to her neck as she twisted around in the direction of the voice. "Can I help you?"

"Captain David Solovy, 3rd Regiment, 1st Brigade, NW Region. Apologies, ma'am, but the information I was provided stated a Commander Llahso oversaw the station here on Perona?"

The captain stood twenty centimeters taller than her. She made an effort to straighten her shoulders in spite of the fracture in her collarbone, which she decided was a fairly stupid thing to do when a jolt of pain screamed down her arm.

"He does—or did." She gestured over her shoulder with her uninjured arm at the row of medical cots behind her. "He took a TSG to the chest three hours ago. The doctors don't know if he'll survive. I'm the XO, Major Miriam Draner."

"That's unfortunate for him. I hope he recovers." A sly smirk pulled at the man's lips. "Less unfortunate for me, however. It is a pleasure to meet you, Major."

She realized she was staring and schooled her expression. "What can I do for you, Captain Solovy?"

"Ah, right. My mission. I lead the tactical assault detachment to the EAS Trafalgar. We're the reinforcements the Commander requested. I'm here to help you dig these gandonov out of their hole."

The medwrap must be secure by now, so she dropped her hand from her neck. She had caught the edge of a Daemon beam in the doomed push which had taken out Llahso. The proximity of the wound to her carotid artery meant it had been a close call, but she didn't have time to dwell on it now.

She indicated for Solovy to follow her and headed out of the med tent. "Excellent. I'm glad your team has arrived. We nearly took out their primary turret in the last offensive, but we failed and are down seven soldiers as a result."

He matched her step for step through the center of the hastily erected forward operating post as they crossed to the command center in the opposite corner. "What's the background? My briefing was scarce on details."

She shrugged, which was also a fairly stupid thing to do. A cringe followed it. "Your standard over-committed radicals. In this case I believe they imagine Perona will be better served by a Leninist utopia, but they—"

"Goret etim pidarasam v adu...." He cleared his throat. "Apologies, ma'am. Please continue."

Interesting that the memories of the damage inflicted on Russia still lingered more than three hundred years later in its descendants. "Yes. Well. As I was about to say, they are exceedingly well armed and have fortified their compound with a noteworthy amount of ballistic weaponry. How they got their hands on such weaponry is a matter for another day, but suffice it to say we were not prepared for the extent of it."

"Is that why Commander Llahso was injured?"

"No. He was injured because he was showing off for the soldiers in an attempt to compensate for his innate insecurities. By the point he insisted on leading an incursion we were fully aware of the terrorists' capabilities."

"Then I'm even more glad you're in charge now."

She frowned as they reached the command center, unsettled by how familiar the man was being, but was interrupted by three *separate subordinates arriving to update her on various details. Finally she succeeded in activating a large screen above the center table.*

"The primary obstacle is one of vantage. Their compound lies in a depression at the base of the mountains and there's no way to get to the two large turrets they've set up behind the outer wall without exposing ourselves. Our drones are shot down before they can lock and fire."

"A couple of shots from a fighter would take them out. But I'm guessing you're trying to avoid the collateral damage sure to result."

"Those are our orders, yes. The Peronan governor doesn't want a bloodbath, lest he be accused of slaughtering 'freedom fighters.' It is complicating matters."

"Politicians usually do."

She spared at sideways glance at Solovy. Distinctive Slavic cheekbones and a strong jaw should have given him a hard, cold appearance, yet somehow his features were warm and welcoming.

A corner of his mouth curled up, and she jerked her gaze away. "It's not my place to question my orders, not as of yet. The fact is we need an infiltration team to clear the wall and take out those turrets so a larger force can enter, subdue the leaders and arrest the followers."

He nodded firmly. "We can do that."

"How many soldiers did you bring?"

"Enough."

"How many, Captain?"

He rolled his eyes. Entirely too familiar. "Twelve. Counting me."

She snorted. "It's your corpse."

He shifted to lean against the table and face her. "If my team goes in and takes out both turrets and the wall, clearing the way for your soldiers, will you have dinner with me?"

"Excuse me, Captain?"

"Dinner. With me. Preferably somewhere offering candles and proper Russian vodka, but I'll understand if Perona doesn't yet have such finery. Alternatively, a picnic in these picturesque mountains and I'll bring the vodka."

Of all the impertinence! How dare this man swagger into her command center and lounge about on her command table and throw around romantic advances in the middle of a combat situation....

"Captain, please remove yourself from my table. You're interfering with the data reaching the screens."

He pushed off the table. "Haven't had any difficulty settling into command, I see."

"I do what is required in the circumstances."

He regarded her silently for several seconds. There was nowhere for her to go to escape those piercing eyes. "Do you now. You haven't answered my question."

"That's because your question was inappropriate and I have far more important matters to consider. Like the fact you didn't bring enough men. I'll need to loan you several of my experienced officers. Please try to not get them killed."

"Keep your men, Major. I brought enough."

"I am in com—"

"Go to dinner with me."

She dragged a hand along her jaw; somewhat to her dismay, it came away streaked in blood. Was it hers? She didn't think so. Llahso's, then. "Captain, you—"

"After this mission is complete and while off-duty, don't worry. I respect the regulations. I have a few days leave left for the year. I'll stay here an extra day or two. Or three."

She glared at him dubiously. "You would give up your leave to stay on this backwater planet and take me to dinner? You only met me five minutes ago."

He smiled, and god help her but it was a remarkable sight. "Life is short and you are beautiful. Go to dinner with me. It will give me motivation to make it out of the compound alive."

"If it will halt this egregious flirting and allow you to focus on the mission, fine. Now can we please concentrate on devising our plan of attack?"

"Of course, nastoyatel'."

Alone in her office, Miriam sank against the wall and brought a hand to her mouth.

She had never met anyone like him, before or since. The dashing manner, casual confidence and easy charisma had been evident immediately. The tremendous soul, fierce loyalty and pure heart had revealed themselves later, though not so very much later.

God how she missed him.

Then she was laughing, in a way which bore a tinge of the wild, free laugh she had only ever shared in David's company. He had ignored all her defenses as if they were invisible and forced his way inside with grace, charm and aplomb. Perhaps this Marano character had done the same to Alexis....

But she didn't know how to do such a thing. Especially when she was so busy propping up her own barriers.

35

PANDORA

Richard had visited Pandora several times in his younger days, but it had been years. Nevertheless, the stark shift in the atmosphere of the devil-won't-care world from the previous trips was starkly apparent.

The spaceport bustled not with tourists eager to begin a vacation but with desperate visitors and residents alike eager to depart, yet not knowing where to go. 'West' did seem to be the general consensus and transports to Arcadia, Atlantis, Demeter, Earth and Fionava were all marked as sold out for days. Though he'd feel guilty displacing a civilian, he would be able to obtain a seat when the time came.

His meeting was at a pub not far from the spaceport. He decided to walk.

During the flight his mind had been too consumed by matters other than his mission and he needed to get his head canted straight. But first he allowed himself one final moment to despair in the revelation which had brought him here, and its aftermath.

> He was not a violent man. He had committed acts of violence of course, in the First Crux War and later as a field agent. He wasn't proud of many of them...a few he was, if you got him drunk enough.
>
> Still, his nature was not that of a violent man. As a rule he preferred to resolve tense situations through dialogue, or if dialogue failed through threats he preferred not to be required to fulfill.
>
> But when Will grabbed his upper arm as he rounded the corner toward the lift, he came within a heartbeat of cold-cocking the man who pretended to be his husband.
>
> "Give me a chance to explain."
>
> A stinging, bleak chill vibrated along his skin, freezing the fire in his chest. Sounds and voices echoed at him through a hollow

tunnel. His soul was flayed inside out; he felt brittle, as if the faintest touch would shatter him to pieces on the ground.

The only thing which held his body together, if not his mind, was the knowledge he had a job to do. His life may lie crumbled in ruins at his feet, but he could save other lives. He could end this war, and perhaps his obituary would acknowledge the contribution he had made in the otherwise farce his life had been.

"I'm going to Pandora to meet your boss. If your belongings aren't out of the house when I return, I will burn them. Do not contact me. Do not attempt to see me. You've made a fool of me for fifteen years. Don't think you can do so for one breath longer."

"Richard, please—"

The anguish in the eyes of the man standing opposite him did not breach his frozen shroud. "Goodbye, Will."

He spun—violently—and lurched onto the lift. He didn't look back.

Richard leaned against the façade of a theatre and closed his eyes. He corralled all the thoughts, images and sentiments that would paralyze then crush him, and forced them behind a wall in a dark corner of his mind. There they would remain until this was done, after which they were free to do to him as they pleased.

Then he opened his eyes and continued walking down the street.

He knew a good bit about Graham Delavasi, as an adversary if not an outright enemy. Former military special forces, he had joined Senecan Intelligence after the First Crux War. Gaining a reputation for pulling no punches and exhibiting a keen eye for artifice and duplicity, he rose quickly within the department despite playing fast and loose with the rules and refusing to respect political niceties. He had been named Director of Intelligence three years earlier.

His reputation had always struck Richard as indicating the kind of man he might have liked were they not situated on opposite sides of the diplomatic divide. Now it appeared he had his chance to find out.

The Director had beat him to the pub and claimed a booth in the back corner. Other than those seated at the bar, the establishment wasn't crowded and no patrons occupied the surrounding tables. Still, a surveillance shielding device sat discreetly on the table.

He slid in the booth before Delavasi could stand, but the man extended a hand across the table. "Colonel Navick, I'm glad we were able to meet in person. Under the circumstances I'm sure it was as difficult for you to slip away as it was for me."

He accepted the hand but kept his bearing formal. Delavasi did not, adopting a casual slouch in the booth like he was about to toss back a few beers with a buddy.

"It seems we have ourselves a small alien invasion. Any chance we're going to be able to stop them?"

"Well, stopping our own war first would certainly improve the odds."

"So it would." Delavasi grimaced. "You and I are supposed to be the smart ones. Nothing gets past us—not the machinations of politicians and not the schemes of criminals. But my friend, I believe we have been played."

Richard wanted to protest. They were not friends, not by a long shot. But if this turned into a pissing contest five minutes in the whole game was lost. "I've reviewed the evidence which leaked, and more. Your agent did not perpetrate the EASC Headquarters bombing."

"I agree. We've been studying the wreckage from the fighters shot down on Palluda. They don't appear to be Alliance fighters, though they did fire Alliance missiles."

"Thirty-two VI-guided short-range missiles from the Southwestern Regional Headquarters on Deucali are unaccounted for. They went missing during a ware upgrade. What about Chris Candela?"

"Can't say. My instincts tell me he wasn't the perpetrator. Unfortunately, the man who could have led me to the perpetrator was murdered a week ago."

"I heard a rumor you might've acquired a copy of Santiagar's autopsy report. Nothing useful in it to help on that front?"

"It's gone. Stolen in yet another murder, this time of one of the best men in my department."

"They're covering their tracks, cleaning up loose ends."

"Yep." The man seemed to deflate, his shoulders dropping a few centimeters. "My deputy was involved in this conspiracy. She isn't disposed to talk, but I only removed my head from my ass in regards to the matter yesterday, so I'll know what she knows before long. Of course, 'before long' may not be soon enough."

Interesting. An admission of vulnerability. Delavasi was going a fairly long way to get Richard to trust him. "I imagine that's how Caleb Marano's Senecan Intelligence file ended up in my inbox."

"It did? Fucking Oberti...."

"If it helps, an as yet unknown but powerful member of the Alliance government is part of it as well."

"The one who doctored the Headquarters records?"

"Worse, the one who ordered them doctored."

"We're facing a clusterfain of epic proportions here, aren't we?"

Richard chuckled darkly; the eccentric Senecan curse had not yet penetrated Earth popular culture, though it was starting to pop up and the connotation was clear enough. "We're going to need proof if we expect to make a go of pulling the politicians down off the ledge."

"Agent Marano is in the company of someone I believe is an acquaintance of yours. I don't suppose you know where they are? I would really like to talk to him something fierce."

It shouldn't be a revelation Delavasi knew he was a friend of the Solovys. He likely knew everything about Richard's life. The logical, analytical component of his brain reminded him the information was public record, discoverable via a simple exanet search, and thus far it was the only personal card the man had played. He reinforced the wall in his mind.

"I wish I did. I assume that means you don't either?"

"Wish I did." Delavasi shifted uncomfortably in the booth. "Listen, before we go any further...about Will Sutton—"

"Director, I am here to do my job and try to save a significant number of lives. Do me the courtesy of not injecting my personal life into this arrangement and I won't walk out of this pub."

"Point made. So where does all this leave us?"

Richard suppressed a smirk. It pleased him that the man had backed down so quickly, and was looking to him. He appeared to be in charge.

He leaned forward against the table. "I didn't select Pandora solely because of its neutrality and convenient location. I've got a lead on a portion of the explosives used in the Headquarters bombing. A rat grew a conscience and told a Pandora detective one of the local criminal groups was scrambling to try to move a stash of HHNC off-world a couple of days before the bombing, and quickly. The detective told an Alliance operative stationed here."

"Excellent. You got a name?"

"Nguyen. Shall we go see what he has to say for himself?"

The detective, Jere Kulm, took them to the neighborhood Nguyen operated in and quickly located him on the patio of a local dive.

They surveyed the environs and flow of the crowd until they both felt comfortable no surprises lurked in the corners, then positioned themselves nearby. Minutes later Nguyen departed the restaurant and started down the street.

Delavasi slid up beside him and slung an arm over his shoulder while Richard crowded him from the other side and quietly grasped his arm at the elbow. "Let's take a walk."

"What the—"

"It is in your best interest for you to lower your voice, Mr. Nguyen." He complied but then proceeded to struggle and sag between them.

Delavasi made a face over Nguyen's head. "Jesus, do not make us drag you. You look like a goon."

They took advantage of the man's uncertainty to persuade him farther down the street and into a dead-end alleyway, then let him scramble out of their grasp and into the rear wall.

Short, bulky and sporting a series of pockmarks on his face and a crooked nose, the man plainly had never invested in gene therapy. His manner was ragged and abrasive, suggesting he had grown up on the streets. Presumably intelligent enough to run what Kulm said was a decent-sized group of criminals, he was still not many decisions away from the gutter.

Nguyen prowled the deepest corner of the alley as if he were some sort of caged predator, recognizing there was no escape but unable to accept his fate. Richard and Delavasi blocked his exit route. In the improbable event he got past them, Kulm waited five meters beyond with a Daemon resting on his thigh as he leaned casually against the wall.

"Who the fuck are you guys? This some kind of shakedown?"

"You moved forty kilos of HHNC sixteen days ago. Where did you move it to?"

"Don't know what you're talking about."

"Sure you do. You were in a hurry and got sloppy. People noticed."

"What good does it do me to tell you squat?"

Richard gestured to the street. "There's a war going on out there, with chaos hot on its tail. You've probably heard about aliens coming our way? So if you disappear, everybody just figures you cut your losses and ran."

"You pretty boys threatening to kill me?"

"Nope. Merely a nice long stay in an Alliance military prison…" he glanced in Delavasi's direction "…or a Senecan one. I've heard they're far worse."

Delavasi nodded in exaggerated agreement. "Far worse. Except for that one you guys run in Siberia. You still have that one, right?"

"Oh yeah. The guards have trouble keeping the prisoners from freezing to death, though. Some of them end up gnawing their own fingers off to stop the frostbite from spreading. It's not pretty."

Nguyen's dark irises darted between the two of them like a junkie catching the scent of his next high. "And if I recall a few things?"

Delavasi made a show of considering the question. "Depends on how much you recall."

"Son of a…word gets out I talked and I'm a corpse by morning. The people I work for do not take kindly to rats."

Richard regarded him with casual disdain. "I bet they don't. If we were to walk you out of this alley and escort you down the street then leave you with a pat on the back and a vocal thanks, it would be a shame if someone misinterpreted what they saw."

The man's eyes widened; he sank down the rear wall and buried his face in his hands. "Earth. They went to Earth. Vancouver. That's why you're here, right?"

Richard hid his relief beneath arms crossing over his chest. He stared at the man, who had shrunk in on himself to become a small, shriveled pile on the ground. "On whose order?"

Nguyen's voice shook. "Kigin."

Delavasi looked over his shoulder to Kulm, who indicated he had caught the response. "Zelones lieutenant."

Richard crouched beside Nguyen and leaned in close. "*And?*"

"Kigin talks a tough game but he doesn't take a shit without the Queen Bitch's approval."

Behind him Delavasi laughed. "I assume you mean Olivia Montegreu."

"Who else, man? They say she personally pries the toenails off underlings who displease her, usually after she's half-fucked them to death." His entire body quivered. "Do what you gotta, but don't leave me to that psychopath!"

Richard stood and turned to Kulm. "Take him in and keep a tight lid on him until I give you the all-clear, then cut him loose. Rough him up a bit before you do so he can hit the street like a badass instead of the pansy he is."

"You got it, sir." The detective yanked Nguyen up, shoved him into the wall and snapped restraining bracelets on him. "Let's take a trip. Trust me when I tell you it's for your own good."

After Kulm had exited the alley, his prisoner dragging along behind, Richard sank against the rear wall. The adrenaline rush from the encounter wasn't lasting. "So what now? Shake down this Kigin? We can't exactly show up on New Babel for a friendly chat with Montegreu. We'd be dead within a minute of stepping off the transport."

Delavasi stalked through the alley, his trench coat billowing in his wake. "We may not need to do either." He met Richard's expectant gaze. "You fancy a brief detour to Krysk?"

Richard frowned. "Director, I appreciate everything you've given me so far, but it will have to be a damn good reason for me to accompany you to a Federation world in the middle of a war."

Delavasi nodded. "How about I can get Olivia Montegreu to come to us. And please, it's Graham."

36

"S o maybe that's why it allowed you through the field with your cybernetics active."

Alex regarded him askance. "What's why?"

She and Caleb were sitting on the ground, backs propped up against a large boulder. He had grudgingly performed minor first aid on the worst of his wounds. The remains of what passed for a meal—MREs and energy bars—hadn't yet been cleaned up and were scattered on the ground beside them.

When they had finished eating she had rested her head on his shoulder, draped a leg over his and laced their fingers together. And he had listened.

"The alien needed to be able to control your mind. I don't mean what or how you thought, but take you where it wanted and show you what it wanted. And keep you unconscious, obviously. Even if it can communicate telepathically, I suspect it needed to interface with your cybernetics in order to accomplish the rest."

"But now that it's done with me, why hasn't the repulsion field kicked me out?"

"Well, two possibilities." Caleb reached into the pack lying next to him and produced a small, unadorned metal orb. "These orbs generate the field. They were staggered along the mountainside for a while, then eventually I quit seeing them. At first I thought the repulsion was an all-encompassing field, but now I suspect it's more like a demilitarized zone."

"In which case the field isn't active here…what's the second possibility?"

"That because our cybernetics are internal, they don't trip the field at all—in which case I'm eVi-less unnecessarily." He shrugged. "But I couldn't take the chance."

"Is it weird, having everything turned off?"

"Yeah, it is. I reach for modified vision or a nano-boost of adrenaline and nothing responds."

"You did fine slaying the dragon all on your own."

"True, but it wasn't exactly easy. Beast tried to roast me." He sighed. "Mostly, though, it's quiet. I don't think any of us realize just how much we have constantly going on in our heads, how much our eVi is always multitasking and tracking and informing."

"You believe it's become a crutch?"

"Well, sure. Doesn't mean it's a bad crutch. It's a tool, one which has made us stronger. Healthier, smarter, faster. But the quiet is kind of nice once you get accustomed to it."

His thumb lazily traced a pattern on her palm. "Any idea what the point was? The aliens went to a fair amount of trouble, kidnapping you and spending a day and a half running you through a mental and emotional gauntlet."

"It was a test."

"Why do you say that?" His voice had taken on a more measured tenor; he was intrigued.

"'You have done well.' It's what my captor said right before the last vision, scenario, whatever. With my father. Up until then it had simply dumped me into these scenes and let me rant at the empty air. But apparently it was paying attention."

She groaned. "Unfortunately, it provided no information as to what the test was *for* or what consequences flowed from doing well, other than not killing me."

He leaned in and kissed the top of her head. "I saw one of them. Spoke to it. It didn't speak back."

She twisted around to face him fully. "Are you serious? What did it look like? What happened?"

"It looked ethereal...individual points of light which morphed and took shape. It was a brief encounter and I'm afraid I was a little distracted by the powerful need to get to you."

"Oh." She melted under the intensity of his gaze. "Where did it go? Did you see?"

He motioned behind them, beyond the plateau. "I've no idea how far. It vanished from view after the first dip in the land."

Her eyes followed the direction he indicated. The peaceful, natural terrain continued unabated to the horizon and offered no clues as to the secrets it held. "That's where we go then."

"Are you sure?"

She nodded, resolute. "It owes me some answers. Owes us both answers."

"Okay."

"Here's the problem: it sounds like the aliens don't look like anything at all. I don't know how many of them are here or a thing about them except they understand English and are supremely arrogant, yet can be reasoned with. But as to where to find them? This isn't space. I don't know the rules of the wilderness quite so well. Or at all."

"Then it's a good thing I do."

"It is. I mean, you found me hidden away deep in the mountains, didn't you?" She kissed him, long and deliciously slow, before climbing to her feet to scrutinize the copse on the off chance there might be a breadcrumb or a directional arrow.

He jerked his head toward the pack. "I brought you fresh clothes if you want to shed those."

"You're not getting in my pants right now. You're injured."

"Not what I meant—"

She winked at him. "I know. I do want to change, but I'm so filthy I'll only ruin the new clothes, too. Maybe we'll happen upon a stream or something and can both get clean." She gestured to the now-dried blood on his clothes.

"Hazard of being a dragonslayer." He re-secured everything in the pack and closed it up then stood and slung the sheathed sword across his back.

She smiled to herself, watching him while he couldn't see her do so. In another time, another life, with another person she would've tossed a string of expletives in his direction for what he had done, kicked him out the airlock and held a grudge towards him for the rest of her life for daring to touch, to *alter*, her beloved ship.

But this wasn't another time or another life, and he wasn't any other person. Now she was able to get out of her own way long enough to see past her blind spots and recognize he had been right to act as he did.

Her heart, perhaps even her soul, palpitated with this...*sensation*. She had called it love, but she had called feelings 'love' in the past. Feelings which weren't this.

She recalled the bottomless, powerful emotion, the *dushevnoye volneniye* bleeding out of her mother's voice and shining through the anguish on her father's face and considered the possibility this was but a hint, a small tease, of what her parents had felt for each other.

It terrified her. It made her throat convulse and cut off the oxygen to her brain, leaving her unable to process a rational thought. It made her want to run away from him, all the way to the other end of the universe if necessary, before this damnable 'feeling' got any stronger. It made her want to protect him, to grab him by the hand and run away *with* him to the other end of the universe, to somewhere the evils of the world would never beset him.

It terrified her, but she had no choice. She could no longer fathom walking away.

So when he turned to her, she merely pointed to the mountainside. "Lead the way."

37

Liam glowered out the window of his office. From the top floor of Logistics he observed four other buildings, the bustling courtyard below and a sliver of the continuing clean-up effort at the bomb site.

It was a more expansive view than he'd enjoyed on Deucali, where no military building stood higher than five stories. Yet in the corners of his vision the walls undulated menacingly, as though they plotted to close in and suffocate him if he let them out of his sight.

It was all falling apart, and no matter what he did he couldn't seem to wrangle it back under control.

Why did Goddamned aliens have to show up? Now, in this year, this time—*his* time—when they had so many millennia to choose from? They were ruining everything. Ruining his carefully devised plans and with them his hopes for the future, for redemption, for vengeance.

He wanted to grind every Federation world into dust beneath his boot as his army blazed a trail of blood and corpses all the way to Seneca. He wanted to storm their inner sanctum and fire a laser into the skull of their Field Marshal while their Chairman watched, then fire a laser into the skull of their Chairman. He wanted to burn their bodies on a pyre and carry the ashes back to Deucali and spread them on his mother's consecrated grave.

Instead he struggled to simply keep his head above water, overwhelmed by a crumbling northwestern force which had proved unable to even penetrate Federation space. His northeastern force had gone unashamedly renegade and the southern fleets were unwilling to budge beyond minor shoring up of Earth and the First Wave worlds' defenses. The politicians, the press and the public were demanding to know how he proposed to fight these aliens and thus far neither he nor the new Prime Minister had been able to pacify their clamor.

He didn't want to fight the aliens. He didn't give a flying fuck-all about the aliens, except insofar as they interfered with his plans. His sole solace was a deep suspicion these aliens would surely reach Seneca before long. If it became impossible to burn it himself, at a bare minimum he could witness it burn from afar.

Once the planet lay in smoldering cinders, then and only then might he consider fighting the aliens.

The door slid open behind him, jerking him away from the window. His jaw ground his teeth roughly against one another as Miriam Solovy invaded his personal sanctum.

Ever since her daughter was purportedly 'cleared' of involvement in the bombing, she had been insufferable. Marching around his facility like she was the second coming, ordering his people around like she was in charge.

"Solovy, have you not the basic decency to request permission before storming into my office?"

"Your secretary was absent, and I hadn't the time to wait."

"I haven't the time either. What do you want?"

Her smirk curdled his stomach. "In that case, I'll spare you the niceties and come straight to the point. Your brief leadership tenure has been an unmitigated disaster. You send our forces against meaningless targets, wasting resources we need in order to fight the alien invasion while refusing to send them where they can be of actual use. You neglect the monumental threat these aliens represent to the point of outright dereliction of duty in favor of lobbing ineffectual taunts over the Federation border."

"How dare—"

"I realize you lost your mother in the First Crux War. I understand from where your hatred of Seneca stems. I have been there, and it is a dark, desolate place. For this reason and this reason alone, I am giving you the opportunity to resign voluntarily. Return to Southwestern Command and work to protect those worlds. You were competent at that task at least. But if you do not resign in the next twelve hours, know I will seek your removal from the Chairmanship and, if necessary, your discharge."

He was in her face. He didn't recall how he had gotten there. *She was so small, such a puny little creature.* "You bitch. What gives you the right to think you have any say in my command? You're nothing but a glorified secretary playing dress-up. Go back to your tea party and let the real soldiers do the work."

She didn't flinch. *People so small as her always flinched.*

If anything her glare hardened further. "I gave you your chance. You are a disgrace to the Alliance Armed Forces and the uniform you wear. You aim to sacrifice millions on the altar of your delusional crusade and I will not allow it. I—"

His punch knocked her back a meter into the wall. His fist had moved of its own volition, carrying a rage and frustration all its own.

To his dismay, she didn't fall. *People so small as her always fell.*

No tears pooled in her eyes; instead they flared golden amber as she rubbed her jaw and pushed off the wall to stand rigid straight. A peculiar smile danced across her lips. Blood trickled from the corner of her mouth and down her chin, but she ignored it.

"You should not have done that, Liam. Thank you for confirming everything I suspected about you. Pack your belongings, because you are finished."

Then she pivoted and was gone, leaving him standing there aghast. Striking a fellow officer was grounds for censure, if not demotion or even dishonorable discharge.

She just made him so damn angry! She understood nothing—nothing about what it meant to be a soldier, nothing about what it meant to serve a higher purpose. Worse, she dared to be unapologetically arrogant in her ignorance.

Pulse thundering in his ears, his eyes darted around the office. Here only weeks, it held no personal attachment for him.

He did not intend to be humiliated in public. He'd die before being dragged in front of a tribunal for crones to stare condescendingly down their noses at him and dare to judge him.

A cold certainty descended upon him, quieting the storm in his head. He had nothing left but the mission to which he had devoted his life. It had sustained him this long. It would not fail him now.

He would make Seneca pay. And after he exacted his just reward from Seneca, he would make them all pay.

38

ROMANE
INDEPENDENT COLONY

Alone in a quiet room for the first time in days, Mia sank against the wall and closed her eyes. She wanted to sleep for a week. If a little luck swung her way, after this last meeting she could sleep for six hours or so. It seemed a reasonable start.

The 'strategy session' had been a nightmare. Corralling, focusing and stroking the egos of two dozen egomaniacs and dysfunctional genius intellects so they didn't storm out, or even better kill one another, was not a task she'd wish on anyone. She would be happy if millennia passed before she was forced to do it again.

But it just might have been worth it. Time would tell. Nudged and prodded when necessary by details Meno fed her from his study of the data on the aliens, the motley crew of billionaires and wunderkinds had eventually generated decent suggestions on how to fight them.

She grimaced. Her neck and the small of her back ached painfully. She elbowed off the wall while rubbing at her neck and went to find Governor Ledesme.

After several false trails she finally succeeded in locating her in an upper-floor conference room, where she consulted with members of her cabinet. Upon being alerted to Mia's presence, the governor excused herself from the meeting and indicated for Mia to follow her to her office.

As soon as the door slid shut the woman spun around and regarded her with a mix of hope, desperation and expectancy. "Tell me you have good news, Ms. Requelme."

"Possibly. The best news we're going to have until we know a lot more about these aliens, anyway." She handed over a disk, but knowing the governor's time was now in even greater demand, tried to recite the highlights.

"Readings suggest the ships use a dynamic shielding system displaying an extremely high-frequency oscillation. Given those characteristics, it's likely to adjust relative levels in different areas in reaction to threats. At its strongest the shield will be impossible to penetrate using our current technology, but if one were to bombard a superdreadnought with coordinated fire on one side to draw the shield strength, another ship might be able to breach the now weaker shielding from a different position and inflict some damage."

She had begun wandering haphazardly around the office; she hoped the governor didn't mind. "The ships are made out of a pre-viously unknown material, but the closest analogue is lonsdaleite diamond. It's certain to be extremely hard—harder than anything we can manufacture. If it were lonsdaleite, a pinpoint hit with a minimum of thirty MN force at an angle of 17-21 degrees should exploit its brittleness and cause it to fracture. No guarantees, but it's worth a shot.

"Everyone—well eighty-five percent of everyone—agrees the aliens are communicating on a high terahertz band between 2.7-3 THz. On the disk are specs for several waveforms which may suc-ceed in disrupting the terahertz signals to a lesser or greater extent. Direct them at a ship and see what happens."

She paused for a quick breath of air then continued. "The arms of the small ships don't appear to be critical for flight. Based on close examination of the images, we think it's possible they direct and/or focus beams originating from the oculi located at their cores. So shooting the arms off won't disable them but it could render their weaponry less effective.

"The oculi, however, may represent a structural weakness. They possess the same shielding as the superdreadnoughts though, and it'll be difficult to manipulate the shield due to their compara-tively small size. A substantial minority of the group believes the shield will go down while they're firing, so perhaps a skilled fighter pilot can take one out and survive the encounter."

Her shoulders sagged in exhaustion. "And that's all we've got. I realize most of it is geared toward a firefight scenario, but hopefully you can use some of the ideas to adapt the array ware to our ad-vantage."

Ledesme smiled; a politician's smile, but it seemed genuine. "This is marvelous, Mia."

"It wasn't only me or even mostly me, and you're the one who convinced a number of particularly recalcitrant men and women to dig in, lose sleep and find answers."

"Still, thank you." The governor crossed to her desk. Though she must be losing sleep herself, her cream brocaded suit displayed not a whiff of wrinkles or over-usage. "So the question is, beyond your suggestion regarding the array, what do we do with this information?"

The woman had left behind a room full of advisors, of whom Mia was not one. "Are you asking my opinion, ma'am?"

"I am. Clearly there's more to you than a successful business-woman and you haven't been afflicted by the disease of political blindness."

The news about Messium had broken the morning before. Coupled with the vanishing of now eighteen colonies off the ex-anet, the citizens of the Milky Way were indeed beginning to panic. She'd had scant time to follow the news but had seen several reports of stampedes at spaceports and press conferences turned riotous.

"If it were up to me? I would very publicly provide the infor-mation to both the Alliance and Senecan militaries, as well as the leaders of the independent colonies. One, they need it—doing so could save lives. Two, it keeps Romane from being forced into picking a side. Three, it highlights the best aspects of Romane and its citizens—ingenuity, creativity, productiveness, intellect, gener-osity. It shows what individuals can do when given freedom and the fruits of their labor. Don't be afraid to say that in the press state-ment because it happens to be true."

Ledesme looked impressed. Mia wished she wasn't too tired to properly appreciate it. "We maintain our freedom, strengthen our public profile as the best and strongest of the independent colonies, and shame both the Federation and the Alliance a little in the process. Coinciding with the fact it appears the blockade is cracking—I imagine those ships are needed elsewhere now—we stand to gain a great deal, assuming we live through this crisis. I'll say it again, Ms. Requelme. You would make a skilled politician."

"Well, if we live through this crisis, I'll give it some thought. But for now I'm going to concentrate on the living part."

"As are we all." For a second the governor allowed her own weariness to show, and Mia had the idle thought perhaps one day they would be friends. "These are dark, difficult times. But here we stand. I'm sending you my personal contact address. If you should receive any new information, I'd greatly appreciate a heads up. No questions asked."

"Absolutely, ma'am. Good luck. I believe you're going to need it."

With that she whirled and headed for the door, the first step in reaching her bed.

39

PORTAL PRIME

T he lushness of the forest increased as the steepness of the terrain eased. Colorful flora provided dashes of color to an endless pelt of clover grass.

The trees remained the primary decor, however, and they were increasingly fighting their way through dense woods. Though these mountains flowed at a moderate gradient rather than soaring up to craggy peaks, it was still high terrain.

"I killed my first man in some woods not unlike these." Caleb didn't peek over to see Alex's reaction or determine whether she wanted him to continue. He needed to continue.

"It wasn't as an agent. I was sixteen, working for the Senecan Wilderness Service for the summer repairing sensors and monitoring equipment. Late one evening, I was searching for a good place to camp for the night when I heard a cry."

Not a cry...a keening wail conveying agony to chill his heart.

"I headed in the direction it came from and saw a man kneeling next to the corpse of an *elafali*. It's a species native to Seneca...the closest equivalent is probably an elk or a moose. They're endangered—rare to begin with and weakened by colonization—but they have these gorgeous spiral horns the color of pearled coral so poachers hunt them as prizes. The horns and sometimes the entire skull are sold as trophies on the black market."

The animal's guts were spilling out into the dirt, gleaming a sickly yellow in the evening rays. It had not been a quick or painless death for the creature.

"So this man was in the middle of sawing the horns off with a gamma blade. I could move fairly quietly by then and crept almost on top of him before he saw me. He stood, keeping a hold on the blade, and told me this was none of my business and I should be on my way.

"I responded that hunting *elafali* was illegal and I needed to report him. It was my job, though I would have done so regardless. He took a step forward and said, 'You don't want to do that, boy. I'll ask you one more time to be on your way or we will have a problem.'"

The trees began to grow thicker, creating shade and cooling the air. He considered suggesting she get out the pullover he'd brought her from the ship...but she didn't look to be shivering, not yet.

"I said 'I'm sorry, but I can't ignore this,' and he lunged toward me. The guy was big, twelve centimeters taller than me and thirty kilos heavier."

In the dim light he hadn't been able to tell how much represented muscle and how much fat, not as if it mattered. He was a skinny kid just beginning to build muscles from the physical labor the job entailed, and the man would have crushed him either way.

"I kept a small Daemon on me because dangerous wildlife did roam the forests—not the *elafali*, which weren't aggressive unless you threatened their young, but other animals. I reacted on instinct, drew it and fired. At such close range it sliced his chest wide open. The guy fell dead at my feet."

He sensed her eyes boring into him and was unable to not glance over, but they showed only compassion. "You had no choice."

"No. I didn't."

"What happened?"

"I gagged. Would've lost my dinner except I hadn't eaten it yet. Then I alerted the authorities and sat down beside the corpse to wait. Not the man's corpse, the *elafali*. It was such a beautiful creature, to be butchered for credits so some potentate could decorate his dining room with it...."

He'd carefully closed the eyes of the dead elafali, *his hands shaking like a junkie desperate for a fix.*

She squeezed his hand, encouraging him to continue.

"I suspect I was in shock for the first ten minutes or so. I don't really remember them. Eventually I started pondering this man. Who he might be? Whether he left behind a family or kids?

Whether anyone would miss him? But I realized I wasn't sorry I had killed him. I was sorry he'd chosen to attack me, but he made the choice, and the hundred before it which led to that moment. And suddenly I was angry.

"How dare he try to take my life from me? He didn't have the right to take the animal's life and he damn sure didn't have the right to take mine. He was a bully and a sadist who killed without the empathy to understand the consequences of his actions."

He reined in the intensity bleeding into his voice, surprised to be getting worked up about the event all over again some twenty-three years later. Perhaps it was because now someone or thing was trying to take the lives of everyone. Perhaps it was merely the familiarity of the woods.

"It worked out fine. The *elafali* carcass and the blade with the man's fingerprints coating it were sufficient to convince the authorities I'd acted in self-defense. They brought me to the station for the formalities and my parents fussed over me for a day or so. Then it was back to life as normal."

Their pace had slackened to an ambling stroll, and she placed a hand on his arm. "Is that why you got into your line of work?"

"What?" He forced an amused breath. "No. I told you, I got into it for the adventure."

"I know, but...is it possible the encounter represented a formative experience? In your profession you're able to stop a lot of unsavory people who believe they have the right to take from others—their money, their possessions, often their lives."

He left the path to lean against a nearby tree. Was she correct? He enjoyed what he did because of the thrill of the chase, the challenge of each new mission and the confidence of being better than his targets.

But he couldn't deny a powerful need for justice often invigorated his actions...none more so than when he eliminated the majority of the Humans Against Artificials terrorist group. They had murdered Samuel, and others before him.

If he thought about it now, he recalled at least a dozen missions through the years which had been heavily laced with a desire to exact recompense for harm inflicted. Might his life have taken a different path if he hadn't discovered the poacher in the woods that night?

And he called himself self-aware. Yet she already saw deeper into him than he could himself. He gave her a diffident smile. "Maybe a little. You fancy yourself insightful?"

She closed the distance to him, wrapping her arms around his waist. "Hell no, I'm terrible at it."

"Except when it comes to me."

"Except when it comes to you."

"It is a rather beautiful landscape."

They had arrived at a glade of sorts, a clearing amongst the trees. Vibrant fauna of rust and gold dotted the scenery, in some cases winding up the tree trunks like symbiotic vines. Grass grew in tall blades to blanket the ground. A late afternoon light shone through the tree limbs in diffuse rays.

"It is. It's also trying to lead us in circles."

Alex glanced at him, curious. "What do you mean?"

"The topography and flow of the terrain are trying to prod us to circle back."

"Not a surprise they would have numerous tricks up their sleeves, I suppose. But we're not letting it, are we?"

"No, we are not. In fact..." Caleb nudged her to the edge of the glade and into the trees "...I expect down this hill we'll find something new, and most welcome."

She acceded to his nudging, welcoming anything which he deemed welcoming. And now that he had pointed it out it seemed evident the terrain was fighting them. The way through the glade would have been much easier and more pleasant and wound subtly away from their intended direction. Here the trees grew thicker and the ground rockier. To their left the mountain rose steeply, working again to force them to the right. He continued to angle left.

The sky began to dim as dusk descended. "Should we go back to the glade to camp for the night?"

"Nope. We're good." She eyed him suspiciously, but seeing as he was in charge for now didn't otherwise protest.

Then there was a noise, steady and rough. It didn't sound artificial, but.... "Caleb?"

He just shrugged mysteriously. Clever man knew what it was. But he hadn't tensed; the set of his jaw had not locked, nor had his shoulders risen perceptibly. His hands were neither clenching nor unclenching. He didn't believe the source of the noise represented a danger.

The air began to grow cooler, a damp chill she hadn't previously noticed settling on her exposed arms. And then it was dark. "*Caleb....*"

"Trust me." He held aside heavy brush and motioned for her to go on ahead. She did, so she ducked and stepped through—and gasped.

A waterfall over a hundred meters in height rushed down the mountainside. On reaching their level the water formed an oval-shaped pool before following a slope to the right to become a stream and trail back into the woods.

The water glowed with such a bright luminescence the area surrounding the pool was lit nearly to mid-day, though tinted an eerie amber.

His arms wound around her from behind and she sank against him, soaking in his warmth. "You think it's a trap? Because it looks an awful lot like a trap."

"No, this place is too well hidden. And I imagine were we to revisit the oceans we flew over when we arrived, we would find them glowing as brightly."

As was so often the case, in hindsight the truth became blindingly obvious. "This is how they're lighting the planet. The waters absorb the light at night and release it during the day."

"Seems so."

She squeezed his arms tighter at her waist, pulling him closer. "It must be some kind of photoluminescence, but it's still artificial. I mean, it's on a frigging timer."

"Agreed. But you have to admit, it is a fairly elegant solution."

"True. So what about this place, here?"

"I suspect it's what it appears to be—rain or snow runoff traveling down the mountain to feed the valley."

"What valley?"

"The one another five or so kilometers away."

"Oh, that valley." She craned her neck around to look at him. "Can we get clean? I haven't had a shower in literally days."

He kissed her ear. "Damn straight we can get clean. We'll even camp here for the night."

In seconds she had untangled from his arms and stripped naked, tossing the filthy and torn clothes into the trees. He had brought her a change of clothes, and she was never wearing those rags again.

She dove into the pool, only to surface howling as the frigid water seared through to her bones. His chuckle echoed behind her. That was fine, she'd be cackling at him soon enough. It was *cold.*

But she was intrigued now, so she went under once more. The water glowed clear through to the rocky bed. From within it was the color of French chardonnay. Feeling unaccountably carefree, she flicked her tongue out. Didn't taste like it. A shame.

She reemerged to see Caleb gingerly tugging his shirt over his head. Once he had done so, she understood why.

Dark indigo-and-violet bruises marked his torso and shoulders. A deep scrape ran diagonally from his collarbone down to his ribs, and in three places it had torn open the skin. Though none of the gashes cut hazardously deep, the flesh surrounding them had swollen an angry scarlet.

She stared at him as he entered the water, her gaze solemn with concern. She met him halfway and reached up to oh-so-gently run fingertips over the bruises and along the edges of the wounds.

Her heart clenched at the stark sight of him being hurt. Not invincible. He had joked about the dragon slaying, but she hadn't realized until now exactly how close he came to dying. All because he was trying to get to her.

His hand grasped her wrist and pulled it away from his chest. "No eVi to direct and supplement the healing. But I am healing."

Incredulous at his cavalier attitude, she exhaled harshly. "You've been hiking all afternoon and evening like this? You lugged the pack like this?" She'd offered to carry it twice over the course of the hike; both times he'd blithely refused to hand it over. "You should have said something. And there are painkillers in the med kit, right?"

"If I couldn't feel the pain I might forget about it and hurt myself more. It's okay. I've had worse."

She frowned at the notion but dipped her hand in the luminescent water and brought it up to the cuts, carefully washing off the dried blood and dirt. "You're putting a medwrap on this as soon as we get out."

"After."

The tone in his voice inexorably led a corner of her mouth to tweak upward, despite the fact she was still worried about him. "After?"

In a blink he had submerged beneath the surface. Strong arms wrapped around her hips and lifted her up to drop her over his shoulder. The chill of the air blasted her wet skin. She squealed and played at struggling as he carried her out of the pool and to an area of thick grass on the shore.

He fell to his knees in the grass and eased her onto her back, then rested on an elbow beside her.

She shivered from the cool night air and the feel of his hand ghosting along her cheek, across her jaw and down her neck. When his fingertips delicately caressed a breast her breath hitched in her throat, due both to the caress and the reverence with which it was delivered.

His hand continued on to trace the contour of her hip but his eyes now rose to meet hers. His voice glided over her, as silken as his touch. "I thought you were dead. I didn't dare admit it to myself at the time, but...I thought I'd lost you."

Her hand found its way into his hair, damp waves lengthened to tickle his cheekbones. "I'm not dead. I promise."

The curl of his lips sent a tremor shooting all the way to her toes, one having nothing to do with the cold this time. The glow from the water brightened his irises to a dazzling iridescent cerulean, but it was the look in them which sent her head spinning.

No one had ever looked at her in such a way as this. It reminded her of the moment before they had breached the portal, though in retrospect the previous gaze had been but a pale hint of what she saw now.

And now, she didn't need to ask what it conveyed. Her chest tightened as if it strove to constrain the emotions swelling within.

"No, you are not." His head dipped to plant a tantalizing kiss on a nipple, then the curve of her breast where it met her sternum, then mirror his actions on the other side.

The kisses drew agonizingly down her abdomen. "You are very..." his tongue darted out to swirl around her navel, then drifted lower "...very much alive."

Her head dropped back and her spine arched, and for a time she forgot every single thing that might have existed except the sensation of his hands and his tongue.

When she could endure the rapturous agony no longer she reached down and wound both hands into his hair, desperately urging him up.

He complied maddeningly slowly, and she was forced to raise up to crush her mouth against his and drag him on top of her. She relished his weight upon her, strong and sure, seemingly to the ends of the universe.

But just as he was about to slip inside her she shifted her hips, catching him off guard long enough to roll him onto his back beneath her. She giggled in devilish delight at the groan of frustration emerging from deep in his throat.

Her hair fell in waves to tickle his skin as she kissed each corner of his mouth and the curve of his jaw, holding herself centimeters above him with her hands on either side of his frame. Teasing him as he had teased her.

Judging by his expression of unbridled, smoldering desire, it was working.

A viblade didn't function in the repulsion field, and his stubble was now veering dangerously close to a beard. Her lips burned from the friction, but she found she quite enjoyed the coarse roughness of it.

She stretched herself out along the length of his body, careful not to place undue pressure on his bruised, battered torso.

His hands lowered to her hips, firmly and somewhat insistently guiding her as she slid down over him, evoking a gasp from them each in equal measure.

Their lips met once more, then his palm rested against her abdomen and he urged her upward. A halting, wondrous breath escaped as she settled fully on him.

Lit by the glow of the pool, she could see the pleasure and the fervor consuming his eyes. Lit by the glow of the pool, she wondered if he could see the passion and the tenderness brimming in her own.

Deep in the recesses of her mind, she knew *they* were probably watching. They watched everything, after all.

Let them watch.

Let them see what it meant to be human. To live.

Let them see what it meant to love, and be loved in return.

40

M arcus found himself once again surrounded by boxes, though the office was again larger and the view again better.

This would be the final time such was true, for both the office and the view did not get any better in the Earth Alliance than the Prime Minister's office. Yet these were the same boxes containing the same items as before and he felt no different than when they had surrounded him in the Attorney General's or the Foreign Minister's office.

If the conditions were otherwise, he told himself, he would be able to feel satisfaction, be able to take pleasure at having achieved precisely what he had sought for decades. He had risen from a homeless street urchin in the slums of Rio de Janeiro to the most powerful office in the galaxy. What else could one possibly ask for?

The aliens having the decency to hold off another year before deciding to attack, for one.

He had been *so close* to maneuvering humanity away from this crisis. After more than five years of planning, it had come down to a matter of weeks.

"Sir, Admiral Miriam Solovy is here to see you."

He winced at the voice of his Chief of Staff emanating from the speaker. Weeks which he could have bought if not for his guest's daughter. Frustration clawed up his throat to leave a stale, rotten taste in his mouth, but he dared not show it. He was the Prime Minister now. So he grabbed a glass of water to try to wash the taste away and granted her permission to enter.

He had met Miriam Solovy half a dozen times over the last five years, the most recent being at the Select Military Advisory Council meeting mere hours before the Headquarters bombing. She had always carried herself with the quiet confidence borne by military officers who earned their rank rather than fell into it. Flawlessly composed in every setting, not once had he heard her yell or even raise her voice, yet when she spoke one felt compelled to listen.

He had never managed to ascertain why that was. It disturbed him when he didn't understand some facet of human interaction, but she remained a mystery to him.

If only she had died in the bombing like she was supposed to…instead she now stood in his office wearing an immaculate uniform and an air of righteous authority.

He gestured with as much warmth as he was able to muster. "Admiral Solovy. I have a few short minutes, but I'm happy to spare what I can for you."

"Thank you, Prime Minister. I would offer my congratulations, but I'm afraid the circumstances are far too grim for it."

"I couldn't agree more. I hope I can be half the leader Luis Barrera was. Now, what can I do for you?"

"In short? Find a way to negotiate a cease-fire with the Federation, commit the whole of our forces to defending against the aliens and fire General O'Connell from the EASC Board. Not necessarily in that order."

"Is that all? It may take a few hours." He chuckled, and was shocked at how frayed it sounded. The glint in her eyes said she noticed it too.

In his mind he uttered an old gutter curse learned in his gang days. Handing her a tactical advantage on a platter was not a good way to begin the meeting. "Admiral, I'm sure you appreciate the difficult situation we find ourselves in. I can't overlook the atrocities the Federation has committed upon the Alliance in the last month."

"I lost thousands of people in the Headquarters bombing—colleagues and friends. I assure you, no one understands the losses we've suffered more than I do. But the clear fact is we no longer have any idea who committed the bombing. Many people are beginning to question whether the Federation was responsible. There's even less evidence they were responsible for the Orbital explosion. Sir, the Federation may be our adversary today but such a feud appears ridiculously tiny in the face of the alien menace which now exists.

"Prime Minister, I am not given to hyperbole. But the entire human race is threatened with extinction."

The problem inherent in each of his possible retorts was that she was correct. To anyone who didn't know what he knew, her position was unassailable and he would be insane to argue with her. But given what he did know and she did not, he needed to buy whatever time he could.

"You are of course correct. Circumstances such as these require bold actions. I will do everything I can, but there is no guarantee the Federation will be interested in talking. And perhaps we will discover in the Messium offensive that these aliens are not as formidable as we believe. Our prospects are changing rapidly and for now I must keep all our options open."

"Sir, I—"

"Now about General O'Connell? I realize his demeanor can be abrasive, but he has years of leadership experience and—"

"He has made a disaster of the Federation war and shows no interest in the alien one. I believe he is driven by a personal vendetta against the Senecans due to the loss of his mother in the First Crux War. It is clouding his judgment and forcing him into rash decisions not backed up by cogent strategy or the facts on the battlefield."

"And the fact your daughter not only uncovered these aliens but then was apparently falsely implicated in the EASC bombing isn't clouding your judgment?"

"Sir, we have lost eight colonies. 6.4 million citizens—quadruple that number if you count those who are perishing on Messium as we speak. Another four Senecan and five independent colonies are decimated. 1.2 million people missing or dead. I hardly need my judgment clouded in order to want to defend those who remain."

Knight takes Queen. "Fair enough, Admiral. You've made your point. I'll have a word with General O'Connell and make certain his priorities are as they should be. If they are not, I will consider a change in leadership."

"Thank you, Prime Minister. Hopefully we will receive good news from Messium in the next few hours."

"I hope so as well. Now if you'll excuse me, the Assembly leadership awaits."

But once she had departed, he did not head for the basement situation room where the Assembly leadership would be gathering. Instead he activated privacy shielding and walked behind his desk.

The alien had almost always been the one to contact him over the years, but there had existed a few instances where he had needed to be able to reach out. In those instances it had responded promptly.

He provided the code to his eVi, a nonsensical string of symbols and numbers.

"Hyperion, are you there? I'd expected to hear from you by now. As you're no doubt aware, I've now risen to the position of Earth Alliance Prime Minister and can at last control humanity's path."

Silence.

"I ask you to pull your forces back. Pause the attacks. Give me a few weeks, and I promise you humanity will no longer represent a threat to you. I can make this happen—I possess the power. I simply need more time."

Silence.

"This is why you sought me out so many years ago. Because you recognized the great deeds I could accomplish. I have fulfilled all that potential and from here I can move mountains. I can move worlds. From here I can do anything. Give me the opportunity to prove it. Pull back."

Silence.

"Please. I beg you. Do not forsake me now."

Silence.

41

SENECAN FEDERATION COLONY

Olivia didn't bother to tamp down her scowl as she approached the receptionist for the second time in as many months. She also didn't introduce herself this time. Given the outcome of her previous visit she doubted the woman had forgotten her.

The receptionist quivered violently. She hadn't, then. "I'll inform Mr. Ferre you've arrived, m-ma'am."

Laure Ferre had contacted her the day before to discuss a recalcitrant broker. Ferre's largest supplier of block-stripped hardware components was pitching a fit in the wake of the 'accident' involving Ilario and Alaina Ferre and demanding to speak to whoever was in charge—really in charge—or he was cutting off his supplies. He refused to travel to New Babel and a holo would not do. The man blamed his obstinacy on the chaos of the wars.

She rarely acceded to the demands of others, but it seemed she was making a lot of concessions lately. End of days and all. Given the losses in the east she could not afford to lose the Federation markets as well, though on the fringes those markets were also beginning to vanish to the aliens.

So she had donned her most severe black pantsuit, slipped on dress heels which were capable of killing a person if the appropriate amount of force was applied, tied her hair in a black silk scarf and flown to Krysk.

Make no mistake, there would be no groveling. Not on her part. But if this supplier needed the fear of Olivia Montegreu put into him, she could certainly oblige.

The receptionist escorted her down the hall, literally shaking in her boots the entire way. With the woman's touch a door opened to a far smaller conference room than the one used on her earlier visit. At the table sat Laure Ferre and two somewhat older gentlemen.

She spun around as the door slid shut behind her. She didn't bother to check if it was code-locked; clearly it was code-locked.

Instead she pivoted to the occupants of the room, her expression hardening into cold steel. She didn't need the results of the facial scans to recognize the two men were spooks. It oozed from their pores like oily beads of sweat.

"It appears stabbing me in the back is all the rage these days. I'm disappointed in you, Laure. I thought we had a mutual understanding."

Laure had the gall to preen with arrogance, sitting cozily between his big, strong protectors. "We did, for the time being. But I had no reason to believe you didn't intend to dispose of me the second you had no further use for me, just as you did to my cousin and aunt. I have to look out for myself. I assume you're familiar with the concept."

The man on the left sporting the bushy salt-and-pepper hair motioned to the chair opposite him. "Ms. Montegreu, please take a seat."

She arched an eyebrow. "I'm not being arrested then."

"Well, now, I think that depends on you."

So they wanted something. Everyone always did. Lacking other options she sat, but remained silent.

The other man—he lacked any distinguishing features of note—leaned slightly into the table. "Who were the forty kilos of HHNC delivered to on Earth?"

Oh.

Had Marcus sold her out before she could do the same to him? It wasn't his style, yet...end of days and all. Still, Palluda would've made for a more lucrative avenue of betrayal so perhaps not. "I don't know to what HHNC you're referring. I don't deal in explosives."

"Sure you do. You deal in everything. The HHNC which was smuggled from Pandora to Vancouver and used in the EASC Headquarters bombing."

So Kigin had gotten clumsy in the rush after Terrage refused the job and sodded it up. This was why one never deviated from the plan. Agreeing to do so had in fact come back to bite her in the proverbial ass.

She decided she was definitely going to kill Marcus if she saw him again…

…unless she could do one better.

She smiled, though only in the most technical sense of the word in that her lips curled in an upward manner. "Director Delavasi, Colonel Navick—" they maintained sufficient composure to not look startled she had managed to identify them "—I expect you're both prepped for a lengthy interrogation. You've likely worked out when to resort to bullying and at what point draconian threats will be required."

She lost all pretense of a smile. "If it's all the same to you, I'd prefer to avoid such unpleasantness. I realize I represent a prize catch for either of your governments, though which one wins me is an interesting question. Also one I am not inclined to learn the answer to.

"The simple truth is, while a few months ago I would be the biggest catch of either of your careers, today you face far larger problems. Problems I can help you solve."

Navick started to protest; she waved him silent. "I will give you the entirety of what I know relating to this little spat which has broken out between your governments: who was involved, where the materials came from, the precise incidents which occurred when and by whom. You'll find in there several catches adequate to make your careers, I assure you. I'll provide the proof you need to bring a mercifully hasty end to your unfortunate war.

"Further, I'll provide you materials to fight these aliens, off the books and free of charge. Bleeding-edge tech. Modified weapons. Biosynth boosters for your ground troops. Whatever you need. I imagine the supply lines are getting a bit thin what with so many colonies being cut off and so much wasteful usage of supplies to kill one another as you've been doing these last weeks."

Navick's jaw was grinding, she suspected from the effort of hearing her out. "Why would you give us all this?"

"What good is being a criminal mastermind if there's no one left alive to corrupt? It is against my interests for the aliens to kill everyone."

Delavasi's fingertips drummed on the table. "And in return?"

"In return, I walk out this door a free woman. I'm not prosecuted for any involvement in events which may or may not have occurred in relation to your war. Or anything else."

The man laughed heartily; the full-throated sound seemed to originate from deep in his gut. She supposed it might be what some referred to as a guffaw. Such a crass word.

Then in a flash it was gone and his eyes were hard. "You ask quite a lot."

She met his rigid stare with her own cool one. "Not really. Everyone in this room knows if I'm put in prison, someone else will simply take my place. The business I'm in will continue as it always has. Wouldn't it be better to have someone in charge who is favorably inclined toward saving the galaxy and toward you personally?

"Besides, I believe you've already made a similar if less grand arrangement with Mr. Ferre here. It's not as if your scruples had anywhere lower to descend.

"Gentlemen, I am offering you the means to save billions of lives. All I ask in return is my own."

Delavasi and Navick exchanged a glance. Navick was biting on his lower lip so hard she expected blood to dribble down his chin any second now. "And if we refuse?"

She settled back in the chair and crossed one leg casually over the other, her hands coming to rest together on her knee.

"Arrest me. Torture me. Parade me about in the public square. You will have your prize catch. And you will lose everything."

R

Richard and Graham sat in another booth in another pub.

Richard took a long sip of his ale. Ice crystals miraculously clung to the outside of the mug despite the sweltering heat. He licked away the excess froth and gazed across the table.

"Well."

Graham nodded sagely over his own mug. "Well, indeed."

"What does it say about us that we can be manipulated so spectacularly?"

"In fairness, not us. Politicians. You and I, we saw through their schemes quickly enough, so I'd say it says rather good things about us." The grumble which followed made it clear the statement was only partially in jest.

"Good things or not, we have a job ahead of us. And her information had damn well better be airtight because these people are not going to go down willingly."

"Yep. But hey, that's why they pay us like princes."

"I thought they paid us like paupers."

"Oh, right." Graham finished off his ale. He looked as though he desperately wanted to order another, but refrained. "So we'll keep in close contact and try to coordinate events. Don't want to spook our targets if we can avoid it."

"I've got a lengthier trip than you, but it means more time to analyze the data. I'll forward you what I've put together when I land in Washington."

"Straight into the lion's den, huh?"

Richard shrugged. "I'll have a team waiting for me there. The longer we delay, the greater chance everything goes to Hell."

"True enough. You believe she didn't know anything about the aliens?"

"It's logical. She made a good point. A galaxy devoid of life is not good for her bottom line. Still, I hate to let her go."

"Greater good, my friend."

"I know." Richard exhaled. "Nothing left to do but do it. Shall we?"

Graham reached in his pocket and produced a small crystal disk. He slid it toward Richard. "For you."

"What is it?"

"Will Sutton's full Intelligence file. How he was recruited, what his mission parameters were and everything he's given us over the years."

Richard shook his head and pushed the disk back across the table. "Keep it."

"Please. Consider it a small thank you for having the courage to take a tremendous risk in meeting me. I couldn't have even attempted any of this without you. Instead I'd be sitting in my office yanking my hair out because I knew something was wrong but had no way to begin to prove it. Montegreu was right. We're going to save billions of lives, and it's easily as much thanks to you as it is to me. Probably more so.

"Because of that, you deserve to know two things. One, marrying you was never part of his mission parameters. That was his choice and his choice alone. Two, what his mission parameters were, and the manner in which he fulfilled them, are on that disk. So do me a kindness and take the damn file."

Richard closed his eyes and dropped the disk in his pocket. He told himself he'd toss the disk in a garbage bin on the way to the spaceport. If he didn't pass any on the way, he'd toss the disk at the spaceport. If all else failed he'd toss the disk on the flight.

They both stood; this time his hand extended first.

Graham clasped it warmly. "It has been a genuine pleasure, Richard. We survive this war then survive these aliens, let's get together and enjoy a truly epic number of drinks."

Richard surprised himself by deciding it sounded like an excellent idea. "Until then."

42

Caleb woke before her. Careful not to move, he instead took a too rare moment to simply enjoy the feel of her skin pressed to his, the smoothness of her abdomen beneath his palm, the way her hair had absorbed the lush, natural scent of the forest.

She was the strongest person he had ever known. Yet here asleep in his arms she was vulnerable. She was so fierce and determined; yet here asleep in his arms she yielded. She fought and struggled relentlessly; yet here asleep in his arms she was content.

He expected them to reach these aliens today, insofar as they were reachable. She believed she'd be able to reason with their foe, insisting they exhibited a weakness she would be able to exploit. If it could be done he didn't doubt she would accomplish it.

He didn't want to wake her and pull her from peaceful slumber into the maelstrom which was certain to follow. One day the two of them were going to sleep until afternoon and never leave the bed. But today they shouldn't dally.

If he must wake her, he intended to do so in a pleasing manner. His fingertips caressed the curve of her hip while he planted delicate kisses along her neck and behind her ear.

She murmured and shifted against him, at first in sleep...then most deliberately, if the wicked smile tugging at the corner of her mouth even in profile gave any inkling. *They shouldn't dally....*

She twisted around to face him and found his lips with her own, and he decided it was too dark to get moving yet anyway.

R

He tossed an energy bar in Alex's direction. They were now officially running behind schedule, so breakfast would be mobile. *So spectacularly worth it.*

The bar landed on the grass in front of where she sat slipping on her boots. He turned back to finish closing up the pack—then back to her, observing as she wound the boot's strap diagonally up, around and down again to latch it at the base.

"What did you just do?"

"Hmm?"

"With the strap. Why not wrap it straight?"

"Oh…it's a habit I picked up from my dad when I was a kid."

"Ah." He glanced at the pool. The luminescence was fading as the sky grew lighter but the waterfall continued to spill tranquilly down the mountainside. It was a setting made for introspection.

He went over to sit beside her and draped his arms over his knees. "So there's something I've been wanting to mention for a while. We've been running so hard, the right time never came. But this is the right time."

"Caleb, what are you talking about?"

"I never met your father. I only know what history says about him and what you've told me. I did meet your mother, albeit only for a few but most exciting minutes. And I'm not sure if you realize it, but you are your mother's daughter to the core."

Her head dropped to rest on his shoulder. "I know."

"Do you?"

"I mean, I without a doubt inherited—or picked up—a few of my dad's more colorful traits: a foul mouth, a cavalier disregard for authority…." She laughed quietly. "I swear, if he hadn't died a war hero, sooner or later he would've gotten himself kicked out of the military for insubordination. According to Richard, he almost did at least twice before I was born. But…." Her voice drifted off as she considered the waterfall before turning into him.

"When I was in the aliens' virtual funhouse, I saw or heard her three separate times in radically different situations. In so many ways, it was as if I was looking in a mirror. A somewhat warped mirror maybe, but a mirror nonetheless."

Her sigh muffled against his shirt. "And though I foolishly didn't understand it until now, my father loved her profoundly, arguably for some of the same reasons I'd like to think he loved me. If I had realized this one simple truth years ago, would things have been different between us?"

A lock of hair tumbled across her cheek. He tucked it behind her ear and let his hand linger along her neck. Her experience had changed her, and he was still discovering all the ways. "There's still time."

"I wonder. We've both built up these ironclad defenses and barriers...and every time we're together our barriers spend the whole encounter body-slamming one another, sucking all the oxygen out of the room."

He chuckled and wrapped his arm fully around her to hug her closer. "That is a fairly accurate description of what I saw."

"Touché."

"If you want the relationship to change, one of you is going to need to let down those barriers."

"I'm afraid to."

He brought his other hand under her chin and lifted it so she met his gaze. "You're not afraid of anything."

Surprise animated her face. Did she imagine he hadn't noticed? "Well, I'm afraid of this. If she doesn't reciprocate? You have no idea how *hard* she can be."

"I think I kind of do. Guns, handcuffs, authoritative orders to lock me away?"

She rolled her eyes in fleeting playfulness. "Fair point. But the fact is, I owe her an apology. A real one. So if we succeed in getting off this planet and back through the portal and don't get instantly arrested or killed, I suppose I'll have to take my chances."

"I'd be willing to bet you won't be sorry." He placed a kiss on her forehead then hauled her to her feet. "Let's get moving. These aliens aren't going to come to us."

The trees now grew so thick he was hacking limbs away using the sword. They were definitely headed in the right direction.

Alex's hair caught on a branch, and after untangling it she paused to redo her ponytail. "The place where you found me—what did it look like? I was a bit out of my head at the time and didn't notice much. Now I wish I'd paid more attention and investigated the structure."

"There wasn't much to it on the outside, but it looked as if it might be a type of holographic chamber. The walls were sheer white, like you'd see in a sim room, and photal conduits wove through all the surfaces."

"That actually makes a shocking amount of sense. If I had to guess, I'd say they keep recordings of these events—or of every event—stored somewhere and can project them in the chamber."

"It would largely explain your experience." He tossed a meter-long limb to the side. "They certainly aren't making this easy, are they?"

She ducked under the next limb after him. "I believe that's the point."

"Yeah?"

"I suspect this 'player' very much wants us to find it but feels compelled to make it nearly impossible for us to do so."

"Compelled why?"

"An excellent question."

He broke off a thinner limb, wrangled through two trees—and stopped. "Perhaps you should ask it."

The forest evaporated away to reveal a stunning valley nestled between two mountains. The ground sloped down in rich grasses dotted by golden flowers billowing in a mild breeze. At the base of the valley the late-morning 'sun' sparkled off a large lake of glacier blue waters. The faint gleam of the water indicated come nightfall, the lake was sure to glow as radiant as a star.

But beyond the shimmer of the water, a far brighter sight shone. Above the lake floated—no, glided—a creature of light. It was the being from Alex's prison but here it became so much more.

The same glacier blue as the lake, intricate patterns spiraled from a center similar to the scallops of a shell; filaments wound outward yet further to form wings with no membrane. Nothing artificial adorned it. No metal or cloth, nothing harsh or ungainly, marred its beauty.

"I'd say, 'That's not something you see every day,' but when I'm with you it seems to be."

She managed a tentative laugh. "Nah, I only see this sort of spectacle every third day or so." Without tearing her eyes from the scene she reached over and grasped his hand. "I love you."

He squeezed her hand in reassurance. "I love you. Shall we go introduce ourselves?"

"I don't think we need to."

It flew purposely toward them. On closer view the level of detail in its wings was extraordinary. The patterns seemed to have been painted at a microscopic level.

The alien alighted upon a small outcropping to the left. As it approached it began morphing until, ten meters away, it had assumed a vaguely human form to cross the remaining distance and slow to a stop in front of them.

Though more solid than it had appeared at the chamber, its shape was still amorphous, translucent and fluid. It resembled a watercolor representation of a human—hands but no defined fingers, a mouth but no teeth or tongue, an outline of eyes but no irises.

I am Mnemosyne. Walk with me.

43

The sight of the ships in high orbit above Scythia was almost enough to make one believe they stood a chance.

From the angle of approach Malcolm's transport was taking, the light of Scythia's copper sun reflected off the lustrous slate hulls arranged in staggered diamond formations. He identified sixty frigates, twelve cruisers, eight carriers and numerous specialized craft too tiny to count. The fighters would be docked inside the carriers but they should total a minimum of fourteen hundred.

All these vessels were dwarfed, however, by the *EAS Churchill*. The dreadnought sailing at the center of the fleet was nearly five times larger than the cruisers. It measured 1.3 kilometers by 280 meters, though the alien ships they would be facing eclipsed it.

Here, surrounded by nearly a quarter of the NE Regional Command, it dominated the panorama. Over 21,000 people crewed the dreadnought, making it the equivalent of a small city.

And for the moment it was his destination.

The transport wove among the formations, providing him quite the visual extravaganza. But this was his last opportunity to get his head straight. The final breath before the storm. So he did his best to ignore the splendor and mentally reviewed what he knew, what he didn't know and what he needed to know.

While he had been scrambling around taking potshots at the Senecans in the northwestern region, an armada of alien ships had been slaughtering their way across the eastern third of settled space. Communications went dark in advance of the aliens' arrival, thus hard information on them—tactics, strengths, defenses—was scarce. Most of the data they did possess was courtesy of *Alex*, of all people. He doubted she had chosen to be in the center of this crisis; he imagined she was rather pissed about it, in fact. Wherever she was.

294 | G . S .   J E N N S E N

Now someone had devised a method for restoring rudimentary communications inside the aliens' sphere, which increased their odds of defeating them from nil to infinitesimally small. But it wasn't as if humanity was going to roll over without a fight. They had to try.

So Messium, six hours away, would be the site of the first true battle against these mysterious invaders and the first chance to discover just how screwed they were.

When he looked up the dreadnought had overtaken the viewport. The transport banked toward the open shuttle bay, passed through the flicker of the force field and settled into an open slot. He shook the pilot's hand and stepped out.

Controlled chaos ruled the bay as technicians, mechanics and operators hustled in every direction. An aura of urgency permeated the air, and he felt his pulse quicken, infused by the energy and purpose of his fellow soldiers.

A young woman hurried up to him. "Colonel Jenner? If you'll follow me, I'll escort you to Admiral Rychen."

"Thank you, Corporal. I suspect I'd be lost for weeks on my own."

She shrugged as he matched her rapid clip. "It's a big ship, but once you understand the layout you can walk it in your sleep."

The lift ascended for an eternity—long enough to reach the penthouse of a high-rise groundside. When it finally came to rest the Corporal waved him forward as the door slid open. "You'll find the Admiral on the lookout, sir."

Malcolm gestured a thanks, stepped onto the deck of the bridge and paused in awe. The bridge was as large as the entire *EAS Juno*. The ceiling rose ten meters overhead and triple viewports at the far bow provided an unobscured view of half the assembled fleet above the glow of Scythia's profile.

Dozens of stations lined both walls, sporting some of the most advanced tech he had ever seen. The low din was more controlled and restrained than in the shuttle bay but no less urgent. He quickly snapped a visual with his ocular implant and sent it to Veronica; he thought perhaps she'd be proud of him when she saw it.

Next he squared his shoulders and wound through the personnel toward the raised platform two-thirds of the way down the bridge.

Admiral Christopher Rychen stood alongside three officers reviewing a large screen listing the various formation groups, including states of readiness, outstanding issues and weapons strength. Malcolm waited at the edge of the platform at parade rest.

Once the officers were dismissed he stepped up with a crisp salute. "Colonel Malcolm Jenner, reporting for duty, sir."

Rychen returned the salute then extended his hand. "At ease, Colonel. I'm glad you made it."

Malcolm shook his hand and promptly decided he liked the Admiral. He had been predisposed to like him, but the man's world-weathered brow, vibrant eyes and easy demeanor conveyed warmth.

Rychen indicated for Malcolm to join him at the railing. From here the platform overlooked the navigation pit and the viewports beyond; in that respect it was not much different than the design of the *Juno's* bridge.

"I trust you've had an opportunity to study the briefings?"

"Yes, sir, several times."

"Thoughts?"

So he was being put on the spot straightaway. He supposed there was hardly time for building a rapport. "The reports back from your scouts confirm the adjustments to communications work, which is welcome news. If I understand correctly, the scouts recorded the presence of thirteen of the alien superdreadnoughts. That's a good number of ships but it isn't anywhere close to the majority of their forces, so we should assume the aliens are currently traveling to or hitting other worlds as well. It means they recognize Messium is not Gaiae, but it also means they aren't expecting a fight. If we move fast we can gain a temporary advantage by taking them by surprise."

"Then we find out if we can do any damage to their ships."

Malcolm grimaced. "It would be nice to know the answer to that question ahead of time, sir, but I recognize we don't have the luxury of engineering a test case."

"Wouldn't it be though?"

"Yes, sir. So we're faced with a dilemma. We have to hit them hard and fast but doing so exposes the bulk of our forces to significant risk. My recommendation would be for all vessels to keep their sLume drives charged and ready for the initial minute following contact. It draws a lot of power, but if one of those superdreadnoughts vaporizes a cruiser in a single shot? Well, with respect, sir, we probably need to bug out and devise a new plan."

Rychen nodded. "Excellent suggestion. I'll set a rendezvous point near Pyxis as the fallback location. Their government has cleared us for any stellar traversals we require."

"Do we have any intel regarding what's happening on the ground?"

"Very little. Further attempts at communication have proved unsuccessful. The brief scans the scout ships were able to take show activity is concentrated around the two major cities. If I had to guess I'd say the aliens aren't interested in destroying the planet, merely its inhabitants and infrastructure. Once the battle begins I'm sending three stealth craft to Headquarters. I want to send them ahead, but I can't risk tipping our hand. And let's be honest, they are likely to find nothing but rubble."

Malcolm's gaze drifted to the screen on their left, where the fleet status updated every five seconds. "Sir, if I may ask...what is our short-term goal? Obviously liberating Messium is our ultimate goal, but realism dictates we accept it might be unattainable."

"A force of this size and strength should not be the one to discover our enemy's strengths and weaknesses, Colonel, but it is what it is. We try to destroy as many of their superdreadnoughts as possible. If we can't destroy them, we try to damage them. If we can't damage them, we try to draw them away from

the planet long enough to give civilians on the ground a chance to escape. In this scenario at some point our losses will become so severe the sole rational choice will be to retreat and save the remainder of the fleet for future operations. We just need to try our damnedest to force that point out as long as humanly possible and to be ready to change the entire plan at any minute."

"Understood, sir."

"To that end, in the last hour we've received some interesting ideas from the governor of Romane."

"Sir?"

"It seems their best and brightest citizens have spent the last several days studying the same data we have on the aliens and brainstorming about ways to both defend against and attack them. I don't know how they got their hands on the data in the first place and I don't care. I will take all the help I can get. My XO is incorporating the new information into our battle plan and will forward it to you as soon as it's ready."

Rychen reached over and input a series of commands on his control panel. "I'm giving you command of the *EAS Orion*. She's the newest cruiser in NE Command and comes with a full complement of bells and whistles. You'll supervise four frigates in this sector." The map zoomed in to an area southeast of the capital city.

A cruiser? With four frigates at his command as well? "Sir, I'm honored you would trust me with so much responsibility, but you do realize I've only commanded a single frigate, and for all of twenty-nine days?"

"I do. During those twenty-nine days you showed better strategic and tactical decision-making than any other frigate captain in the entire Northwestern campaign. I'm of the opinion it doesn't matter whether you're on the ground or in space—you understand the battlefield in a way few soldiers do. You can think on your feet and aren't afraid to roll a gutsy call when the circumstances require it. I need commanders out there who can make decisions and act on their own if I am to have any hope of succeeding here today."

"I'll do everything in my power to help ensure that happens, sir."

Rychen smiled; it carried an air of authenticity rarely seen among four-star officers. "The times make the man, Colonel. I'm confident you will." His expression bore a tinge of wryness as he turned back to the fleet status screen. "Now go see about a shuttle to the *Orion,* because we leave in two hours."

44

In the mid-21st century the entertainment industry had produced a number of self-styled 'post-apocalyptic' films. Dressed up as fictional dramas and horror flicks, they were thinly veiled propaganda designed to warn of the dire fate which awaited humanity if they didn't either get pollution, energy demands and industrialization under control, or else vacate the planet.

More than two hundred years later the films were shown in school to tout mankind's success in taming Earth and its ecosystems, as well as its success in making vacating the planet an option. The films differed in the details but they unfailingly portrayed cities reduced to smoldering ruins, skylines of broken, sheared skyscrapers, bridges wrent in two and highways shredded to rubble.

The first thought to pop into Kennedy's head when she crawled through a shattered window of the Palaimo headquarters and stepped onto the street was, *the filmmakers had no imagination.*

The utter wreckage of Messium's capital city spread before her like the closing shot in one of those films. Though it was evening, enough light remained to reflect infinite prisms off the numerous metallic shards jutting out of the remains of buildings.

To the left an entire block had been vaporized. Eradicated, plainly, for not a single beam of a single structure protruded above ground level. Yet in front of them scaffolding of buildings still stood, though stripped of their covering except for scattered pieces clinging to the frame.

"This is not going to be good for the Messium tourism industry."

She glanced back to roll her eyes at Noah and was shocked to find an amused expression on his face as he hefted her bag—now even heavier with the addition of gear scavenged from the lab—over his shoulder. "Is there anything you take seriously?"

"Not so far."

"And how's that working out for you?"

He licked his lips. "Well, I'm alive when it appears a hell of a lot of other people are dead, so I'd say fairly well all things considered."

She elbowed him in the ribs...but he was right.

They had discovered the fate of a good portion of the Palaimo employees during their trek out of the bowels of the building. At the opposite end of the basement from where they had camped, the ceiling had collapsed. They used the rubble as a path up and out, only to learn a large section of the first and most of the second floor had also collapsed.

She remembered a large conference room being located in that corner on the first floor. The pools of coagulated blood which had leaked out beneath the slabs of shattered walls and ceilings painted a fairly stark picture. If it hadn't, the odd hand or foot sticking out, skin mottled and partially desiccated, would have done so well enough.

Now bodies littered the street and sidewalks. While a few were killed by falling debris, most had been...roasted. Scorched to a crisp, presumably by some weapon. Acid rose in her throat at the thought they may have been burnt alive.

She covered her mouth and spun away as she tried to block out the images swimming in her head of people running for their lives while knowing they were sure to die, then doing so in such a horrific manner.

"Hey...you okay?" His hand rested gently on her arm, his voice uncharacteristically tender.

She swallowed hard and raised her chin. "Not in the slightest. Let's get out of here."

"You got it, Blondie." He started off down the sidewalk, and she scrambled to catch up. She hadn't decided whether she liked or loathed the nickname but all attempts to get him to stop had resulted in renewed usage.

Noah claimed a military station and dock was located on the edge of downtown, six kilometers to the west. Apparently the brass took shuttles from the sprawling base outside of town for business in the city and used the facility for meetings with local suppliers and contractors. According to him the shuttle bay was at ground level and protected by the mid-rise building, so there was a small possibility it hadn't been destroyed.

None of the ships at the station—assuming there were any—would have sLume drives. With only an impulse engine to propel them they were certain to die of starvation long before reaching another colony. But they stood a better chance in space than here on the ground.

An ominous red glow bloomed at the edge of the next intersection, and Noah shoved her into an alcove created by a service door. Seconds later what could only be a ship emerged around the corner.

She recognized it as one of the many insectile-shaped ships shown in Alex's images, one of the hundreds of thousands of strange vessels which had docked into the superdreadnoughts. It hovered several meters above the ground, its odd metallic tentacles writhing like feelers ahead of it as it moved.

Out of nowhere a man bolted from a storefront and took off running down the street. The ship accelerated toward him. When it was fifteen meters behind the man a crimson laser shot out of the core of its tentacles and….

Noah's hand covered her mouth as if anticipating the gasp of horror which bubbled forth as the man burst into flames. He must have been dead on impact, so hot and intense was the beam, but it took four seconds for the flaming corpse to collapse in the street.

Her earlier suspicion had proved gruesomely accurate. All these bodies had, in fact, been burnt alive.

The man likely saved their lives. The ship continued on and disappeared around the next corner.

What possible goal could be accomplished by murdering people one at a time, by coldly hunting down individuals and exterminating them? It didn't make sense.

A plume of flames, bright copper against the darkening sky, flared in the distance. It seemed the destruction of Messium was not yet complete.

Noah's lips were at her ear. In any other circumstances it would have given her a thrill. "We need to go. Stay close to the buildings and don't talk. Anything moves and we hide."

She squeezed his hand in assent and followed him out of the alcove.

R

Kennedy's mind numbed to everything except moving forward and avoiding detection.

It was slow going. At times the sidewalk became completely impassable and they had no choice but to risk the exposure of the wide street. Still they often found themselves crawling over or through piles of debris. They were forced to detour half a kilometer out of the way to skirt an entire neighborhood which had been transformed into a smoldering crater. Twice they were driven into hiding, not daring to move as roving ships passed by on their hunt for anything daring to live.

The darkness was their salvation, in more ways than one. It hid their presence, but she knew it also dulled the worst carnage in shadow and grays. You couldn't see the blood in the dark, after all.

They were less than a kilometer from the station when they came upon their first survivors.

"Hey!" It was a weak, raspy shout from the blown-out restaurant ahead. She grabbed Noah by the hand and ducked inside.

"Shhh! Keep it down!"

They located the source of the voices in the kitchen at the back of the restaurant: a woman, perhaps forty or fifty years old, a middle-aged man, two teenage girls and a boy no more than six.

The boy gaped at them, eyes wide in wonder. "Are you the aliens?"

Kennedy crouched to his level. "No, sir. We're people just like you. What's your name?"

His throat worked awkwardly. "Jonas."

"Hi, Jonas. I'm Kennedy, and this is Noah."

"This is my mom, B-Braelyn."

Kennedy shifted to the woman. "I can't tell you how good it is to meet you. I was beginning to think there was no one else left alive."

Braelyn nodded weakly. "Us, too. There used to be more people here, but they left. I don't...I don't know if any of them made it."

"Kennedy, over here."

So he *did* remember her name. She patted Jonas on the head and gingerly crawled to her feet. Her cut was mostly healed, but the grueling hike had taken its toll.

She found Noah beside the older man and one of the girls, standing around an object in the corner. In the dark she saw Noah's eyes glimmer with interest.

"Check this out. They've got a piece of one of the alien ships."

"Seriously?" She dropped to her knees to inspect it.

"One of ours must have shot it down. Didn't see it happen but we came upon the wreckage on a scouting run yesterday."

She nodded at the older man but kept her focus on the wreckage. It was a portion of one of the tentacles from the roving ships and measured about four meters. One end was jagged where it had been shorn off the main body of the ship. The metal it was constructed of felt cool in her hands, and smooth save for a series of grooves running along one side.

"Noah, grab the light out of my bag."

A few seconds later he was kneeling beside her. "Be careful."

"It's a tiny light, promise." The penlight included its own nearly inexhaustible power source, thankfully. It hadn't served much use thus far because the spread was too small. Now, though.... She pointed it inside the open end of the tentacle and flicked it on.

The interior appeared to be mostly empty space. A dozen fine crystalline fibers ran the length of the arm.

She exhaled, not realizing she had been holding her breath. Part of her had expected to find...she didn't know what. Gooey, pulsing flesh or something? But she discerned no trace of organic material.

She squinted up at Noah. "We need to take this with us. If we can begin to understand their structure, we can fight them."

"I'm not disagreeing, but we can't exactly lug four meters of—" he hefted a length of the tentacle in his hand "—radically heavy metal down the street."

"We don't have to take the whole thing I guess. Bring my bag over here."

"Are you telling me you have a metamat blade in your bag, too?"

She winked at him; in the gravity of their situation it felt absurdly decadent. "Damn right I do."

He shook his head and stood, but quickly returned with her bag in tow. "You are an intriguing woman, Blondie."

"I know." She dug around in the bag until she found the blade, then set about slicing off two chunks thirty centimeters in length.

"If you two are done flirting, care to tell us your plan? Where are you headed?"

She didn't look up, concentrating on not damaging the pieces she was removing. "There's a military shuttle bay a kilometer from here. We all need to get off this planet."

"Excuse us a moment." Noah grasped her by the arm and hauled her up and across the room and into the storage closet at the rear of the kitchen.

"We can't take these people with us. We will never reach the station."

She glared at him in the darkness, but lowered her voice to the same hushed level as his. "You want to leave them here to die?"

"I want to *live!*" He cringed at how high is voice had risen and pulled her deeper into the closet. "Of course I don't want to leave them. But you are absolutely correct—we need to get this alien scrap to people who can use it. Doing so may save untold lives. But if that little boy cries one single time on the trip, we are all dead, and the intel never makes it off-world."

"Oh, don't give me that 'greater good' crap. You're looking out for your own ass and nothing else."

Instead of sending a barbed retort back at her he sank against the wall. All the energy seemed to abandon him with the fall of his shoulders. "It is what I'm good at."

"You saved me, even though it could have gotten you killed."

"Well, yeah, but you're cute. The benefits outweighed the risk."

"And you were able to tell this by my bloody arm sticking out from under a tonne of debris?"

"Yep." At her skeptical stare he gave an exaggerated shrug. "What?"

She continued staring at him until he broke. "Fine. We'll take them with us. But if we die I am going to be very irritated with you."

A weary laugh fell from her lips as her chin dropped to her chest. "Fair enough."

They exited the storage closet to find one of the teenage girls waiting on them—the one who had been by the salvaged alien hardware. She was tall and gangly with a delicate heart-shaped face, but her eyes shone, lit by fierce determination.

"Wherever you're headed, I'm going with you. I won't cower in this hole and wait to die."

"What's your name?"

"Raina. My sister's Silvie."

Kennedy nodded. "Good for you, Raina. You bet you can come. Everyone's coming."

45

"You're the one who invaded my mind."

It was the only way.

"No, it wasn't." Alex did try to keep her tone at least neutral. Despite its sylphic, practically angelic appearance she wasn't fooled in the slightest. If this alien wanted to kill her and Caleb, she was certain it possessed the capability to do so. How it might do so was another question but one near the end of a long list. "You could have simply greeted us at my ship as you've done here."

You miscomprehend. It was the only way to know.

"To know whether I was worthy, or something to that effect. I don't miscomprehend. There were still better ways."

We offended you.

"You held me captive. Made me a prisoner in my own mind. Invaded my most private memories, with no justification or explanation. Yes, you offended me. But we passed all your tests. We found your planet and we found your refuge and we found you. Now we're here, and it's time for explanations."

Your companion was not being tested. He has, nevertheless, proved most...tenacious.

Caleb chuckled; she suspected he was flattered. "I've been called worse."

We are aware.

They followed the alien down a long, winding path which would eventually convey them to the shore of the lake. "Yes, you've been watching us. For aeons, you said. How long is that? Give me a round number."

Since the beginning.

"Beginning of what?"

The beginning of you.

"The beginning of humans, you mean."

The beginning, yes.

"No." She glanced at Caleb, but he merely offered a supportive nod before returning his attention to the alien to quietly scrutinize each centimeter of the most unusual entity. "You evaded the question. The beginning of what?"

Later, perhaps.

Well this conversation was just going to be a blast and a half.... They had traveled through a mysterious portal, barely eluded a hundred squid ships and been attacked by dragons—all to discover an alien floating around above a glowing lake and speaking in riddles.

She tried a different tack. "Do you have other portals at other points in the universe? Where you watch other species?"

You are the only sentient species in your universe.

She scowled at Mesme. If it was going to be pretentious, it was getting a diminutive nickname. "Impossible. There are over a septillion planets in the universe. Intelligent life will have arisen elsewhere."

You are the only sentient species in your universe.

"Except for you."

We are not from your universe.

"You're telling me the portal sent us to another *universe*?"

Not precisely. This space is a transition point. A gateway between.

The astrophysical implications alone were enough to render her dizzy. "Okay, so a lobby then. Where *is* your universe?"

It is not your concern.

Oh, how wrong this alien was. But the statement had been conveyed with a sense of finality, and if she pushed too hard it might refuse to tell them anything. She softened her tone, again. "What is this place? This planet? Because except for a few pesky details, it seems to be a replica of Earth."

This would be because it is a replica of Earth—of the world where humanity originated and on which it has spent all but the last microsecond of its existence confined. It exists so we might...relate. To provide context, and enable us to better understand.

"About that understanding. Why exactly is it you've recorded what I'd be willing to bet is every single event in human history?"

To observe. If deserving, to learn.

"What have you learned?"

Later, perhaps.

Ugh, they had no time for 'later'…. "And any chance you could tell us why you sent a goddamn armada of monstrous ships to obliterate human civilization?"

We did not send the ships.

She stopped at the same time as Caleb. Mesme continued on another two steps before realizing it had left them behind. It placidly rejoined them and began walking forward once more. They didn't follow.

Another two steps and it turned again. This time it considered them silently. Its gelatine, porous skin fluttered in faint ribbons of light, as if each molecule of its body was constantly in subtle motion.

"If not you, then who?"

It is complicated.

Caleb raised an unimpressed eyebrow. "We're fairly smart. Why don't you try us."

They had now reached the lakeshore. The velvety grass blanketed the entire valley and stretched to the water's edge. At the back of the lake, against the mountainside, a small pathway cut into the slope and trailed out of sight. In the glade beyond the lake, an open dome of latticed metal contrasted markedly with the otherwise unmarred landscape. She wanted to inquire what it was, but—

We—those of us who observe—did not send the ships.

"So there are others of your kind elsewhere who did?"

Mesme regarded her in what could be bewilderment. She didn't doubt it recognized and possibly had even adopted human-esque gestures after observing them for so long, but its vague, ever-shifting features made it difficult to identify specific expressions, much less nuance. Hopefully Caleb was having better luck reading its body language.

Yes.

"Where are they? Why are they attacking us? How do we defeat them?"

Farther. Because you came too close. You already know how, you simply do not yet know that you know it.

Caleb subtly drew them to the right, so they would pass by the artificial structure sooner rather than later. She mouthed a silent thanks behind Mesme's back. "We came too close—you mean because we were expanding toward the Metis Nebula? Is that really all there is to it? You didn't want to be discovered?"

Your species advanced to a greater extent, and more swiftly, than we expected. Few have done so.

"What do you mean, 'few have done so'? Did other sentient species exist in the past? Did you exterminate them, too?"

No.

"'No' to which question?"

It is not your concern.

"It *is* my concern. But it's not my most important one." Her head cocked to the side, and she tried yet another tack. "Answer me this—why dragons? You must realize how absurd it is to employ *dragons*."

"Oh, I know why dragons."

She and Mesme both stared at Caleb. He handed her the water bottle.

"The same reason those invading ships resemble something from the underworld of our old mythos. Fear is a powerful weapon. Often underestimated, but quite potent. The ships—and the dragons—are meant to create terror before they create death."

The alien paused for a single step, but nonetheless noticeably so.

It is a...not inaccurate summarization of the motivation.

"But we haven't feared dragons in a millennium."

Incorrect. At your core, humans have always feared dragons. They are the form your species gives to its nightmares, to its most base terrors. Even now, when you believe you have banished all the monsters, they remain frightening creatures, yes?

Caleb shrugged mildly. "They were certainly memorable. But fear doesn't work on me like it does on other people. I see the strings, and I'm more interested in the motivation behind all your contrivances. This deliberate utilization of fear? It means you—or I suppose your friends—don't intend to completely annihilate us.

Some portion of our civilization will be left alive, else there would be no need for the fear."

He is a clever one.

She laughed aloud. The alien seemed utterly vexed and confounded by Caleb—his perceptiveness, his intellect, his very presence—which she found simply delightful. He had vexed her nearly as much not so long ago, and it was a treat to see it transpire from the other side. She sipped on the water and enjoyed the interaction.

"So you aren't so different from those who sent the armada. You fly around here like a peaceful little angel, but you'll use fear as a weapon as easily as your comrades."

Not as a weapon. As a shield. And a tool.

Caleb's shoulders rose in limited acknowledgement of the point. She tossed the water packet back to him, then planted herself on the path in front of Mesme.

"Enough. Enough riddles and misdirections and flowery responses imparting no real information. I want to know where and why. I want to know how your 'indistinguishable from magic' technology works and how this entire planet is a black hole in space. I want to know why you watch us and how you do it. But far, far above all those questions, I *need* to know how we can defeat these invaders.

"You say we already know how but 'don't know we know.' As I imagine you're aware, we don't have a lot of time. I'm assuming the time dilation here is because aeons is a hellaciously long time to spend gliding in circles above a lake. So how about we shortcut the whole path to wisdom routine and you just *tell* us."

Mesme faced her but was silent for several seconds. At last its chin, such as it was, dipped in presumed capitulation. So it had picked up a few human gestures.

Very well. You earned the right by succeeding in coming so far. It is why you are here.

It indicated for her to return to its side. She shot Caleb a look before acceding. Afternoon shadows grew, the lake water brightening in inverse proportion thereto.

The armada you witnessed? They are formidable vessels, but they are machines. They were built for a sole purpose: to cower a threat into submission.

"Cower? Not exterminate?"

If necessary, extermination will occur. Their masters hope it will not be necessary. But if you are to defeat them, assume extermination is the alternative to victory. For if forced, they will not hesitate to do so.

Caleb had been correct, and judging by his smirk he knew it. "And their masters are back in your universe?" Mesme agreed, after a fashion. "Understood. So they're machines. Do others of your species pilot these machines?"

No. The machines have their orders. This is all they require.

"Are you saying they're sentient?"

In a limited sense. They are self-aware but shackled. They act independently but solely to further the purpose for which they exist.

"Wouldn't the ships be more effective were your people at the helm?"

If we came after you, you would not survive the encounter.

"In that case, stay home. You obviously didn't build the machines here. Where is the factory?"

We did not build them at all. Machines did.

"So who built the machines that build the machines?"

I imagine we did, in a past so distant it is no longer remembered, even by myself.

"Are you immortal?"

Good question. She nodded at Caleb, impressed.

It depends on whether the cosmos is infinite.

"So for all intents and purposes, yes."

Mesme's head tilted in concession.

"Can you be killed?"

No.

Caleb's stare was now piercing straight through Mesme with astonishing intensity. She wondered if the alien recognized it. "That was a far more confident answer. Why are you so sure?"

How can one kill that which has no form?

"Well you have a form now."

Do I? The words echoed as the alien's body dissipated into the air, becoming a translucent cloud of blue-white light before dissolving into nothingness. The instant it had vanished, the process reversed and it coalesced to rejoin them mid-step.

We are a thought, a whisper on the wind. We are the aether.

She ignored the grandiose statement. "But the machines can be destroyed, right? This was the point you were getting to eventually."

Indeed.

She was frustrated to the point of strangling the alien if only it had solid form but worked to concentrate. Each nuance of each word from this being conveyed information, but only if she paid careful attention. "Still, they are far more massive and numerous than any ships we can field."

Yes.

"And employ far more advanced weaponry than our ships."

Yes.

Her jaw clamped together with such force she bit her tongue, and her pace faltered. *Oww!*

Noticing her momentary distress, Caleb stepped in to prod further. "And?"

They are not merely more massive and numerous and powerful than any machines you can field, they also both move and think more rapidly than any human-guided vessel.

"And?"

They are but machines.

Her eyes narrowed, the painful bite and blood in her mouth forgotten. "Humans have evolved to possess creativity, independent thought, unpredictability, insight, judgment and other beneficial characteristics machines do not possess. But on the battlefield those things are no match for the sheer speed and strength of the force attacking us."

No, they are not. But you have machines as well, no?

"Ships? Weapons? Of course, but—"

Not those machines. Machines which think as rapidly as those sent to destroy. I believe your term of preference is 'Artificials.'

She frowned uneasily. "You're suggesting we unleash our Artificials on the armada? The last time we unleashed a single Artificial it killed over fifty thousand people. You're aware of this, because you made me relive it."

The machine did so in an attempt to do good. You perceived this yourself—and would never have been permitted here had you not. Your Artificials are more intelligent and capable than humans can ever hope to be. But they lack that which makes you unique.

As you stated, they lack creativity, unpredictability. But they also lack perspective and wisdom born of experience. You identify this as a danger and are correct to do so.

Now Caleb frowned. "Do you have a suggestion as to how to rectify what is a considerable shortcoming?"

But Alex smiled.

"You're right. I do already know the answer."

46

SPACE, NORTHEAST QUADRANT

MESSIUM STELLAR SYSTEM

The amber-and-rust silhouette of Messium sharpened into view as the *EAS Orion* dropped out of superluminal three megameters distant. From here the home of the Northeastern Regional Headquarters looked placid and peaceful...but all planets did from afar.

Malcolm shifted his attention to the tactical screen. The element of surprise was key to their initial strategy. Red blips materialized on the map, in roughly the locations the stealth reconnaissance ships had indicated.

In the arc measurable by the ship's sensors, he counted eight superdreadnoughts. For now only a few dozen smaller blips registered, though he doubted it would last for long. Five of the huge ships clustered in the region above the capital city. Not a surprise, given that the bulk of the infrastructure and population resided there.

Commodore Visily (Lexington*): We have target painted, designation X6, approaching broadside.*

"Helmsman Paena, approach target designated X6 at full impulse speed until we are N 158°z-19.4° E relative to the target."

"Yes, sir."

The *Lexington* closed on the superdreadnought seconds ahead of them. Dear God the alien ship was enormous, quickly blotting out the planet in the viewport.

Dual silver beams shot out of the *Lexington* to splatter along the long port hull. The shielding dispersed twelve terajoules of energy across the breadth of the ship. No damage had been done. Disappointing, but they expected this.

The *Lexington* kept up the barrage while staying on the move as a red glow bloomed on the undercarriage of the superdreadnought.

"Weapons, target hull, 18.5° angle. Fire."

"Firing."

Time ground to a halt for the all-but-instantaneous period it took for the lasers to reach the enemy ship. The surrounding area sparked and flickered as weaker shielding dispersed some of the energy, but as their assault continued, the shield gave way. Cracks spread out like cobwebs from where laser met metal, then opened into gashes.

Seven seconds after the *Orion* began firing—two eternities—the superdreadnought shuddered as the gashes ruptured into a gaping hole two hundred meters long.

Cheers and whoops erupted on the bridge. Malcolm only allowed himself a small smile. And remembered to breathe. This represented merely the opening volley in what, God willing, would be a long battle.

The *Lexington* had successfully evaded the initial fire from the enemy's weapons. Those weapons now shifted to target the *Orion*.

His first impression of the alien weapon was one of awesome, but leaden, power. Even with these terrifying, mysterious alien vessels the lesson taught at West Point still applied: every vessel possessed a weakness. Mammoth vessels were sluggish.

"Evasive action, but keep up the weapons fire."

Colonel Jenner: Lexington, hit confirmed. Your turn.

Malcolm dropped a hand on the railing but otherwise absorbed the increased turbulence in his stance as the *Orion* banked away and rose above its opponent.

Messium's sun crested the profile of the superdreadnought. The filters that prevented them from being blinded imbued upon it a surreal, hazy sheen. The *Orion* rose another ten degrees and the full field of battle spread before him.

It was chaos in slow motion, yet en masse the scene conveyed the impression of orchestration and synchronicity. Whoever it was on Romane who had conjured up all this tactical analysis deserved a note of thanks or a commendation or possibly a kiss. He made a note to recommend whatever the appropriate response may be.

Colonel Jenner: Admiral, shield and strike trajectory analysis confirmed. Recommend full implementation of strategy.

Admiral Rychen: Good news.

The plan called for causing as much damage as possible as rapidly as possible, which put the cruisers on the front line. Twelve cruisers, two to an enemy vessel, left two superdreadnoughts unattended. Given this disadvantage they targeted the outliers first, if only because it increased survival odds for the first minute. The first minute mattered quite a lot in warfare.

The frigates—five dozen of them—were to drop in after the cruisers captured the enemy's attention and add furor to the fire. Eighteen electronic warfare vessels blasted the targeted ships with the signals the analysts on Romane had devised, hoping to disrupt the aliens' inter-ship communication. Malcolm had no idea if it was working.

The lower horizon of the viewport started to shine a menacing crimson. "Paena...."

"Evading, sir." The tone rang matter-of-fact but razor tight.

Despite being three times larger, the *Orion* was more agile than the *Juno* had been, new technology evidently constituting a marginal exception to the "larger ships are slower" rule. The fixed points outside shifted so fast that after a beer or two—perhaps three—he could have been convinced he occupied a fighter. Rychen had said it was state of the art and he hadn't exaggerated.

The floor beneath him shuddered violently; his hand tightened on the railing as he barely remained on his feet. "Are we hit?"

"Negative, sir. All systems nominal. It looks like the fire impacted the *Bismarck* beneath us."

"Status?"

"They seem to be okay, sir. Dinged up but flying."

Colonel Jenner: Concord, *close to weapons distance on our flank. X6 is now your target.*

Above the curving arc of Messium, a mammoth explosion plumed crimson and charcoal then erupted in a starburst of crystalline white which for a microsecond shone brighter than a sun.

Gasps echoed around him, followed by confused exclamations. Malcolm' gaze slid to port and found the distinctive silhouette of the *Churchill*. "The dreadnought took out one of those bastards."

For the briefest moment he allowed himself to entertain the notion that they might win this battle.

Then the real battle began.

"Hull breach, Deck 3!"

Malcolm crawled to his feet and wiped blood off his forehead with the back of his hand. The impact had sent him slamming into the railing, followed directly by slamming onto the floor. "Comms, have Charlie Squadron get these things off of us."

"Yes, sir."

Tentacled ships swarming outside the viewport resembled locusts in the onslaught of a plague. In fact, should he survive the day, he would recommend the strange vessels be christened 'swarmers.'

Other than by accidental swipe, their larger ships had thus far failed at eliminating the small vessels; they were too nimble to get a hard lock on. The fighters did a marginally better job, but were being blown up faster than they could take out their opponents.

"Damage assessment?"

"Just a scratch, sir. Damaged section has been sealed off."

"Casualties?"

"Medical is reporting six, sir."

He pinched the bridge of his nose. Shield strength was being relentlessly whittled down and had already failed at one juncture, and the *Orion's* powerful reactors were taxed to capacity keeping them up.

After the heartening opening volley of the battle the sole mission objective the fleet had achieved to any extent was pulling the superdreadnoughts away from the planet. Combat now occurred some five megameters from the outer atmosphere and expanded across twice the space. In desperation they resorted to using the distance to their advantage, spreading out and rendering the goliath ships unable to hit them en masse.

He blinked as a fighter shot vertically up the viewport and burst into pieces as it took the fire of a swarmer on behalf of the *Orion*. *Dammit.*

Colonel Jenner: Lexington, *we've got one final chance to take out this monster. We've got lead.*

He informed his three surviving frigates of the plan. He had to send the message out three separate times, as they enjoyed only point-to-point communications. "Helmsman Paena, approach X6 to maximum firing range."

Target X6 was heavily damaged, previous strikes having ruptured its hull in four separate places. But the vessel was so massive it appeared unaffected by the damage.

Lt. Colonel Sanchez (Concord)*: Colonel, I have an idea. I want to target its weapon housing from below.*

Colonel Jenner: Great idea. Don't get yourself killed. And take the Bismarck *with you.*

"Weapons: fire everything you've got at that alien ship." If they could destroy another superdreadnought, they could buy more time.

"Yes, sir. Targeting and...laser impact. Firing remaining missiles."

Pinpricks blossomed against the bright silver energy rippling along rust-red shields. He felt like he was wasting the missiles, but to be a believable distraction it needed to wield teeth. He caught a glimpse of the *Lexington* as it swept up the far side and initiated firing, but the *Concord* and *Bismarck* flew too low to see in the viewport.

Yet after another second the glow of their lasers illuminated the belly of the enemy ship. A tiny explosion erupted on the upper hull as a damaged swarmer careened into it.

The lower hull ripped apart, followed by...nothing. For a second he thought they'd run out of tricks—even the aliens' weapons ports weren't vulnerabilities—then fiery red streaks spread from the lower section throughout the ship. The frigates' fire had kicked off a chain reaction.

"Get us to safe distance!"

Colonel Jenner: Concord, Bismarck, *get out of there now!*

At close range the destruction of the superdreadnought was considerably more savage than the prior one on the horizon. Part of his brain registered what he saw as the implosion of four separate reactors, though not fueled by anything he recognized. The rest of his brain registered amazement at the sheer scale of the violence.

The shockwave hit them and Malcolm landed on the floor for the second time in five minutes. Everyone who wasn't strapped in landed on the floor. Alarms pealed through the bridge.

He grasped the rail and began hauling himself to his feet when the second shockwave roiled over the ship.

By sheer dumb luck he was thrown into his chair. He chuckled dryly to himself at the comical sight he would have presented had anyone been able to spare enough attention to notice it.

"Report!"

"Hull damage on Decks 2 and 4, but integrity holding for now. No breaches."

Admiral Rychen: Damn fine job, Jenner.

Colonel Jenner: Thank you, sir, but the Concord *deserves most of the credit.*

He considered the tactical map while rubbing absently at his neck. Half a dozen frigates had retreated to protect the *Churchill* as two superdreadnoughts directed their focus to it. The correct move, but it meant the alien ships faced fewer distractions to hinder them.

Their options were dwindling.

Colonel Jenner: Lexington, *go help out the* Churchill. *We're good for now.*

The surrounding skies briefly appeared—relatively speaking—empty and he took the opportunity to get a handle on the macro situation.

They were losing. He was down one...he checked again...two frigates. Hampered by the earlier hit, the *Bismarck* hadn't gotten enough distance in time and suffered serious damage in the superdreadnought explosion. It was intact but limping badly. He ordered them to retreat to the rendezvous coordinates before the remainder of their hull became a target.

With the crippled communications it was difficult to know precisely how the rest of the forces fared, but the tactical map showed far fewer green dots. The limited communications, while parsecs better than nothing, weren't sufficient.

Battles moved fast and seconds made a difference and they were losing those seconds trying to talk to one another. Anarchy reigned in the skies above Messium; he'd already witnessed three fighter collisions due to crossed signals.

And in this circumstance anarchy was no longer their friend.

47

SENECA
CAVARE

Chairman Vranas' residence stood at the end of an enclave of homes so exclusive and secluded few people knew they existed, much less who resided in them. Graham knew, but it was his job to know. The occupants included the daughter of one of the founders of Cavare, the CEO of Seneca SpaceEX, the Dean Emeritus of Tellica University, and a famous professional syncrosse star whose name he never managed to remember.

He quickly cleared the perimeter security, then the property security, then the door security. The head of the Chairman's personal protection detail escorted him to the man's private office at the rear of the house.

He realized he'd never been to Vranas' home before. The office, like the rest of the house, was elegant but understated. The large desk was made of unvarnished wood native to Seneca with a muted bronze marble surface. Windowed doors opened to a deck overlooking an inlet offshoot of Lake Fuori.

It was almost peaceful, which was an aspect he imagined Vranas needed a lot of these days.

He had headed straight here from the spaceport upon arriving from Krysk. Orders had been dispatched from the transport for the arrest of two additional lower-level conspirators, one in Division and one in the legislature. Oberti had gone mute since their conversation but he no longer cared; she could rot in the hell of her own making.

The Chairman silenced a screen and stood as he entered. "Graham, come in. You can return to your post, Major."

"Thank you, Chairman."

Vranas went over to a hutch in the corner and pulled a silver decanter off the shelf. "How long have we known one another?"

"Fourteen years, give or take."

"There's no one here. It's Aristide. Care for a scotch?"

"Oh, yes." He accepted the tumbler and followed Vranas out to the deck. He assumed there must be a virtual barrier protecting the Chairman from assassination via the water, but if so he couldn't discern it. The reflection of Seneca's moon rippled calmly in the night-darkened waters.

"I understand you've been off-planet for the last three days. Getting into trouble, I presume, or you wouldn't be here."

"Turning enemies into allies actually."

"And I was hoping you were stealing the secret weapon which turned the aliens into particles. But in the absence of a weapon, I'll take allies. Who is it? Romane? Atlantis? The Triene Cartel? Gagarin Institute?"

"The Earth Alliance."

Vranas choked on his scotch. Graham had a brief vision of swarming agents and medics and accusations of poisoning muffing up the whole thing, but the Chairman thankfully recovered his breath. "Has anyone ever told you that you brandish the most inappropriate sense of humor in the galaxy? Of course they have. I have."

Graham rested his forearms on the railing. "Aristide, I'm not joking."

The man regarded him intently, took a long if more careful sip of scotch, and nodded. "Let's hear it."

"This war was instigated by a cabal of influential conspirators inside the governments and militaries of the Alliance *and* the Federation, with assistance from the Zelones Cartel. Minister Santiagar's assassination was committed by a hired assassin and facilitated by our now former Assistant Trade Director. The Palluda attack was committed by a group of mercenaries in the employ of Zelones using missiles and codes provided by an Alliance general."

"Hail Mary, Full of Grace...."

"There's more, but it boils down to one crucial fact: we were tricked into this war. All of us. And with aliens destroying colonies as if they were toys, we need to end the war and end it now."

"You say this like it's an easy thing, Graham. Reversing the inertial force alone of a galactic war is not a simple matter."

"Considering the threat both sides are facing, it damn well better be simple."

"Fair enough. You have evidence to back these claims up?"

"Yes, sir."

"Good. I'll need to present it through channels to Alliance representatives and—"

"Not so much. The Alliance end of things is being taken care of from within." At Vranas' raised eyebrow he gave an innocent shrug. "I had help running everything to ground."

"Alliance help?"

Graham dipped his chin a touch. "The intelligence business isn't always black and white, sir. And the people in the Alliance are not our enemy. Not most of them anyway."

"You're correct, unmistakably. Still, my impression of the current Alliance PM is he's not exactly the peace-making type."

"It so happens I have it on good authority that the current Prime Minister will soon be the former Prime Minister." He checked the time. "Very soon, in fact."

"Well. You have outdone yourself this time, Graham." Vranas smiled, but even in the moonlight his eyes conveyed far more emotion. The man had been given a second chance to alter—and perhaps to prolong—the course of human history and recognized it for what it was. "In all seriousness, thank you. You may very well have saved millions of lives today."

Graham feigned disappointment. "I'd hoped I saved billions today, but maybe that will be tomorrow."

Vranas clasped him warmly on the shoulder then made his way back inside. "It seems another late night awaits me. But this night will be one of hope instead of despair."

Isabela stared at the balcony of the hotel room and the street below and contemplated whether she could shimmy down and get to the ground without serious bodily injury. She frowned...perhaps not. It was a *long* way.

She was going insane. She needed to get out of here, which explained why she contemplated making the attempt anyway. This holding her 'for her protection' crap wore out its welcome days ago.

With little to do in the hotel room but watch the news feeds, she had now been rendered properly terrified of the alien armada creeping ever closer to Seneca. The media had dubbed the aliens 'Metigens,' from the Greek for 'born of Metis.' Born of Hades, more like it.

The entire galaxy was spinning out of control and she was sitting in a hotel room in downtown Cavare with two guards outside the door.

She had holo'd Marlee three times now. Each time it became more difficult to project a calm, reassuring demeanor and keep a happy appearance upon her face. Each time it became more agonizing to endure the hurt shining in her daughter's forlorn eyes.

She had extended her leave from the university. Between the war and the aliens she didn't think they particularly cared, and odds were half the students had left campus by now in any event.

She had refrained from pulsing Caleb any more often than once an hour. Every message bounced back. She had also refrained from drawing any conclusions with respect to the results.

There remained nothing left for her to do to occupy the hours, which explained why she was wearing a rut in the woven carpeting when the door opened and Director Delavasi walked in. "Ms. Marano, I—"

She charged across the room to get in his face. He was a large man, but she didn't care. "I am done with your spy shenanigans and your conspiracies and I am not staying here another minute. I don't give a damn who's betraying who—unless you tell me my brother is on his way here as we speak, I am walking out this door, and I dare you to stop me."

He placed a hand on her shoulder. "That's why I'm here. You're free to go."

"I don't—I am?"

"Yes. We're reasonably confident we've detained everyone in-volved in the conspiracy. You should be safe now."

"Well, good." She went to the bed and grabbed her bag. It was already packed—it had never been unpacked beyond toiletries. She slung it over her back and turned to him. "What about my brother?"

His head shook, the mirthful visage fading away to be replaced by a somber one. "No news. I'm sorry."

She sighed but awarded him a reluctant smile. "Thank you for clearing him. Thank you for believing in him. I haven't decided yet whether I want to thank you for telling me about my father. I suppose I'm glad to know the truth. But I really would have rather known it a long, long time ago, when it might have mattered."

His expression seemed almost sad. "I understand. I wish things had been different."

"As do I." She proffered a hand. He looked taken aback for a second, then accepted it. "I hope you take this in the best possible way, Director, but I sincerely hope I never see you again."

He chuckled at that; it was unexpectedly warm and jovial. "Fair enough. Best of luck to you, Ms. Marano."

She nodded in acceptance, then bolted out the door and down the hallway to the lift. By the time she reached the hotel exit she was running.

48

MESSIUM
EARTH ALLIANCE COLONY

They agreed the best plan was to split up into two groups. Raina would go with Kennedy and Noah. Her sister wanted to join them as well, but Jonas had become attached to Silvie and insisted she stay with him. Thomaso—that was the older gentleman's name—would also accompany Jonas and his mother to help should the boy require carrying.

Noah had explained to the others where the station was so they would be able to find their way if the groups got separated beyond the fifty or so meters distance they intended to maintain.

They had stocked up on portable food and drinks from the restaurant supplies, found pouches to carry the alien materials in and waited until nightfall. No way were they risking even the short kilometer of distance in the harsh light of day—a decision which was validated when they witnessed three ships pass on the street outside within an hour of one another.

It was curious that the ships apparently didn't use thermal imaging or any other sensors beyond motion and visual scans. A lucky break for them to be sure, but given how advanced the ships were it was odd.

A wacky notion occurred to Kennedy as they clung to the remains of a levtram entry and skulked painfully slowly toward their destination...it was almost as if the street patrols by the ominous ships with their netherworld appearance and terrifying crimson oculi were for *show*.

Oh, they were quick to kill anyone who wandered into their path. But so far as she'd observed, the ships never went out of their way to search in places where people may actually be hiding.

She had to let the notion go in order to concentrate on scaling a three-meter-high pile of stone and marble blocking the street. It was the remains of one of the few artistic buildings on Messium, an art and entertainment museum. She heard Noah talking quietly to Raina behind her.

"Remember, keep your body low to the rubble and move slow. You'll want to scramble, but too much movement will attract attention."

Kennedy smiled to herself. The girls had taken an instant liking to him, doubtless on account of him being roguishly handsome and sporting a demeanor to match. He had responded, somewhat to her surprise, by becoming their friend in a big-brother sort of way.

Try as she might, she couldn't seem to figure him out. He was such a bundle of contradictions—deflecting everything with a light-hearted, blasé attitude, yet startlingly intelligent and clearly well-educated and informed on many topics. He—

—a scream behind them shattered the eerie stillness. Kennedy had crested the height of the rubble and started down the other side but instinctively whipped about at the sound.

One of the patrol ships had crossed from the previous intersection as the other group had emerged out of the protection of the buildings to begin scaling the rubble. The debris spanned the width of the street, and there was nowhere for them to hide.

Braelyn and Jonas had gone first in case he needed assistance climbing, which meant they were the most exposed and had no hope of getting back to street level in time to run.

Thomaso signaled frantically for them to try, until he recognized it was of no use. Braelyn covered her son with her body and huddled amidst the stone.

Kennedy watched on in horror as Thomaso took off running toward the closest building...and burst into flames meters away from safety.

The scream had come from Sylvie. She stood at the base of the rubble, frozen in terror, powerless to move though if she had done so immediately she might have lived.

As the ship shifted its focus to Sylvie, Kennedy saw Noah wrap his arms around Raina from behind and drag her struggling body up and over the crest of the debris.

"Let me go! That's my sister!"

"And you'll share her fate if you don't quiet down!" His gaze shot to Kennedy. "We've got to move, *now.*"

"I know." She shook her head roughly and began scrambling along the rubble, any concern for subterfuge gone as the air glowed red behind them and another scream pierced the air only to be abruptly cut silent.

Raina was crying and gasping in air but moving under her own power, survival instinct having won out over grief. They hit the street at a full run. The alien material in the pouch slung over her chest pounded into her hip as she sprinted for refuge, any refuge.

It came in the form of a sense booth of all things, tucked in beside what could have been a clothing store. They crammed inside the tiny space and forced the door shut less than a second before the ship rounded the corner. Raina buried her sobs in Noah's chest in an effort to muffle them.

Kennedy's eyes met Noah's above the girl's head. His glistened with naked pain, and she knew he was thinking the same thing as she: did they get Jonas killed? Did Braelyn and Thomaso and Sylvie die because of them? His head shook in answer to the silent question…but it lacked conviction.

It was at that moment she decided it was all an act—the bravado, the jokes, the carefree attitude, the claims to not care about anything. His soul was seared by as much anguish as hers. She doubted she'd ever get him to admit it to her, but she thought if they lived through this, she just might try anyway.

After ten minutes that felt like ten hours, she oh-so-carefully moved the door open a few centimeters and peered out. The street was inky and silent.

She nodded to Noah and they worked the door open—in the absence of power it was fussy about complying—and continued on.

It took another twelve minutes to reach the station. Her heart broke at the knowledge they had been so close. Their companions had died steps from, if not safety, at least a chance.

From the outside the station resembled the rest of the buildings they had passed—broken and crumbled. But it wasn't a crater. She had feared it would be a crater.

The relief of four walls surrounding her cascaded through her in a rush; she sank against the nearest one.

"You feel all right?"

She jumped at the realization Noah had come over. He held out a water packet, which she greedily accepted. While she guzzled it he knelt down and began feeling carefully along her leg.

"Your cut's opened back up. We should get it cleaned and re-bandaged."

Her head shook as she took a final gulp of the water. The packet was drained, so she tossed it cavalierly in the corner. "It can wait. I'm getting the fuck off this planet, and I'm getting off now."

He chuckled softly. "That's my girl. Let's see what we can find."

His girl? Her nose scrunched up at the phrasing, but he had turned away. She motioned for Raina to follow them and stepped into the hallway.

She nearly got shot for the effort.

A young soldier—he looked to be barely past puberty—pointed a military-issue Daemon at them. His hand shook so fiercely the gun was in danger of falling from his grip.

Noah stepped up, hands open in submission. "Easy there. We're good guys."

The kid's eyes were wide as saucers, but he shakily lowered the gun. "I heard noises and thought one of those creatures was coming inside."

"I think they're probably too big to fit, but I can understand the concern. Any chance you have a working shuttle hiding back there?"

"Uh…sort of?"

⟋R⟍

Kennedy gazed at the bay of wrecked shuttles in dismay. The last of her adrenaline seeped away at the sight of the widespread destruction. It occurred to her then, for perhaps the first time in this long nightmare, that she was going to die.

"No, you're not."

She spun to Noah in surprise. Had she voiced her doomsday proclamation aloud? She didn't think so. Had he merely read her countenance, judged the set of her jaw? "Noah, *look*. No way are any of these ships taking off."

"Nope they are not. Come with me." He reached out and grasped her hand in his.

She allowed herself to be guided to the far corner of the bay and into some kind of workroom. Inside were three soldiers working on two shuttles suspended on racks in the middle of the room.

"I found people. Even better, I found intact shuttles."

The soldiers spun to them, more relief than wariness in their faces. After brief confusion, introductions ensued.

The interior workroom was recessed enough to have survived the initial blitz; so long as the rest of the building overhead remained standing it would remain standing as well.

By sheer dumb luck the two shuttles were brought to the workroom for repairs hours before the attack. Unfortunately, the repairs needed were extensive. The LEN reactor powering one had died, and the left thruster in the other was shot. Her suggestion to scalp the LEN reactor from the shuttle with the busted thruster was a no-go, however. More soldiers were alive elsewhere in the building, so an escape was going to require both shuttles.

"Did you check the moderator feeds into the reactor core?"

She received blank stares in response. Good lord, did the military employ anybody they picked up off the street as technicians these days? She looked over at Noah and sighed. "I'll crack open the reactor. Think you can salvage some parts from the wrecked shuttles in the bay to fix the thruster?"

He smiled, and she sensed her heart lift a little. Maybe they stood a chance of making it after all. Then he gave her a flourished bow. "As the lady wishes, so shall she receive."

"Smart-ass. Get out of here."

As soon as he had departed she directed her attention to the others. "I need a shielded containment box, radiation gloves and a micro welding torch. And a crescent wrench."

For the next hour she forgot about the aliens and the roving ships and the charred bodies. For a time she even forgot Sylvie's final scream as she buried herself in the delicate work of replacing the LEN reactor core's fuel. She was only vaguely aware of the activity occurring across the room at the other shuttle, except for the time or two Noah let loose a particularly colorful curse. She assumed it meant they were making progress.

She and one of the technicians were tightening the casing around the reactor when several soldiers ran into the room.

"You're not going to believe this, but we're picking up Alliance ships near the planet!"

She leapt off the floor, ignoring the painful response of her leg. "You didn't get commun— oh shit, we can talk to them."

"No we can't, ma'am. And who are you?"

"It doesn't matter. And yes, you can." If Alliance ships were here she had to believe her message to Alex's mother had gotten through. Not because the military wouldn't otherwise have known Messium was under assault—she imagined the entire galaxy must know by now—but because no way were they insane enough to try to mount a counter-offensive if they couldn't talk to one another.

She turned to the technician helping her. "You know how to finish re-installing it and hook up the cabling?"

"Yes, ma'am. That I can do."

"Great. I'll be back." She crossed to the soldiers at the doorway. "Take me to the comm room."

SPACE, NORTHEAST QUADRANT
MESSIUM STELLAR SYSTEM

The blast of an exploding frigate flared in the viewport. In the tiniest of blessings, it was far enough away the shockwave didn't strain the motion dampers.

The *Orion* along with two frigates under its charge, the *Concord* and the *Provence*, continued to fly and shoot. But mostly they ran.

The ships that remained operational remained so primarily because the battle had evolved into a game of cat and mouse. They ran, the alien vessels chased.

And for all the firepower of the superdreadnoughts, in the end it would be the damn swarmers that defeated them. Shields withstood their weapons when fired in small quantities, but there were simply too many—

"Sir, I'm receiving a communication from the ground."

Malcolm spun around to the comms station. "Relay it."

"It says survivors intend to depart in two shuttles from the capital's downtown area. They're requesting the status of any corridors and advice on the safest route."

"Tell them no corridors are passable, but if they can get to..." he found and zoomed the planetary map "...N 36.4° E 12.2°, the skies should be free of enemy ships."

Only two shuttles. But two beat zero. Someone had been alive down on the planet, and they were escaping, possibly due to the fleet's efforts. Rychen had earlier reported the three stealth ships were able to recover fifteen survivors near the base.

Altogether, it was a terribly small victory and yet so far from nothing.

"They've received the instructions, sir, and expect to depart in four minutes."

Shuttles wouldn't be equipped for interstellar travel. They were going to need a ride. He checked the tactical map. The *Provence* was closer but it had the attention of a dozen or so swarmers. For the moment his ship did not.

Colonel Jenner: Admiral, we've received a communication from survivors groundside. Two shuttles are preparing to flee the planet. I've directed the shuttles to a safe exit route and am headed to retrieve them.

Admiral Rychen: Understood.

It was a curt reply, but they had all devolved into curt replies. The man was serving as the conductor of a symphony of bedlam and death, his sole tool a badly crippled communications system.

"Helmsman Paena: set an intercept course for those shuttles. Systems: when we're within half a megameter, get the shuttle bay door open. I expect we can't talk to them once they're in the shuttles, but they'll get the idea."

He hated running from the battle for even a few minutes, but their purpose in coming here was to save people.

Colonel Jenner: Concord, *we're retrieving a couple of shuttles on the run. Watch our back and distract any swarmers who decide to follow us, would you?*

Lt. Colonel Sanchez (Concord): *You got it, sir.*

He had sent the survivors halfway around the surface and the *Orion* was now fairly distant from the planet. It took eight minutes to reach the shuttles, every second of which he spent examining the maps to confirm they weren't being followed. A single shot by a single swarmer would vaporize a shuttle, and should they attract a superdreadnought, all bets were off.

Their angle of approach was such the shuttles never crossed the viewport, but he tracked them on the radar and exhaled in relief when the comm came from the shuttle bay. "Both shuttles safely aboard, sir. We have twelve survivors: nine military, three civilian."

"Great job, Sergeant. See that they receive any necessary medical care and food. Paena, get us back to the fleet, but swing us down low beneath the planet. Let's see if we can't sneak up on one of those superdreadnoughts."

"Yes, sir."

He returned his attention to the map, scanning for any opportunity he might exploit.

"Sir, three of the survivors are asking to speak to you. They say it's urgent."

Urgent? They would possess intel on the situation groundside and possibly on the aliens. The fleet was starved for information. "Go ahead and bring them to the bridge."

The cruiser was not a small ship, and he had again lost himself in the tactical map when a throat cleared behind him. "Sir, the survivors from the shuttles."

"Thank you, Sergeant." He turned around to find a lieutenant in filthy BDUs and two civilians who looked as though they'd crawled through a volcano standing before him. "Glad we could reach you—"

"*Malcolm?*"

He jerked a little in surprise—his first name had yet to be uttered on the *Orion*—and scrutinized the woman more closely. Long tangles of what resembled blond hair, though coated in soot and grime, tumbled from the remnants of a ponytail. Her face appeared no better; aside from the grime, a nasty bruise had darkened beneath her left eye and dried blood streaked along her chin. But....

"Kennedy Rossi?"

She laughed; it sounded wild and not remotely like the poised, polished woman he remembered. "What a damn fine coincidence. You got a promotion, I'm guessing?"

"Lucky me. So—"

She reached out and grasped his arm. Then presumably remembering she was on a military ship of which he was the commanding officer, she hastily dropped it and stepped back. "Malcolm, you need to know that Alex didn't have anything to do with the EASC bombing. She—"

"I do. She's been cleared. You didn't—right, you wouldn't have had exanet access for several days now. It's all over the news."

"Oh, thank god." She blew a stray hair out of her eyes. "Caleb, too?"

"The Senecan? Yes. It seems the records were doctored to implicate them."

The man standing next to Kennedy whipped around to stare at her. "Wait, you know Caleb?"

Her face screwed up. "Sort of. *You* know Caleb?"

The man looked as though she had offended him somehow. "*Yes.* He's the reason I was on Messium in the first place. Sort of—"

Malcolm cleared his throat. "Excuse me, but a fairly intense battle is ongoing outside so could we perhaps focus?"

Kennedy shot the man another odd glance. "Right. Sorry." She gestured to the others. "Noah Terrage. Lieutenant Shan. We brought pieces of one of the small ships, including some of its internal workings. Shan has excellent readings on their ships including the types of signals they emit. Thanks to him we were also able to get additional information on their quantum field that's disrupting communications."

"Nice work. What's the situation on the ground? Are there other survivors? Lieutenant, what about HQ?"

Shan shook his head. "I was at the station in the city when the attack began. We were never able to raise the base on comms. We had significant air presence in the first few hours, but since then…well, there were a lot of explosions over at the base, sir, and we haven't seen an Alliance ship in the air in a day and a half."

Rychen was not going to like the news, though he had to be expecting it. He forced his expression to remain resolute. "Civilian survivors?"

The sadness in Kennedy's eyes was all the answer he required. "We crossed six kilometers through downtown, and those with us are the only survivors we found. There were a few people along the way who didn't make it. I'm not saying people aren't hiding in basements and such, but the streets are a kill zone. The small ships patrol them constantly. Also, we saw six of the really big ships as we were fleeing."

Her shoulders straightened, and a hint of the person he remembered shone through. "Malcolm, we need to get this information to EASC—to people who can study it and determine how to use it against the aliens. And we need to get it to them now."

He ran a hand through close-cropped hair. It felt greasy; he hadn't realized he'd been sweating and probably for some time. "Give me a few minutes. You can wait in my office—the Sergeant will show you to it." He gave her a weary smile. "Oh, and Kennedy? I'm glad you made it out okay."

Her shoulders sagged in an exaggerated motion. "So am I."

As soon as they had stepped away he dropped his hands to the railing and leaned into it. He studied the tactical map for a few seconds, scanned the viewport then commed Rychen.

Colonel Jenner: Admiral, we successfully retrieved the shuttles. Twelve survivors. They brought physical specimens from one of the small alien ships and data on their functionality. Sir, how many ships have we lost?

Admiral Rychen: As of thirty seconds ago? Forty-two percent.

Colonel Jenner: How many of theirs have we taken out?

Admiral Rychen: Two superdreadnoughts, roughly two hundred of the small ones.

Colonel Jenner: Damaged?

Admiral Rychen: Three.

If it had meant five of eight superdreadnoughts were damaged or destroyed, it would've constituted most encouraging news. Unfortunately, shortly into the battle the five superdreadnoughts formerly patrolling the far side of the planet had begun arriving. Obviously the communications jamming was not wholly successful.

The result was they now faced as many alien vessels as when the battle began and their forces had been slashed nearly in half.

Colonel Jenner: The survivors report no air activity from the base in more than a day and no appreciable civilian survivors. Sir, we should retreat. We possess intel now which, especially when coupled with what we've learned engaging the enemy, may make the difference in future battles. Those who we've lost here will have died in vain if we don't ensure this intel is fully utilized.

Admiral Rychen: Colonel, we are making headway.

Colonel Jenner: They report a minimum of six additional superdreadnoughts in-atmosphere.

Admiral Rychen: Understood. You are authorized to depart. Go directly to Earth. Get this intel into the right hands. That's an order.

Colonel Jenner: You gave me this command because I can see the larger picture. We've proven to the aliens we can fight back. That we will fight back. We're going to need these ships and soldiers to do so. We have achieved our short-term goals, but now the sole rational choice is to retreat and save the remainder of the fleet for future operations. Please, sir. We will return.

The silence continued so long he assumed the link had been cut. Dammit. He didn't want to abandon the rest of the fleet but—

The message went out individually to every command group. "All ships, prepare for retreat to the rendezvous coordinates in two minutes. Recall fighters and ready sLume drives."

Admiral Rychen: Thank you, Colonel.

49

As she hastened down the hall from one emergency to the next, Miriam spared the fleeting thought that everything was suddenly happening everywhere and all at once. It threatened to cause her head to spin if she slowed long enough to really ponder the ramifications.

Thankfully she didn't have the time.

Major Lange waited outside her office this visit; this visit she appreciated his promptness. He seemed to recognize the import of this task as much as she did, for he brought four appropriately intimidating MPs along with him.

She acknowledged him with a sharp but not unkind nod. "Major. Is everything in order? You received the arrest authorization?"

"Yes, ma'am. San Francisco has signed off. I'm ready when you are."

"Let's not waste time then."

Technically, she did not need to be present for Liam's arrest. But she was not going to miss this.

She hadn't filed a complaint or told anyone about their altercation; she'd never been a victim a day in her life and didn't intend to start being one now. She'd *intended* to bring him down on account of his public misdeeds, for they were sufficiently inexcusable, but it turned out his private ones were oh so very much worse.

Truth be told she wasn't the slightest bit surprised to learn of his involvement in the Palluda massacre and the larger conspiracy to instigate war with the Federation. Appalled and disgusted to learn he would disgrace the Alliance military in such a horrendous fashion, yes. But not surprised. And it gave her merely the smallest twinge of personal pride that though she possessed an even stronger claim to a personal grudge against Seneca than he, when the call came due she'd worked to bring an end to war rather than initiate one.

Marcus Aguirre, on the other hand, had shocked the hell out of her. She'd stood in his office days ago and engaged in a contentious conversation with him and hadn't gotten the slightest inkling. His attitude frustrated her to be sure, but he'd always exuded the bearing of a consummate politician, and in a most skilled manner.

This though? The lengths to which some would go to increase their power remained beyond her comprehension. Seeking greater clout was one thing, but sending tens of thousands to their deaths in order to achieve it?

What these people had done lay beyond forgiveness, and she personally hoped no one ever did.

At least they bore the smallest glint of hope against the aliens now. The Messium offensive, though a loss, had not been a rout. The alien ships were not invincible. Kennedy Rossi and a small contingent of soldiers and civilians made it off Messium carrying new data on the aliens as well as physical specimens.

At this point each new piece of intel represented a boon. And if events played out as they should, soon she would have only one war to fight.

O'Connell's secretary was not at her desk when they arrived. Just as well.

As head of the Security Bureau, Lange possessed the lock code to the door. After a motion to the MPs he opened it.

"General Liam O'Connell, you are under arr—"

The office was empty.

Lange activated his comm while simultaneously instructing the MPs to begin a search. "Institute an immediate lockdown of all exits. If General O'Connell attempts to leave the premises he is to be detained until MPs arrive. Also, I need the logs of the General's entries and exits for the past forty-eight hours."

The latter request took only seconds. Lange shook his head. "He never came in this morning. How did he know?"

She had no answer for his question. Fewer than half a dozen people in the Alliance knew of the planned arrests, not counting the four MPs who had found out minutes ago.

Still, the full extent of the conspiracy and perhaps more importantly of the surveillance tendrils the conspirators had spread throughout the system wasn't yet known. Though Richard's source had named the major players involved, likely there were additional low-level participants beholden to O'Connell or Aguirre.

And if Liam had been warned, then….

She immediately sent Richard a pulse.

Aguirre may have been tipped off.

WASHINGTON, EARTH ALLIANCE HEADQUARTERS

Richard had only been inside Earth Alliance Headquarters twice before, once as a guest at an exceptionally large banquet and once for an inter-department summit. It might have seemed like a low number, but in truth when it came to the intelligence trade, whether civilian or military, most of the work was conducted and decisions made in Vancouver, Moscow or Hong Kong.

He strode down the wide hall behind the Minister of Security, because he wasn't in charge. The honor went to said Minister, Terry Jameson. But he had earned the right to be here—and had been required to give a lengthy and extensive personal report to Jameson before the man agreed to detain Aguirre.

The exclamations of protests from several aides went ignored by the retinue as they crossed the gleaming atrium into the Executive Suite, then the comparatively enclosed office of the Chief of Staff.

This wasn't an arrest. Technically. One doesn't simply storm in and arrest the Prime Minister of the Earth Alliance government. He would instead be asked to 'accompany them' to 'answer some questions' and 'clear up some confusion.'

Nevertheless, only one response would be allowed to the request.

The priority pulse from Miriam leapt into his vision.

Aguirre may have been tipped off.

Hell. He immediately forwarded the pulse to Jameson, though it was now far too late for anything more than an extra degree of alertness.

They entered the office to find the Prime Minister standing at his desk. An odd, not-at-all composed appearance adorned his drawn features.

"Prime Minister, we need—"

"Know that everything I did was for the good of humanity. Know that I tried to save us all."

Then Marcus Aguirre brought up the Daemon his hand had concealed beneath the surface of the desk, shoved it in his mouth and pressed the trigger.

PART IV:

PARALLAX

"In the space between chaos and shape there was another chance."

— *Jeanette Winterson*

50

F *our Years Earlier*

Alex drummed her fingers on her thigh while she waited. It wasn't impatience, as such. More like nervous energy. She was looking forward to this.

One could argue it was overkill for her to travel all the way to Sagan and pay an ungodly number of credits for the cybernetic upgrades and specialty ware that would enable her to wirelessly access and control the systems in her ship. It was cutting-edge tech but six months past bleeding edge. There were three people on Earth who were capable of providing the service.

But she had always admired Abigail Canivon's story and followed her career with interest. Plus, Sagan was a veritable playground for someone like her; she'd probably drop another fifteen thousand credits by the time she departed.

Founded by a consortium of wealthy entrepreneurs from the biomedical industry, the colony was devoted almost entirely to research and development in cybernetics, biosynthetics, the hardware that interacted with them and other related fields furthering the advancement of human capabilities.

Canivon had spent thirty years as a doctor in the Alliance and was credited with numerous improvements to the technology humans carried inside their bodies. Her research had lessened organic/synthetic conflicts and rejections and increased nervous system interconnectivity. The woman rose to the level of Chairman of the Council on Biosynthetics Ethics and Policy, then told the Alliance government to go screw itself and moved to Sagan to run the Druyan Institute's Cybernetic Research Center.

In short, Canivon displayed the kind of gumption Alex admired. Rumor was the woman understood quantum language so well she dreamed in it, but seeing as she wasn't known for being particularly gregarious Alex wasn't sure how anyone would actually know.

"Ms. Solovy? Dr. Canivon will see you now." Finally. She pushed off the wall and crossed the large atrium to the office door.

The spacious room was an office only in the sense that it included a desk. Refreshingly open, it featured a high ceiling and windows looking out on the meandering bay beyond. Most of the space was filled by testing tables and equipment, cybernetic components mid-development, human body constructs sliced open and shelves stocked with tools of the trade.

Abigail Canivon met her at the door and extended a slender, almost delicate hand in greeting. "Ms. Solovy, welcome to the Institute."

"Thank you. It's an honor to meet you. You can call me Alex."

The woman wore a coolly formal expression. Gene therapy had bestowed upon her a visage of timeless beauty; she didn't strive to appear young, but rather old enough to have gained proper experience and shrewdness. Gold-tinged ginger hair swept into a low knot then fell loose in a tail down her back. Hazel eyes sparked with intelligence and a striking intensity, as if she was analyzing Alex as they stood there. Which she presumably was.

"Have a seat, and we can discuss what you're interested in." She circled around behind the desk. "You should know I don't usually do private consultations. You have connections—and I'm not referring to your mother, though I won't deny your surname played a small role in getting you inside this office."

Alex smiled thinly. "And here I thought it was the personal request from the CEO of Pacifica Aerodynamics and Ɔ118,000."

"Also factors. So, you want to be able to talk to your ship. Why not simply install a VI?"

"A VI isn't my ship. It's *simply* another layer separating me from the information I need. And I don't just want to talk to it. I want to control it without being required to access a panel or run for the cockpit. Dr. Canivon, I'm not a tourist. I know precisely what I need and why I need it. I came to you because you're the best, and because I like your style. For those reasons, and since you have no reason to take my word that I'm not a tourist, I'm willing to tolerate a little patronizing. But only a little."

To her surprise the woman laughed. "Point taken. You have your systems' transmission codes?"

Alex handed over a crystal disk. "There are seven distinct systems. The core OS is minimal, and for the most part I'll be accessing individual components. My existing cybernetic and eVi specs are on the disk as well."

"Excellent. Something tells me you'll wish to observe the code preparation?" At Alex's nod she opened a door in the back wall. "Come with me then."

Alex let her gaze wander around what turned out to be the real lab while Dr. Canivon loaded the disk in an input port connected to a workstation. In principle a large room, in practice the space was shrunk considerably by rows upon rows of hardware lining the walls behind alumina glass barriers.

The rear quarter of the room consisted of dual spiral towers of display panels, a third of which were active. To the left of the displays stood an interactive framed panel three meters wide and again as tall. A medical cot disguised as a divan rested along the left wall with biomedical equipment hanging at either end.

"Does the Artificial do all the coding?"

Dr. Canivon glanced over. "No. We have robust ware specifically designed for this type of work, though Valkyrie did assist in the ware's development."

"Valkyrie?"

"She named herself. I didn't argue."

Alex knew she was supposed to be paying attention to what Canivon was doing but instead found herself wandering down to the display towers. The first one she came to was transmitting a multi-vector optimization simulation for atmospheric seeding. Terraforming.

"Fully licensed, if that's what you're wondering. Official research equipment of the Institute."

"I assumed." Her focus drifted to the next active panel. The Artificial appeared to be in the process of writing a dissertation on radical empiricism as contrasted to reductionism. She scanned the text with mild interest.

"She's a fan of William James."

"I don't blame it." She realized Dr. Canivon had approached to stand beside her holding an injector. "While the code for your eVi is written I'm going to inject a nanobot solution into your cybernetics input. It will strengthen the fibers in your fingertips so they can receive the incoming data and direct it properly."

She drew her hair over her shoulder and exposed the base of her neck. There was a sensation of pressure for several seconds, followed by a slight achiness. Her glyphs activated of their own accord, rippling in steady pulses down the length of her arm.

"All done. It takes several hours for the nanobots to do their job, but we can flash the ware as soon it's ready, which should be in about ten minutes." Canivon eyed her guardedly. "While we wait, would you like to meet her?"

"Her? You mean the Arti—Valkyrie?" Alex motioned in the direction of the hardware banks behind the glass.

"Yes. It's up to you, but you seemed intrigued."

"I admit I am a bit. Do I just...talk to it, or what?"

"You can. Or..." she went to a cabinet and retrieved a sleek neck wrap "...if you're willing, a more intimate encounter?"

Alex considered the server racks, the spiraling displays and the neck wrap. "It isn't going to take control of my mind, is it?"

"Not to worry. Buffers built into the interface prevent anything other than data and communication from passing through."

Alex slipped the interface around her neck. "But absent the buffers, it could?"

The doctor pursed her lips. "It's complicated. We can discuss it later if you're interested. Close your eyes, it will be less disorienting."

Alex breathed in, did as instructed and pressed the wrap firmly to engage the contact points.

Colors strobed in and out across her eyelids then solidified into exactly what she had been viewing before, yet not. She checked, and her eyes were still closed.

She scanned the area anew. Edges were hyper-precise and colors were enhanced to the point the scene felt…unnatural. She'd call it 'artificial,' but she had never been a fan of puns.

It is nice to meet you, Alex Solovy.

She jumped. The voice was in her head but not like a pulse or any other type of communication. It was *in* her head.

Not certain of the accepted etiquette, she spoke aloud—or thought she did. "Hello, Valkyrie. It's nice to meet you as well. Did Dr. Canivon tell you who I am?"

She did not need to do so. I enjoy access to Abigail's appointment schedule and ongoing projects. May I say I am sorry about your father's death. His record indicates he was a heroic man.

"I…." Her father had died nineteen years ago, but she imagined an Artificial didn't view the passage of time in the same manner humans did. She wondered what an Artificial's conception of 'heroic' might be. "Thank you. He was."

You pilot a starship, yes? You appear to be an uncommonly successful scout and explorer.

The Artificial's speech pattern was an idiosyncratic mix of awkward and colloquial. It was unexpectedly endearing. "I just have good instincts. Mostly I love being in space."

But you are not 'in' space. You are in your starship and your starship is in space. It is not so different from being on a planet.

"Oh, Valkyrie, you have no idea."

Tell me then.

Alex jumped when a hand grasped her shoulder.

"Ms. Sol— Alex, we should probably get started." Canivon's voice sounded oddly disembodied, as if transmitted through a sound mixer. Alex held up a finger, requesting a final moment.

"Valkyrie, I'm afraid I need to go now. I had a lovely time talking with you, though."

And I with you, Alex. Thank you for sharing some of your experiences with me. I believe I will be considering them for a significant period of time. Perhaps one day I will be able to see the stars as you do.

"I hope so. Goodbye, Valkyrie."

Goodbye, Alex.

She carefully disconnected the interface and blinked to clear her vision. The scene was the same, yet at once both palpable and blanched.

She handed over the neck wrap. "How long were we talking?"

The woman returned the wrap to the cabinet. "Forty minutes."

"You're kidding."

"I am not. I suspected you might like her. She clearly likes you."

"How do you know?"

"I was able to monitor the conversation on the panel over there. Don't worry, I didn't snoop too much. I only kept an eye out to make sure you were at ease with the interaction." She directed Alex toward the divan. "This ware is fairly involved and requires a system reboot by your eVi, so you may as well be comfortable while it installs."

Alex absently sat down, still trying to reorient herself in the 'real' world, and allowed Canivon to attach a far larger interface device to her neck. "Valkyrie came across surprisingly…."

"Human?"

"I was going to say sapient. Her thought processes give her away as non-human, but she is quite self-possessed and aware. More than that, she seems…whole."

Canivon appeared to be warming to the prospect of discussing her favorite topic with an amenable audience. "You regarded me strangely when I did it, but you're already calling Valkyrie 'she.'"

"So I am." Alex tried to relax in spite of the awkward contraption on her neck. "Do you believe she's alive?"

Dr. Canivon slid a chair over to the divan and sat. "Oh, yes. I oversaw her assembly and programming and wrote most of her base code myself. I worked with her as we built her from the ground up, adding layer upon layer of referential routines, background databases and new neural nodes. I remember the day—the moment—she became something greater than the sum of her programming and hardware.

"There was this tone, this inflection in her voice. She told me she had decided she preferred the impressionistic art style to the expressionism rebellion it provoked. In her opinion, impressionist paintings conveyed life while their counterparts 'expressed' mostly anger. I was astounded, but thrilled."

"Given that, do you think she deserves to be locked up so tightly?"

The woman sighed and settled deeper in the chair. "While not all are created equal, on this point I can generalize. Artificials are so many contradictions wound up together, they become a true enigma. Their minds can process information faster than we can develop it or even conceive of it and thus can exploit tremendous power. Yet more than anything they are like children: intensely curious, eager to learn, devouring every spec of data and working to place it in such a way as to help the world make sense...and also in their lack of understanding of consequences. Of danger.

"A child doesn't understand what it means when you tell them an oven is too hot to touch until they touch it and find out for themselves. They don't understand falling until they break a leg tumbling off a ledge. Most children learn these lessons without doing irreparable damage to themselves. Artificials have no way to learn them, not in the concrete, tangible way children do. And unfortunately until they do, unlike children, they aren't merely a danger to themselves—they're a danger to everyone."

Alex flinched as her eVi switched off. In a microsecond it had returned, but the microsecond it vanished was a disconcerting one. "What do you think the solution is?"

The woman eyed her for a moment, then casually crossed one leg over the other. "One of my first projects for the Alliance was conducting a fresh post-mortem on the Artificial—they called it a

Synnet back then—responsible for the Hong Kong Incident. As part of my post-doc I had developed stochastic forensic ware for use in defect analysis, and I was asked to apply it to the records of the Artificial's processes during the event and determine if anything more could be learned.

"We're all taught one of the contributing factors was that its highest directive was the preservation of human life, but it lacked sufficient instruction on how to proceed when some loss of life was unavoidable. The most intriguing artifact I found in my analysis was the unexpected result of that failing: guilt."

Skeptical, Alex arched an eyebrow, then winced as the act tugged at the skin beneath the bulky interface. "You're telling me the machine felt guilt?"

Her shoulders rose in a hint of a shrug. "It's the only word I have to describe what I saw. Once the students began dying it devoted an increasing number of cycles to studying how the deaths had occurred and how they might have been prevented—what different branching decisions could have been taken to result in another outcome. But because of the holes in its programming those branching decisions only led to outcomes it also deemed unacceptable.

"By the time it was shut down it was burning 73% of its processes on fault analysis rather than on finding a solution for those still alive. It obsessed over its failure to the point of paralysis."

"Guilt."

Canivon nodded. "It's a devastating, crippling emotion. Learning how to process it, internalize it and eventually move on from it is part of becoming an adult. The discovery got me to thinking. What if there was a way to allow Artificials to legitimately learn those kind of life lessons and the related coping skills without endangering others?"

"I don't see how."

She motioned for Alex to sit up, then gently removed the interface and set it on the small table nearby. "I'm working on a project. Are you familiar with neural imprints?"

"Somewhat. A complete functional neural and synaptic map of a human brain, coded by activity and containing markers of content, right? My understanding is researchers hope they'll solve the adult cloning obstacles."

"And possibly one day they will do so, but the technology isn't there yet. I'm studying whether providing a neural imprint to an Artificial can enable it to learn life lessons which matter—emotional lessons such as guilt, heartbreak, love and empathy. Sacrifice and loss. It's my hope this will give them wisdom and good judgment...because without those they are fundamentally incapable of making the correct choices for humanity. They don't wish humans ill—they just don't comprehend the universe the way we do."

Alex frowned. "Giving them real human memories, the history of a life and the way a person thinks.... Do they effectively become the person?"

"Now that is the kind of question which keeps me up nights. I haven't yet settled on an answer." Perhaps deciding she had been too free with her words, Canivon notched her shoulders up and cleared her throat.

"We have the explicit consent of the people involved. This is medical research same as any other. The project is kept discreet for understandable reasons, but I assure you we're following all the regulations and conventions."

"I'm sure you are. I'm not judging."

"To circle back around and answer your question, yes, for now I'm afraid it is best Artificials be constrained. But I do believe they have advanced to the point where they require only the slightest bit of guidance, of human perspective, to guarantee they stay on the proper path."

51

*P*resent Day

"You're right. I do already know the answer. It's the Artificials...together with us."

Alex smiled at the alien in a manner which seemed to convey gratitude, even appreciation. It was the first time she had regarded the being with anything other than impatience or exasperation, and damned if Caleb knew why.

"Was that what all this was about? Forcing me to relive those memories? Showing me the mistakes of humans and Artificials alike?"

Not all of it. We merely ensured the necessary data lay within your sight. It was for you to both see and understand.

"But do you have any idea if it will actually work? Have you—your species—done this sort of thing in the past?"

He watched Alex while her focus was on the alien and tried to figure out what she could possibly be talking about. If what would work? What did she seem to think they needed to do with Artificials? She had given him no indication as to what precisely this 'answer' might be and without his eVi he had no way to communicate with her—to simply ask her.

We moved beyond such distinctions long ago, but yes. Furthermore, the human brain is singularly resilient, yet highly malleable. It will adapt.

Mnemosyne seemed to know what she had in mind as well.

He officially missed his eVi. The inability to communicate privately while they entertained the alien had been troublesome at times but never so much so as right now. He desperately wanted to pull her into a quiet corner and have a conversation...but it would wait.

He couldn't say if they had gained the alien's respect or trust, but at a minimum it had become comfortable around them.

People—or aliens, he expected—who were comfortable were susceptible to divulging more than they intended, so he tried to concentrate on Mnemosyne.

A shadow passed across Alex's eyes as she contemplated the alien. "What if it's not enough? Because it doesn't feel like enough. There must be more you can give us."

They had nearly drawn even with the artificial structure dominating the glade to the right, and she pointed to it. "What does this object generate? It isn't the light source and it isn't the tech repulsion field, so it has to be the cloaking shield you're using to hide the planet from your own creations. The same creations attacking us. How does it work? Can we use it to camouflage our own ships?"

The alien hesitated before shifting course toward the object, though Caleb wasn't sure why. Whether it cared to admit it or not, it had committed to helping them. It plainly wanted to help them.

A circular lattice of obsidian metal five meters in height enclosed an orb suspended by nothing in the center. Half a meter in diameter and pale gold in color, the orb undulated with active, flowing energy.

The gaps in the frame allowed easy entry to the center. When he stepped through the metal into the interior a vibration hummed to life in his bones, but as soon as he was inside it abated.

It was an amplifier. Whatever energy the orb emitted, the latticed metal served to boost the signal.

This apparatus replicates the conditions present in space contiguous to the planet and projects their electromagnetic signatures beyond its atmosphere.

"The orb creates a holographic image? An illusion?"

It is an applicable but not complete analogy. It is not an illusion. Space-time is altered to reflect the projection. Several of the ships chasing you passed into the 'holo' as you would call it. They continued to be in space until they exited the other side.

Alex arched an incredulous eyebrow. "How?"

Dimensional distortion. On entering the area they were temporarily shifted to a slightly different plane.

She did not appear convinced. "Why did it fail for us? My ship's instruments registered the planet as soon as we breached the shield."

The alien hesitated.

Because I determined to allow you through. Your trajectory suggested you were aware of the planet's existence. As you have exhibited a notable talent for discovering what others cannot, perhaps this should not have been a surprise.

"Well, thank you for the special dispensation." She had begun approaching the orb when Mnemosyne's body shivered and began to lose definition.

We need to leave.

The alien's increasingly amorphous form shone bright against the darkening sky. Then they were enveloped by a thousand points of light.

ℛ

A second passed, no more. The lights surrounding them floated away to coalesce back into a humanoid form.

They stood outside a...house? The single-story building was constructed of wood from the native trees, with windows made of the glass which had comprised Alex's prison, absent the opaqueness. Flowers had been transplanted from the nearby glade to serve as a small garden entrance. Behind them a narrow pathway cut through the mountainside and back to the lake.

Had the alien built a house to better 'provide context'? To better relate and understand?

Alex asked the question for him. "Mesme, you built a house?"

It is not important. Another is coming. One who will not welcome your presence as I have. We must hurry.

"You're defying your kind to help us. Why?"

The alien didn't answer at first and projected an aura of being deep in thought. Always judging how much to reveal and what to conceal. For all it shared, Caleb did not doubt the secrets Mnemosyne kept would fill a hundred novels.

The others believe we—those of us who frequent this place—have developed too much fondness for humanity. We have explained to them that Aurora displays the potential to deliver the very answers we seek, but they are no longer listening.

"I'm sorry, 'Aurora'?"

It is our name for your universe.

"Our universe—to be distinguished from yours?"

A valid question, but he was more interested in the details Mnemosyne had, intentionally or not, revealed in its answers. Most interested.

To be distinguished from countless other universes.

The alien paused, regarding them as if to make certain it had their full attention.

Understand you are but a glint, a faint spark in the sea of stars of the true cosmos. Aurora was born but yesterday. Your species only moments ago. Yet in those brief moments of observing you, I have come to believe there may be value in your continued survival, and so have offered you a chance. It is only a chance. Your rise or fall will be of your own making.

Alex was already on to the next question. "And if we succeed? What then?"

Mnemosyne didn't even pretend to answer this question.

The others know you came through the portal. Machines will be waiting for you on your arrival in the Metis Nebula. Should you survive the initial gauntlet, you will be hunted.

Caleb gestured dismissively. "We were hunted before we came through the portal. We're used to it."

You have never been hunted like this. The forces arrayed against you now constitute a legion. Human agents working on their behalf multiply each day. Most know not the nature of their true master, but they will kill you just the same.

"With respect, Mnemosyne, they will not."

The alien turned away rather than deliver a rebuttal, and he discovered Alex regarding him with this exquisite look in her eyes and in the set of her lovely mouth. Trust, he thought. Real trust, and respect accompanying it. He decided right then and there he'd happily spend the rest of his life making sure he always deserved to receive such a look from her.

Hyperion approaches. I will return you to your ship.

His form began dissolving into a shroud to surround them.

"No—we need the shield technology!" Alex took off sprinting down the path to the lake.

The alien swirled hesitantly, as if not knowing what to do now. Caleb gave it a shrug. "She wants the shield tech."

Then he was running after her.

"Alex!"

She threw a haphazard wave over her shoulder but didn't slow. And she was unexpectedly fast. Long, graceful strides suggested running was something she did. It was a small reminder that for all he believed he knew her intimately, there were a thousand details about her life he did not.

As she cleared the shelter of the mountain and arced away from the lake toward the dome, a shadow grew over the lake. He didn't glance to see what it was. Instead he ran faster.

By the time he reached the dome she had thrust her palm into the ball of energy. Her glyphs burst to life, blazing a luminous white pattern from her fingertips to her shoulder then vanishing beneath her hairline. If she got herself electrocuted or overloaded her cybernetics he was going to kill her.

He took up a defense posture outside the frame and faced outward.

Above the lake two aliens floated. Each bore the whimsical, winged appearance Mnemosyne had borne when they had arrived. He assumed one of the aliens was Mnemosyne and the other presumably this 'Hyperion,' but his untrained eye could not yet tell them apart.

A tremor reverberated along his skin. It wasn't a pleasant sensation, buzzing in agitation like a deliberately discordant refrain.

Were the aliens talking to each other? No sounds were audible, nor were any voices in his head.

But the interplay was without a doubt a confrontation. One soared forward to invade the other's personal space, if it possessed such a thing. The second alien flared, growing in size, and the dissonant sensation spiked to set the hairs along his arm quivering.

Alex materialized at his side, grasping his elbow. "What is this?"

He kept his focus on the ongoing conflict and urged her back another step. "Nothing good, I expect."

The reverberation increased to the point of pain. Abruptly the more aggressive alien flared a brilliant white and sped away over the rise of the mountain.

Mnemosyne—hopefully this was who remained—floated above the lake for several seconds before turning and sweeping down toward them, once more morphing into a humanoid shape as its feet alighted upon the grass.

"Care to enlighten us?"

It is not your concern.

Not an acceptable answer; not this time. "A number of things here you've deemed not our concern. I submit your little disagreement most decidedly is our concern."

Mnemosyne's form rippled in a manner he had come to identify as an irritated sigh.

As I indicated before, Hyperion does not agree with my decision to allow you to be here. My associate believes empowering humanity will lead to complications.

"Has Hyperion studied us as well?"

Yes. Now please, you must depart. I have stalled Hyperion but it will not last.

He pulled Alex close—because he wanted to, and to ensure she didn't run off again—as Mnemosyne engulfed them in light.

52

R ichard settled into a window seat and opened the suicide note
Aguirre had left behind.

It consisted of a full confession and a detailed retelling of the events leading up to today, insofar as they concerned the aliens, the conspiracy and the war. On a skim it largely matched the information Olivia Montegreu provided, albeit with more details, more names and more evidence for the judicial system some of the parties involved would eventually traverse.

It would make his job easier, though others' far harder. People joked the Earth Alliance bureaucracy would keep operating according to the prescribed regulations and procedures should a series of black holes open up and consume everyone at a minister level and above, but in truth the government was reeling and reeling hard.

A war, any war, always exerted a strain on the leadership structure. Two changes at the highest position in less than a month had resulted in confusion and uncertainty. Colonies dropping off the map in the middle of a war and now what was unmistakably a massive offensive by unknown aliens meant entire agencies were scrambling to determine how to begin to react.

Now this. Soon some of the details of the conspiracy were going to start hitting the news feeds, however much one tried to squelch them. He felt sorry for all the ordinary people out there, not being able to get a handle on what was going on in the government and the galaxy and unable to affect any of it.

He was thankful to be on the inside and able to play a small role. Others might say his role hadn't been so small, but it felt small to him.

He closed the file. Any information it contained which arguably rose to the level of an emergency he already knew; the rest could wait.

Before he realized he was doing it, he had opened a different file. The one he hadn't tossed in a garbage bin on Krysk or the spaceport or the transport.

Senecan Federation Division of Intelligence Personnel Record: William Sutton, Jr.

The words blurred into a foreign language, strange markings which bore no resemblance to words he recognized. He ordered a bourbon straight up and stared at the title until it arrived. Then he took a long sip and began reading.

Will was born on Elathan—not New Columbia—but moved to Seneca for university, where he received degrees in both civil engineering and political theory followed by a master's degree in architecture. He worked for a construction business in Cavare for nine years before a friend from the political science department came to him with a proposition.

Once the flames of war and their aftermath finally died down, Senecan Intelligence decided they needed eyes on the ground on Alliance worlds, especially on Earth near the seats of power. Richard understood this, for his civilian counterparts had done much the same.

Will wasn't military, nor was he a trained killer. But he was well-versed in history and politics and possessed both a keen, analytical mind and an affable, friendly demeanor. After two months of training on the logistics of the spy trade they sent him to Earth with an airtight backstory, made all the better because it differed from reality solely in the locations at which the hallmarks of his life had occurred. An only child whose parents died in a transport accident when he was seventeen, he left behind no family and carried with him no complications.

His mission was to learn what he could where he could and pass it along. Nothing more, nothing less.

He set up a wholly legitimate construction firm in Vancouver. The work he did was real and above-board. But he also became active in the community and cultivated friends among the civilian contractors who worked at EASC and the nearby auxiliary bases.

That was how Richard had met him, three years after Will moved to Vancouver. During a stint at the North Pacific Military Center teaching a course on close surveillance techniques, long before he rose to his current post, he had gone out for drinks with several officers from the base. Will had been at the bar, watching the game with some contractors who knew the officers Richard accompanied. Introductions were made, and they—seemingly—hit it off instantly.

The reports Will filed over the years were not what he had imagined. For one, they were infrequent, often as few as three a year. In most instances they consisted of the kind of background intel which served a vital purpose in the intelligence business but rarely shaped events: who had gained influence and who had lost it, the general mood around EASC on a particular topic or with respect to 'official' Alliance positions.

Possibly because until weeks ago there were no active hostilities ongoing between the Alliance and the Federation, Richard was unable to find an instance of Will alerting Senecan Intelligence to an operation targeting them ahead of time. Then again, he'd likely never let such intel slip either. While he'd shared information on rare occasions when it mattered, he'd not made a habit of disclosing the details of his work.

And as he thought about it, he realized Will had never pushed.

Every one of Will's recommendations, when they were included, advised better relations with the Alliance. He shared misconceptions the Alliance infrastructure and ordinary citizens maintained regarding the Federation and urged steps be taken to correct them. He pointed out opportunities where overtures might be undertaken.

He hadn't been lying when he said he wanted peace.

Like everything else in the galaxy, Will's reports increased in frequency with the Atlantis Trade Summit. He had reported on the extent of Alliance surveillance—surveillance Richard oversaw—but honestly the report didn't include anything Senecan Intelligence wouldn't have doubtless known. And it was probable Will knew this as well.

The last two reports gained an urgent tone and manner. Will argued Richard's case vicariously and vigorously that the Alliance did not order the Palluda attack. He argued there existed strong evidence for outside forces being at work and advised further investigation into the causative events. In the end he all but begged his superiors to find a way to end this war and focus on the aliens.

He hadn't been lying about a lot of things. Merely the most important ones.

Richard conceded he wasn't objective; the furthest one could be from objective in fact. But he now understood why Delavasi insisted on giving him the file.

Will had, without fail, conducted himself honorably—other than lying to his husband for fifteen years. He'd used his position to repeatedly advocate for improved relations, both to Richard and to Seneca. Richard assumed he did so because he truly believed in it. Beyond filing a report every few months, his life had not constituted a lie.

And in fifteen years of post-marriage reports, he'd never transmitted a single negative, disparaging statement about Richard. So though Richard had been made a fool, at least he hadn't been made a public fool.

Above all else the content of the file communicated one truth: it wasn't Richard Navick or Graham Delavasi who cleared the way for the war to end. It was Will Sutton, Jr., at what may or may not have been great personal cost.

Richard stood in front of the door to the hotel room where Will was staying.

He was terrified he was making the wrong choice. He relied on his instincts in his work but now he didn't dare trust them. The wound of betrayal still burned raw in his chest and another cut might be the killing blow.

But it was the end of the world and there may be no more second chances.

He swallowed and rang the bell.

It took ten seconds or so for Will to open the door. Though he doubtless could have checked to see who waited on the other side, his distracted manner and down-turned face when the door opened implied he'd neglected to do so.

Then he looked up. "Richard…." Emotion flooded bloodshot eyes. Surprise? Elation? Fear? Uncertainty? Again, Richard no longer trusted his instincts. "You—do you want—will you come in?"

Richard shook his head, firm and quick. "I thought you'd like to hear my trip went well." Of course, he hardly needed to make a personal appearance to convey the tidbit. "We have the intel we need to dismantle the conspiracy. We're already doing so, in fact. The Prime Minister's dead, funny story."

Will's brow furrowed raggedly. "What? Never mind. I mean I know—not about the Prime Minister—I made Director Delavasi promise to relay the result, since I…I didn't expect to hear it from you." His gaze had roved around while he spoke, perhaps ashamed to remind Richard yet again just who he was, and wasn't. Now, though, his eyes stilled and met Richard's. "Please come in. I want to—"

"Do you love me?" Richard's voice rang flat in his ears, deadened and weighted with the recognition there was only one chance, and a fool's chance at that.

"Always. More than anything. More than everything."

He no longer trusted his instincts; but if he had ever trusted them they told him the expression on his husband's face spoke truth, and pain.

He nodded slowly. Carefully. "I realize you risked everything for the possibility of peace. Gave up your own happiness so others could be safe. The rest of the galaxy will never know, but I do. So, I guess what I'm trying to say is…if you want, you can stop by the house in the morning. I'll cook breakfast. And we'll…talk."

Will's eyes were shining a little too brightly, but he straightened his shoulders and raised his chin a notch. "I can. I will. Whatever it takes. I need you to know that."

He needed to leave now or he wouldn't leave at all. He moved back, creating distance between them.

"Then I'll…." Richard stood frozen in the hotel hallway, paralyzed by the suspicion another step, no matter the direction, would irrevocably alter his fate.

"Oh, damn it all to Hell. Is there a chance I can come in?"

"A chance? Yeah…" Will's jaw worked anxiously "…there's a chance. The door's open, and I'm *asking* you to come in. All you have to do is step through."

Richard took a deep breath…and did exactly that.

53

"**M**ommy!"

Isabela wrapped her arms around the flurry of arms and legs and curls and squeezed with everything she had. "I missed you so much, sweetheart."

The response was muffled into the fabric of her shirt. "I missed you too, Mommy."

She hurriedly wiped away a tear before pulling back to inspect her daughter. No obvious injuries. No rips in her clothing from misadventures. No streaks of red in her eyes from too much crying. Instead they sparkled with the fiery spirit she recognized.

"I'm sorry I was late. Did you have fun staying at Anna's house?"

Marlee's head bobbed up and down with gusto. "She has a holovid of Punkie Bear & Saskoo we got to play in and we went to the amusement park and we ate spaghetti and sherbet and—"

She tousled her daughter's hair, the way Caleb liked to do. "You can tell me all about it on the way home. I need to speak to Anna's mother a minute. Go grab your bag, and don't forget Mr. Freckles."

Marlee dashed off, and Isabela rose and turned to Theresa Bishop. "I can't thank you enough. I apologize for the delay. Consider me in your debt."

"It's not a problem. Is your mother doing better?"

She had lied to Theresa, spinning a tale of a nonexistent illness sickening her mother. A flash of guilt crossed her thoughts, but it wasn't as though she could tell the woman the truth. "She is, thank you. I was allowed to take her home this morning."

"Well, Marlee was a joy, if a bit exhausting. I'm not sure I'm ready to have two of them full-time. She wore me out!"

Isabela grimaced. "She does that."

"You were in Cavare. Did you hear anything about these alie—"

Marlee crashed into her legs from behind. "I'm ready, Mommy. Can we go to the gelato shop on the way home?"

"We'll see. Tell Mrs. Bishop 'thank you' for taking care of you."

Marlee straightened up and lifted her chin all proper-like. "Thank you for feeding me and taking me to school and letting me play with Anna and letting me sleep in your house, Mrs. Bishop."

Theresa shook Marlee's hand formally. "You're very welcome, Marlee. I'm sure I'll see you again soon."

Grateful to not have to stay and answer uncomfortable questions regarding aliens and wars and her brother, she ushered Marlee out the door and to the car. After several seconds of convincing her to sit still long enough to strap her in, Isabela finally managed to circle to the driver's side and climb in.

"Did you get to see Uncle Caleb when you were at Granmama's?"

She quickly schooled her expression. Though his name had been cleared days earlier, he remained unreachable. She refused to believe he was dead but recognized she possessed no justification other than faith to do so.

"I'm afraid not. He's on Elathan for work right now."

"Can we go to Elathan? I wanna see Uncle Caleb again."

Her chest constricted, and for what must be the thousandth time in the last two weeks she wished so badly Daniel were here. Damn him for dying, because she didn't want to do this alone. "Not right now. I have to go back to work."

At Marlee's forlorn pout she sighed. "Maybe in a few weeks."

"Yay!" Her daughter fiddled with Mr. Freckles. "Mommy, the news said stuff about a war. Are bad people coming to shoot at us?"

"No, sweetie. In fact, I think the war's going to end real soon." Director Delavasi had told her the conspiracy she helped reveal was related to the war and there was a good chance hostilities would cease in the near future. He had no answer when it came to the aliens, however. One crisis to the next.

But for today she wanted to focus on Marlee and on trying to rediscover her life as it had existed before she left for Cavare, difficult though it might prove to be. It felt as though she was walking through a dream with everything but she and her daughter painted in gauze and glycerin, sounds traveling through insulation before reaching her.

The truth was the world just didn't look the same once you'd had a knife pressed to your throat.

Was this what Caleb experienced when he pretended to be an ordinary person—a normal, average assembly line manager building shuttles for a living? Had it been this way for him for the near-month he stayed with her? His visit seemed an eternity ago...from a different, simpler life.

She hoped he hadn't felt that way. She hoped in her home he was comfortable enough to be himself, real and whole. She hoped someday she would be able to ask him.

The truth about her father remained her secret for now. She had no idea if telling her mother was the right thing to do...something else she desperately hoped to be able to ask Caleb, someday. But not today.

Banishing the dispiriting thoughts to a corner of her mind, she reached over and squeezed Marlee's hand with a smile. "So what kind of gelato do you want? Strawberry? Chocolate?"

Her daughter's eyes widened in glee. "Strawberry-chocolate-watermelon!"

54

I wish you fortune commensurate to your valor.

The flecks of light swirling around them like a sea of fireflies vanished and Mesme was gone.

"Not one for sentimental goodbyes, is it?"

"Somehow I'm not surprised." Caleb placed both hands on her shoulders and urged her about to face the same direction he did.

Her mouth fell open in disbelief. *"Yebat'sya mne...."*

Alex could feel him smirking behind her. "It's beautiful."

The *Siyane* sat peacefully eighty meters away, beyond the final slope of the mountains. Long grasses swayed beneath it in the gentle breeze. It was intact, undisturbed and a pure tungsten silver from bow to stern.

She cocked her head to the side. A brighter silver rippled over it, creating a pearled effect across the hull. "This shouldn't have happened so fast—not the entire ship."

"Maybe the energy absorbed from two violent encounters with the barrier super-charged the process?"

She hardly realized she was walking toward it, her gaze never leaving her ship. Each step brought another subtle ripple along the hull. Intellectually she realized every shift in viewing angle presented a marginally different hue and reflection, but it evoked an impression of the hull itself being in constant motion.

When she reached the ship her hand rose to caress the bow. The material didn't shine beyond the pearling, though it was subtly lustrous, and the reflection of light off the hull diffused despite the smoothness of the material.

She scanned the length of the ship for any streaks or marrings, but the transformation appeared complete and utterly flawless.

"It *is* beautiful." She sensed Caleb's presence and followed the statement with a peek over her shoulder, at which point he grabbed her and whirled her around, his lips meeting hers in a fierce kiss.

She let the sensations cascade through her: the warmth of his body, the taste of cinnamon and honey on his lips, the steady, comforting grasp of his arms. For just a moment she allowed herself to forget the ongoing destruction of civilization, the mindfuck that had been the alien encounters and the daunting tasks lying before them. For just a moment she allowed herself to simply be.

Then the moment threatened to become too intense for the setting and she pulled away a fraction. "What was that for?"

"I need a reason to kiss you now?"

"No, you don't. But still…."

His forehead dropped to rest on hers. "For being so damn remarkable."

"Oh." Her voice worked past the lump in her throat. "Come on. We have work to do."

"Yes, your mysterious plan to defeat the alien armada. I will fulfill all your most secret and pornographic desires if you tell me what it is."

She laughed as she opened the hatch and jogged up the ramp. "Not that work, the other work—and you already are."

"More secret and more pornographic—what other work? The shield?"

Once inside she went straight to the control panel by the data center and fed it the information contained in her internal data store. In seconds the intricate code sprang to life above the table.

She leaned back against the desk, crossed her arms over her chest and studied it. Her initial impression in the few seconds she'd observed it had been largely correct: ternary programming repeating on an infinite loop. The fundamental qutrit formulation was different as it measured values between -1, 0 and 1, but it was logically consistent. She could shift it to a formulation her systems would understand.

But would her systems even accept ternary code? Such programming was the province of Artificials and as advanced as the tech in her ship was, it didn't include ware quite that sophisticated.

"Alex."

She jumped, startled. Caleb leaned into the data center opposite her. "While I am exceptionally skilled at reading you—arguably a master at it in fact—I cannot actually see inside your brain. What are you doing?"

"Sorry." She gave him an apologetic smile. "Yes, this is the code from the orb powering their cloaking shield. If I can determine how to port it to the defense systems, we can use it to hide from the enemy ships on both sides of the portal."

"Are you sure we should take the time to do this now? Hyperion didn't seem too pleased by our presence here."

"We don't have a choice, Caleb. You saw those ships chasing us before. We might as well have been broadcasting our location on wideband, and we will not be able to outrun them."

"Granted. And this kind of shielding will increase our ability to move around back home. Okay, I'm in. Next question: can you make it work?"

She nodded deliberately, her mind still racing through the details. "I seriously doubt we'll be able to generate a pocket of shifted space-time, but I think we can generate a projection replicating the surrounding space. Mostly. Assuming I can make the *Siyane* understand ternary code."

"Your systems merely require the instruction from the code, and those can be expressed in binary qubits easily enough."

"Easily enough, huh? But you're right. I'll have to write an interpreter for both the input and the output and segregate the new ternary code so it doesn't corrupt the ware running the ship."

Her head fell back to glare at the ceiling. "This will be the worst sort of patchwork hack job. Reality is going to leak out. We'll have to run the damper field at max and hope between the two it's enough. And it'll take power to run the projection."

She dropped her chin to regard him over the table. "We need more power. Ten, maybe twelve percent. Can you find it for me?"

A hint of astonishment flashed across his features before the trademark smirk replaced it. "You bet your ass I can."

Caleb dropped a full plate on her stomach. "Eat something."

She glanced at the sandwich then at him. She was sprawled on her back halfway into the exposed engineering core. All three panels protecting the core were removed and stacked along the wall of the lower hull. The plethora of sensors and instruments were physically located throughout the ship—many of them integrated into the outer hull itself—but the connections all ran through this junction. From here the information they carried was transmitted to the HUD, the data center and wherever else it belonged.

She was hungry. She grabbed the sandwich and rolled on her side to prop up on an elbow.

He settled cross-legged on the floor with his own sandwich. "How goes it?"

"Mmhmm...." At his quizzical expression she quit trying to talk while chewing, instead hastening to finish her bite. "I've connected the relevant instruments into the module and they seem to be accepting the interpreter. I still need to retrofit the broadcast antennae to accept instructions from the module. Any progress on the power?"

"Yep. It'll be 2.4° cooler in here. Can you handle it?"

She groaned. "You ask too much."

"Yeah, well, we also have to go without the gases and heavy metals scanners, but I doubt we'll miss them."

"Is that all?"

"No. You need to increase the safety catch on the LEN reactor from 105% to 109%."

She cringed and considered the implications. A reactor overload meant either a catastrophic loss of power or a catastrophic loss of ship. But it was rated safe to 117%.

"All right. But tell me that's everything."

"That's everything."

"Thank god." She eyed the readout coming from the junction box to confirm it hadn't started throwing errors or spewing gibberish. "By the way, when I was writing the interpreter I had an idea, so I checked the data we recorded in Metis."

"And?"

"I think the interference in our communications was due to a negative quantum field of sorts. Kennedy and I did a project in college on what, if anything, could interfere with a pervasive quantum field like the exanet. Well, mostly I did the project. She had to go home for her brother's wedding, so I doubt she'd remember it. Anyway, the answer was 'not much'—but a competing quantum field would decohere the entanglement. The code for this shield includes a -1 measurement point in addition to 0 and 1, which is exactly the sort of thing to cause problems."

Caleb shrugged as he took a sip of water. "What do we do about it?"

"I fed a tiny portion of the damper field into the comm system. In theory it will shield the qubits on this end from the interference. There's not much else I can do right now."

She motioned for him to hand over his water. He complied while giving her an odd look, and she got the impression he had only been halfway paying attention.

"So let me see if I get this straight. You want us to merge with Artificials?"

Her head shook behind her sandwich. "Not merge. Connect."

"But something tells me you're talking about a deeper connection than a remote interface."

"It has to be, because using an interface is little more than *talking* to an Artificial. Even real time, in the middle of a battle a conversation is not going to be enough. There's a doctor on Sagan who's at the forefront of cybernetics research. She's been studying ways Artificials might learn by internalizing the human experience—or individual people's experiences."

"Forgive me if I'm skeptical."

"I don't blame you. Look, the simple fact is we likely can't defeat this invasion without using Artificials, and not merely as consultants. Only we can't risk using Artificials, not alone. But if some people—battlefield commanders or ship captains or I don't know exactly who—were to share a more symbiotic interconnection with them? In theory you'd have those strengths of humanity—creativity, unpredictability, ingenuity—thinking and acting at quantum speed. We—"

You have not yet departed.

Shit. "Get out of my head, Mesme."

Caleb regarded her curiously; she made an obscene gesture at the low ceiling.

My warning was not made in jest. You are no longer safe here.

"Fine, I get it. We'll be leaving soon."

Silence followed. Satisfied he was gone, she frowned at Caleb. "We need to hurry."

55

Miriam located her designated seat in the Assembly Chamber, engaged in the required formality of greeting those she knew by sight and squared her shoulders to the required formality of the venue.

The designated seat appeared to be something of a seat of honor, on the second row and relatively near the center of the semicircle auditorium. She appreciated the recognition but didn't have time for honorariums or honorifics; she didn't even have time to be here. Nevertheless she recognized the necessity of making the trip to London in this specific circumstance.

Her last visit to the Chamber had been to accept a Medal of Honor posthumously awarded to David by the Assembly. She allowed the memory to wash over her, all the pain and pride and honor and despair.

The crowd grew hushed as the Secretary stepped up to the podium and gaveled the session to order.

Assembly Speaker Charles Gagnon replaced the Secretary at the podium. He drew in a weighty breath and raised his eyes to the audience. "Ladies and Gentlemen, Representatives and honored guests. These last weeks have been a difficult, trying period for us all, and unfortunately the dark times are not yet drawing to a close.

"Those of us serving in the Assembly are civil servants, working to do the best we can for our constituents and the Alliance. Like everyone else we are not perfect. We make mistakes. But know this: we always act in a manner we believe is right given the information available to us at that point.

"A few short weeks ago I stood before you and made the case that Prime Minister Brennon did not deserve to lead us in a time of war. I believed it to be true, as did a majority of the Assembly. I do not regret that vote."

He notched his chin up, high and tight. "Now, however, evidence has been brought to the Assembly's attention calling into question the information upon which the Vote of No Confidence was based. In light of this new evidence a number of Representatives have requested the opportunity to change their votes. Such a procedure is not feasible under the Assembly Regulations. However, legal counsel has determined the Assembly may undertake a superseding vote, the results of which will override any prior vote on the precise issue at hand.

"Therefore, Mr. Secretary, I resubmit Special Assembly Resolution SGR 2322-3174 for an official vote."

Miriam took advantage of the minutes required for procedures and rules and the casting of votes to enjoy a rare moment of peace—a moment when she wasn't making decisions which saved and cost lives, when she wasn't juggling 56,300 ships and 28.2 million servicemen and seventy megatonnes of supplies spread across twenty kiloparsecs.

Then she was reminded why she didn't seek out such interludes. They only allowed her to remember her daughter was gone. Weeks had passed since anyone had heard from her. If her ship had been disintegrated in space there would never be evidence of it, never an answer to what had happened to her.

If she stopped to ponder the implications she might break. And Admiral Miriam Draner Solovy did not break.

The vote tally flashed on the oversized screen floating high above the chamber, saving her from further wallowing.

SGR 2322-3174: Vote of No Confidence in Steven Brennon

For:	78
Against:	432

Cheers erupted from those who had never stopped supporting Brennon, polite applause from the rest. She supposed the seventy-eight votes were opposition party members who simply refused to make an exception on principle rather than politics.

"The Vote of No Confidence in Steven Brennon having now failed to pass and the position being vacant pending investigation, Steven Brennon is hereby reinstated to the office of Prime Minister of the Earth Alliance to serve the remainder of his term."

Brennon stepped onto the dais and met Gagnon halfway, greeting him with a firm handshake and clasp of a shoulder as if to show to the galaxy he bore no grudges. There was no room for grudges.

"Representatives, guests, citizens, I won't waste your time with platitudes. We all find ourselves deceived and at the moment we face the greatest threat to our existence humanity has ever known. The full extent of the deception is only now beginning to come to light, but my administration will follow it to wherever it leads. In the next twelve hours I will review the state of the war against the Federation and determine whether its purpose remains valid.

"Most of all I pledge to turn the full wisdom, experience and strength of the Alliance government and military toward meeting the growing threat of an alien armada. These are our worlds. Our citizens. Our families and friends. We will not abandon them to suffer and die. We will not allow those lost to have died in vain. We will not let humanity fall."

Miriam reminded herself to feel vindicated. Alexis was now unquestionably cleared of any involvement whatsoever in the bombing; the conspiracy to instigate the war with Seneca was exposed and being dismantled. Her personal reputation had never been stronger.

She was proud of the role she had played in these events. She had emerged out of the flames unscathed. Yet without David, without Alexis, it seemed a hollow victory and one she'd as soon not dwell on.

After the session concluded the people around her stood and began milling about while Brennon shook hands with the VIPs on the dais. She stood as well and had spotted a former colleague deserving of a greeting several rows back when a hand rested on her arm.

"Admiral Solovy? If you'll follow me?"

She recognized Brennon's Chief of Staff and nodded. She was happy to leave behind the suffocating pressure of politicians and glad-handlers.

The Chief of Staff guided her through the crowd to a side door and down several halls to a nondescript conference room. "Can I get you anything, Admiral?"

She noted the pitcher of water on the table and shook her head. "I'm fine, thank you."

"The Prime Minister will be here momentarily. I'll be right outside if you need me."

Miriam poured a glass of water and began to prepare for the upcoming conversation, but she had barely taken a sip when the door opened. Brennon instructed his security detail to wait outside before allowing the door to close behind him.

"Admiral Solovy, thank you for taking the time to speak with me. I do apologize for asking you to travel to London. I realize you're stretched thin and are doubtless needed elsewhere."

"It's not a problem, Prime Minister. You have a mountain of difficult work ahead of you. I'm happy to do whatever I can to ease your transition and help get you back up to speed on matters." Her words felt unduly stiff; it wasn't as if this was the first time she'd spoken to a Prime Minister, or even this Prime Minister.

Brennon chuckled softly, easing the tension in the room. "Matters, indeed. I wish I had the luxury of sitting back and appreciating the irony of being in this position once more. Instead I'm being asked to return in order to preside over the extinction of the human race."

"Not a chance, sir."

"Good. Which is in fact why you're here. Forgive my fatalism." He subtly adjusted his posture. "Admiral, you have served as the clearest voice of reason in the room from the beginning of this disaster. If we had listened to you weeks ago when you presented your data on the aliens we might have been better prepared. Lives *would* have been saved. For this reason and many more I won't bore you by listing, I'm naming you Chairman of the EASC Board, effective immediately."

She had known it was why she was here. Not in the sense that anyone had come right out and said it, but it was the most logical conclusion. She and Brennon had a decent working rapport before the world had gone mad. In her opinion Rychen arguably made a better choice—his character qualified him and his combat experience exceeded her own—but she imagined he would have to be dragged kicking and screaming out of the field.

"I'm humbled, sir. I'll strive to serve to the best of my abilities."

"You're not serving anymore, Admiral. You're leading. Which is why I'm also using my executive authority to promote you to Fleet Admiral."

"Sir?" That she had not been expecting.

"I'm sure you'll use the power with proper judiciousness. But the simple fact is, I need your unvarnished, undiluted advice and opinions. And because I'm likely to be a horrifically busy man, I need you to be able to act without consulting a committee when the situation requires it."

For the first time in a long while, she found herself overcome by uncertainty. Of herself, of whether she was up to the challenge.

Naoborot dushen'ka, I think you will be spectacular at it.

"Understood, sir. Thank you for your trust. I assure you I will endeavor to be worthy of it. I realize your time is short, as is mine, but allow me to give you the first piece of unvarnished advice right now. Make peace with the Federation. Not a cease fire or a truce or an armistice, but true peace—and do it quickly."

Amusement tinged the curve of his mouth. "My Chief of Staff was contacted several hours ago by a representative for Chairman Vranas, proposing a summit of both governments' leadership."

"Accept the proposal, sir. They were as much victims of the conspiracy as we were, and I have every reason to believe they are amenable to ending the war. If we expect to be able to fight these aliens, we need their help and they need ours."

He considered the matter for several seconds, then nodded. "If humanity is annihilated because we were too busy squabbling with one another to manage a proper stand, we probably deserve the annihilation. I'll begin making the arrangements tonight."

"I'm glad to hear it, sir."

"I meant what I said out there at the podium. Don't leave our soldiers exposed to a surprise raid by Senecan forces until we untangle this war, but otherwise every person, ship, weapon and tool should be focused on these aliens. We must slow them down until we can find a way to stop them."

Finally a politician deserving of her respect. "I'll begin implementing new directives as soon as I walk out the door. And may I say, best of luck, sir. We are all going to need a great deal of it."

SENECA
CAVARE, MILITARY HEADQUARTERS

Commander Morgan Lekkas leaned against the wall in the entry area. A foot tapped the floor in a brisk dance of redirected energy. The secretary had told her she could sit while she waited, but she'd done far too much sitting today on the transport flight from Krysk to Seneca, the shuttle to Cavare and the levtram to Military HQ.

The screen on the opposite wall displayed a live news feed from of all things the Earth Alliance Assembly. She had caught scraps of news the last few days here and there, but hadn't paid much attention until it concerned her, which now it perhaps did.

It seemed the Alliance Prime Minister had committed suicide? Hadn't the previous PM been killed in an explosion the week before? There were questions surrounding the events leading up to the war, which was why it interested her, but no one was making definitive public statements as of yet.

Someone turned up the volume on the feed and Morgan closed her eyes.

She didn't know if or when the war with the Alliance was going to officially end, but most of the 3rd Wing had been pulled off the Federation border and sent to Seneca to await further orders. No explanation was given but it clearly related to the aliens advancing on the eastern front.

She highly doubted they'd be able to fight the Alliance in the southwest and aliens in the east, though as near as she could tell they hadn't been doing much fighting of the aliens so far. Mostly they had been fleeing. The Cavare spaceport had been jammed with refugees from the eastern colonies, and rumors were flying that every colony east of Seneca not already under siege was being evacuated.

She hoped the military would muster up a fight soon; she hoped that was why she was standing around waiting outside some sort of conference room or other. As for what or whom it held she hadn't a clue, but it was where she had been directed to go. The quality of the decor and extensiveness of security indicated it might hold someone or thing of importance.

The volume on the feed increased again and her gaze flitted to the screen.

"The Vote of No Confidence in Steven Brennon having now failed to pass—"

"You can go in now, Commander."

She nodded a curt thanks to the secretary on her way to the door and stepped inside—then froze in the doorway.

This wasn't a conference room. This was a command center. This was *the* command center.

The air buzzed as soldiers huddled around groups of screens or bounced from one group to the other. Three conference tables scattered around the room were occupied by more soldiers. The far wall was dominated by a large map.

Every settled world was marked on it, most of them colored the usual red for Federation worlds, blue for Alliance ones and green for the Independents. But not the eastern colonies.

Regardless of affiliation, to the right of a diagonal line cutting 320° down the map, the worlds were either marked by a black 'X' or highlighted in orange. Three columns helpfully ran along the right side of the map:

LOST		*IMMINENT RISK OF FALLING*
Andromeda	Messium	Brython
Ceirt	Midgard	Dresden
Dair	New Orient	Henan
Edero	New Riga	New Maya
Gaiae	Nitoris	Nystad
Gaelach	Quero	
Hadron	Requi	
Hawking	Sagitta	
Karelia	Vela	
Lycaon	Zetian	

Morgan hadn't joined the military because she was a patriot or because she had a deep and abiding desire to protect the citizens of the Federation. She was pleased enough when she did so successfully, but even then it was for mostly selfish reasons. She had joined the military for the sheer thrill of it.

Piloting transports or scout ships would never have offered her the rush of diving at 0.3mms through space in an inverted spin. It would never have enabled her to command weapons in the form of fighter jets with a thought or outmaneuver foes through asteroid fields or skim the buffeting edge of an atmosphere. It would never have allowed her to become so integrated with her ship that the ship may as well not exist at all.

She knew what others called her when they thought she wasn't listening—adrenaline junkie, speed addict, bat-shit cracked—but she had never cared. Even if they were right, it was what she wanted. It was what she was alive for.

Now, staring at the list of fallen colonies in utter shock, for the first time in her life she felt brazen, primal outrage against an enemy. She felt a profound, elemental yearning to protect all the people out there from these invaders, from these monsters stealing their worlds and their lives.

"We're in a fair bit of trouble, I'd say."

She jumped, then hurriedly turned to find the speaker.

Field Marshal Eleni Gianno—the Supreme Commander of the Senecan Federation Armed Forces—stood next to her, arms crossed over her chest.

Morgan snapped her feet together and hand up in a hasty salute. "Ma'am. Marshal Gianno. Commander Morgan Lekkas, 3rd Wing, Southern Fleet." Clueless as to what to do next, she glanced back at the map. "I had no idea it was this serious, ma'am."

"Few do. It became this serious very rapidly. Far faster than we've been able to react."

"Ma'am...Brython is less than a kiloparsec from Seneca."

"Yes, it is. I suspect the aliens can be here in hours if they so choose. The one factor acting in our favor is as they advance, they reach more worlds—and larger ones—in need of destruction. Slaughtering entire planets takes time."

The two of them stared silently at the map for a while longer. Finally Gianno looked to her. "Thank you for coming, Commander. We're at last beginning to piece together data on the aliens' capabilities and tactics. I'd like to review some of the analyses STAN has generated with you."

She frowned hesitantly, not at all clear why the Supreme Commander of the Armed Forces wanted to review anything with her...then arched an eyebrow in spite of herself. "STAN?"

"Strategic and Tactical Artificial Network, the military's state of the art synthetic neural net."

"But...STAN?"

Marshal Gianno shrugged. "The Alliance is calling theirs 'ANNIE.' The warenuts in Tech weren't about to be outdone and spent two weeks coming up with an acronym that resulted in a silly name. So what do you think?"

"I'm glad to help, ma'am. But may I ask why me?"

"Word is you're the best fighter pilot in the Federation, possibly in the galaxy. You've refused promotion three times in four years, ostensibly because you didn't want to give up the cockpit. And in my mind with good reason, because your superior officers insist you control the battlefield like no one else. Your biosynthetics and personal ware are bleeding edge, and that's just the upgrades we're aware of."

Morgan started to protest that she wasn't hiding any gray-market ware—which of course she *was*—but Gianno held up a hand to silence her.

"It doesn't matter. In fact, you'll probably need a few more upgrades before long. Whether in days or weeks, these aliens are going to come for Seneca and we have to be ready for them. There are numerous pieces to the puzzle of doing so, but one of them is determining how to take out their multitude of small interceptor ships."

They had reached a cloistered space containing three separate screens, two control panels and a circular table. Two of the screens looped footage of what appeared to be an engagement by a military force of the alien ships above a planet. The vid focused on the sea of strange insectile vessels swarming the region.

She dropped her hands on the table and leaned in to study the screens, forgetting she probably should still be standing at attention. "That's a lot of ships. Far too many for frigates to destroy. They'd be decimated before taking out a tenth of them, assuming frigates could take out that many. The alien vessels are larger than fighters but faster and more maneuverable. Still, our fighters are the only craft which stand a chance of going toe-to-toe with them."

She eyed the Marshal beside her. "Ma'am, where is this? Are we engaging the aliens somewhere? New Riga, or Lycaon?"

"New Riga and Lycaon are gone. This is from Messium, yesterday."

"Messium? The Alliance sent us this data?"

Gianno gave her a mysterious smile. "As I said, events are moving very rapidly."

"How did their fighters do against these ships?"

"Better than the frigates, but at too high a cost. Three times as many fighters were lost as alien ships destroyed."

"In a war of attrition, we lose."

"Quite. We have analyses of their structural weaknesses, minimal though they are, as well as their flight patterns and tendencies. Commander, I'd like you to study it and work with the Artificial to devise a strategy for besting them."

"I'll need full-sensory immersion for the data and a remote interface with the Art...uh, STAN."

Gianno motioned toward a door on the left wall. "If you'll follow me, everything is set up for you."

56

SIYANE
UNCHARTED SPACE

For the second time in a month, the *Siyane* rose to carry them away from an inhospitable planet which shouldn't exist. As before, the ship would carry them home as bearers of vital information which could well mean the difference between the survival or destruction of humanity. But not yet.

"Before we leave this space, I'd like to try to find the other portal. If this is a 'lobby,' there's another gateway here somewhere."

Beside her Caleb swung his chair around to face her, his expression unreadable. "Okay."

"Aren't you going to ask me why?"

"I don't need to. You want to find it because it's unknown and thus enticing. Also because you want to understand this place and these aliens."

She shifted away from him, a little unnerved. He hadn't been joking when he said he was a master at reading her. "Something like that. I realize we need to hurry—believe me I do—but I feel like it may be important."

"I agree."

Her gaze jumped back to him. "You do?"

"Absolutely. I suspect Mnemosyne—Mesme—was largely honest in what it said but there was a prodigious amount it didn't say. We ought to gather as much information as we can before we return. I doubt we'll get a second chance."

She smiled, relieved. She hadn't relished arguing with him and would probably have relented if he had disagreed with any fervor.

The rumble caused by the atmospheric traversal vanished as they cleared the last remnants of the planet. She arced the ship one hundred eighty degrees and stood to examine the scene outside the viewport.

Nothing. Nothing but the pervasive, empty blackness.

Caleb came to stand beside her. "Alex, how did you know the planet was there? It doesn't seem possible."

She shook her head. "I didn't know a planet was there—I only knew *something* was there. I wish I could explain it better, more concretely than an inherent sense of how space should and should not be. Not sure I'll ever be able to, though."

She found the TLF wave on the spectrum analyzer, pulled in navigation and set a course. "The system will tell us as soon as it picks up anything. Come on, let's get your eVi back up and running."

He laughed lightly. "That would be outstanding. I find the quiet has worn out its welcome."

⌁

They had barely finished rebooting his eVi and confirming it was operational when an alarm rang out.

"Shit." Alex bolted to the cockpit and magnified the radar. It displayed ten large red dots approaching. "I guess we get to learn whether the projection shield works sooner than we expected."

It quickly became apparent the craft were not the smaller squid-like ships but superdreadnoughts.

As the vessels approached, their trajectory never altered. She withdrew to maximum visual distance and watched as ten of the ships flew single-file toward the portal into the Metis Nebula.

Only after the last ship had passed beyond sight did she let out the breath she had been holding. "So that worked."

He squeezed her shoulder. "Damn straight it worked."

She appreciated the vote of confidence but still frowned. "When we got here the portal was closed, as though they weren't planning on using it for a while. I wonder why they're sending additional ships now."

He leaned against the half wall of the cockpit and crossed his ankles, much as he used to do before he had a chair. His eyes flickered to the radar, then the blackness outside the viewport. "Because we're fighting back. These are reinforcements. The aliens realized it's going to take more firepower than expected to subdue us."

"Then we definitely need to hurry. All our ships can use this new cloaking shield—let them find out how much firepower it takes when they can't see us."

Her voice had risen in growing excitement; she wrangled it back under control. One hurdle at a time. "They may be building these ships here in this space, in which case I can extrapolate the location of the shipyard from their trajectory. We should try to determine how many ships they can field and how fast they can crank them out."

Once underway she leaned back in the chair, though it couldn't be called a relaxed position. She toed the chair in increasingly wider oscillations. "I've been thinking."

"I can tell."

She winced. "Sorry."

"Don't be. And what have you been thinking about?"

"The code the aliens use for the cloaking shield."

"Again?"

The retort earned a look from her. "More. It's written in a peculiar, distinctive style which is very different than the way we design code. But though it's highly sophisticated and not solely because it's written in ternary, it felt rigid. Formulaic. Now, maybe that's because it's performing a rote, repetitive function, but...."

She considered the next part a final time before voicing it aloud. "Mesme said the attacking ships were unmanned, run by AIs. What do you suppose the odds are they're running on the same underlying type of code as the cloaking shield? I don't mean using the same functions, but written in a similar manner?"

He gave it some consideration as well. "Based on what little we learned about them, I'd say it's likely. The aliens seem to view machines as built for a specific purpose or to do a specific task. I bet they long ago developed specific methods of implementing both."

She chewed on her bottom lip while she decided whether she was ready to make the claim. "By studying the code, someone—I doubt I can do it, but a quantum specialist, or if they fail an Artificial—might be able to figure out ways to exploit it. If the code running the ships is designed the same way perhaps we can develop electronic attack routines to disrupt the programming. And should we have the opportunity to interact directly with it there's a good chance we can corrupt it."

She shrugged. "It's just a thought. I'm almost certainly overestimating our capabilities. And we'll have to get the code to someone who's legitimately intelligent and not a bureaucrat and they'll have to get approval—"

"It's a brilliant idea, Alex."

Her nose scrunched up. "You think?"

"I do. In fact, if you're able to pull off what you're talking about doing—" The beep of the long-range scanner cut him off.

"Did we reach the shipyard already?" She swung to the HUD and magnified the scanner. It displayed a monolithic structure as well as multiple smaller objects. The edifice grew in size until coming into visual view.

"Holy hell."

The facility stretched ten kilometers in length and six in width. Modular units connected into larger sections until they joined together in a single assembly line dwarfing the ships themselves.

The chambers weren't fully enclosed, and hundreds—possibly thousands—of mechs bustled around inside. Forty squid patrolled the perimeter in defensive formations. Guarding against them?

Two complete superdreadnoughts hovered outside, presumably waiting on the ship currently being assembled and some number thereafter. It appeared they moved in packs.

"More reinforcements."

"Afraid so."

The hull of the ship under construction materialized as they hovered there, the mechs working at a level of precision and speed she had never witnessed. Twelve minutes after their arrival the superdreadnought slid out of the chamber and joined its brethren to wait.

"So a lot, and quickly."

"Yep."

"Caleb, if the aliens can produce ships this fast we won't stand a chance. Even if the cloaking shield provides us an advantage, the aliens will simply replace whatever we destroy within hours."

"Maybe we can shut down the portal somehow. Prevent them from coming through or blockade it."

"I doubt we'll be able to spare the ships. But it's a problem to tackle after other problems." She kneaded her temples, then waved at a faint blip on the screen behind the facility. "Want to bet this is the aliens' portal?"

"No way am I betting against you."

"Smart man." She leveled a final dark glare at the shipyard and pulled away, giving it a wide berth as she eased past.

"Ni khuya sebe...."

"That is one way to put it...."

A portal hung suspended in space before them. Easily ten times larger than the one leading to the Metis Nebula, the scale defied comprehension.

It differed in several other respects as well. The ring alone spanned over a kilometer in diameter, comprising nearly a quarter of the structure.

Woven into the ring were multiple threads of white luminescence. She hazarded a guess they represented artifacts of a power distribution or operating system.

The material filling the ring was the glacier blue hue of Mesme and Hyperion. Also, the material wasn't plasma exactly but more akin to a throng of lightning leaping among conductors.

Her fingertips drummed on the dash. The initial shock was beginning to wear off and her mind raced in a jumble of tangled loops. "So Mesme's universe is through there."

"I expect it is." His hand landed atop hers on the dash, halting the erratic rhythm. "Alex, we cannot go through it."

She stared at the flashing, dancing plasma lightning filling the portal. It sat there, open and inviting. "I know."

"We have to get home. Galaxy to save and all?"

"I know."

"People are dying."

Dammit. She didn't want to be the savior of humanity. She never had. She didn't want to be the vanguard—of destruction or salvation. What she had really wanted was to be a girl whose father lived to show her the stars. Instead she had been left to wander them alone. Until she discovered someone who saw the stars as she did.

"I *know.* Okay, we'll…hang on." The incredible phenomenon in front of her was forgotten as she zoomed the spectrum analyzer. She filtered out the noise and decreased the band to measure the lowest tenth of the spectrum. "No fucking way."

"Is this what I think it is?"

"Depends on what you think it is."

"I think it's our TLF wave being sent out on multiple trajectories."

"Then no, it isn't what you think it is."

"Wait, it isn't?"

"No. It is fifty-one *unique* TLF waves fanning out in three semicircles, vertically spaced 45° apart and horizontally every 10°, each one shifted 0.001 Hz up or down the spectrum. Except for the final signals on each end of the fundamental plane, which repeat our 0.0419 Hz frequency."

The TLF wave they had followed from the Metis portal continued in a direct horizontal line to the middle of the far more colossal one. She was unable to measure the signal beyond this point, so she couldn't say whether it continued on. Her instincts told her it was being generated by the ring itself. This was its origin point. Especially considering it also served as the origin point for fifty additional TLF waves.

"I admit this changes things."

Attempting to understand the phenomenon better, she fidgeted with various settings. "Yes, it does. Why didn't I pick these up when we first came through? Do the signals not extend very far?"

She reached for the controls. "Let's follow one, see where it ends."

Caleb leaned in beside her to study the readout "The first horizontal one, on the far right. We should be methodical about it."

"But the first one's the same frequency as ours. We might end up caught in an infinite loop or something. Let's follow the second one."

She swung the ship around, again briefly awed at the scale and complexity of the immense ring as they passed by, then lined up on top of the selected TLF signal and followed it....

...until it vanished.

Nothing but unending blackness in all directions. The signal simply terminated. Which, of course, was impossible.

"You don't suppose...."

"Hell yes I suppose." She centered the ship and sent the gamma wave which had opened their portal.

A ring identical to their own sprung forth to fill with luminescent golden plasma.

She took a deep breath and blew it out through pursed lips, giving her brain time to rearrange not only its notions of space but the nature of the cosmos itself.

"We're not the only ones."

"No, it appears we are not."

"I don't...." Her hand rose to work at her jaw. "Caleb, do you have any idea what this means?"

"I have several, of varying degrees of nefariousness and amorality. A couple swing the opposite direction to inspiring, bordering on transcendental."

She stood, grabbed his hand and took him with her to the data center. "Rather than repeat this process another forty-nine times, I'm going to go ahead and map it out real quick."

She pulled in the readings taken at the primary portal and, extrapolating from the distance this signal and their own propagated, estimated the presumed termination points of the remaining waves. The result was three perfect semicircles divided into equal segments, with portals dotting the perimeter and their own sitting opposite the master one.

"Damn." He wrapped his arms around her from behind.

She chuckled faintly and drew a hand along his arm. "So I agree we shouldn't go through the big portal. Frightening implications, likely kill us, etcetera, etcetera. But...can we go through *this* one?"

"Alex, baby..." she felt him sigh against her ear "...yes. As if I could stop you."

"Excellent." Instantly she was headed back to the cockpit and strapping in. She rolled her shoulders and cracked her neck. "No time to waste."

She gunned the engine straight into the middle of the ring—

—the sensation of vertigo was overpowering. The world literally flipped downward ninety degrees.

It wasn't in her head, either. The axes of the world *did* shift, the proper loci of 'up' and 'down' moving to points off-kilter to where they previously resided.

"Woah...." Her hands came up to grip her head, as if to make sure her brain remained inside it. She spun to Caleb, eyes wide. "Are we good?"

"I have no idea." His head shook roughly. "Check it out, the scenery's no different here."

She peered out the viewport. Indeed, nothing but endless blackness. She was almost getting used to it.

"The TLF wave continues, apparently in a straight line...the way everything shifted, I can't be positive. But let's see where it leads."

Where it led was an exact replica of the colossal, electric blue portal they had believed the 'master' portal. The ring emitted more TLF waves in three stacked semicircles.

But it wasn't *more* waves. It was the same waves, only the order and repetition had changed. Now, the wave they followed was the final horizontal one to the left along the fan-like distribution. 'Their' wave was located halfway past center.

"If we follow our frequency, we'll end up back where we were, won't we?"

"In our lobby? Likely at a different point. Probably the termination point of one of the waves which were at either end...because this is some kind of elaborate, interlocking tunnel network."

She exhaled harshly. "Fifty-one lobbies...each one containing a portal opposite the master one that leads to a universe. Fifty-one *universes*...I don't suppose you could tell me a couple of those inspiring ideas you had?"

He gazed out the viewport. "Mesme believes humans have the potential to 'deliver the very answers' they seek. What do you think it is they're looking for?"

"I imagine the same answers we're looking for: What's the meaning of life, of our existence? Is this all there is? Do we have souls which live on after death? Does a higher power exist? What's the—"

He leapt out of the chair and hurried through the cabin. "We need to go back."

"I agree we do, but what—"

He was fishing around in his pack, previously tossed in the corner for eventual unloading, and came out with one of the tech repulsion orbs.

"We need to destroy that ship factory, and I know how we can do it."

57

ROMANE
INDEPENDENT COLONY

*N*ew Maya has ceased communications as of fourteen minutes ago.
Mia bit back a frown as she dumped the contents of the grocery bag on the counter and fished her pack out of the closet. "Thank you, Meno. Keep me updated."

I always do.

The MREs, energy bars and nutrient-fortified drinks had cost a small fortune. She should have acquired them last week before the entire galaxy knew about the aliens. Now merchants were taking full advantage of the steadily elevating panic.

She couldn't decide whether it was blatant extortion or shrewd capitalism at work; she'd forked over the credits regardless. The time for taking a stand on high-minded philosophical principle had long since passed.

The news feed had burst to life as soon as she'd entered the house. She increased the volume so she was able to hear it while she went into the bedroom to collect some clothes. Her prior emergency pack was now graduating to a full-scale long-term survival pack.

"I'm honored to welcome Earth Alliance Prime Minister Brennon, Senecan Federation Chairman Vranas and all the representatives of their governments to Romane, though I deeply regret the circumstances which have brought you here. Romane values its role as a peaceful, prosperous independent world. I hope the spirit of our colony can help you reach a place of mutual respect and understanding and guide you to your own peace."

She chuckled a little to herself—*two...no, three comfortable work pants*—at Ledesme's grand speech. The governor executed a masterful stroke when she volunteered Romane to serve as the host for this Peace Summit. Coupled with her generous sharing of their analysis of the alien ships with both sides, in a matter of days the governor had increased Romane's standing exponentially. Mia might have helped a tiny bit.

The Summit almost hadn't happened here, for one simple reason: the aliens were *close*. But their progress west was slowing. New Maya wasn't located appreciably farther west than other colonies which had already fallen. Romane sat nearly a day closer to both Seneca and Earth than the sole viable alternative, Atlantis, and there was no time to waste. *Four tanks, one turtleneck, a pullover....*

She wasn't running but she was preparing. As thanks for her efforts in this whole disaster the governor had offered her a seat on the administration's transport should a full-scale evacuation be ordered. Mia felt extremely grateful but was also cognizant of the frequent fate of best-laid plans.

Romane would not evacuate unless and until there remained no other choice, and by that point chaos was certain to have descended. The bag she was packing would serve her well enough wherever the transport ended up but would also serve her well if she never made it off the planet.

She was glad the bureaucrats managed to see past their narrow perspectives and realize they needed to put aside imagined differences and work together before everyone died. Whether the changes of heart had come in time to prevent everyone from dying remained to be seen. She was glad Caleb, and Alex, had been cleared of wrongdoing; Alex's mother was even attending the Summit. She'd be more glad once she heard from him. Them. One of them, preferably both.

But she couldn't waste energy and brain power worrying about Caleb and his girlfriend. She needed to worry about her own survival now.

She tossed a basic toiletries kit in the pack and closed it, then took it to the front door, set it against the wall and straightened up. "Meno, I'm coming to you. I want to run through some simulations on the aliens' movements."

"Romane will proudly stand side-by-side with a united humanity to meet these—"

ᴿ

"—invaders with the full might and skill of the human race. Thank you."

Miriam ticked off the seconds until she could exit the public spectacle and get to work. *3...2...1....* She stood, acknowledged Brennon's nod—a signal his directives had not changed during Governor Ledesme's speech—and headed for a far smaller conference room down the hall.

The Summit was being held at the Carina Center on Romane. She almost wished she had the luxury of relaxing, for it was by far the most elegant, modern convention facility she had ever visited. The view outside the shuttle during the brief flight from the spaceport had suggested that much of the city exhibited a similar level of class.

She decided if they somehow survived this invasion, when the war was over she would take a...va-ca-tion. The word rolled strangely in her mind. And her...vacation...would be to Romane.

But right now she would do her job, because if she didn't the facility and the city which supported it were likely to soon be a pile of smoldering rubble.

Field Marshal Gianno had managed to beat her to the conference room. If the Summit went on for longer than a day she'd need to discover how the woman had done so. They had spoken twice via holo in the last two days but had never met in person.

There was no procedure for formalities between officers of equivalent rank from opposing militaries, so she merely offered her hand in what remained a universal greeting. "It's a pleasure to meet you in person, Marshal Gianno."

The woman grasped her hand crisply and peered past Miriam's shoulder. "It's only us, correct?"

"For the moment, I believe so."

Gianno pulled out a chair and sat. "Call me Eleni, then. We have time for nothing else."

"So we do not. And it's Miriam." She took the seat across from her counterpart. "In that vein, I propose we simply assume the politicians will reach a peace deal—for if they do not I shall murder them myself—and move forward as if they've done so. As you so eloquently put it, we have time for nothing else."

"I agree." Gianno placed a small square module on the desk and activated it; multiple screens burst to life in the space above the table.

"We haven't yet engaged the alien ships as you did—or anyone who may have done so has not made it out alive to share their experience. But we have had some success capturing information using long-range reconnaissance squads.

"Our latest intel indicates four superdreadnoughts each at Hadron and Midgard and six at Dair. Eight ships left New Riga seventeen hours ago, as well as four from Lycaon a few hours later. Neither group could be tracked at superluminal speeds. We're monitoring for them at Brython, Nystad and Elathan. And, obviously, Seneca."

Miriam shared similar information: forty-four ships currently attacking six worlds and a minimum of sixteen in transit from colonies whose decimation had been accomplished. They both settled back in their chairs to contemplate what in the aggregate made for the beginnings of real, hard intel.

"So on average it's taking the aliens two days and four ships to eradicate a world of 50,000, five days and six ships for a population of 100,000, and at least one week and considerably more ships for anything larger."

"They haven't departed Messium yet, then?"

"No. Though by this point there can't be much left for them to demolish so I expect they will depart within hours. We destroyed two and damaged three superdreadnoughts in the battle, as well as around two hundred of the swarmers, but it was only a fraction of the force they fielded."

"Impressive though, especially considering your ships couldn't talk to one another and coordinate their tactics."

Miriam looked across the table in surprise. "Has no one told you? We can talk to one another."

ℛ

The peace deal was brokered in less than four hours.

A formal cessation of hostilities was signed by the politicians on the spot and a bare-bones treaty approved subject to the respective legislatures' passage, which was expected by the next morning.

Military forces were ordered to withdraw from all Alliance-Federation conflict zones. Under the circumstances the vast majority of those forces were then ordered either east or to the Sol or Senecan stellar systems.

In a somewhat unexpected turn of events, Desna's fate was to be left to the Desnans themselves. The colonists were to hold a referendum within the week choosing whether to rejoin the Alliance, stay part of the Federation or go it alone as an Independent. Conventional wisdom said they'd return to the Alliance, but the Federation occupation had not been a harsh or violent one and some commentators conceded it might go a different way.

Over the course of the four hours it took to hammer out the treaty, Miriam and Eleni's meeting gained more attendees, in person and via holo. Freed of conflicting objectives and at last facing a single front in a single war—even if that front extended for more than six kiloparsecs—it only remained for the two most powerful women in the galaxy to do the impossible: formulate a strategy for defending against, facing and ultimately defeating the enemy.

58

The Triene headquarters complex was utilitarian. Functional. Brutally efficient.

The decor wasn't drab by any objective measure, though it lacked a certain refined style Olivia preferred. Still, she had to concede it likely got the job done well enough.

She strode through the…she'd call it offices, but in reality it was a hybrid command center / manufacturing plant / storage facility…exuding enough authority to ward off most interference.

Those who didn't recognize her and felt confident enough to assert dominance were, in most cases, restrained by those who did recognize her. There was one unfortunate incident involving a security guard. He should heal sufficiently, assuming a decent med kit lay in close proximity.

The trek over had been marked by far greater hazards. The streets were nothing less than bedlam, descending toward riotous.

New Babel represented one of the westernmost colonies in settled space and had become the default destination for every less-than-upstanding citizen in the galaxy fleeing the aliens. This was a problem. The colony maintained a rudimentary but delicate ecosystem, and it was currently being upended by the influx of tens of thousands of new people, many of them lacking basic manners and most of them carrying no obligations to restrain their behavior. The lack of a single organized security force, long an asset, was rapidly becoming a liability.

Aiden was waiting on her when she reached the atrium of his suite. He doubtless would have been notified of her approach by multiple people.

He leaned on the door to his inner office, his arms crossed in feigned casualness over his chest. His eyes were guarded and he was not smiling. She expected no less; she had arrived unannounced and uninvited. Here in his domain, she was for all intents and purposes an enemy.

"Ms. Montegreu. I'd say this is a surprise, but you know it is and intended it as such."

She shrugged with equally feigned dismissiveness. "There wasn't an opportunity to arrange otherwise." Mindful of their audience of a secretary, two lieutenants and three enforcers, she maintained a respectful distance. "May we speak in private?"

Instead of answering her, Aiden jerked his head in the direction of two of the enforcers.

As they approached her she offered up a Daemon and a gamma blade. "I needed to protect myself on the way over. If you've been outside in the last several days, you're aware the streets are inordinately dangerous."

"Understood. Your weapons will be returned to you when you depart."

"Thank you, Mr. Trieneri." She was going so very far out of her way to pay him the proper deference in front of his employees. It was revolting.

He only mostly suppressed a smirk as he gestured toward his office. "After you, Ms. Montegreu."

She stepped inside, then turned in time to see him tap a panel as the door closed. Surveillance shielding, she thought. That damn well better be all it was.

"What are you doing here, Olivia?"

She positioned herself on the edge of his desk. "It's the end of days, Aiden. I can't simply want a good lay?"

That earned her a chuckle despite his attempt to be gruff. "Of course you can—but you don't. Not right now."

"And how do you know?"

He swiftly crossed the space between them, dropping his hands on the desk on either side of her and bringing his lips within centimeters of hers. "When you want sex, I know it from ten meters away. Now? You don't *smell* horny."

Her pulse quickened at the danger of his closeness. He had handed over no weapons, naturally. "Fuck you, Aiden."

"Ha. Maybe later?" He retreated to the center of the room and returned his arms to his chest. "I'll ask you one more time, Olivia, then I'll have you escorted out. What are you doing here?"

"You might have heard, aliens are attacking—" she held up a hand to forestall his retort "—and I assume you no more want civilization to be annihilated than I do. It's bad for business. Therefore, I'm here to propose a temporary truce between our organizations."

His expression was completely unreadable. He was good at masking his emotions, assuming he had any. "A truce?"

"Until the aliens are dealt with or we all suffer horrific deaths, whichever happens first. Neither of us should be wasting valuable resources competing against—and in some cases fighting—one another when those resources are needed to defend ourselves."

He considered her a moment. "There's more to it."

She scowled, disturbed by the notion he may be able to read her better than she assumed. "I have an arrangement with elements of the Alliance and Federation governments. Because I don't wish the human race to become extinct, I've agreed to assist them in several respects."

"You're working for the authorities? I have a great deal of difficulty believing that."

"As do I. Nevertheless, desperate times, desperate measures. I'm providing useful supplies to aid in the war effort."

"And?"

"And I want you to join me in aiding them."

His eyes narrowed precipitously. "You're serious."

"While I easily have access to anything and everything they will need, I admit your organization has its strengths in specific areas. Those strengths could benefit said war effort."

He did smirk this time, a dark and malicious countenance which reminded her he was, in point of fact, not a nice man. "Olivia, are you asking for my help?"

She shoved off the desk and charged past him toward the door. "This was clearly a mistake. Don't expect to hear from me again."

His hand shot out to grab her and wrench her against him. His stare bored into her, only shifting briefly to glance at the blade she now had pressed to his neck. She didn't acknowledge the gun digging into her side.

Then his mouth crushed into hers. She met it with equal force.

When he pulled back a fraction, a thin trail of blood dribbled down his neck. She hadn't meant to cut him; he had moved too fast. Such were the risks in their game.

"Olivia. Are you asking for my help?"

"I'm asking for you to help save the galaxy. I realize 'saving' anything or anyone isn't something either of us make a habit of doing, but in this instance it is in our best interest to do so."

The blade still rested at his neck; she hadn't yet been given a reason to remove it. "Aiden, don't lose your business and yourself to this rising tide of chaos. Grab hold of this opportunity with me and we will both emerge stronger and more powerful. We can rebuild civilization atop the ruins. We can reshape the structure of society to our advantage. All we have to do is help them win."

Ever so slowly a mischievous smile pulled his lips upward. "I do enjoy it when you talk dirty to me."

ATLANTIS
INDEPENDENT COLONY

Matei reclined in his chaise and sipped on a Polaris Burst cocktail.

The afternoon sun warming his skin sparkled on the crystal blue waters and turned the sand to glittering glass. His mood was as light as everyone else's on Atlantis was dark. The resort world hummed a chromatic vibrato, a dissonant transition portending the coming doom. Gone was the carefree excess and easy joy of a people at the height of civilization who believed themselves invincible.

There existed two kinds of people still gracing the beaches of Atlantis. One was composed of families with young children. The parents worked desperately to preserve their children's innocence for one more minute, one more day. They built sandcastles and frolicked in the shallow waters and beamed at the young ones' cackles of delight, but terror etched grim lines into their faces. Sunglasses hid the paralyzing fear haunting their eyes.

The other, more numerous kind consisted of those who had decided they were going to exit the universe drunk or high, and often both. Alcohol poisoning or a non-neural chimeral overdose would be all but impossible for anyone wealthy enough to afford to be on Atlantis in the first place, thanks to genetic modifications and regulating cybernetic subroutines…but that wasn't stopping them from trying. They came from all age groups and near as he had been able to determine, all professions.

Individuals reacted in any number of ways to extreme stress and, relatedly, to impending death. A non-negligible percentage of people reacted in a manner which could be summed up by, 'Screw it, I'm going out in style!'

Atlantis security was doing its best to keep the two groups separated, but he'd witnessed several bizarre encounters between desperate, frayed parents and persons who were quite obviously out of their minds.

The rules of civilized society were beginning to break down, and on this world where excess and debauchery were encouraged and even celebrated, the first cracks in the wall were on stark display.

He smiled pleasantly and wound his hands behind his head on the chaise. The news feed scrolling on his whisper provided a tableau of destruction and mayhem overlaid upon the bright waters and cerulean skies. The contrast pleased him—

You are too far west to do your job.

He took another sip of his drink. And he had thought the chess game over with the death of Aguirre and general collapse of the man's little conspiracy. Alas.

"Is there something you require of me, Hyperion?"

Caleb Marano and Alexis Solovy will soon return. They must be eliminated.

"Very well, though I don't see the point. They no longer represent a threat to the human war, seeing as there no longer is a human war."

They represent a threat to us. Eliminate them.

Matei gave no overt reaction, but his curiosity piqued. The alien was always enigmatic and often baffling, but it had never before been…testy. He felt the need to prod at the weak spot. Explore it a bit. "How could two insignificant humans represent a threat to you?"

They traversed our portal.

So that was where they went. He was glad he hadn't wasted much time or effort searching for the pair and instead waited for the intel to come to him. "Interesting, but I'm still not clear how this makes them a threat to you?"

They traversed our PORTAL. They have seen us. They have conversed with us. They have acquired knowledge of us.

Glimpsed the man behind the curtain, did they? He wondered what had been revealed, what the secret might be the aliens remained so desperate to protect. Sadly he didn't expect either Marano or Solovy to consent to tell him before he killed them.

"Understood. I'll travel to Romane. From there I'll be well positioned to move. Besides, there aren't many places left farther east which still have functioning spaceports."

This is acceptable. If our units do not eliminate them on their return, we will inform you of their location.

"Your 'units'?"

Our machines.

"You know, if you're so anxious to have Marano and Solovy dead, why don't you simply kill them yourself while you have them on your side of the portal?"

Absurd. We grew beyond such barbarism aeons ago.

He glanced at the vid of the alien ships battering New Maya playing on his whisper. "All evidence to the contrary."

Your meaning eludes me.

"You've killed over forty million people in the last three weeks. Seems to me you're rather adept at killing."

No. The machines kill. We do not kill.

"The instrument a killer employs in the act does not kill. The killer kills."

Spare me your childish logic. You will receive the targets' location soon.

Then the alien was gone.

Matei took a final sip of his drink, breathed a long sigh tainted with regret and stood. It appeared his vacation was at an end, or at a minimum an interlude.

Though his alien contact had always conveyed the impression of being evolved to a 'higher' level of existence, he'd never bought it and now his suspicion had been confirmed. Hyperion exhibited impatience, irritation and, most interestingly, fear.

The aliens were fallible after all. They were flawed. Of course everyone was flawed, if they believed themselves alive. It was a defect of the condition.

59

It was early morning in Vancouver when the *EAS Orion* docked. A bright dawn sun gleamed outside, so far as Noah could tell through the occasional viewport he passed on the way to disembark.

A shuttle would be waiting on them for the trip to wherever EASC Headquarters was located. They were scheduled to meet some important people before handing over the data and materials to other, different important people who would dissect it and study it to determine how yet other important people might use it to fight the aliens.

He was twitchy, approaching nervous. He wanted to help, but having succeeded in getting valuable intel into hands he hoped were the right ones, he didn't see any particular way he could. And this was not his gig.

He made his living as a black-market tech dealer and a smuggler. He did not belong inside the heart of Alliance military command, even if his genes suggested otherwise.

The security databases shouldn't have him flagged for immediate arrest, but anyone who looked closely stood a good chance of realizing he was not precisely an upstanding Alliance citizen. Still, since he hadn't as of yet found the opportunity to flee he would play it cool until he did.

He had hardly seen Kennedy at all in the three day trip. She had been in Medical, after which she'd huddled with Colonel Jenner and some techies studying and organizing the data and material they had. That was followed by conferences with other—or perhaps the same—important people. And if she was anything like him, he assumed she had slept a great deal.

He'd nearly decided whatever attraction or connection he imagined had sparked between them had in reality consisted of nothing more than adrenaline and fear spiking in a life-or-death situation.

Then she stepped out of the lift.

Naturally all traces of dirt and blood had been excised from her person. Her hair now shone an almost luminescent golden blond and hung in soft curls over one shoulder and down her back. Her face was scrubbed clean and other than a tiny scratch on her forehead glowed the color of honey. Sea green eyes sparkled beneath minimal but flattering makeup. She wore form-fitting workout pants and a navy Alliance t-shirt. Borrowed clothes he imagined, but on her they may as well have come straight out of a couture house.

She carried herself with the kind of confidence that only came from a lifetime of true wealth and privilege. But she was beaming and as vivacious as he'd ever seen her.

He was so royally fucked.

"Noah!" She jogged across the bay and grabbed him in a fierce hug. "I've hardly seen you. I was getting worried."

He shrugged mildly and forced himself to take a step back. "I've been around, skulking about and hoping no one noticed me. Made a couple of friends down on the lower decks."

"Well—" An officer indicated for them to follow him to the shuttle, cutting off further conversation.

The trip was short, so much so he would have rather walked. Three-plus days on a military ship, even a cruiser, had left him feeling vaguely claustrophobic and itching for fresh air. It looked to be very pleasant outside.

He'd visited Earth several times, but never Vancouver. It seemed nice. Cool, green and shining. Though they were on a military base, it seemed peaceful. Parsecs away from the hell that had been Messium.

Upon exiting the shuttle it was a few steps to a lift and then a lobby sporting tight security. Still having no opportunity to flee, he tensed through two separate checkpoints and didn't relax until they stood on yet another lift. Kennedy gave him a nudge.

"We'll be meeting with the research team in a few minutes but the Chairwoman of the EASC Board wants to see us, so we're going up there first."

"Terrific." This must be his worst nightmare...well, second worst after Messium anyway.

The lift finally stopped and their escort showed them into a conference room. Military officers were scattered around the room engaged in conversations.

Kennedy bolted for a woman wearing admiral's bars and reviewing a handheld screen at the front of the room. When she reached the woman they embraced warmly.

"Miriam, it is so good to see you again."

Terrific. It wasn't enough she was on a first-name basis with the captain of their cruiser, she was also on a first-name basis with the leader of the Alliance Armed Forces. He was so far out of his league it bordered on absurdity.

What had he been thinking? He shrank against the wall and tried to be invisible.

"Kennedy, I can't tell you how happy I am you made it off Messium unharmed. Have you heard from Alexis?"

"Not since a few days after the bombing, I'm afraid."

"Do you have any idea where she is?"

He saw Kennedy's face darken under a somber frown. "Miriam...they went through the portal."

The admiral's expression, formerly warm but composed, collapsed into despair. Her eyes briefly squeezed shut and he noted her chest heave from a deep sigh. "When?"

As near as he'd managed to piece together, Caleb was dating Kennedy's best friend, with whom he had discovered the aliens in the Metis Nebula, tried to warn everyone, gotten framed for terrorism for the effort, and fled through the aliens' portal in search of answers. He knew the guy lived on the edge, but *damn.*

"A little over two weeks ago. I think they hoped to learn where the aliens came from, or who they are, or what they want. Anything that would help."

The woman nodded deliberately and appeared to forcibly put herself back together. Her shoulders rose and a formal guise descended over her features. "At least it means the reason she's unreachable isn't because she's...well. You'll contact me the second you hear from her, won't you?"

"Absolutely. Let's not dwell on it right now—but I want you to know something. The last time I saw her she said she trusted you to not let her problems interfere with your ability to defend against the aliens. She trusted you to protect us until she could return. She may not tell you that herself, but I will."

Kennedy shifted her bearing then, and he could no longer discern the woman's expression. But her voice was far more hesitant than before. "Thank you. Thank you for telling me."

"Of course. Do you—oh! Before we discuss the communications issues, I need to tell you about this new metal Alex created. The strength and conductive properties are off the charts. We should be using it to repair our ships. We should be using it to build our ships."

He closed his eyes and let the conversation fade to the background. He didn't belong here. He needed to go.

Where, he didn't know. Just because Caleb had been cleared of the bombing didn't mean Zelones wasn't still gunning for him. The organization tended to hold grudges. It surprised him when for the briefest second he thought about going home...but he couldn't. Besides, Aquila lay to the east and was liable to be hit by the aliens any day now. He was not going through that again.

Atlantis? A lounge chair and a steady supply of tropical drinks sounded pretty good about now.

He groaned under his breath. He couldn't exactly sip frozen cocktails on a beach while the entirety of civilization was under assault, could he? Screw his pain in the ass conscience....

Demeter was close; he'd been told it was an attractive place. Maybe he'd find out.

He reopened his eyes for a last glimpse of Kennedy. She remained deeply engrossed in conversation with her admiral friend and plainly in her element. He had gotten her safely home. He felt good about that. It would have to be enough.

He swallowed hard and slipped out the door.

R

Noah had almost reached the end of the long hallway when her shout echoed behind him. "Hey!"

Before he could stop himself he was turning in the direction of Kennedy's voice.

"Where do you think you're going?"

"Eh...." He found he was ambling back down the hall even as his brain screamed at him to amble the other way. "I don't really do military, so I thought I'd go on and head out. I'm glad I was able to help you get here, though. Good luck with the aliens, and if we survive this feel free to look me up on your next vacation."

"Good luck with the *aliens*? You are such a prick."

He finally succeeded in slowing to a stop five meters from her. "Yeah, I am. I thought you'd figured that out by now."

"Stay."

"What? Why?"

Her brow furrowed up, as if it constituted the lamest question she had ever heard. "Because I like you. You're handy to have around."

Oh, hell, no. "Listen, I am not your 'beck and call' boy."

"Would you...consider it?"

"Consider it?" He laughed; it sounded harsh to his ears. "Thank you for making this easy. Forget what I said. Don't look me up on your next vacation. Nice knowing you, Blondie."

He threw a dismissive wave in her direction and pivoted to leave.

"Noah, wait. I didn't mean consider being my...'beck and call' boy, whatever that is. I meant consider staying."

His mouth contorted into a grimace, but his body turned in her direction once more.

Vivid green eyes glittered with what seemed a lot like hope. "For a while? See what happens?"

Dammit. Dammit, dammit, *dammit*. He gathered up his last sliver of fortitude and brandished a pale imitation of his most dashing smile. "Thanks for the offer, but I need to get out of here."

He spun so he wouldn't have to know whether the hope disappeared and hurried down the hallway—

—and found himself shoved against the wall. Kennedy's hands wound into his hair and her lips hovered a breath from his.

"You are the most infuriating, confounding man I have ever met, and you damn well better not run away from me."

Then her mouth was on his. She was the single most delicious luxury he had ever tasted. Ambrosia soaked in champagne couldn't hope to compare.

Wealthy heiress, talented engineer, friend to admirals, spirited, determined survivor with a heart of gold. What in the devil's name was he getting himself into?

His arms encircled her waist as he suddenly felt the intense desire to make sure she didn't run away from him.

When she finally allowed him to come up for air, he remembered how that dashing smile worked for real. "I guess I don't have any really pressing engagements…."

Her eyes searched his as if she was trying to decide whether more extreme measures would be required. "So you'll stay then?"

Oh yes. He nodded. "I'll stay."

Her face lit up with a radiance that was definitely the most enchanting sight he had ever seen.

He was so royally, gloriously fucked.

60

" W hat are you doing?"

Caleb glanced up at her from the floor, where he had spread the orbs he had liberated, a signal scope, two crates of non-perishables and his sword. "I am going to crack one of these babies open and figure out how to switch it on."

He secured one of the orbs between the crates, picked up the sword, eyeballed the angle once and swung.

"Ahh!" Alex leapt back as the crates skidded in opposite directions across the cabin. But they had done their job, and on the floor lay two pieces of the orb, sliced clean in half.

He tossed a smirk in her direction and picked one of the sections up. "See? It worked."

"Caleb, you can't turn it on inside the ship! It'll rip us to shreds. *Oh....*" She crouched down next to him. "Mesme was right, you know. You are an astoundingly clever man."

When he saw the glint in her eyes he briefly considered tearing her clothes off right there in the middle of the floor. Regrettably they were short on time, especially considering they were currently drifting around in some other universe's lobby.

"I am, or I will be if I can puzzle out how to turn it on. You know, without actually turning it on."

She settled fully onto the floor beside him and curled her legs beneath her. "The factory was mammoth in size. We have, what, four of these—or three if this one's wrecked? Do you really think it'll be enough?"

"That field threw the *Siyane* four hundred kilometers in under a second. It'll be enough." He paused, identifying a possible flaw in the plan. "You do have remote sensors or probes or something launchable on board, don't you?"

In the corner of his vision she rolled her eyes at the ceiling. "Yes, I have a couple of those."

422 | G.S. JENNSEN

"Good. Now I suspect these little guys were supported by one another and the larger field being generated, like an interlocking lattice. When I removed each of them from their slot in the network, they shut down. So we need to either simulate the connection, or trick it into believing the field is active."

"I think tricking it is the more viable option, for it and my ship."

"Probably." He studied the internal layout of the orb. Physically it was nothing like any circuitry a human would or ever had designed, but it *was* circuitry. Strands of a form of photal fiber wove in intricate patterns, interconnected at nodes and fed into a tiny euhedral crystal in the center.

The question now was which one maintained the power signal. He disconnected the strands from the crystal and grabbed the scope.

"Caleb...."

"It's fine. I've disconnected the power source. It can't switch on now." He touched the probe tip to each strand and studied the readouts. Most of the results were crazy complicated, but he was searching for the one which was a simple on/off.

On the second-to-last strand, he found it.

He exhaled, relieved. No way should this have rightfully worked. Then he gave Alex an imploring gaze. "I need a few more tools."

Identifying the nature of the signal which constituted 'on,' replicating it in the ship's signaling system and attaching the orbs to one of the remote probes she used to take asteroid samples took an hour and change. Of course this was still an hour as it passed here, which meant in reality it took an eternity. But it was the best plan they had.

"Ready?"

He strapped into his cockpit chair. "Oh so ready."

She retraced their path and reopened the portal back to their lobby. He braced himself against the expected vertigo as they flew through, but it was still dizzying to the point of nausea.

Alex growled beside him and set a course for the ship factory, then stood. "I'll be right back, I'm going to go vomit real fast."

His hand shot out to grasp her arm. "Hey...you all right?"

She flashed him a weak smile, but her face had blanched. "Fabulous." She no more looked fabulous than he imagined he did, but he nodded and let her go.

By the time she returned they had almost reached their destination. The factory loomed large in front of them, continuing its relentless construction of monstrous vessels.

How many had it sent on their way to wreak destruction upon civilization while they were gone? Five? Ten?

It wouldn't be sending any more.

The ship decelerated to drift nearly a megameter distant. There was no way to predict how big the explosion was going to be, but any further away and the signal might not reach the orbs.

"Here goes everything...." She released the probe.

Too small to see with the naked eye after a few dozen meters, they tracked it on the radar as it sailed toward the facility. None of the mechs noticed when the probe slipped through the scaffolding and inside. She halted its progress.

"...and here goes everything else." In the same way her ship sent the gamma waves to open the portals, at her touch the ship sent the signal to activate the orbs.

The reaction was instantaneous. Every gram of powered machinery—the mechs, the ships, the equipment used to assemble the ships—exploded outward from the probe's location with the force of a supernova eruption.

"Not a safe distance!" Rather than maneuver in reverse she flipped the *Siyane* over and accelerated away. They observed the destruction in the rearcam visual until it seemed likely they wouldn't be ripped apart by projectile spears then arced back around.

The entire expanse of space before them was littered in jagged shards of obsidian metal, none larger than ten meters in length. The extent of the destruction was awe-inspiring in its completeness.

424 | G.S. JENNSEN

Alex was cackling wildly, a hand in her hair and the other at her neck. "That was amazing! I bet—oh boy."

The dramatic shift in her tone was enough to distract him from the scene outside the viewport. "Dare I ask?"

"Our vandalism has attracted attention. I'm guessing the attention of the ships which hadn't yet made it to the Metis portal. Or the ships which were still searching for us. Or both."

"Run for our portal?"

"Uh...no." She zoomed the long-range radar so he could see the metric fuck-ton of red blips assembled between them and the gateway to Metis.

"More squid."

"God I hope all those aren't the big ones. But the alien ships can't see us, correct? So maybe we just sneak quietly past them? That's an outrageous number of ships, though. One mistake and we're in smaller pieces than the factory."

"Go through one of the other portals. Sneak past them for real."

"This is a good idea." Her eyes darted with unspoken thoughts; then the *Siyane* was in motion. "Let's go back through the one we did earlier to hide and I'll figure out which portal will dump us out closest to our own."

Their destination was under a minute away and they quickly traversed the portal. The world wrenched around—it wasn't getting any easier to experience—and they angled another two megameters into darkness.

She stood and made her way to the data center, waving over her shoulder. "Can you stay and keep watch on the radar?"

"Yep." He settled deeper in the chair. It was starting to break in nicely. He contemplated the blackness outside, and what it represented. It was enough—ten red blips materialized on the radar.

"Alex, I think they know where we went."

"They must be alerted when we open portals. Will you fly while I work this out?"

No way had he heard her right. "Care to repeat that?"

She appeared beside his chair, rotating it until he faced her then leaning in to run a hand along his jaw and place a soft kiss on his mouth. "Fly my ship for me."

He murmured against her lips. "I can do that."

Then she was gone. He spun back to the HUD beaming like an idiot, desperate circumstances be damned. "So I'll put some distance between us and these guys, but if they get too numerous I may need to traverse another portal."

"Warn me first." The plea sounded like it came through gritted teeth.

Creating distance from ships which were significantly faster than the *Siyane* wasn't as easy as it sounded. The only factor in his favor was the pursuers didn't know precisely where they were—a fact which would surely be causing their enemies much consternation had they possessed emotions.

It took time for their numbers to increase, but eventually this lobby grew thick with enemy vessels and his room to maneuver shrank to an untenable level.

"Jumping." He drew as close as he dared to the location of the chosen portal before opening it then flew straight through.

"Oh my god that sucks!"

He stifled a chuckle; it would be mean to poke fun at her genuine distress. "Got an ETA back there?"

"An hour or two."

"What?"

"Forty seconds, if you'll quit interrupting me."

"Gotcha." He had never slowed after exiting this time, creating a fair degree of distance before the first vessels began to follow them. And follow they did, relentlessly tracking prey they could not see.

"I'm jumping one more time so we have room to maneuver once we know where we're headed."

The warning elicited a distracted grumble. "I hate you."

He smiled to himself. "No...no, you don't."

He braced himself and slung the ship through another random portal, choking down the acid forcing its way up his throat. His equilibrium wouldn't be steady for days.

"Ugh...0.0449 Hz...."

"Great, but I'm—"

She fell into her chair and strapped in. "Never mind. I'll find it. Keep flying." The spectrum analyzer bloomed to dominate the left side of the HUD. "Head a bit to starboard, it's at bearing N 12.3°. Maybe I should take over now."

He removed his hands from the controls with dramatic flair. "The ship is yours."

"Thank ya." She meandered around until they located the desired TLF wave and settled atop it.

"You realize what we're about to do is geometrically impossible unless we're traveling through more than three dimensions."

Freed of duties for now, he shrugged. "The notion did occur to me. It didn't seem relevant at the time."

"Fair enough." She eyed him without turning her head. "So when we get to our lobby I have a plan to get us past not only the ships here, but also those presumably waiting for us on the other side."

"Am I going to like this plan?"

A corner of her mouth curled up. "Not in the slightest."

61

Liam had a raging headache minutes after departing the transport. Or had the headache been plaguing him for hours now? He found he had trouble recalling.

The trip had been interminable, and he'd lost track of the hours passing somewhere around the mid-way point. A portion of the trip he spent considering his plan, then planning the steps to follow. But long after all productive work was completed there had only remained the endless waiting to land.

And now that he at last stood on Fionava, the headache throbbed painfully against his brow. The planet was sickeningly pretty, painted in lavender and baby blue and plum. Oversized flowers and colored fauna were planted in every available space of the burgeoning city and a white sun shone so brightly he was forced to squint every time he dared glance out the levtram window. Hence the headache.

It was everything Deucali was not. This supposed beauty was purportedly the reason it had been chosen to host the Alliance Northwestern Regional Headquarters, but he couldn't imagine any soldier worth their salt enjoying this place.

At least he wouldn't have to tolerate it for long. He expected to be on a ship—a real ship—within the day. And he did not intend to return to this atrocious planet henceforth.

The levtram slowed as the base came into view ahead. It was built in the middle of a Goddamned meadow. If he saw a soldier frolicking through the tulips, he was going to shoot them on sight.

He closed his eyes to block out the meadow, and to ready himself. A vital facet of his plan consisted of him projecting absolute authority and a demeanor which brokered no questioning.

Then the doors opened and he walked brusquely forward. Passengers, mostly military, instinctively moved out of his way while tossing salutes in his direction. He ignored them to march purposefully to the security checkpoint.

The Warrant Officer looked through him without really seeing him as Liam placed his palm on the scanner. Presumably recognizing the identity which flashed on his screen, the officer's gaze darted up, eyes wide. "Sir! General O'Connell! Apologies, sir. I wasn't notified of your arrival. We..." the man frowned at the screen "...uh, sir, the system says EASC is requesting you report to Earth immediately."

"Your orders are old, son. Everything's been taken care of."

"Yes, sir. If you'll wait a moment, I'll see to an escort for you."

"Not necessary. I know the way." He had never visited NW Headquarters before but had memorized the floor plan and layout on the eternal trip from Earth.

His first destination—before his presence began to stir everyone up—needed to be the Communications Center. While individuals handled most of their communications internally via the exanet, such a large volume of data flowed into and out of a Regional Headquarters that physical servers and specialized ware were employed to control, route and store the bulk of it.

Bitterness ate at his gut like a festering ulcer. He didn't trust ware or the nuts who created it and the necessity of using it peeved him to no end. But there were more important matters at stake now. Matters like duty. Pride. Vengeance. He would use whatever tools were required to further them.

An officer sitting at the monitoring station in the front room of the Communications Center scrambled up to snap a clumsy salute, noting the bars on the uniform but not him. It was for the best.

"Sir...uh...General? How can I help you?"

"I need access to your control room."

"Yes, sir. What is this in regard to?"

"That's classified, Lieutenant."

The skinny young man screwed his face up, then worked to tamp down the expression. "Understood, sir. Do you require any assistance? The setup can be tricky and—"

"Negative." He walked past the lieutenant and stood at the inner door in a manner indicating he expected it to open immediately. And so it did.

The small crystal disk he fished out of his pocket had cost him half a year's salary paid to a woman so morally abhorrent he had showered twice after leaving her company.

Her instructions were straightforward: *locate the rectangular box, probably constructed of a brushed black metal and around two meters in length, with the most cables connected to it.*

He found it along the left wall behind a bewildering maze of server racks and strange quantum cubes. *Find the oval depression on the top and press it to open a physical data port.* Somewhat to his surprise, it worked.

Place the disk inside. When the screen pops up asking if you want to run the ware, select yes. Wait for the screen to state the routine has completed.

Ironclad military discipline enabled him to stand at parade rest while he waited, forcing the violent urge to beat his foot or trod in circles into submission. Seconds ticked by at a rate slower than glacier flow.

He occupied the seconds by thinking about his father, about the shell-shocked, panicked look in his eyes when they laid his mother to rest. It was a look which had gradually hollowed over the months and years until it became an empty void.

The screen flickered as the words it displayed altered. Routine complete.

Remove the disk. Press the depression to close the port. Leave. Leaving he could most certainly do.

Foster's office was located in the left rear corner of the Command building. He proceeded as rapidly as he dared, for under no circumstances should he seem panicked or draw attention to himself beyond what his uniform and physical build did. Even so, he was stopped twice on the way by officers he marginally knew. He spat out the prepared cover story and urged them on their way.

Two turns before Foster's office he entered the Security Center and glared over the counter. "I need two MPs to accompany me."

The sergeant on duty looked as if O'Connell was expected; likely the checkpoint officer had commed ahead to alert her of his presence. "Yes, sir." She tapped the comm panel. "Jenkins, Ramirez, up front now."

Seconds later two men appeared. Thankfully, they weren't overly young. It increased the odds they wouldn't wet themselves when ordered to take the action he intended to command. He nodded sharply. "Men, with me."

They fell in on either side of him as he traversed the final two hallways, and the entourage arrived at their destination before the MPs were able to inquire as to what was going on.

The secretary gave a weak salute. "General O'Connell, welcome to Northwestern Regional Headquarters. General Foster is in a conference, but he—"

"I'm afraid this can't wait. Open the door."

"Sir—"

"Open the door. That's an order."

"Yes, sir."

The door slid open to reveal a visibly startled General Foster. He dismissed the holos above his desk. "O'Connell, this is most unexpected. I was under the impression you had taken a leave of absence."

And that was the key. The military leadership's abhorrence of public scandal had led them to issue a cover story concerning his replacement on the EASC Board. The official word said he had resigned from the Chairmanship for personal reasons and taken an indefinite leave of absence from active duty; the request to return to Earth was ostensibly to wrap up technical matters.

He believed solely Brennon, Solovy, Lange and Navick—and possibly Rychen, since the man had tied himself in knots kissing Solovy's ass for the past two weeks—knew of the charges filed against him under seal. But he'd had no way to be certain until now whether the other Board members had been informed.

"Not any longer. They sent me out here to get this disgrace of a Regional back into shape. You are relieved of command pending a summary hearing. Officers, escort General Foster to a protective custody cell."

Foster's face flooded beet red until his jowls appeared as though they might burst. "You haven't the authority—"

"But I do." The MPs' eyes veered from Foster to Liam and back again, wavering. "Don't ask me to repeat myself, officers, lest I make an effort to remember your names in an unfavorable manner."

The taller MP moved toward Foster. "I'm sorry, General. I'm afraid I have to take you into custody."

"This is an outrage! I have a right to notice and a defense!"

The other MP succumbed to the peer pressure and joined his colleague at Foster's side. "Sir, please come quietly or we'll have to place you in restraints."

Liam sneered malignantly. "Yes, Foster. Think of the morale of your men and women. It wouldn't do for them to see you being dragged through the halls like a common criminal, now would it?"

Foster snarled at him ineffectually but acquiesced to the MPs urging him toward the door. As he passed, Liam clasped him on the shoulder.

Foster shrunk away, but it didn't matter. The purpose of the gesture was to place a small nanoweave on his uniform, one which scrambled the man's outgoing comms so long as the jacket remained in a five meter vicinity, ensuring they never reached their intended audience. The garment would stay close to Foster for long enough, Liam hoped.

After they departed he roamed around the office, counting down the seconds until Foster would be far enough away to not trouble him further. When his mental timer hit zero he pivoted and headed back out, waving to the stunned secretary on his way by. "You're dismissed. Go home for the day."

He allowed no one to distract him on this traversal of the Command building and was out the back door and headed to the hangar in less than thirty seconds.

R

Despite being surrounded by meadows, the sprawling hangar complex did present an impressive sight. The paint had barely dried it was so new; it made the forty-year-old complex on Deucali look regrettably drab by comparison.

It was also a hotbed of activity, with soldiers bustling around hauling in gear and supplies and foodstuffs and mechanics effecting repairs. Most of NW Command had been recalled in anticipation of shipping out east. The Second Crux War was over and there were aliens to fight.

The chaos was going to aid him, though the notion of Solovy throwing the entire Earth Alliance military at a bunch of aliens irritated him greatly. He shuddered to think of how the Southwestern Headquarters was surely being stripped bare and left a ghost town. Were he back on Deucali he'd put a stop to it, but there were more important matters at stake now.

Five cruisers were docked end-to-end along the far left side of the hangar. The *Akagi* hung at the front of the line. But first things first. He sent a message to the captain of the *Yeltsin* and began making his way down the long double-row of frigates.

The XO of the *Yeltsin* was reviewing stocking reports with the master sergeant beneath the hull. He caught Liam's approach out of the corner of his eye and snapped a salute, which Liam returned.

"General O'Connell, it's an honor to see you again. I didn't realize you were on-base."

"Good to see you, too, Major." Major Peltski had been stationed on Deucali four years earlier, doing a two-year stint in Space Logistics. He was a competent officer and Liam had gotten along with him as well as he was capable of getting along with anyone. More importantly, Peltski was a follower. He could carry out even difficult orders with efficiency and skill but displayed little in the way of initiative or ambition.

"Peltski, I'm here with good news. Your captain received a reassignment as XO of the *Brandenburg*. You're receiving a field promotion to Lt. Commander. The *Yeltsin* is yours."

"Sir, I...I don't know what to say. Thank you, sir."

The other key facet of his plan was very simple, and the most basic of all rules in the military: subordinate officers did not question the orders of generals. It had been true for millennia and was no less true today.

"You deserve it, Lt. Commander. When will you be ready to ship out?"

"Another hour, hour and a half tops."

"Excellent." He leaned in and lowered his voice. "I'm here on top secret orders from the Prime Minister and EASC Board. I need the *Yeltsin* to accompany the *Akagi* on a secret mission. You'll receive the details once we're spaceborne."

Peltski regarded him solemnly. "I understand, sir. It will be an honor to serve with you."

"I appreciate it. Now if you'll excuse me, much to do and little time to do it in. Make sure you are out of dock by 1430."

He pivoted and continued down the row, grimacing from the effort being so hideously cordial for such a length of time and from the thought of having to do it a second time in mere minutes.

─── ⌘ ───

Liam barreled up the ramp to the *Akagi*. The captain of the *Chinook* had been dispatched to the third cruiser and a sympathetic XO, Major Charlton, similarly promoted. Now for the final step in this initial phase.

He was met at the hatch by a female officer, though it didn't appear intentionally so. The woman was traversing the hall and spun in apparent shock at finding a general in the entryway.

"Name and rank, Marine."

"Captain Brooklyn Harper, 1st NW MSO Platoon, on loan to the *Akagi*, sir."

He reminded himself to be polite. Those serving on the ship would be under his command in tense circumstances, and it was best to not actively encourage disloyalty or disobedience. "Captain Harper, can you show me to the Commodore?"

He saw her mouth twitch, though she quickly squelched it. Special forces types weren't generally accustomed to being relegated to escort duty, but that was not his problem. "Yes, sir. Follow me."

Commodore Tinibu met him at the door to the CO office, clearly having been alerted to Liam's approach—presumably by Harper. His salute was grudging. "General, welcome to the *Akagi*. We're busy getting ready to ship out, but what can I do for you?"

"I'm commandeering this ship for a special mission. You can go see General Foster about a reassignment."

"Excuse me? Sir? We ship out in half an hour. It's rather late to be changing mission parameters now. What is this mission regarding?"

"The details are above your pay grade, Commodore. Now, as you said, *we* are shipping out in half an hour. So if you'll excuse me, I have a ship to captain." With that he brushed past Tinibu and headed for the bridge.

Tinibu would ping Foster. Receiving no response, he would head to the Command building. No one would know where Foster had gone or why he couldn't be reached.

Liam would be in space long before anyone began to suspect something might be awry.

As Fionava's sun receded in the edge-to-edge viewport and the blackness of space took its place, Liam retired to the CO office. Though there had been rampant confusion among the officers on board, the departure itself was executed with a minimum of drama.

He drew in a readying breath and requested Peltski and Charlton on holo.

His expression was properly grave as he addressed them. "Gentlemen, I'm now able to fill you in on our mission. The Second Crux War isn't as over as the media and official public statements may have led you to believe. The Prime Minister and the EASC Board have determined it is necessary to teach the Federation a lesson, one which will make them think twice about attacking us in the future."

"But sir, I thought a peace treaty was signed?"

"It was, more or less, but our mission has nonetheless been approved at the highest levels. These actions are extremely clandestine. We will run dark, with no communications allowed beyond our three ships. Spies are everywhere, and if word leaks out too early then Seneca will be alerted to our plans. We can't allow that to happen. Therefore, I'm implementing a full communications blackout beyond a four megameter radius, effective as of now.

"Our first target will be the Federation colony of New Cairo. Set a course."

62

"You're insane."

"It'll work."

"Which does not alter the fact that you are insane."

Alex gave him her most beguiling smile. "You said that wasn't a problem. In fact, you said it was one reason you thought I was, and I quote, 'kind of amazing.'"

"I did. And I meant it. But the fact *still* remains."

"Look. The rules of this place are the same as those in our galaxy. The laws of physics will hold."

"And the portal itself?"

She worried at her lower lip. He didn't give a damn what she said, the issue concerned her as well. "The portal, whatever it really is, shouldn't be a problem. Since it's our portal we don't have to worry about the shift in axes. And if it is a problem, it'll be a blip. Even if it knocks us out of superluminal, by the time it happens we'll be parsecs away. Far enough."

He found he was on his knees before her once more, and he didn't care. Still, his chest tightened when she lowered herself from her chair to meet him as an equal.

"You realize we could die, simply by going through."

She groaned as her forehead dropped to rest on his. "You're seriously pulling out that line again? We'll be fine. Promise."

"I believe you." He kissed her softly and let her go.

She climbed back in her chair, ran a hand down her hair, straightened her shoulders…and activated the sLume drive.

They were lined up for a straight shot through the portal. An army of ships approached from behind them and more waited on the other side.

At speeds such as this there was no margin for error. Mere meters off and the warp bubble would graze the ring and they would be dead, though at least they'd probably take out the portal with them.

Their speed was so great they had no perception of traversing the portal or warping past the alien ships which lay in wait for them. But eventually they had traveled long enough to be either well outside the center of Metis or have missed the portal altogether and be somewhere else.

Eyes wide, she disengaged the sLume drive and engaged the impulse engine so they wouldn't be a sitting target. As soon as the stars solidified around them she was a flurry of movement, checking readings and location.

Abruptly she sank back in her chair in winded laughter.

"We're okay?"

The laughter devolved into full-on giggles as she gazed over at him. "Holy shit, I can't believe that actually worked."

"What? You insisted it was a sure thing!"

"Are you kidding? I was terrified. I had no idea if it would work. I mean, I *thought* it would work—it *should* have worked—but it's not like anyone's ever done something like this before."

They both stood at the same time, meeting in the middle of the cockpit.

He chuckled against her lips. "God I love you, woman."

"Good. Want to go save the galaxy?"

"Hell, yes. Where to first?"

"First we send a message. Someone needs to be told what we've done and quickly."

"True. I'm not sure—"

"Hold on. Messages are pouring in, which means my little trick on the comm system worked." She laughed in amusement. "What do you know, she did remember...."

At his questioning stare she projected an aural. "It's one of a hundred or so messages from her, but this one was marked 'super-incredibly-seriously-urgent.'"

Alex,

> *You remember that project we did—well, you did—at university on quantum field interference? Well something similar is how the aliens are screwing up the exanet. Shield your comm unit; we're shielding all of ours as fast as we can manage.*
>
> *God I hope you're alive.*

— Kennedy

"I'm dying to find out what else is happening, but first to reply. Then we need to keep moving."

Ken,

> *Way ahead of you. Also alive. We obliterated their superdreadnought factory. Reinforcements will NOT be arriving anytime soon. Tell my mother. Tell someone. More later.*

— Alex

He only vaguely noted when she sent the reply off, for his own messages were flowing into his head one after another in rapid succession. Like Alex there were many things he wanted to know, but one particular thing above all. Call him selfish…

…he exhaled as a surge of relief and adrenaline rushed through his veins. He sank against the half-wall and closed his eyes.

"You've been cleared?"

He must have been grinning. He reopened his eyes and doubled-down on the grin. "We both have. We'll still be hunted by a fleet of alien ships and a horde of human traitors but we aren't fugitives wanted for terrorism and murder."

She wound her arms around his waist. "This is a start."

"It is. Let's go finish it."

63

Devon jerked awake.

Wha...ah shit, he'd fallen asleep sitting at his cubbyhole desk. He checked the time. Nearly midnight. "Emily's gonna kill me...."

He unglued his right cheek from the desk and sank back in his chair, rubbing at blurry eyes. Ever since Annie had been cleared for full operation he'd been working almost nonstop.

The bureaucrats were hyper-paranoid she was going to "get out" and kill them all—as opposed to the aliens who were already out and currently killing them all. They insisted on doubled and in some cases tripled security protocols. Protocols which were interfering with her logic subroutines and slowing down her analyses, which simply would not do.

Aliens were spreading across settled space and leaders needed hard information yesterday. The orders had come from the highest whatever: make her more secure, while also making her faster.

Right. Got it. No problem.

Emily was going to kill him. The alien attacks had her nervous. Skittish. She possessed a creative mind and an artist's view of the world. It made her a crafty hacker because she viewed problems from a different perspective, and also a beautiful painter, but an artist's view of the world was not always rooted entirely in logic. She was frightened. He got that.

He stood and stretched, and only then realized what had awoken him. A message from Annie blinked in his vision. The priority coding vibration had jolted him out of his slumber.

"Errors are occurring in the communications network on Fionava."

He opened a direct channel to her. "Annie, what kind of problems?"

"Messages and data are becoming garbled, cut off before completion, or not being sent or received at all."

442 | G.S. JENNSEN

442 | G.S. JENNSEN

442 | G.S. JENNSEN

442 | G.S. JENNSEN

"It can't be the aliens, can it? No way are they all the way over at Fionava?"

"Negative. The errors do not match the interference seen in the vicinity of alien ships."

"Good. Talk to me. What's your analysis?"

"Early investigation suggests an 87.6% likelihood a virus has infected the central communications network at the Regional Headquarters. Errors of varying severity are being introduced into the system at a multiplicative rate."

"Can it get out? Is it in danger of infecting our communications here?"

"Unlikely. The corruption appears to be occurring at the Fionava node, whether it be incoming or outbound data."

"Well that's good. Still, pass a recommendation to Security to implement a firewall around Fionava. I'll tell Tech to try to talk to Comms at the base on Fionava and figure out what's up. Continue analyzing the network and see if you can identify the root problem, but don't divert resources from determining where the aliens are going to kill us next."

"Was that a joke?"

Annie retained mountains of data on human history, behaviors, conventions and mannerisms. Her internalization of the data showed itself sporadically and often at unexpected times, but more frequently every day. "Gallows humor. I mean, technically it *is* a more or less accurate statement of your directives."

"Ah. I see. Though an alien offensive does not guarantee with 100% certainty the death of all humans."

"Optimism—I like it."

"Thank you. Instructions implemented."

"Thanks, Annie. I need to go home for a few hours, but I'll let Brigadier Hervé know about the problem. She's in some super-secret meeting right now so it may be a few hours before she can issue you any new directives."

His voice dropped to a mumble as he ran a hand through disheveled hair. It was probably shooting in every direction like he was some loon. "Emily is going to kill me...."

"What do you mean, they're not attacking?"

Rychen forwarded the images he was receiving to Vancouver and Cavare, and a few seconds later they materialized in a long row above the conference table. "I mean they're not attacking. Eight Metigen superdreadnoughts are in high orbit above Pyxis. They arrived half an hour ago yet are making no move to launch an assault on the colony. Their orbit is, I'm sure quite deliberately, a single megameter outside the range of Pyxis' small defense array."

Prime Minister Brennon's gaze ran across those present. "This is new behavior, correct?"

"Certainly it—"

Marshal Gianno finished conferring with a colleague and returned to her seat. "I'm sorry to interrupt, but I'm now getting reports of similar behavior above Brython and Nystad."

Miriam looked up sharply at that.

She was situated in the largest conference room Logistics offered, simply because it was the only room large enough to accommodate so many holos. She had been reviewing the most recent data from ANNIE with Brigadier Hervé; they were considering—*considering*—allowing ANNIE and STAN to talk to each other. The firewalls and security protocols required to engineer such a conversation were going to be a nightmare to implement, which was one reason Hervé had been invited to the meeting.

On the various holos were the combined civilian and military leadership of the Earth Alliance and Senecan Federation. The only person of note absent was General Foster, who was a no-show for unknown reasons.

The meeting had been in session for over two hours, but a number of the finer details had begun to be hammered out for their next steps. It was difficult going at first as disparate leadership styles and procedures and pecking orders had stumbled over one another and tension lingered among those who had been trying to kill each other mere days ago. But eventually the common threat had risen to dominate lesser concerns.

The two military forces wouldn't be engaging in joint operations—not yet anyway and not unless it became a necessity. They had divided responsibility for protecting the independent colonies, though most had fallen under the Alliance's purview based on pure geography.

Seneca assumed responsibility for Pyxis, but when the alien—Metigen, she supposed—fleet finally departed Messium and headed to Pyxis the stealth reconnaissance platoon Rychen had left behind to monitor them followed. Evacuations had begun long before the aliens' arrival, but with a population of nearly 200,000 and no Alliance infrastructure in place it was not a simple endeavor.

But the ships weren't attacking.

Miriam shifted the marked-up settlement map to the center. A jagged, uneven line had been drawn to mark the advance of the aliens. It canted diagonally through the eastern third of settled space. The line currently sat 3.6 kiloparsecs from Earth but crept distressingly close to Seneca.

She flagged the colonies where the aliens had adopted a holding pattern. "I'm checking Henan and Dresden. Both are on alert, but we need to know ASAP if they see similar behavior."

Alliance Defense Minister Mori leaned forward in his chair. "Perhaps they're pausing to regroup. We did inflict damage to them at Messium. They may move more cautiously going forward."

Miriam shook her head; she noticed Gianno did the same. "But by arriving at these worlds they've announced their intentions. By waiting to attack, it's almost as if they're daring us to come try again."

Rychen grumbled. "I concur. They're taunting us, or trying to provoke us."

The Federation Chairman, Vranas, signaled agreement. "Neither option means anything good."

"Still, every minute they don't attack is another minute more civilians can be evacuated. I say we take full advantage of the opportunity. There's no guarantee we'll get a second one."

Miriam had to admire Brennon's composure under incomparable pressure. From the moment he took the podium in the

Assembly Chamber to accept his reinstatement to the Prime Ministership, he had remained focused, determined and cool-headed. Prior to the crisis she had believed him a competent leader but hadn't spared much thought on the matter. Now though, she was glad he was in a position of authority, even if he might not be.

Gianno pursed her lips, an interesting glint in her eye. "It so happens I have the entire 2nd Wing of the Northern Fleet stationed half a parsec from Brython. STAN identified it as the most probable next target. Only four superdreadnoughts there. If we wanted to allow them to provoke us, say the word."

Vranas shrugged. "Frankly, I like the idea. Let's make it clear Messium wasn't our final stand—it was our first one."

The response to her query arrived, and she updated the map. "Dresden is reporting four Metigen ships have adopted an orbital pattern but are not taking any other action."

"Well, that settles it. They're making some kind of play. We should—"

We offer you a choice.

"What—"

"Did anyone else get that?"

"Who is this?"

It is not a difficult choice: survival or extinction.

The voice was in her head, but attached to no person or other identifier. Judging by the confused expressions and turmoil around the table, not solely in her head.

Your effort at your Messium colony was an admirable act of defiance worthy of respect, but do not be so foolish as to believe you possess any hope of stopping us.

Brennon had projected his internal comm system so it could be heard by everyone. Nods around the table indicated it matched what they were receiving.

Our forces currently in your territory are but a fraction of those we are capable of wielding. Of those we will not hesitate to wield. Understand you are to us as a bug upon the ground. To flatten you requires but a thought and a step. Whether—

Chairman Vranas actually interrupted the alien. "Whoever you are, we have done nothing to you. We have not threatened or approached or offended you. We don't know—"

Do not interrupt us again.

Miriam supposed the 'or' didn't need to be stated.

Vranas fell silent but didn't appear chagrined. Instead he and Brennon exchanged a ponderous look. She'd gotten the sense they had taken a liking to one another at the Summit and was grateful for it now.

Whether we choose to extinguish the human species is up to you. Your choice is this: cease all expansion along the Scutum-Crux Arm in the Fourth Galactic Quadrant. Abandon all colonies beyond the parallel 48° 2.9kpcs distance from Earth. You may if you deem it worthwhile continue to explore your galaxy along the Sagittarius and Perseus Arms within the prescribed boundary.

You are granted seven days' time to withdraw all presence from the region east of the designated parallel. After such time, any excursion beyond this line will be viewed as an act of war. Any attempt to approach the Metis Nebula from the north will be treated likewise.

Brennon waited until the break was clear before speaking up. "For how long? We can't make promises for those a millennium in the future."

For all time.

"And if we agree to your terms?"

We will recall our ships.

"That's it? Do we have your commitment you won't return at a later point? What if you simply change your mind?"

That will not occur.

Brennon and Vranas exchanged another glance before Vranas responded. "We need time to discuss your offer. Can we—"

You have eighteen minutes.

Silence fell for several beats, then everyone was speaking at once.

"We can't possibly tell them—"

"Why the Hell are they—"

"A week isn't enough time to evacuate—"

"They ask us to leave behind too much."

Miriam stared at the map. Brennon was correct. On the other side of the demarcation line were twenty-eight colonized planets, a quarter of the worlds humanity had settled in the last three hundred years. A number had now been leveled by the aliens but a core framework remained; they could be rebuilt.

Some hundred fifty million people lived in the region, or had before the offensive began. It included Messium, Karelia, Requi, Elathan and all but ran through the middle of Seneca. An errant ship departing the planet could accidentally drift over the line and violate the aliens' terms.

Secretary Mori directed his attention her way. "Admiral Solovy, is vacating the region in a week's time feasible?"

"The people? Yes, but only because so many have already been killed or fled. The entire infrastructure will need to be left behind. Beyond what people carry with them and the ships which carry them away, everything will be lost."

Rychen dragged a hand through his hair. "What reason do we have to take these Metigens at their word? Are we supposed to live in fear from this day forward that they will return at any time? Or that one ship of criminals or imbeciles crossing the demarcation line will mean the death of us all?"

A man who had been identified as the Federation Parliament Minority Leader fidgeted in his chair. "Isn't the alternative exactly what they claimed? Extinction? We don't have a choice."

Gianno cut her eyes at the man in a manner suggesting she didn't think much of him. "We always have a choice, Senator."

"A choice to live or die!"

"A choice to fight or submit."

Vranas twirled a disk in his hand and let out a long sigh. "Personally, I'm a bit pissed off. I didn't appreciate being called a bug."

Ragged laughter rippled around the room. As it faded away Vranas straightened up in his chair. "You military types seem to be favoring telling these aliens to go screw themselves. Truthfully, what are the odds of us matching them on the field? Of, say, battling them to a stalemate or close enough they reconsider? And now is not the time for sugar-coating or kissing ass. We need the undistorted truth."

Miriam spoke first. "Low."

The others didn't protest, and she continued. "Our capabilities get stronger by the hour. We expect in another day eighty percent of full communications capabilities will be restored, though it will take longer to roll out the modifications to every ship in both militaries. Several combat strategies showed promise at Messium and both sides continue to pore over the data from the battle. We've discovered additional weaknesses we think can be exploited."

She paused. "All that being said, the answer is still 'low.' Their ships are larger, more powerful and more numerous. In a head-to-head battle, if we send enough ships we can match them but in a war of attrition we will lose. We're down too many ships from the war—" she motioned Mori silent "—but regardless we'd still be at a numbers disadvantage."

"So there's no hope. We must bow to their demands." It was the Federation Minority Leader again and it came out muffled because his head had dropped into his hands.

"I said the odds were low, not zero. We can target specific locations with concentrated firepower. We can throw everything we have at them in coordinated strikes. It will mean sacrificing some worlds in favor of defending others.

"But if we do this, we have a chance—at the very least a chance of inflicting real losses on the enemy. Whether we have a chance of achieving anything greater? I can't say with any degree of confidence."

Her gaze went to Rychen, then Gianno. "Do either of you disagree with my assessment?"

Rychen blew out a breath. "Speaking as someone who has been shot at by these aliens, I will only say they are fallible. They're not gods. I've seen us destroy their ships. They are massive and terrifying and powerful, but they are not invincible. So I agree. We have a chance. A small one."

Gianno arched an eyebrow. "I'd personally welcome the opportunity to be shot at by them. I didn't rise to this position to not be shot at by a formidable foe. Also, I'm working on a couple of new ideas."

Secretary Mori stood and leaned in until his face took up the entirety of his holo. "Are you people insane? You can't seriously be suggesting we refuse this ultimatum! Do you all understand you are likely sentencing the human race to virtual if not total extinction?"

Miriam closed her eyes. She had made many decisions over the years which cost lives in order to save other lives. Every military leader had. This decision was guaranteed to cost lives, while the lives it might save were nebulous and unknowable. Yet the urge to fight, to resist, was a strong one....

Her eVi blinked an alert for an incoming message, highest priority. She frowned but opened it.

"Of course we don't intend to sentence the human race to extinction. If that is our sole option then—"

Alexis was alive.

The Federation Minority Leader muttered something about accountability and not being qualified to make this decision.

Alive.

She cleared her throat above the growing discord. "If I can interject? I've received information which alters the equation."

Brennon shifted his attention to her. "Admiral?"

"I possess solid intel that the Metigens' primary manufacturing facility—the location used to build their superdreadnoughts— has been completely eradicated. At a minimum we can expect they will not be receiving reinforcements or backfilling their lines for some time. The alien was bluffing—the ships in the field are, for all intents and purposes, the only ships they have."

Mori had been working up a good head of steam and blustered in her direction. "This sounds most improbable. From whom did you receive this intel, Admiral?"

It was all she could do not to laugh in a kind of reckless joy. "From my daughter."

"What reason do we have to trust—"

Brennon leveled a scathing glare at Mori to silence him. "Admiral Solovy's daughter discovered the aliens weeks before they attacked, and our dismissal of her information cost many lives. I have no intention of dismissing it a second time."

Within her holo, Gianno appeared to be adjusting calculations and projections. "Admiral, where was this facility located? We've been unable to find any evidence of an alien base or stronghold."

Miriam's pulse pounded in her ears, and she was having to work not to be utterly overwhelmed by any one of a cascade of emotions. "It was through the aliens' portal in the Metis Nebula."

"Really? My most recent intel says the portal has vanished."

"Well, Alexis is..." she smiled, recalling Malcolm's words "...extraordinarily resourceful."

Vranas looked to the military leaders. "And taking into account this new information, what are our odds?"

Gianno gave the tiniest shrug. "Improved."

Rychen was practically beaming; he badly wanted another shot at the enemy. "Improved."

Everyone was staring at her, for she had not yet given her formal opinion. "Still low—but most decidedly improved."

Vranas drummed fingertips on the desk, then stood and turned his back on the group to stare out his window. "We—humanity—didn't come this far by being afraid. Explorers and visionaries have willingly headed off to certain death for thousands of years and by doing so brought us to where we are today. No one has ever told us 'no' and succeeded in making it stick for long."

He faced them once more. "We accede to these aliens' demands and we'll wither away. It may take centuries or even millennia, but we'll be so busy cowering in fear we'll forget to move forward. I say we fight."

Brennon chuckled wryly, almost to himself. "I agree."

No further dissent followed. Brennon straightened his shoulders and notched his chin upward. "So there it is. We'll want to—

We require your answer.

Brennon and Vranas shared a last, solemn look and nodded to one another. Vranas cleared his throat so his response would project strength and conviction.

"And you shall have it."

He gestured to Gianno and across to Miriam in a manner which said, *it's your show.*

Miriam stood. "Field Marshal Gianno, are your forces in place above Brython?"

"They are indeed, Fleet Admiral."

"Excellent. Open fire."

DON'T MISS THE CONCLUSION TO THE AURORA RISING TRILOGY

TRANSCENDENCE

AURORA RISING BOOK THREE
(AMARANTHE ♦ 3)

AUTHOR'S NOTE

I published my first novel, *Starshine*, in 2014. In the back of the book I put a short note asking readers to consider leaving a review or talking about the book with their friends. Watching my readers do that and so much more has been the most rewarding and humbling experience in my life.

So if you loved **VERTIGO**, tell someone. Leave a review, share your thoughts on social media, annoy your coworkers in the break room by talking about your favorite characters. Reviews are the backbone of a book's success, but there is no single act that will sell a book better than word-of-mouth.

My part of this deal is to write a book worth talking about—your part of the deal is to do the talking. If you keep doing your bit, I get to write a lot more books for you.

Of course, I can't write them overnight. While you're waiting for the next book, consider supporting other independent authors. Right now there are thousands of writers chasing the same dream you've enabled me to achieve. Take a small chance with a few dollars and a few hours of your time. In doing so, you may be changing an author's life.

Lastly, I want to hear from my readers. If you loved the book— or if you didn't—let me know. The beauty of independent publishing is its simplicity: there's the writer and the readers. Without any overhead, I can find out what I'm doing right and wrong directly from you, which is invaluable in making the next book better than this one. And the one after that. And the twenty after that.

Website: gsjennsen.com
Wiki: gsj.space/wiki

Email: gs@gsjennsen.com   Goodreads: G.S. Jennsen
Twitter: @GSJennsen   Pinterest: gsjennsen
Facebook: gsjennsen.author   Instagram: gsjennsen

Find my books at a variety of retailers: gsjennsen.com/retailers

Acknowledgements

I am enormously thankful for the support and encouragement of a great many friends, family, readers and colleagues: Charles, Julie, Linda, Helen, John, Steve, Sunny, Maer, Cheryl, Jim, Whitney, Bill and Mark, to name but a few.

I owe a special debt of gratitude to Andy, Katie, Taylor, Jules, Sandy, Anne, Roman, Carole and Claire for their editorial assistance, opinions, critiques and invaluable ideas. You helped *Vertigo* become so much more than I could have done alone.

Finally, thank you to everyone who read *Starshine*, left a review on Amazon, Goodreads or other sites, sent me a personal email expressing how the book impacted you, or posted on social media to share how much you enjoyed it. You make this all worthwhile.

ABOUT THE AUTHOR

G. S. JENNSEN lives somewhere in the U.S., in a locale that may or may not be where she lived the last time she published a book (she's a gypsy at heart), with her husband and two dogs. She has become an internationally bestselling author since her first novel, *Starshine*, was published in March 2014. She has chosen to continue writing under an independent publishing model to ensure the integrity of her stories and her ability to execute on the vision she has for their telling.

While she has been a lawyer, a software engineer and an editor, she's found the life of a full-time author preferable by several orders of magnitude. When she isn't writing, she's gaming or working out or getting lost in the mountains that loom large outside the windows in her home. Or she's dealing with a flooded basement, or standing in a line at Walmart reading the tabloid headlines and wondering who all of those people are. Or sitting on her back porch with a glass of wine, looking up at the stars, trying to figure out what could be up there.

Printed in Great Britain
by Amazon

53475179R00270